**Praise for *New York Times* bestselling author
Lindsay McKenna**

"McKenna provides heartbreakingly tender romantic
development that will move readers to tears. Her military
background lends authenticity to this outstanding tale,
and readers will fall in love with the upstanding hero and
his fierce determination to save the woman he loves."
—*Publishers Weekly* on *Never Surrender*

"Talented Lindsay McKenna delivers excitement and
romance in equal measure."
—*RT Book Reviews* on *Protecting His Own*

"Lindsay McKenna will have you flying with the daring
and deadly women pilots who risk their lives… Buckle in
for the ride of your life."
—*Writers Unlimited* on *Heart of Stone*

**Praise for *New York Times* bestselling author
Joan Johnston**

"A guaranteed good read."
—*New York Times* bestselling author Heather Graham

"Joan Johnston does short contemporary Westerns to
perfection."
—*Publishers Weekly*

"Joan Johnston continually gives us everything we want…
fabulous details and atmosphere, memorable characters,
a story that you wish would never end, and lots of tension
and sensuality."
—*RT Book Reviews*

NEW YORK TIMES BESTSELLING AUTHORS

LINDSAY McKENNA

& JOAN JOHNSTON

HEART OF THE EAGLE
&
HAWK'S WAY: ADAM

ISBN-13: 978-1-335-04000-8

Heart of the Eagle & Hawk's Way: Adam

Copyright © 2019 by Harlequin Books S.A.

The publisher acknowledges the copyright holders of the individual works as follows:

Heart of the Eagle
Copyright © 1986 by Lindsay McKenna

Hawk's Way: Adam
Originally published as The Rancher and the Runaway Bride
Copyright © 1993 by Joan Mertens Johnston

Recycling programs for this product may not exist in your area.

Printed in U.S.A.

www.Harlequin.com

CONTENTS

Lindsay McKenna is proud to have served her country in the US Navy as an aerographer's mate third class—also known as a weather forecaster. She was a pioneer in the military romance subgenre and loves to combine heart-pounding action with soulful and poignant romance. True to her military roots, she is the originator of the long-running and reader-favorite Morgan's Mercenaries series. She does extensive hands-on research, including flying in aircraft such as a P3-B Orion sub-hunter and a B-52 bomber. She was the first romance writer to sign her books in the Pentagon bookstore. Visit her online at lindsaymckenna.com.

Books by Lindsay McKenna

Shadow Warriors

Running Fire
Taking Fire
Never Surrender
Breaking Point
Degree of Risk

Jackson Hole, Wyoming

Out Rider
Night Hawk
Wolf Haven
High Country Rebel
The Loner

Visit the Author Profile page
at Harlequin.com for more titles.

HEART OF THE EAGLE

Lindsay McKenna

To my mother, Ruth May Gent, who took four turkeys
and taught them how to be eagles…

Chapter 1

What the hell! He didn't have time to think, only react. There, coming down the muddied ranch road, was a fully grown golden eagle. The raptor's wings were outstretched, talons bared as he skimmed the earth toward his prey, a zigzagging jackrabbit. Simultaneously, Jim slammed on the brakes of his Blazer and hit the horn. The eagle was so intent on capturing its prey that it had not seen his truck come up and over the crest of the same road.

The Blazer slewed sideways. The eagle screamed indignantly, its amber eyes glaring as it barely missed the truck and sailed skyward. Jim eased the Blazer to the side of the road, drew in a deep breath and loosened his grip on the steering wheel. He watched the bird for a few moments, puzzled by its actions. Then, grabbing the pair of binoculars he always carried with him, he eased out of the truck. His scuffed cowboy boots sank into the mud and snow on the road. He glanced at the watch on his wrist; he had a few minutes before he had to make the appointment.

Crossing the deeply rutted gravel road, Jim walked to the grassy ledge on the opposite side. He followed the movements of the magnificent golden eagle as it spiraled lazily below the gray clouds that hung like a blanket above the valley. The late April weather was sharp and Jim pulled his sheepskin coat tighter as he halted at the edge of the drop-off that slid into a shallow slope of the valley. Lifting his binoculars, he trained them on the raptor. His mouth pulled into a pursed line as he followed the eagle as it stooped into a deep dive and plummeted into attack position.

Expecting that the eagle had found another quarry, Jim followed the dive. Instead, at the last moment, the eagle exploded into a flurry of braking movements with its seven-foot wing spread, beating countermotions as it slowed down its approach to the outstretched arm of a woman.

What the hell! Twice in the span of five minutes he'd been taken by surprise. The eagle had no jesses or leather straps dangling from its yellow legs to evidence that it was domesticated for falconry. Without realizing it, Jim was holding his breath. As the eagle landed, he saw the woman bend her knees to take the bird's weight and velocity. She wore a soft leather gauntlet type of glove that extended from her left hand up to her elbow to protect her from the razor-sharp talons of the raptor as it settled on her arm. Jim watched as her entire body absorbed the tremendous impact of the eagle's landing, the woman nearly dropping to a kneeling position so that she didn't lose her precarious balance.

Jim felt his heart rate accelerate. Beautiful! My God, they're beautiful together. Part of it was from the primal beauty of the wild eagle. Part was the thrill of watching the slender woman, who reminded him more of a graceful deer, as she slowly stood to her full height. Even the heavy sheepskin coat couldn't hide the grace of her carriage. A deer and an eagle. Natural enemies. Now natural partners. The morning…no, the day, was turning out to be one of incredible surprise, and the rare, intrinsic beauty of the moment simply tore the breath from his tense body.

Jim moved his binoculars from the woman and her eagle. There was a black horse standing nearby, ground tied at the far end of the large meadow. Beyond rose the Rocky Mountains, still clothed in snow at the higher elevations. He returned his attention to the woman, hoping that she had turned around by now. His black brows knit as he concentrated on her face. Was it? No, it couldn't be. Dr. Dahlia Gordon was a staunch opponent of falconry. It couldn't be her. And yet, Jim could vividly recall that one moment they had met in the past. Dal Gordon had a haunting, expressive face that was imprinted in his mind. Yes, it was her…

A slow smile edged his mouth as he watched her walk with the eagle resting imperiously on her arm. My God, the raptor was huge! A weak streamer of sunlight chose that moment to slice through the leaden clouds and strike the meadow. The eagle's dark brown body blazed to life in a molten bronze color. Jim watched in appreciation as the sun struck Dal Gordon's shoulder-length spice-colored hair, bringing more of a flush to her pale features. How long was it? he mused. He had heard Dr. Gordon speak three years before in Washington, D.C. on saving the predatory birds that were being callously slaughtered in the Rockies. Despite the ravages of her recent divorce, she was still one of the most beautiful women he had ever seen.

Jim lowered the binoculars, a deprecating smile pulling at one corner of his mouth. His light brown eyes narrowed as he watched the woman and eagle. It was a thrill to be undetected and witness the harmony between her and the magnificent predatory bird. Was it her eagle? How had she gotten it? Jim glanced at his watch. It was time to go. Reluctantly, taking one last look at them, he turned and crossed the road to the Blazer. Some of his happiness backwashed. In half an hour he would be facing her and asking her for help. Would she give it? Jim got in, settling the black felt cowboy hat on hair of the same color. His hands tightened momentarily around the wheel as he started the engine. She had to help. Without her, his entire plan would be destroyed.

"Yes?"

Jim removed his hat as he stared across the doorway at a woman in her early sixties who was built like an overly plump pigeon. "I'm Jim Tremain, from the Department of the Interior. I have an appointment to see Dr. Dahlia Gordon at ten."

The woman's small mouth puckered. "You mean Dr. Kincaid?" she challenged, eyeing him.

The divorce. "Yes, I guess so."

"Humph! Dal didn't say she was expectin' anyone." Her blue eyes narrowed suspiciously. "You got some ID?"

He dug out his wallet, producing the evidence. The housekeeper appeared mollified—to a degree. She reminded Jim of a keg of dynamite ready to go off. Or perhaps a guard dog would be a more appropriate comparison, he thought, smiling to himself.

"I had my secretary call and confirm the appointment two days ago," he said, trying to smooth her ruffled feathers. "I'm from Denver, the regional office."

She stared up at him. "Well... I don't know. She isn't here right now. And if she was expectin' someone, she wouldn't have left."

Patience, Jim reminded himself. He gave her a slight smile. "I saw her down in a meadow as I drove up here to the Triple K."

"All right, come on in, Mr. Tremain."

Jim stepped into the foyer, immediately at ease in the rambling ranch-style home. As the housekeeper escorted him from the cedar foyer, through the living room, which housed a huge stone fireplace, and then to the study, Jim collected his impressions.

"You can wait here. Dr. Kincaid ought to be comin' back shortly."

Jim placed his hat on the well-used leather couch, inhaling the scent of the large, brooding study, whose walls were lined with books. "Thank you."

The housekeeper hovered at the door, her pinched features softening a bit. "Coffee?"

Jim shook his head. "No, thanks."

"No tellin' when she'll get here, Mr. Tremain."

"That's all right, I'll wait."

She shrugged her shoulders. "Have it your way, Mr. Tremain. I'll be in the kitchen if you need anything."

His smile was genuine. "Thank you, Mrs...."

"Millie. I'm the housekeeper for the Kincaid family."

"I see."

Millie gave him one last predatory look before she left. Jim shrugged out of his sheepskin coat and draped it over the arm of the couch. He drank in the atmosphere of the quiet study, impressed with the titles of the books: most ranchers wouldn't be interested in Tolstoy or Shakespeare. But someone was and he wondered who. Above the bookshelves were many brilliantly colored photographs of the wildlife that no doubt inhabited the forty-thousand-acre Triple K Ranch. Jim found himself applauding the hanging of photographs of the animals on the walls, rather than their stuffed heads. Yes, the Kincaids were known for their strong conservation efforts, and were longtime friends to the Department of the Interior.

He sauntered out of the study and into an adjoining alcove. More slats of sun were peeking through the overcast as Jim looked out the window at the ceaseless activity of cowboys on horseback and the brown-and-white Hereford cattle they were herding. Ten acres on the south side of the house were enclosed in paddock after paddock of milling animals. It was time for the cows to calve, and Jim spotted more than one wobbly kneed youngster sticking close to its mother.

His sharp hearing caught the opening and closing of a door. The housekeeper's voice was barely discernible. Jim realized his hands were damp, and he laughed at himself for such an uncharacteristic show of nerves. Turning back to the window, he once again forced his concentration on the scene outside.

In the kitchen Dal shrugged out of her coat, handing it to Millie. "Who did he say he was?" she asked.

Her left arm ached where Nar had gripped her. He had been upset about something; otherwise, he wouldn't have bruised her with the powerful grip of his blue-black talons that could easily have shredded her kidskin gauntlet as well as put puncture holes through the thick sleeve of her sheepskin coat. While she absently rubbed her arm, her sapphire eyes darkened.

"Jim Tremain. From the Department of the Interior. I thought you said you wanted to rest, Dal. No more travel, no more lectures. Just to rest from that…that awful divorce," Millie said, sputtering.

Dal touched her brow. The divorce. Six months of freedom from a daily hell. She still wasn't herself. Inwardly, she wasn't ready to meet anyone. Not yet. "It's all right, Millie. You know me, no memory."

"Humph! That's 'cause of that no-good ex-husband of yours. Runnin' you into the ground like he did."

"That's over now, Millie," she began tiredly, not wanting to discuss it ever again. Dal glanced down at herself; she didn't look very presentable in her blue jeans and long-sleeved white blouse, with her hair in tangled disarray about her shoulders. Compressing her full lips, Dal touched her hair. God, Jack had beaten her down so far, she even forgot to tend to herself beyond the most necessary of tasks needed for daily survival. "Well, Mr. Tremain is going to see me the way I am," she muttered to the housekeeper. "I don't remember the appointment. But that's nothing new. Where did you say he was?"

"In your brother's study. Like some coffee and a freshly made roll?"

Dal touched her ribs. She ought to eat more, she

knew. Her brother, Rafe, was on her constantly to regain the lost weight. "No, just coffee, Millie."

"I'll bring it in to you, lamb."

Managing a smile of thanks, Dal headed toward the
south wing of the ranch house. The cheerful crackle
of a fire soothed her sudden raw-nerved feeling. How
could she have forgotten an appointment? Especially
when she had refused to see anyone over the past six
months? Running her slender fingers through her cin-
namon-colored hair, Dal stepped into the library.

Her irritation with herself was torn away as she came
to a halt. A man dressed like a wrangler rather than a
businessman stood with book in hand. It wasn't his
appearance as much as the aura surrounding him that
caught Dal completely off guard. The cougarlike lean-
ness to his body shouted of someone who braved the
elements regularly—and won. Her eyes moved up his
tightly muscled frame, taking in the faded blue jeans
that emphasized his long thighs and narrow hips. Unconsciously, she licked her lower lip. The pale-blue
long-sleeved shirt emphasized the powerful breadth
of his chest and shoulders. Her heart began an uneven
pounding as her gaze met and held his. Clear, light
brown eyes flecked with gold gently held her in check.
A tremor passed through Dal and suddenly she felt pan-
icky. This man, whoever he was, was affecting her on
levels she had thought were destroyed long ago.

She didn't want to admit that she was drawn to his
large, intelligent eyes, which smoldered with some unknown emotion in their honey-colored depths. Or was
she attracted by the harsh, chiseled planes of his face,
which made him appear hawklike? Immediately, in
her chaotic thoughts, Dal thought he resembled Nar,

her golden eagle: dangerous, beautiful in a breathtaking male way and excruciatingly masculine. Was it the deep tan and his softly curled black hair that made him look dangerous to her? She was perplexed. It was only April in Colorado and no one had seen enough sun to get a tan yet.

Was he Indian? No. Part, perhaps? Yes, as evidenced by the high cheekbones and the oval-shaped face, which was completed by a mildly stubborn chin. Her gaze fell to the hands that cradled the leather-bound book; long, tapered hands that were large knuckled and almost artistic looking. Hands that held the book so gently that Dal found herself wondering what it would be like to be held by him.

What an idiotic thought! she upbraided herself, giving herself a mental shake for the scattered feelings that this stranger evoked in her. With a slight, embarrassed smile, Dal said, "I'm Dr. Dal Kincaid." She watched as he placed the book back onto the shelf and turned to take her hand.

"Jim Tremain, doctor. I'm the regional supervisor with the Department of the Interior." Her hand was slender and the fingertips cool to his touch. She was just as tense as he was, he realized. Did it show on him as obviously as it did on her? The nervous gesture of her tongue caressing her full lower lip sent an unbidden tremor through him. Jim released her hand, thinking she was like a delicate-boned bird. And then his eyes narrowed as he began to drink in her present condition: she was far too underweight, with dark smudges beneath her luminous blue eyes. The flesh across her cheekbones was stretched with fatigue and appeared almost translucent. Jim found himself wanting to hold her, to tell her that everything was going to be all right....

"I'm sorry I'm late. Millie told me we had an appointment." She gave a forced laugh and gestured for him to take the wing chair near the desk. "Lately my memory hasn't been what it should be. If you'll take a seat, Millie is bringing us coffee." Dal touched her breast as she rounded the desk, her heart pounding like a trapped animal. But one look into his eyes and she began to relax. He wasn't the predator he seemed to be, she thought, relieved. She had been married to a man who had turned into one;

that was enough. No, only Tremain's countenance was that of a hawk. His eyes contained kindness. And understanding. Those two discoveries helped Dal relax in his presence as she walked to the desk and sat down.

Jim waited until she sat down before taking the chair opposite the desk. The tiffany-style lamp suspended over the massive cherry furniture highlighted her spice-colored hair, bringing out strands of nutmeg shot through with gold. He found himself wondering if it was as thick and silky as it looked, lying with a slight curl across her shoulders. "No problem." He smiled, the stoic planes of his face easing. "As a matter of fact, I wouldn't have traded my drive up to the Triple K for anything, if you want the truth."

"Oh?" Her smile was in response to his. He had a wonderfully shaped mouth, Dal thought. Neither too thin nor too thick; his lower lip was full and somewhat flat. She wanted to know if he was Indian, but had the good manners not to ask him.

"I was about three miles from the main ranch house when I crested a small rise and saw this golden eagle heading straight for me." He watched her blue eyes widen. Did she realize how beautiful she was? Probably not, Jim decided. There was an artless femininity to Dal that couldn't be bought or worn at any price. She wore no makeup on her heart-shaped face—the red of her lips combined with the blush now creeping across her cheeks all that she needed.

"Oh, my God... Nar!"

"Nar?"

"Yes, the golden eagle. He disappeared over the hill near the ranch road and I lost sight of him. When he came back, he was upset." She touched her left arm, rubbing it gently to ease the remembered throbbing from her flesh.

Jim crossed his legs, enjoying her sudden emergence from her guarded stance. Her eyes had been lifeless, as if a part of her had been destroyed. Now he saw cobalt sparks in their depths, and breathed easier. She was pale and exhausted looking and it bothered him. "He's yours?" he asked, a hint of teasing in his voice. "The famous Dr. Kincaid who advocates freedom for all predators, with a golden eagle on her arm?"

Dal felt heat flow up from her neck and sweep across her face. She managed a slight smile. Since Jim Tremain was from the Department of the Interior, he had to know a great deal about wildlife conservation. For a moment, she studied him, searching her memory. A man like him would be hard to forget, and some vague spark of recognition flashed in her mind. Where had she seen him before? "Nar belongs to no one, Mr. Tremain. He's wild by nature, although he comes to visit me every morning."

"Call me Jim," he invited. "And what does the name Nar mean?"

A slight tingle flowed through her. His voice was husky and intimate. She sat up, clasping her hands in front of her on the desk. "That's Arabic for fire. His plumage, when the sun strikes it just right, becomes like molten fire. I rescued Nar from sure death seven years ago."

"Tell me about it."

Dal took a deep breath, finding herself comfortable with a man for the first time in a long while. Jack had made her distrustful of all men and their intentions. All except her brother, Rafe. And now, Jim. Funny, she mused, that she wanted to be on a first-name basis with him, when at all other times she wanted an arm's length between her and any other male.

"I was with my older brother, Rafe, and we were taking notes on where the nests of the golden eagle and redtailed hawk were located on the ranch one summer. We came up to the base of a cliff and I spotted Nar floundering in the brush. Apparently something had frightened him and he had fallen out of his nest on the cliff, or else the wind had pushed him out. We couldn't climb up the cliff to put him back into his nest, so we brought him back here." Some of the sadness fled from her eyes as Dal recalled that special day in her life.

"He was nothing but a fuzzball of gray down. When I dismounted and went over to rescue him, he sat perfectly still. I had expected him to try and escape when I leaned down, but he seemed to realize I wouldn't hurt him. There was instant trust and it hasn't stopped to this day."

Jim nodded, enjoying her sudden warmth when she

talked about the eagle. What had nearly destroyed her? She appeared tentative, almost frightened. Why? "You have no jesses on him, I noticed."

"No. I think it's wrong to keep a hawk or eagle tied to a block, only to fly them against game. It's a cruel form of imprisonment, to me. Nar comes and goes as he pleases. He usually comes to greet me every morning if I happen to be here at the ranch. Even during those six years when I was married and away, Nar would fly over.

"So this eagle imprinted and adopted you as his mother?" he said, making a guess.

Dal looked at him closely. He knew a great deal more about predators than she had given him credit for. A knock at the study door erased her next question.

Millie came in bearing a tray of freshly made cinnamon rolls glazed with butter and two mugs of steaming coffee. She handed each of them a mug and a plate with a roll, then left, but not before giving Dal a stern look that said, "You'd better eat that roll or else...."

Dal laughed softly. "I think Millie has decided we're both underweight and need to gain a few pounds."

Jim grinned, inhaling the spicy aroma of the roll, and suddenly felt hungry. "You definitely need to put on some weight, doctor."

"Call me Dal. Everyone else does." And then her heart banged at the base of her throat. *Why had she said that? Because,* her heart responded, *Jim Tremain is trustworthy.* Nervously, Dal picked at the roll, not really hungry, only wanting to camouflage her unexpected friendliness with a man who was a total stranger.

The next few minutes were spent in silence as they tackled their cinnamon rolls. Dal poured cream and sugar into her coffee, noticing that Jim drank his black.

Then, wiping her hands on a napkin, she returned to business.

"So, what does the Interior Department want, Jim?"

He put his plate on the tray and stood up, coffee mug in hand. Some of the hardness returned to the planes of his face as he studied her. "I know this is probably going to be painful to discuss, Dal."

Her arched brows moved downward. "What is?"

Jim took a sip of his coffee and set it on the tray. Typical of any cowboy, he allowed his hands to hang loosely on his hips. "Five years ago you and the department started a project to bring goshawks from Canada to nest here in the Rockies."

"Yes, and it's been a success."

Jim nodded. "A little too successful, it seems, Dal."

"What do you mean?"

"The Triple K has a high number of hawks and eagles that are natural to this area."

"We have red tails, golden eagles and Cooper's hawk."

"Plus the goshawks."

Dal nodded, resting her chin against her hands, watching him. She felt the sudden shift in energy around him. His walk belied the tension in him as he crossed the oriental rug that lay in front of the desk. His mouth, once relaxed with the corners softly turning upward, was pursed. Dal felt her stomach knotting. "I'll be going to the high country in another month to check on all the predator sites, plus log in the new nests," she said.

Jim turned, pinning her with his now umber-colored eyes. "I don't think so, Dal. It could be dangerous at that time."

She lifted her chin, eyes flaring wide. At first she

started to smile and then she saw he was serious. "What do you mean, dangerous?"

"The FBI has been working closely with the government of Canada on a group of poachers who have been stealing goshawk, peregrine, red-tail and golden eagle eggs from northern Canada."

"All right, go on."

"These poachers are a multinational band of men and women who know predatory birds well. Not only that, but they've got outlets for the stolen eggs, or eyases, over in the Middle East. As you know, falconry is a major way of life for the sheikhs and princes of those kingdoms. And now, they have a penchant for the types of birds I just mentioned, to train them into falconry."

Dal nodded grimly. "Falconry is popular in Europe, also."

Jim halted. She looked vulnerable to the point of fragility. What would she do when she found out the rest of the problem? "The demand is on an upswing. You know there's a black market for exotic or imported hawks and falcons. Some people will stop at nothing to acquire a unique specimen— much like the first kid on the block with a new car. The Middle Eastern clients are willing to spend any amount of money to get these eggs or the resulting hatched eyases. If a prince is seen with a golden eagle, then every one of his noblemen wants one, also. The demand becomes astronomical and creates lucrative black-market rings that operate against the law to acquire the birds.

"Basically what's been happening is that such a group is active in North America and has been supplying falcons and eagles to these countries. Like jewel thieves, they're professionals. Many times they'll send

in a team of three people: two who are mountain climbing experts to scale the cliffs to get the eggs or nestlings, and a third member who's an expert on spotting
nests, or is familiar with the nesting habitat of a given
area. They fly in by helicopter and ferry out their stolen
goods. Or, they may go into an area posing as hikers on
a pack trip. They're ingenious and the Royal Canadian
Mounted Police have been close to capturing them, but
they've always eluded them at the last moment."

"And they're operating in the States, too?" Dal asked.

"Yes. Five months ago, information pinpointing certain predator nesting areas was found to be missing
in Washington," he said, watching her closely. "Information that was in a computer to which only a few
knew the access code. The maps showing locations of
these birds, their nesting habitat and exact location were
taken, Dal."

Her brows drew down. "That means the locations
on the Triple K are open for poaching?"

"Those and several other key areas in Wyoming and
Montana."

She pushed her fingers through her hair in an aggra-
vated motion. "Damn these people! If it isn't the ranchers shooting these poor birds, or sheepmen poisoning
them with meat, we have poachers to contend with!"
Her voice took on an anguished edge. "Where is it all
going to end? My God!"

Jim put his hands flat on the surface of the desk,
holding her gaze. "There's more, Dal."

"How can there be?"

"Your ex-husband, Jack Gordon, is suspected of pay-
ing the government employee who took the information
from the computer. Not only that, but evidence leads us

to suspect he will mastermind the U.S. connection to the international poaching ring this year. The FBI has been following this case closely, and photos of Jack Gordon with key members of this ring were taken down in the Virgin Islands early this year. With Gordon's knowledge and skill as a trapper of exotic birds, the poaching would be a piece of cake if he chooses to get involved in it."

Dal blinked once, a gasp escaping as she stared at him. She felt as if someone had hit her in the chest, leaving her heart aching with a blinding jolt of pain. Pain that she was trying to get some distance on and forget. And then Jim Tremain blurred before her eyes as tears silently ran down her drawn cheeks.

"Here," Jim said, placing a linen handkerchief in her hands. He rose, unable to stay that close to her and not reach out and touch those tears that were falling.

"I'm sorry," he muttered and then turned away, unable to absorb the pain so apparent on her suddenly waxen features. He walked toward the door and opened it. He felt stifled and helpless to do anything for Dal. As he turned back toward her, he saw her wiping the last of the tears from her cheeks. She looked like hell.

Dal controlled her breathing, willing back the rest of the tears that wanted to fall. She was vaguely aware of Jim moving toward the liquor cabinet. An avalanche of conflicting emotions ripped through her: anger over what Jack had done and then anger at Jim Tremain for dredging up a part of her life that she wanted to forget.

"Drink this," Jim offered quietly, putting a shot glass filled with apricot brandy in front of her. "Go on...."

Wordlessly, Dal took a hefty gulp, the brandy burning all the way down. But it staunched her tears and steadied her roiling emotions. "Thanks," she murmured, setting the glass down.

"I'm sorry. I know you were recently divorced." Jim's mouth worked into a grim line as she lifted her head and looked at him. "I had a choice: come to you for help or let the FBI start crawling all over the place trying to capture Gordon and his counterpart. I came to you for help because you know the location of all these nesting areas. No one knows predators like you do."

Dal gave him a mirthless smile. "Certain two-legged predators, Mr. Tremain. The feathered variety, not the human ones."

Jim steeled himself. Now it was Mr. Tremain and not Jim. She was on the defensive again, but he couldn't blame her. He kept his husky voice low and steady, as if calming a frantic horse. "My men and I will take care of the other two-legged predators. If you can act as guide, we'll set up a trap that will capture Gordon and his people."

"Am I a suspect, Mr. Tremain?"

"No."

"Why not?"

Jim steadily met her blue eyes. "Given your record of conservation of predators, doctor, I felt you were innocent."

"So someone didn't think I was?"

He met her cool smile. "The FBI considers you questionable. If you want to know."

"And you don't?"

"No."

She gave him a flat glare of disgust. "I'm surprised I'm not an accessory to the fact, Mr. Tremain." Dal rose and paced the study for a minute before meeting his gaze. "Let me get this straight. You want me for a guide in late May to find the location of the eggs or nestlings?"

"Yes."

"And then what?"

"I'll have the men who are at my disposal close in on the ring once we know they're in the area. The eggs of most predators will be hatched by early June, making them prime for poaching. The eyases are best caught just before they learn to fly. I think Gordon will start with the nests in the southern regions and work his way north with the warmer weather. And the Triple K is the farthest south of all the areas."

Dal paced some more, explosive anger building within her. "I came to the Triple K for a long rest, Mr. Tremain. I don't want to play tour guide. I don't want to even think about that ex-husband of mine!" She halted, drawing herself up, her face mirroring her feelings. "Jack wouldn't step on Triple K land. Rafe would kill him and he knows that."

Jim spread his hands in a gesture of peace. "Look, I know this comes as a shock but—"

"I won't do it, Mr. Tremain."

He winced at the anguish in her voice. "I need your help, doctor. If I can't enlist your aid, then the FBI is going to come barreling in here and take over. I don't think your brother would like to get the law entangled in the daily running of his ranch. Right now, there's calving and moving the herds to higher country for the summer. Do you want a bunch of three-piece-suited dudes from D.C. overrunning this place? I know they'll botch the capture of the poachers because they're unfamiliar with the terrain and methods that it will take to capture them. And they'll also make a mess of things here."

Dal glared at him, rubbing her temples with her fingers. "What are you talking about?"

"If you don't agree to help me, they're going to set up operations here at the Triple K. I persuaded the inspector to let me take on the task and see if I could get you to work with us. That way, your brother can go about his business of running his ranch and we'll stay out from underfoot."

"Either way, you'll be here," Dal said bitterly, crossing her arms.

Jim felt his heart wrench. The kind, soft-spoken Dal Kincaid he had seen a short while ago was gone. And he had caused the change. Now, she was defensive and hurting. Whatever trust he had briefly established with her was destroyed. "It's better than the alternative, doctor."

She wanted to scream. She wanted to sob. *Oh, God! Jack, again.* The man whom she had loved at one time and who had learned to love money more than her or their marriage. He had known how to manipulate her emotions until she had felt herself shredded by his razor-blade tactics. Dal knew she had to get hold of herself. She had to think clearly. Fairly. Lifting her head, she looked over at Jim Tremain.

"It's stuffy in here. I want to go outside."

"All right. Let's go."

The April sun was weak but welcome on her face as they crossed the muddy yard between the horse and cow barns. Dal led Jim to a pipe-fenced paddock and placed both elbows on the pipe. The breeze was inconstant, occasionally lifting strands of her hair across her jacketed shoulders. For no identifiable reason, Dal felt an island of momentary peace when Jim Tremain hitched up his foot onto the lowest pipe of the fence. Their elbows almost touched.

"I love coming out here," she confided softly. The paddock contained four brood mares and their newborn foals.

Jim glanced at her. "The babies?"

She nodded, a tremulous smile lifting the corners of her mouth. "The babies," she agreed. "When Rafe took over the operation of the Triple K eight years ago, he replaced the quarter horses with Arabians. They're smaller, but they have more endurance and are as tough as the mustangs that cross our land."

"They're like you, then, doctor."

Dal turned, perplexed by the intimate tone of his voice. She trembled beneath the smile that reached his clear brown eyes. "I don't understand."

"You're as beautiful as they are and you have an inner core of endurance that will see you through."

She laughed, but it was a hollow sound filled with pain. "Oh? And just where did you gain such insight, Mr. Tremain?"

His smile broadened as he held her confused gaze. "My mother. She was a full-blooded Navaho. She was the one who taught me to listen to my heart and not my head. Call it a sixth sense. I just feel that when the going gets rough, you're there with commensurate strength to survive and become stronger because of the experience."

Warmth flowed through Dal, dissolving the icy cold fist in the pit of her stomach. She stood beneath Jim's gentle inspection, lost in the smoldering gold of his eyes, seeing much and unable to decipher all that he said with them. Dal felt breathless and tore her gaze from his, staring at the brood mares instead.

"Right now, Jim," she said in a whisper, "I'm at the end of my rope emotionally. I won't bore you with the travesty of my marriage to Jack Gordon. The past two years of hell have worn me down. I once thought I had a backbone of steel like the rest of the Kincaids, but I don't. Not anymore. I'm raw. I can't take too much emotionally or I'll crack and I know it."

She removed her elbows from the pipe and stood, hands buried deep in the pockets of her jacket as she looked up at him. The brim of his hat shaded his eyes and hid his reaction to her admission. "That's why I'm here at the family ranch, Jim. I'm trying to patch myself together so I can go back out in the world and live again."

Jim raised his hand, taking a strand of hair from her cheek and easing it behind her delicate ear. His voice was thick with emotion when he finally spoke. "If I told you I'd take care of you through this problem we've got with Gordon, would you believe me?"

Chapter 2

Hot scalding tears pricked the backs of Dal's eyes as she stood looking up at Jim. His image blurred and she turned away, walking a few paces, her back to him.

Jim stared at her back, noting the way her shoulders were tensed and drawn up. He had watched her vulnerable eyes darken with a torture known only to herself and had seen her full, generous mouth draw into a line of anguish. What had happened in her marriage to tear her apart like this? Swallowing hard, he waited, his senses cautioning him that if he were to approach her too soon or try in some way to comfort her, she would turn on him. Trust, his senses screamed at him; she trusts no one. No man. He searched his memory for facts regarding Jack Gordon: he was an entrepreneur in the business of birds, capturing rare or colorful species from jungles around the world and selling them to zoos or private patrons. In those six years of marriage, had Gordon used Dal to sharpen his own education and utilized her knowledge to enhance his lucrative, international business?

Dal struggled to force down the lid on the caldrons of emotion that Jim Tremain had torn lose with his one touch. He had shaken her to the core. He wanted to use her just as Jack had at the end of their once happy marriage. Jim was even more dangerous because he knew how to read her and get what he wanted. Jack's methods were always obvious once he had allowed material goods and stature become the center of importance to him. Jim knew that a simple gesture, such as placing a strand of hair behind her ear, would catch her off guard and place her in a more vulnerable position. Anger warred with a heart that said: he did it out of care, not because he wanted to use you. Pressing her fingers to her temples, Dal shut her eyes tightly for a moment, willing all her anger, frustration and pain back into a tightly lidded place in her heart.

She turned, her shoulders sagging as she stared at Jim. As much as she tried, Dal could not find one shred of selfishness in his face. If anything, she was screamingly aware of the tender light that burned in his golden eyes, the laugh lines at their corners and the way his mouth was pursed. *Oh God, no!* she cried inwardly. She had learned to take a secondary role to Jack's aims. But she had no defense against a man who showed her kindness. *It's all a sham,* her mind screamed. *He wants something from you, just like Jack did. Only he's going to take it from you a different way. Jack wanted your knowledge. Jim wants the same thing.*

Dal had not realized that two paths of tears had

streaked down her cheeks as she stood staring at him. It was only when she saw his eyes darken and his mouth part in protest that she became aware of why he was reacting. Quickly wiping the telltale signs away, Dal lifted her head, her azure eyes darkened with confusion.

"No, I wouldn't believe that you or anyone could protect me from Jack. Not now. Not ever," she forced out in a low, quavering tone.

"I'm sorry, I didn't mean to make you cry."

Dal looked blindly toward the paddock, unable to hold his understanding gaze. Jim was dangerous to her and she wanted to run. Run and hide. "I told you, I'm in no shape to help anyone. Not even myself."

Jim moved closer, but not close enough to frighten her into fleeing. She reminded him vividly of a hunted deer standing tautly before him, an almost imperceptible quiver surrounding her. "My mother always told me tears were healing. I see nothing wrong with them."

She snapped her head to the left, glaring at him. "Part of your half-breed heritage, no doubt."

Jim's mouth thinned as he studied her in that glacial moment. *Half-breed.* The word made his mouth go bitter with the taste of his past. He struggled with his anger toward her and then surmounted it. She had hurled the insult at him to get him to stop pressuring her. He drew the cowboy hat down a little lower on his brow, forcing a one-cornered smile. "My half-breed status has gotten me out of more trouble than in," he countered mildly.

"How? By pushing papers in an office for the government!"

Jim leaned languidly against the pipe railing, studying the foals, who were now frolicking around their mothers after their recent meal. "My boss complains

I'm not there enough to push those papers around. Usually, I'm in the field with my people." His gaze moved to her. "I'd rather have the sky for a ceiling and a good horse under me instead of sitting at a desk. How about you? Which do you prefer?"

Dal frowned and licked her lips in a nervous gesture. He was cunning. He had diffused her attack and managed to steer the entire matter into an innocuous but important investigation of her as a person. "I'm sure you have a file on me in your office, Mr. Tremain. There's little I care to add to that."

"We're not the FBI, doctor. The file I have on you is about your educational background, not your personal life." He scowled. "But if you don't allow me to enlist your help on this project, the FBI will come in. I don't think you or your family will want that. It's my opinion that because I and my people know the mountains and habitats, we stand a much better chance of netting the poachers than the FBI will."

Dal clamped her lips together, refusing to be drawn into his soft banter. She liked his voice. It reminded her of a cat's roughened tongue licking her hand, and sent delicious prickles of pleasure through her. She tried to squash all those feelings. "I'll let my brother Rafe decide what's going to happen, Mr. Tremain. It's his ranch. I'm only a guest here."

"All right," he said slowly. "It will be necessary to talk to him, anyway. He's as much a part of this plan as you are."

"Rafe will be back tomorrow morning. He had business in Denver."

"Maybe you can tell me where there might be a motel around here?"

Dal gave him a brief glance. He looked more like a wrangler than a government official. Cowboys had their own code and could be trusted. Jack was a civilian. An outsider. But Jim Tremain wasn't. "There isn't a motel within sixty miles of our ranch."

"I see…."

Guilt twinged in her and Dal was unable to maintain that barrier of anger toward him. She could see his mind working beyond those lion-like eyes, and she watched as he rested his long, tapered fingers on his slender hips. She could discern the Indian blood in him by the sharp planed features of his face and his sun-darkened flesh. Another shaft of guilt struck her: she had called him a half-breed. God, what was wrong with her? She never threw prejudiced comments like that at anyone.

"There's no sense in you driving all the way back to Denver just to come here again tomorrow morning," she heard herself say. "I'll get Millie to fix up one of the spare bedrooms and you can stay here tonight."

Jim's eyes glimmered with some undefined emotion as he met and held her nervous gaze. "That's more than kind of you, doctor. Thank you." So, he thought, there was ground for them to work on after all; he hadn't totally destroyed the possibility of their combining their expertise on the poaching problem.

Shoving her hands in the pockets of her jacket, Dal stared down at the muddy earth. "It's nothing," she muttered, walking past him. "Let me tell Millie you'll be staying."

He watched her walk between the barns and knit his black brows. She was scared of him. As a man? Or as a government emissary? The Kincaids had a sterling reputation of having worked closely with conservation officials in the past on a number of wildlife projects. As Jim ambled around the paddocks, eyeing the horse-flesh in each, he narrowed down Dal's reaction to her distrust of him as a man. That cut down the chances of her agreeing to help him.

Sunlight bathed the valley as the clouds parted, slats shining across the lush land of the Triple K. Jim watched as a group of wranglers coaxed a herd of about a hundred Herefords out of a paddock, heading them in the direction of some upper pasture. He inhaled the crisp spring air, glad to be out of the office and in the field again. And then a rueful smile split his harsh features. Would "guard dog" Millie allow him to stay at the ranch overnight?

"What do you mean he's stayin', Dal?" Millie lifted her head, her chin jutting out stubbornly.

Dal walked farther into the spacious kitchen that was Millie's territory. The red-tiled floor gleamed from a recent waxing, giving the cedar walls even more warmth. She poured herself a glass of water and leaned against the counter. Millie resumed folding the bread dough on the table, flour spotting her plump arms.

"He wants to talk to Rafe about poachers. I didn't have the heart to make him drive sixty miles to a motel and then come all the way back tomorrow morning."

"You know Rafe doesn't like strangers about," Millie chided gruffly.

"I know…."

Millie straightened, put the dough into a bread pan and then transferred it to the countertop. "Still," she muttered, moving back to the table to begin folding another batch of dough, "he doesn't seem all that bad."

Dal raised an eyebrow at the housekeeper. Millie was mountain born and bred. She had an uncanny knack of summing up people on first sight. "What do you mean?"

"He might be with the government, but he's got some horse sense in him. Can see it in those whiskey-colored eyes of his. That man's always thinking. I nearly took his head off at the door earlier and he was like a duck, letting my snaps and snarls roll off his back like water. Didn't let it ruffle him one way or another. He's a man of patience, I can tell you that." And then Millie looked up at her. "The exact opposite of that sidewinder of an ex-husband of yours!"

"What would I do without you around, Millie?" Dal asked with a grin.

"Humph! You might've listened to me when you first dragged Gordon home here to the ranch with you. Your parents didn't like him. Rafe hated him on sight. Even your sister Cathy couldn't stand him."

Dal lost her smile and drank the rest of the water. "Nobody liked him," she agreed quietly. "Except me."

"Humph! What did you know? With you being in love for the first time in your life and Gordon being ten years your senior, he manipulated you just like a hand puppet." Millie's stern features softened momentarily. "But that's all right, lamb. You did love him up until the time he let all that worldwide fame go to his addled brain. The important thing is you're out from under his clutches. I told you then he was a wolf in sheep's clothing, and I was right. We all make mistakes. The important thing is not doing the same thing over again!"

Dal's laugh was strained as she placed the glass in the sink. "No chance of that, Millie. Men and marriage are two things that have been written off my life list."

Millie shot her a know-it-all glance. "Maybe right now, lamb, but you're a woman who needs a partner. You were made for marriage. Your sister Cathy isn't, but you are. You work better in a team harness than as a single."

Dal laughed and went over, hugging the housekeeper. "Oh, Millie…"

Regaining her stern look, Millie pinched Dal's cheek, leaving a bit of flour on it. "Just listen to us, lamb. That's all I ask. Your parents are right in wanting you to stay here to recuperate. So what if you miss a year of teaching at the university? You're hurt bad by this divorce. Just don't shut us out."

Dal nodded, feeling her heart wrench in her chest as she walked slowly around the airy kitchen. "I have been, haven't I?"

Millie nodded. "You need to talk to someone about all this. Ever since you came home, you've kept to yourself. All you do is meet that eagle every morning and go for long horseback rides. Rafe's worried about you…."

Dal turned, her face contorted. "My God, Rafe's got enough on his shoulders, Millie. He just lost his wife and baby a year ago. He doesn't need me crying the blues to him. I didn't lose someone I loved, Millie. Jack killed my love for him. Rafe lost the two most important people in his life. How can I go to him?"

"Sometimes, lamb, healing takes place between two hurt animals. You've seen how cats or dogs will lick each other's wounds to speed their recovery. Maybe you need to do the same thing. Think about it."

Running her fingers through her thick hair, Dal left the kitchen. Millie was right: she did need to confide in someone. But whom? Her parents, God bless them, were more than willing to help her. But they had a marriage that seemed to have been made in heaven—not like the one she had had. How could they understand that Jack's love for her had been replaced with something he considered more important? He had beat her down emotionally until she had almost lost her sense of selfhood. There was Rafe, but he was barely surviving on a daily basis between shouldering the massive responsibilities of the ranch and his own internalized grief he refused to release over the loss of his family. She wouldn't put her burdens on Rafe. She loved him too much to do that. Rafe was the oldest and always felt responsible for her and Cathy. For once, she was going to handle her problems by herself.

There was Cathy, Dal mused, standing at the picture window, staring out at the brilliant sunlight that bathed the green valley before her. Cathy was a mining engineer, a trouble-shooting expert for gem mines around the world. They had never been close as sisters growing up, each going to Rafe instead. Rubbing her temple, Dal admitted to herself that they were both pretty volatile and temperamental, whereas Rafe was an island of continuity, trust and steadfastness. Just like Jim Tremain.

A softened smile touched her lips as she mulled over her insight into Jim. She liked him. Or at least a part of her did. Her silly, blind heart. Her mind, on the other hand, distrusted him completely because he was a man who was able to infiltrate her defenses and reach out and touch her. Her blue eyes grew clouded with worry. What if Rafe decided that she should work with Jim? The brittle, damaged part of her cried out in sheer alarm over that possibility. How could she explain to Rafe that Jim Tremain knew how to get to her? And how could she explain how dangerous that was to her open wounds that hadn't yet begun to heal? Would Rafe understand? Sometimes he was blindly insensitive to the subtle emotions.

Dal was pulled from her reverie as she noticed a dark shape growing larger and larger in the sky. It was Nar! What was he doing back there? She looked at her watch: it was almost noon. Concerned, she pulled on her sheepskin jacket and ran out the back door. Mud sloshed around her cowboy boots as she heard Nar's shrilling cry overhead. The golden eagle swooped down and past her, ruffling her hair from the closeness of his pass as he glided out toward the last of the horse paddocks.

Dal went into an old garage that had a large oak block in the center of its quiet confines. Picking up the protective leather gauntlet, she slipped it over her left hand and arm and walked quickly out beyond the barn. She heard Nar shrilling, and as she rounded the end of the barn she almost collided with Jim Tremain.

"Oh!"

Jim reached out, gripping her arm as she stumbled. "Sorry."

Regaining her balance, Dal kept her eye on the golden eagle that was circling lazily above them. Her heart was pounding and it wasn't from the seventy-five-hundred-foot elevation, either. She was wildly aware of the strength of Jim's hand upon her arm; her senses were screamingly alive as she rested momentarily against his hard, unyielding male body. There was nothing about him that spoke of soft office life. As her right hand rested on his chest, Dal felt the smooth interplay of muscles move beneath his shirt.

"Thanks," she said breathlessly, pulling from his grip.

"Is that the same eagle I saw you with earlier?"

Dal nodded. "Yes. Nar never comes this late in the day. I wonder if something's wrong?"

Jim watched her as she made a series of high-pitched whistling sounds. The golden eagle, which was at least two thousand feet above them, suddenly stooped. Jim's breath caught in his throat as the raptor's wings folded against its body for the dive toward earth, legs outstretched and murderous-looking black talons opened. The power of the eagle was awesome as it fell like a hurtling rocket fired from the sky. Jim held up his hands to warn Dal, but it was too late.

The golden eagle broke his stoop at the last possible second, the backwash from his wings powerful as he hung suspended for a split second before coming to rest on Dal. She held her arm high above her, her knees deeply flexed and legs spread far apart as she took the shock of the eagle's full weight.

Jim looked on in a mixture of terror for her and admiration at the spectacle before him. At that moment, he saw Dal's face light up with such joy that he found his own heart pounding in his chest. Her blue eyes were filled with the fire of life as the eagle mantled, flapping his seven-foot wingspread, hackles raised on its head, and gave a fierce call from his blue-black beak. Jim stood transfixed, privy to something that few people would ever see. Nar folded his massive wings, his feathered legs and yellow feet in sharp contrast to the tanned kidskin glove he gripped, his amber eyes large and intelligent looking.

Dal laughed softly and raised her right hand, gently stroking his feathered breast.

"Poor day hunting, is that it?" she teased the bird.

"His crop is empty," she called to Jim. "That's why he's here."

Nar lifted his majestic head, staring imperiously at Jim. Dal turned. "He doesn't know you, so don't come any closer," she warned quietly.

"No need to worry," he assured her, observing the raptor. "He's got to be heavy."

Dal nodded. "All thirteen pounds of him. He's three feet in length. As you can tell, he's fully matured because he has no white feathers under his wings here. He's still a baby at seven years old."

"He's a big baby," Jim said with a grin.

"A spoiled one. He must have been too upset after meeting you on the crest of that hill to continue hunting."

"He wasn't the only one," Jim drawled, meeting her smile. My God, he thought, she was simply breathtaking. Her cheeks were flushed and her eyes sparkled like dark sapphires. Jim had the urge to reach out and simply cradle her face between his hands and worship those smiling lips with his mouth. Right now, she was a child, as was he. His gaze traveled to the eagle. It was wildlife that brought Dal out of her cloak of distrust for him. He absorbed every nuance of her in those precious moments.

Jim eyed the eagle's grasp on her arm now; Nar was barely gripping it. "When he's upset he grips hard?"

"Yes. Remind me when he decides to leave to show you the scars I have on this arm."

"God, he's magnificent."

Dal met his gaze. "Yes, he is. And he's free."

"And yet you've trained him to sit on your arm."

She shivered beneath the husky excitement in his

voice. Suddenly she was sharing one of the few joys of her life with Jim, and she wanted to. The look of excitement in his eyes told her everything. He was just as elated as she was with the majesty of Nar.

"I started feeding him when he was a baby. When he was old enough to begin to fly, I had to make a lure out of a rabbit skin with raw meat attached to it and teach him how to catch food." She laughed. "I'd swing the lure and he'd sit on my arm looking first at me and then at it. Finally, I'd throw him off my arm and swing the lure and he'd stoop, grabbing it in his talons. After that, I'd take him out to one of the meadows, cast him off into the air and he'd hunt his own rabbits or whatever."

"And he still returns to you after being put back out in the wild?"

"When I got here six months ago, Nar somehow knew I was home again. Every morning he'll be sitting on the block right after sunrise, waiting for me." She gave Jim a shy look. "It's our special time together. Nar flies to the meadow, circling me as I ride on horseback. Then I give him a few scraps of chicken or beef liver and then we play."

"What do you mean 'play'?" Jim had a tough time accepting that the raptor knew the meaning of the word play. There was nothing harmless about the bird.

Her smile widened. "Want to ride with me tomorrow morning at dawn and find out?"

Removing his hat, he scratched his head and thought about the invitation. "He won't attack me? I've heard of other falcons and eagles being so protective of their masters that they'll attack anyone who gets near them."

"Nar won't hurt you. He knows you're a friend and not an enemy," she assured him.

At that moment Nar turned, chirping softly at her, and then raised one wing, preening his molten-bronze feathers. Dal smiled and leaned forward, touching the bird's breast with her cheek. "He's such a pushover," she confided, lifting her head.

Jim nodded, thinking that the eagle had one hell of a deal going for him. Not only was the bird on the receiving end of her affection, she trusted him. He knew that with a murderous beak like that, Nar had only to strike with savage swiftness to quite literally open up half of Dal's face, if he chose. Jim wouldn't want that fierce predator on his arm for any reason...and that left him worried for her sake. Falcons or eagles that had been kept in captivity for years were known to turn moody unexpectedly and strike their owner, inflicting no small degree of damage. Dal's flesh was too soft, too lovely to mar with a scar made by Nar.

"Some pushover," he growled.

"Follow me. I'm going to take him to his block and feed him some beef liver. On some days when food is scarce, he'll make his presence known here at the ranch in no uncertain terms. Millie's chased him away from the henhouse more than once," she added with a laugh. "And Rafe has been ready to strangle him on a number of occasions for frightening the foals as he glides across the paddocks to the garage where his block is."

Jim followed her into the gloom of the garage. As if on some silent cue, Nar stepped like a gentleman from her arm to the large, round wooden block that stood five feet off the concrete floor. Dal rubbed her arm. "God, he's heavy."

"I thought he was going to knock you over when he went into that stoop."

"He has, a number of times," she said with a chuckle, going to the refrigerator. "You figure a thirteen-pound eagle stooping at thirty miles an hour and calculate the force with which he comes in for a landing! Then, when he wraps his claws around your forearm…" She pulled out a package of beef liver, unwrapped it and threw the meat toward Nar. The eagle's right leg shot out, his talons catching the food midair. Then he mantled, flapping his wings. The feathers on his head rose and he shrilled in warning.

Dal reached over, taking Jim's arm. "Come on. Feeding time means leaving him alone. If he thinks you're going to try and take that food away, he'll fly at us."

Not needing any more coaxing, Jim slid his hand beneath Dal's elbow and led her back out into the sunlight. They stood there, watching the eagle for a minute or two. Jim smiled to himself; Dal was standing less than six inches from him and wasn't displaying any of her previous nervousness. He thanked Nar for that.

"Isn't it dangerous raising a bird like that?"

She pulled the glove off her left arm and held out her hand to him. Innumerable white and even recent pinkish scars marred her artistic-looking fingers. Turning her palm over, Dal pointed to a long deep scar that ran the length of her hand. Her voice held a rueful note. "When Nar was six months old he decided to make a meal of Millie's cat, Goodyear. You'll see him around here, I'm sure. He's a long-haired white and yellow cat who stole Millie's heart. Consequently, she overfeeds him, and so we started calling him the Goodyear blimp because he resembled one. I was out with the foals when Nar flew from his aerie on the cliffs about ten miles north of here. It was the middle of the day, so I was surprised to see him. I heard his call first. And then I saw Good-year crossing the hen yard."

Jim matched her grin. "So of course, Nar thought Goodyear was an ideal meal on wheels."

"Exactly! The only thing that saved the blimp was the fact that at that age Nar wasn't expert at stooping and catching his quarry. He managed to skim the ground and caught Goodyear's tail between his claws." Dal hooted with laughter as she recalled the event. "Imagine Millie coming out of the house screaming at the top of her lungs and waving a broom, and the blimp squalling for all of his nine lives, and Nar shrieking because the cat wouldn't stay still."

"So who got to whom first?" Jim asked, enjoying her warmth and camaraderie.

"Thankfully, I did. One thing I learned about predators long ago is that you never take their quarry away from them. I tried to get Nar to let go of Goodyear, who was still squalling, and I was begging Millie not to hit the eagle all at the same time. I put my arm out and I didn't even have a glove on, so I knew I was in trouble. Nar wasn't going to let go, so I reached down and tapped him smartly across the legs. His right leg came up like lightning and he struck at me. Goodyear escaped and I sat hunched in front of Nar with the palm of my hand sliced down to the muscle." She grimaced. "Needless to say, Rafe was ready to shoot Nar before he took me to the hospital for stitches and a tetanus shot."

Jim picked up her hand, gently cradling it between his own. He ran his thumb lightly down the length of the puckered scar. "Did you stop to think he might have struck at you with his beak and blinded you or scarred your face for life…?"

A tingle of unexpected fire leaped to life as he caressed her hand. Dal's mouth grew dry, and she lifted her head and stared up into his dark gold eyes. Eyes of a hawk, her mind whispered. Yes, he was like a hawk, she thought weakly, tendrils of pleasure leaping like hot fire licking through her nerve endings as he met and held her gaze. His fingers were long and warm against the dampness of her own and she felt the callused roughness of his hands. Working hands. Not soft like an office worker's. She blinked once, ensnared within the web of his amber gaze, an ache centering in her breast. Dal sensed his caring, his genuine concern toward her. It was no game. No, the low tremor in his voice that impacted her so headily was completely sincere.

"I...hadn't thought of that," she stammered, withdrawing her hand from his. Dal felt the heat of her blush and cringed inwardly. At thirty she shouldn't be blushing. Just another Kincaid trait, she thought, embarrassed as she saw the beginning of a smile on Jim's mouth.

"Well," he growled softly, "from now on, if you don't think of it, I will. You're too beautiful to have your skin marred by that eagle if he takes a fit of temper again."

She felt as if she were in a pool of golden light that surrounded them in that mesmerizing moment. All sounds ceased to exist except his low voice and the many unspoken messages conveyed by his predator-like gaze. It was so long since a man had honestly cared what happened to her. "Well," she heard herself say in a faraway voice, "Nar isn't temperamental. Some birds are moody, but he isn't. You just can't take the food that he's earned away from him, that's all."

"Dal?" Millie's voice carried across the yard. Dal

gave Jim a quick look, as if relieved that their intimacy had been broken by the interruption.

"Coming, Millie." She managed a slight smile of apology. "Come on, lunch is ready."

"Good," Jim murmured, "I'm starved."

Casting him a suspicious look, Dal tried to read between the lines of his statement. Yes, she had seen hunger burning in the depths of his eyes, and it was all aimed at her. She was trembling and that shocked her. Even her knees were weak as she walked toward the ranch house with him. How could that be? Jim had simply touched her palm. What was going on within her? she wondered. When Jack touched her, her skin crawled and she shrank deep within herself to blot out his advance. But Jim's touch...

Dal tried to analyze the chemistry that existed between them, scared to death.

After lunch Dal excused herself and went into the study to lie down on the couch. She hadn't slept well the previous night, as usual, and she catnapped daily to catch up on the sleep lost during the night. She pulled the orange, blue and green afghan that Millie had knit across her shoulders and drifted off quickly. The study was her one refuge while Jim Tremain was there. Usually, she would take a nap in the living room where the fire crackled and popped with friendly sounds, lulling her to sleep. Now she closed her eyes, wondering what he might think if he knew she slept on the couch every night instead of in a bedroom. What did she care what he thought? Grousing at her inability to make many decisions in her life yet, Dal let it all go, sleep claiming her almost immediately.

Millie woke her near three, stroking her hair in a gentle motion. "Time to get up, lamb."

Dal groaned, stretching and yawning. "Three already?"

"Already," Millie agreed, looking down at her. "What time did you finally get to sleep last night?"

"Around four in the morning," she admitted, her voice thick with sleep as she sat up.

"More nightmares?"

"Didn't you hear me?"

"My room's in the back. You know I don't hear a thing."

Dal rubbed her face tiredly. "Rafe usually does."

Millie nodded, her eyes mirroring her unspoken worry. "Why don't you try and sleep in your own room tonight?"

Her heart suddenly began pounding in her breast and Dal felt herself going all shaky inside. "No... I can't, Millie. Not yet."

"But Mr. Tremain is here. He's a stranger to the house. What if he finds you sleeping out on the couch?"

She shrugged tiredly. "He'll have the guest bedroom next to your room, Millie. I doubt he'll hear a thing if I do wake up. Besides, I'll work late tonight for Rafe, here in the study. By the time I get my bed made up in the living room, Jim... I mean Mr. Tremain, will have already gone to sleep."

"Whatever you say, lamb. Speaking of Mr. Tremain, he's been outdoors most of the time snooping around."

Dal looked up, smiling. "Snooping?" she teased. Millie distrusted everyone in general unless they had been born on the Triple K.

"Poking and prodding. You know. Charlie, the farrier, came in to tell me he was out in the stud barn looking over Rafe's stock."

Rising, then folding the afghan and hanging it neatly on the back of the leather couch, Dal asked, "Is that where he is now?"

"Guess so," Millie groused. "That man's got the curiosity of a cat."

"Probably nine lives, too," Dal said, chuckling. She put her arm around Millie and walked out of the study with her.

"You gonna go find him?"

"Sure. Matter of fact, the day's so nice, I think we'll take a ride. Rafe wanted me to check that new barbed wire fence the hands put up in the southern pasture. Mr. Tremain looks like he might put a leg over a good horse, so let's not disappoint him."

"Humph! Ask me, that man was born to the saddle."

Dal felt lighter, happier. Happy? When had she last felt like this? The feeling was so foreign to her that it sobered her sharply. She divided her attention between the housekeeper and her unexpected revelation. "We'll be back around seven at the latest."

"Just in time for supper."

Dal grabbed her dark brown felt cowboy hat and dropped it on her head. The late April day was turning mild, with the temperature probably somewhere in the high forties, she figured. She was used to below-zero conditions of winter, and forty felt like summer. She decided to leave her sheepskin coat behind, since the long sleeves of her shirt would be warm enough. Then she headed toward the Arabian stallion barn.

Jim looked up as many of the horses whickered simultaneously in greeting. There was Dal, at the entrance to the airy barn, walking toward him. He saw that she looked rested, the shadows gone from beneath her blue eyes. Did she realize how graceful she was? He had a tough time disguising the inner hunger he felt for her as she drew abreast of him.

"I see you've made friends with our three studs," Dal said with a smile as she opened the box stall of a white stallion, led him out to the center of the aisle and placed him in the cross ties. "You ready for a ride with me?"

Jim followed and picked up the tack box from the tack room, handing her a currycomb and taking a brush for himself.

He began brushing down the stallion. "Sure."

She grinned at him, then went to the tack room to find the appropriate saddle. "Trusting soul, aren't you? You don't even ask where we're going or what we'll be doing."

He took the blanket and saddle from her and tacked up the Arab, which pawed restlessly in the ties. Jim's amber eyes were dark and thoughtful as he looked across at Dal. "I'm trusting of some people," he countered.

"And how do you know you can trust me?" Dal taunted softly.

"Your mouth."

She laughed outright, curious as to how he saw her. "My mouth?"

"Or maybe it's your large deerlike eyes. Vulnerable mouth and trusting eyes," he murmured, finishing his task by bridling the horse.

Dal gave him a grim look. "You're serious, aren't you?"

He handed the reins of the horse to her but she shook her head. "He's yours to ride. His name is Flight."

Jim smiled. "Fast, eh?"

"You'll see," she promised, walking down to another stall.

Within minutes Dal had her favorite gray gelding saddled and they were off at a brisk trot toward the southern pasture. Flight pranced sideways, blowing and snorting beneath the capable hand of Jim Tremain. From time to time Dal would drop back slightly and watch him handle the spirited stallion. Millie was right; Jim knew how to ride with the best of them. His thighs were long and powerful against the stallion's barrel, and he rose and fell with each stride of the horse, as if they were one. He was beautiful, Dal decided. The man and the stallion: one and the same with so much spirit fused with pride and maleness.

"You and Flight suit each other admirably," she complimented dryly, riding at his side.

Jim's eyes narrowed as he studied her. "I hope your brother approves of me riding one of his prize stallions."

"Rafe knows I'd never let anyone ride Flight who didn't know what he was doing."

"Is my wrangler side that obvious?"

She grinned. "You've got bowed legs like the rest of us. What do you think?"

His laughter was deep and clear and it freed Dal in a breathless sort of way. When he smiled, the crinkles at the corners of his eyes deepened, and the smile lines around his mouth became grooves that eased the hardness of his features.

"I thought you were going to blame my Navaho blood," he teased.

Dal became more serious, her curiosity overcoming her natural distrust of him. Flight was a volatile animal at best, and yet beneath Jim's firm but sensitive hand the stallion had never once tossed his head or fought the bit. Her gaze rested on Jim's hands, and she recalled him sensitively caressing the flesh of her palm. Her heart beat a little faster as she savored that branding moment earlier.

"I owe you an apology, Jim."

"Oh?"

"I called you a half-breed. I shouldn't have. I'm sorry."

His eyes were filled with amusement. "I didn't take what you said seriously, so don't apologize. You were a little out of sorts, that's all."

Dal cast him a spurious look. "I haven't figured out whether you're a mind reader or not," she muttered.

"Why?"

"Because you know me too well."

"What's wrong with that?"

"Nothing. Everything. Men are insensitive."

His mouth curved into a teasing smile. "Is that like 'all women are catty'?"

She laughed at his generalization. "Touché. Well, I guess I can throw all my labels out the window with you and start all over."

He gave her a heated look. "I think you'd better," he said huskily.

Chapter 3

It was nearly eleven when Jim sauntered into the study that evening. Dal sat at the cherrywood desk, calculator nearby and pen in hand, wrestling with a set of figures in a ledger before her. Her head was bent, one hand resting against her wrinkled brow as she labored over the accounting records. Jim leaned casually against the door frame, a tender light burning in his eyes as he watched Dal. She looked closer to twenty-four years old rather than thirty, he thought ruefully. Her skin had a peach color to it and her cheeks were rosy with good health. Had their ride earlier brought that color to her face? She was a different person when she was on horseback or working with her eagle. At other times, Jim could feel her putting up walls and shrinking behind them. Why? He wanted to find out. If Rafe Kincaid approved of his plan, Dal would be working with him almost constantly.

And then he could gently get her to remove those barriers that she threw up so easily between them.

"I wanted to come in and say good-night," he said softly, so as not to startle her.

Dal raised her head, a tired smile on her full lips. "How long have you been standing there?"

He became concerned with the exhaustion he saw in the depths of her sapphire eyes. "A few minutes."

"You're silent. Like a cougar."

"But not dangerous like one."

Dal brushed several strands of hair from her eyes. "Every man is dangerous."

Easing from his position, Jim walked over to the desk, holding her challenging gaze. A smile relaxed the angles of his face beneath the lamplight. "Give me a chance to prove your generalization isn't always right."

She stared up at him, thinking how ruggedly handsome he was and that there wasn't the aura of male ego around him that she associated with most men. Another blessing of his Indian heritage? Pursing her lips, she returned to the numbers beneath her hands. "Perhaps Indians aren't as concerned with the macho image as most men."

Jim slid his long, tapered fingers across the dark polished wood of the desk, watching her. They had come so far so quickly. Despite her distrust, Dal was opening up to him. Did she realize it? Probably not. "The Navaho revere their women. As a matter of fact, it's a matriarchal society. In your present mood, you'd probably feel very secure in that type of environment."

Dal gave a soft snort and tried to concentrate, but found it impossible. Rightly or wrongly, she was drawn to Jim Tremain's quietness. He was an island of peace in the dangerous currents of emotion she experienced daily. Listening to his cajoling voice, Dal had to fight a tumult of emotions that surfaced as easily as new life in a wintered land under the tender caresses of the sun.

She raised her head and studied him intently. "I think you're a cougar in disguise," she accused.

"Why?"

Dal licked her lips, avoiding his amused gaze. He was stalking her. She could sense it, and her brain was going off in alarm over his veiled statement. "You just are," she answered stubbornly. Damn, why couldn't she concentrate? Gripping the pen until her knuckles whitened, she said, "I have to get this done before Rafe gets back tomorrow."

"Then I'll say good-night."

"Good night." Dal flinched inwardly over her gruffness. Jim made her feel simultaneously uneasy and euphoric. After he had left as silently as he had come, she dropped the pen and rubbed her face with her hands. God, she was so tired. When wasn't she? The thought of having to close her eyes in the darkness of night leaked through her and she tasted terror. Holding her head between her hands, she wondered if she'd ever feel comfortable sleeping at night again. The nightmares always haunted her. During the day she could remain busy enough to keep them at bay. It was only in the silence of the night that they preyed upon her shredded heart.

Near two in the morning Dal had finally dragged herself from the study, taken a hot bath and slipped into her floor-length flannel nightgown. Taking the sheet and blankets from the hall closet, she made her bed on the orange-colored sofa that sat on a sheepskin rug in front of the fire. The hoot of an owl soothed her fears as did the warmth of the crackling blaze. She closed her thick lashes, dark fan shapes against the tautness of her cheeks, and took a long slow breath, slipping into the darkness where she could forget for just a little while....

Hands...they were strong, viselike hands wrapping around her wrists. Pain flared up her wrists, shooting into her arms as Dal felt her limbs being jerked savagely in order to control her. No, no, it was happening again! She moaned and tossed restlessly, the blankets now acting as something that held her powerless against the attack. In her sleep, she pushed them off and they slipped to the rug below the couch. Sweat glistened against her taut features as she heard Jack's snarling voice break through her pleading cry.

"You're staying, you hear me?" he growled. "You think you're going to leave me, you're the crazy one!"

"Ow-w! You're hurting me. Let me go!"

His hands tightened viciously around her wrists as he pinned them above her head. "No way, baby. You're mine. And you're staying." His nostrils flared. "You want some attention? I'll give you some. You keep accusing me of ignoring you all the time...."

Anger soared through the sheer terror as Jack straddled her on the bed. It was dark. So dark...and yet, by the fullness of the moon outside of their bedroom window, she could see the glint of wildness in his narrowed green eyes as he watched her with feral intent. This wasn't the Jack she had married. Where had he gone? Over the years fame and success had become his wife, and she had become nothing more than slave labor for his insatiable appetite to achieve more fame and make more money. Dal tried to throw him off her body, bucking and struggling. Fear gave her even more strength and she screamed. The sounds clawed up and out of her throat, which was now constricted in terror. Even to her own ears, she sounded like an animal that had been stalked and cornered, knowing that it was going to die at any second.

Oh, God, dying... She had died that night. Jack stripped her soul from her and he had done it deliberately, trying to frighten her in order to keep her beneath his control so she wouldn't leave him. A whimper tore from her lips and she thrashed her head to one side, trying to fight off his powerful attack. No! God, no...

"Dal...wake up...you're having a dream...."

Dal's breast heaved with terror as she fought to take air into her lungs and throw Jack off her. He was a large man made of solid muscle. She felt hands on her shoulders and she tried to move away, curling against the back of the couch. Somewhere in her cartwheeling nightmare, part of her was slowly coming awake and telling her they weren't Jack's hands. No, these were a man's hands that were firm with warmth without bringing her more pain.

"Dal, wake up.... Come on, wake..."

She heard his roughened voice soothe the ragged edges of her nightmare. It wasn't Jack's voice...no, it was a man's voice that calmed her instead of instilling more of the revulsion that twisted through her. Dal felt herself being pulled up, felt arms going around her, holding her, rocking her gently within an embrace. A sob escaped her contorted lips as she fought to surface from the nightmare, her fingers digging into warm, hard flesh. Tears squeezed from beneath her tightly shut lashes and Dal was dully aware of them streaking down her cheeks.

"You're all right, Dal.... Just let it go.... You're safe... safe...."

Slowly, Jack's voice and face dissolved into the tears that now flowed unchecked from her. Dal sobbed hard, burying her head beneath his chin, wanting, needing the safety he offered. As she reoriented to the present, the first sensation that struck her muddled senses was Jim's masculine smell combined with the fresh odor of pine. She cringed like a frightened animal against the tensile strength of his bare, well-muscled chest. A myriad of sensations clashed within her reeling state as Dal tried to separate reality from the dream. Her fist clenched and unclenched, her long, slender fingers tentatively moving across his flesh. Jim was real. What was happening was real. And his voice... Dal's sobs lessened as she sank against him, allowing the melodic, unknown language to fall over her raw, screaming senses. The thick, dark honey of his chanting tone was healing to her.

"You're safe, Dal. Nothing's going to harm you anymore. You're home and you're with me...not Jack. It's all over."

A shudder tremored through her. Jim's fingers splayed against her back and he gently began to rub the tension out of her shoulders. Through her nightgown his touch was steadying to her spiraling caldron of emotions as his fingers moved down the deeply indented curve of her spine, freeing all that tension. Dal gulped, aware of the coolness of tears still on her lips as she struggled to gain a complete hold on reality.

She felt him breathing evenly and deeply, and that calmed her more as she forced her eyes open. Gray light filtered through the windows, telling her it was near dawn. A rush of gratefulness coupled with some undefined emotion coursed through Dal as she pushed herself out of Jim Tremain's embrace. She couldn't meet his gaze. Instead, she sat up and buried her face in her hands. He remained close to her.

"I—I'm all right," she heard herself say. Her voice was unsteady.

"You will be in a few minutes," he agreed huskily.

Dal felt fresh, hot tears brim in her eyes as he gently stroked her head. She was like a scared little girl and he seemed to realize that she needed his continual physical touch in order to get a grip on herself. How could he know that? When had she ever welcomed the touch of a man since her travesty of marriage to Jack? Another shudder coursed through her and Dal felt his hands gently settle on her shoulders, beginning to knead her taut, screaming muscles.

"Sit up more," he commanded quietly, "and turn your back toward me."

She did as he asked, melting beneath his sure touch as his fingers worked a special kind of magic to her tense body. "H-how did you know?" she quavered.

"What?"

"That I needed—" She couldn't finish the sentence, shame flowing through her. She wanted to be touched? She'd cringed from any nearness to a male since… Her mind shut the door on Jack's parting act that had severed their marriage. Dal heard Jim's voice and clung to it.

"Any animal in pain needs the touch of its mate. One dog will lick the other's wound. A horse will nuzzle the one who is sick. Humans are no different. Sometimes a healing touch is all that's needed. You need it…."

Her lashes swept down, wet with tears, as she gave herself to his ministrations. His words had slipped from his mouth like a reverent prayer. Dal heard the smile in his voice and ached to turn and see the expression on his features.

"The first time I saw you out in the meadow with Nar you reminded me of a deer. When you rose from your crouched position with him on your arm, I saw how slender and graceful you were," he told her in a low, husky tone. "And like a deer, you had large, liquid eyes that I could read and see the unhappiness within." His hands stilled on her shoulders. "Deer are one of the most helpless of all animals. They have no way to protect themselves from predators. Their strength lies in their ability to run. All they have is their camouflage coloring and their running so that whoever is stalking them won't find them." His hands tightened slightly against her arms.

"You're like that; you've been stalked by someone. My guess would be it was your ex-husband. You've thrown up walls to freeze behind, hoping all men will pass you by and leave you alone." His voice grew deep. "In my eyes, you are like a deer. A woman who needs a gentle hand and who isn't frightened into running away once again."

Dal felt bereft as Jim released her. She could feel the heat from his male body and was wildly aware of his scent: a clean, outdoor scent mingling with the special odor of his skin. It was perfume to her and she took a deep, drugging breath, feeling the last vestiges of the virulent nightmare fading. Slowly, Dal turned around to face him.

If she had expected the natural planes of his face to be hard and unreadable, she was wrong. Dal found tenderness burning like a gold flame deep in the recesses of his shadowed eyes, his mouth relaxed. A lock of black hair had fallen on his brow and she had the wild urge to push it back into place with her fingers. In those moments out of time that spun effortlessly between them, she found herself wanting to fall back into the welcoming embrace of his arms and simply rest her head against his chest.

The thought that she wanted to be held by Jim shocked Dal. Her gaze traveled down from his face to the strong column of his neck to his powerful shoulders and chest. She remembered that he didn't appear to be that well-muscled in clothes, but seeing him clad in only a pair of well-worn jeans, she changed her mind. Indeed, he was like a cougar, lean but compactly built, as if he could uncoil and leap upon a prey with graceful ease.

Her mouth suddenly became dry. For the first time in a long while, she was appreciative of a man in a purely physical sense. There wasn't an ounce of fat upon his deeply bronzed form. Her gaze followed the line of dark hair that traveled from his chest, across his hard stomach and disappeared beneath the waist of the jeans he wore. Male. He was intensely male and Dal found herself wildly drawn to him.

Jim knew that if he had made the slightest move that resembled a pass, she would have shrunk away from him. And if he correctly read her inspection of him, he didn't allow it to interfere in the trust he had magically woven between them. Instead, he shared a slight smile with her, his eyes dark and assessing as he watched her in the ensuing silence.

"How about a cup of hot chocolate? Milk always makes you sleepy." And then he reached out, pulling away several strands of hair that clung to her cheek. "You need to get some rest, Dal."

Just the way her name rolled off his tongue like an endearment made Dal shiver. And it wasn't out of fear. She didn't trust herself to speak and nodded instead.

"Okay, you just lie there and rest. I'll be back in a few minutes," he promised huskily as he rose.

Dal looked up at him, the darkness and firelight dancing across his lean form. He looked frightening as well as beautiful in her eyes. Ruggedly beautiful in a male way that dissolved her fear and replaced it with awe. The soft curl of his black hair only emphasized his harsh features, and yet Dal found solace within his ensnaring golden gaze. He picked up the blankets, tucking them in around her before he left for the kitchen.

She lay propped up on her pillows, staring blankly into the fire, trying to absorb the myriad sensations pulsing around her. It was impossible and Dal tried to tidy up her bed. Jim Tremain was a stranger to her. A man who had walked quietly into her life the previous morning. And now, less than twenty-four hours later, she had given him what little trust hadn't been destroyed by Jack. Swallowing hard against a forming lump, Dal waited for his return, too hollow and wiped clean of terror to do much more than sit and not think.

Jim returned on bare feet, silent as he turned the corner from the hall and walked into the living room. He gave Dal a smile that said, relax, it's all right. And she did, reaching out for the mug when he handed it to her.

"Thank you," she murmured, her voice scratchy.

He sat down on the sheepskin rug, resting his back against the couch near where she sat with her legs tucked up beneath her. The firelight heightened each curve and hollow of his face and Dal found herself staring down at him.

"I found some honey out there. I put that in the chocolate instead of sugar," he offered, lifting his head and
meeting her dark, anguished eyes. God, he thought,
she looked so damned vulnerable. But he stilled any
reaction on his part to take her back into his arms and
hold her. As with any wild animal, touching Dal could
only go so far before she would misinterpret the gesture
as an attempt to entrap her and deny her her freedom.
Her lips parted and he groaned inwardly. He had been
sorely tempted to kiss them when they were contorted
with pain, but had held himself in tight check for her
sake. And for his. Jim smiled when the corners of her
mouth curved slightly upward.

"Just as long as you put it back where you found it,"
she managed with a slight laugh. "Or Millie will know
someone was in her kitchen and all hell will break loose."

Returning his gaze to the fire, Jim sipped the steaming chocolate. "She reminds me of the guard dog type
that would take a wooden spoon to you if you trespassed
on her territory."

Dal tasted the chocolate, finding it just right. A glim-
mer of amusement came to her eyes. The relaxed aura
surrounding them was astonishing. It had to be Jim's
presence; she had never felt so safe or protected. Never.
Too drained and exhausted to question the special feelings embracing her, Dal accepted them and Jim. "You're
right. I'm sure when Millie gets up and sees the pan you
made the chocolate in, she'll sniff around to find out
who didn't wash it and put it away."

His mouth stretched into a full smile. "I'll do that
before I go back to bed. We don't need a snarling housekeeper. It's a bad idea to bite the hand that feeds you."

Dal couldn't stop the laughter that bubbled up from

her throat. "Even as kids growing up here at the ranch we all knew to stay out of Millie's domain. Rafe, who was the greatest cookie snatcher in the world, couldn't always fool Millie. She'd make a batch of chocolate chip cookies, and naturally we'd all be plotting and planning how to get a few before dinner."

Jim glanced up, drowning in her relaxed features. No longer was Dal haunted looking. "Did it work?"

"Not often. And if Millie caught you, then you didn't get any cookies at all."

"Sounds like she ran a tight ship with the three of you around."

"She did, believe me."

Quietness settled between them and Dal drank the mug of hot chocolate, feeling the fingers of sleep starting to pull at her. She glanced at the clock on the mantel above the fireplace. It was almost 5:00 a.m. In another half hour the wranglers would start moving around and the cook would be fueling the wood stove over in the chow hall for the fifteen men who worked on the Triple K. Her thoughts pulled back to Jim. He hadn't asked her about her nightmare. How much had he heard? A tremor of shame flowed through her. If he knew…no… Dal chewed on her lower lip, unable to deal with the humiliation now sweeping through her.

"Jim?" Her voice was like a croak.

He turned, frowning, hearing the sudden strain in her tone. "Yes?"

Dal rubbed her temple, averting her gaze. "Uh… how much—I mean—how did you know I was having a nightmare?" Her hands went damp and sweaty as she gripped the mug tightly.

Jim gave a slight shrug, his expression suddenly less

guarded. "You screamed and I heard it. That's when I came out to see what was wrong."

"But—you've got the room next to Millie's. She never hears me when I wake up screaming."

His eyes sharpened, as intent as an eagle's. "You have these nightmares often?"

Damn! She hadn't meant to imply that. Dal stared down at her mug. "Just…sometimes."

Jim's nostrils flared but he said nothing. "I've been accused of having ears like a dog and the night sight of an owl."

"Your Indian heritage," Dal whispered.

He rose in one fluid motion, leaning over and taking the mug from her hands. "I guess so. Listen, you get some sleep." He wanted to ask her why she was sleeping out on a couch and not in her own bedroom, but thought better of it. Jim gave her a tender smile meant to soothe her sudden nervousness. "Is that ride this morning still on?"

"Yes," she said with a nod as her fingers toyed with the blanket. "But later."

"Sleep as long as you want, Dal," he murmured huskily. "Come and get me when you want to go."

"All right. And Jim?"

He hesitated at the door. "Yes?"

Dal lifted her chin, meeting the golden brown gaze that seemed to reach out and envelop her. "Thanks."

He nodded. "I'll see you when you wake up."

The morning dawned clear with a pale ribbon of rose on the horizon. Dal said little as they walked their horses from the barn area to the open valley before them. She unbuttoned her sheepskin coat, her breath a mist from her mouth and nose. Sliding on the falconer's glove, which almost reached up to the elbow of her left arm, she mounted her gelding.

The silence was complete as they rode from the main ranch area at a slow trot. Thick drops of dew hung on the green blades of grass, frozen in stalks of splendor everywhere they looked. Twin jets of steam shot from their horses' nostrils and the saddle leather creaked pleasantly. Dal glanced at Jim, who rode at her side. His expression mirrored a peacefulness she longed to possess. But after the previous night's episode, there was no peace in her.

Just thinking about being held by him caused heat to sweep up from her neck into her face. Unconsciously, Dal touched her cheek as she relived those stolen moments out of time in his arms. He had held her. Simply comforted her. His arms had gently embraced her to ease her inner pain. And it only served to make her more vulnerable to him. Jim had given to her last night, not taken as Jack had always done.

A high-pitched shriek shattered the quiet of the mountain valley.

"He's here," she said automatically, pulling her horse to a stop and turning toward the sound. Her chin lifted and she saw Nar high above them, his seven-foot wing-spread silhouetted against the apricot-colored dawn light. She smiled as she met and held Jim's gaze. "Stay here. Nar will put on a show for you, I'm sure." With that, she lifted her fingers to her lips, creating a call similar to Nar's.

Jim watched as the golden eagle shrilled back and suddenly folded his wings and stooped. The brown body of the raptor plunged out of the lightening sky like a cannonball. Jim tensed as Dal clapped her heels to her gelding and it took off at a gallop across the grassy valley. The eagle hurtled down at the escaping horse and rider, his beak open and claws extended. At the last possible second, Nar spread his wings, lightly touching Dal's outstretched gloved hand.

It was an unbelievable ballet, Jim thought as he tensely watched the raptor wheel around, skimming the earth by no more than two feet as he came flying back toward Dal. The gelding was obviously used to the antics of the eagle, neither swerving nor slowing his gallop as they raced in a collision course toward each other. Nar shrilled, suddenly swooping a mere foot from the horse, his wing tip barely grazing Dal's hair, which flew back across her shoulders. Her laughter was joyous as the eagle wheeled on his wing and corkscrewed around. Dal reined her gelding to the right in a tight circle, Nar following smoothly, almost touching her shoulder. She guided the horse into a straight line at a dead run, and the eagle easily followed.

As she pulled her gelding to a sliding stop, Dal's laughter was silvery. She threw her arm up above her head and Nar reversed his flight, gently landing and lightly gripping her gloved wrist and arm. He lifted his head, his amber eyes blazing as he shrilled, his call echoing throughout the valley. Dal stroked his breast lightly and the raptor leaned down, moving his beak through her hair, twittering at her like an indulgent parent to a naughty child.

"Ready?" she asked Nar.

The intelligent bird's head tilted, studying her. Nar mantled.

"Okay, big bird, off you go!" Dal drew her entire

arm and shoulder back, stood up in the saddle and flung the heavy eagle off her arm. Nar flapped, the wings snapping in the coolness as he rapidly gained height, climbing up and out of the valley. He wheeled, spiraled and cavorted around her and the horse as they quietly stood in the grassy plain. Coming from one end of the valley, Nar would dive and then barely skim the earth, soaring upward within a foot of them. Jim sat admiring the powerful grace and beauty of the golden eagle from a distance. He didn't know who looked happier: Dal or the predator. Her face was flushed, sapphire eyes alight with joy and her hair in provocative disarray around her face and shoulders. More than once he sucked in a breath, afraid that the eagle had misjudged his distance from Dal. But always the raptor missed her, often by only inches. Once he saw the wing-tip feathers brush her hair and he shivered. What if Nar ever decided to strike out at Dal with those razor-sharp talons of his? He could easily shred the jacket she wore, or worse, injure her.

Nar's attention was taken elsewhere when he spotted a jackrabbit at the edge of the meadow. Dal watched as the raptor took off for his quarry, and turned her horse back toward Jim. The gelding was well rested from his run and cantered easily beneath her.

"Well, what do you think?" she asked breathlessly, pulling up opposite him.

"Beautiful, dangerous and thrilling," he admitted, a slow smile pulling at his mouth. He pushed the hat back on his head, studying her. "You were beautiful, he was dangerous and the whole ten minutes were thrilling. I wouldn't have missed it for the world."

Dal laughed, running her fingers through her hair to

try and tame it back into order. "We've played like this ever since he learned to fly. When he was younger, he would ride out here on my arm and I'd cast him off." She patted her gelding. "Smokey enjoys it, too."

"I could see that. You wouldn't find many horses willing to tolerate an eagle attacking them like that."

"No. Most horses would shy," she agreed, smiling.

Resting his arm on the saddle horn, Jim said, "You're at one with nature and the animals."

Dal pulled her leg across the horn, balancing herself with unconscious ease as she dropped the reins and let Smokey nibble at the grass at his feet. She gazed around her, a soft hint of a smile lingering in her eyes. "Yes, I love the forest and the animals."

"But not the two-legged variety known as men?"

The joy died in her eyes as she met his probing gaze. "No, never them."

He gave her a slight smile. "Wish I was an eagle, then. I envy Nar."

"Why?"

"He's male and he has your trust."

His insight was unsettling to her, but she had found out the night before that his intuitive knowledge of her didn't necessarily mean pain. "Nar gained my trust with long hard hours of working together."

"But you were willing to give him your time," Jim countered huskily.

Dal lifted her leg, slipping her foot back into the stirrup and picking up the reins. "What are you trying to say, Jim?"

He straightened up, his gaze holding hers so that he could see the fear and defensiveness reflected in her luminous eyes. "How do you get a man-fearing horse to trust you again?" he countered.

"You work with him, I suppose."

He gave her a heated look charged with some unknown emotion. "That's right, you do."

Dal looked mystified. "Do Navaho always talk in riddles?"

"When it suits them," he drawled, smiling. Dal was a man-fearing woman right now. And whether she knew it or not, he was going to handle her, force her to work closely with him and regain her trust. If he told her that he knew she would flee from him like the frightened deer she was, and never allow him near her again. But if he could convince Rafe to let him deal with the poaching problem, then Dal would have no choice. "Come on, I'll race you that two miles to the end of the meadow. Let's find out what kind of a rider you really are, lady."

She was thrown off guard by his questions and then his challenge. Gripping the reins, she tossed him a smile. "All right. Let's go!"

Jim matched her smile, allowing her to leap ahead of him. Flight tugged angrily beneath his hand, wanting to outrace the gelding barely a length in front of him. Jim contented himself with letting Dal lead over the pounding two-mile run. The graceful synchronicity between her and the horse was breathtaking. She was free, if only for those heart-pounding minutes as they flew across the emerald carpet of the valley.

Dal pulled up her gelding, a triumphant smile on her flushed face as they circled to a stop at the end of the meadow. "Why do I get the feeling you didn't really try to win?" she asked.

Shrugging easily, Jim ran his fingers down Flight's

arched and damp neck. The stallion was still angry at being held in. "There're other things more important than winning."

"Such as?"

"Hmm, just things. One of these days I might share them with you."

Dal gave him a suspicious look. "Has anyone ever accused you of being closemouthed?"

Jim took off his hat, wiping the sweat from his brow with the back of his sleeve. "A few people. Does it make you uncomfortable?"

She nodded. "Yes. You're the kind of man who's always thinking, and I'd feel safer knowing your thoughts than with you keeping them to yourself."

Settling the hat back on his black hair, he asked, "Do you want to know out of curiosity or for your comfort level?"

Dal walked beside him as they took a well-beaten path back through the pasture toward the barn. Her eyes glimmered with mirth. "My own comfort level," she admitted.

"I like your honesty, Dal Kincaid. It becomes you," he said in a husky tone.

She colored fiercely, feeling as if he had reached out and stroked her as he had done the night before. Dal vividly recalled the firm pressure of his fingers massaging the pain from her shoulders and back. "I don't play games very well, Jim," she muttered.

"Neither do I. We have something else in common."

"Except you won't tell me what you're thinking."

He reined Flight to a stop at the barn and dismounted. "The Navaho believe in peace among people, not dissension or creating fear. If I told you some of my thoughts right now, you'd take flight just like that eagle of yours. I don't want to cause you any more havoc with what I'm thinking."

Holding his amused gaze, Dal dismounted. He was gently baiting her and she felt the same kind of safety she had when he had held her. "I get it. You're being polite and telling me to mind my own business."

"Not really," he murmured, taking the reins to the horses while Dal slid open the door. The change in Dal was startling. The previous day she had made a point of keeping her distance from him. This morning, she walked relaxed at his side, their shoulders almost brushing. "There's a right place and time to say everything," he told her, holding her expectant gaze.

"Is that another Navaho adage?"

He grinned and brought the horses to a stop in the center aisle, so that they could be cross tied and untacked. "No, just common sense."

Dal's laughter pealed through the breezeway, light and silvery. She began to uncinch Smokey's saddle. "You really are different, Jim Tremain."

"Just like you. Don't ever forget that, Dal. We're both horses of a different color."

With a wrinkle of her nose, she lifted the saddle from Smokey. "Is that supposed to be bad or good?"

"Why should it be either? It just is," he said, taking his saddle and following her into the tack room.

Dal nodded thoughtfully. "I've never really looked at life that way," she admitted, sliding the saddle onto the peg. "Everything in my life gets put into the bad or good category. Most of it bad, lately."

"The Navaho way is to see each event as something

to be learned from and accepted," he said, putting the saddle down and tossing the blanket over a rack.

Picking up the tack box, she handed him a grooming brush and cloth to wipe Flight down with. "So life doesn't consist of good and bad events?"

"No. I take each event and each person and ask myself, what will I learn today?"

Smokey nickered softly as Dal approached. She smiled and stroked his broad forehead with a brush where the sweat was trickling down and itching where he couldn't scratch. The gelding leaned gratefully toward her, eyes half-closed in enjoyment. Dal's mouth puckered. "Then I learned plenty from my ex-husband," she said, beginning to rub Smokey vigorously.

Jim rested his arms on the stallion's wide back, gazing over at her. "What was Gordon like?"

Her head snapped up and she met his serious expression. It was a personal question, one that she had never discussed with anyone, not even her parents. Dal could have retorted it's none of your business. Only she got the feeling Jim really wanted to know. He didn't seem the prying type, except with her....

Dal resumed her brushing of the gelding. "I married Jack when I was twenty-three."

"That's pretty young."

"Too young," she agreed grimly. "I was a green college kid who had played catch-me-if-you-can games with guys my own age until Jack came along. He was ten years my senior, extraordinarily handsome and at home in the most expensive business suits." She blew a strand of hair from her eyes, her face glistening with the sweat of her exertion. "To make a painful story very short, I married him three months after I met him. I was moon-eyed over him; it was the first time I'd ever fallen in love...."

Jim took the cloth and wiped down the stallion all the while, listening to the edge of pain in her voice. "And then what happened?"

"He painted a wonderful future for both of us. I was one of the three people at the university majoring in ornithology. I had a straight 4.0 average and was Professor Jacob Warner's assistant. I had trained under one of the most widely recognized ornithologists in the world for four years. Rare and exotic species were my specialty. That and predatory birds." She halted, looking over at Jim, her face flushed. "Jack said we'd make a wonderful team. He wanted to import and export birds from the jungles and sell them to zoos around the world. He lacked the expertise but had the managerial knowledge."

"Are you saying he married you for that?"

She managed a pained smile. "No... I know he loved me in the beginning. At first, we were both excited about the possibility of tramping the jungles of the world with each other, looking for exotic birds."

"It sounds pretty good so far," he said quietly.

"The rose-colored glasses were definitely on," Dal agreed tightly. "We spent the first two years in the Amazon and the Far East chasing birds; I identified them and watched Jack crate them up and send them to zoos. At first, I thought his enthusiasm for the birds was okay. After the third year he got more excited about a blue-crowned hanging parrot from Malaya than about our marriage. He got caught up in the desire to make more and more money. The last two years was a total sham. Somehow, we let our relationship falter and we just grew further and further apart."

Jim continued to brush Flight down, saying little, though his mind worked furiously. Gordon had used her idealism and trust to manipulate her to get what he wanted. Anger rushed through him as he stole a look over at Dal. She appeared distraught over her admission as she worked on the horse. An overwhelming sense of helplessness rushed through him; no wonder she had looked fatigued three years ago when he first met her. Gordon had taken everything from Dal, including her own sense of self, for his own end.

"What about you?"

"Me?" Jim echoed, rising and resting a hand across Flight's wither.

She gave him a slight smile. "Here I am dumping the story of my life on you and I know so little about you. Are you happily married with a bunch of kids?"

It was his turn to smile. "Is that how you see me?"

Dal thoughtfully ran the comb through Smokey's silky mane. "Yes. You look married." And then she gave a self-conscious shrug. "Some men just give you that impression of being happily married."

"I see...."

"Are you?"

He shook his head, brushing Flight's back. The stallion groaned and lifted his head in utter pleasure. "Not yet. I just never met the right woman."

Mustering a smile, Dal murmured, "The woman that gets you will be very lucky."

"Thank you. And I think the man who's able to reach out and get beyond your past experience with your marriage, will also be lucky."

Dal untied Smokey, leading him back to his roomy

stall. "I'm staying single," she promised him. "Marriage isn't for me."

Sliding the box stall door shut on Flight, Jim turned and walked down to where Dal was standing. An enigmatic smile shadowed his well-shaped mouth as he approached her. "Let time heal your outlook on marriage," he said, coming to a halt. God, she looked so enticing with her hair in delicious disarray about her flushed features. Jim wanted to reach out and lightly touch her cheek, just to feel the velvet pliancy of it. There was so much he wanted to do—could have done if Dal wasn't running so scared from him....

Dal lowered her lashes, unable to stand the tenderness burning in his honey-colored eyes. Suddenly, she felt shy and unsure of herself in his presence. "Listen," she began, her voice barely above a whisper, "about last night..."

"It was special," Jim returned huskily.

She lifted her chin, her sapphire eyes luminous with tears as she held his gaze. Whatever had made her think she couldn't trust Jim Tremain? He stood inches from her, his hands thrown languidly on the hips of his well-worn jeans, looking incredibly self-assured and handsome in her eyes. The notion that she even had a shred of trust left in her shook Dal completely. But whatever was left of her pulverized emotions was reaching out like tendrils of new life toward him. This time, Dal didn't fight those feelings as she held his searching gaze.

"Yes...it was very special.... You were special...."

A slow smile pulled at the corners of his mouth. "The sharing of experiences is healing in itself, Dal. You don't need to apologize to me." His voice lowered in timbre. "You allowed me to share a piece, a part of yourself and that was a gift to me."

"Gift?" she repeated thickly, fighting back the tears that wanted to come.

He nodded. "A gift of your life you shared with me. I was glad it happened and I was glad I could be there for you." Jim reached out, lightly stroking the delicate line of her jaw. "Tears shared between two people are the greatest gift of all. They're a sign of ultimate trust, and to the Navaho one of the most important things that can be expressed between two people."

"What? Tears or trust?" Dal asked, trembling beneath his fleeting touch.

"Both. If you can cry openly in my arms, doesn't that signal trust?" he asked quietly. The urge to reach out and gently draw her into the shielding embrace of his arms almost overpowered him. Jim saw the pain and uncertainty in her eyes and longed to ease the anguish in her. He could do it. He knew he could....

"I—never cried around Jack. He thought tears were a sign of weakness." She gave a broken shrug, taking a step away from Jim's powerful presence.

"Some men do think it's a sign of weakness."

"And you?"

"I see them as a sign of trust. Of healing."

"And I suppose you've cried before?" she challenged, remembering all the years with Jack when she'd never seen a man cry.

"Many times," he assured her, taking her by the arm and slowly walking her down the center of the aisle toward the doors.

"Did your mother teach you that it was all right to cry?" Dal was wildly aware of the monitored strength of his hand on her elbow. Jim was so close, so dizzyingly close, and she yearned to move into the safe harbor of his embrace once again. To find once again that healing ground that seemed to have blossomed miraculously between them earlier that morning.

"Yes. As I said before, the Navaho are a people who were ruled by and gave homage to woman. The Navaho men realize women are stronger in some ways than they are, so we try to open our senses like they do. When a woman sheds tears, she becomes cleansed. Our men have watched this for countless centuries and know the wisdom of her ways." He smiled down at her, amusement deep in his eyes. "A man gains strength and wisdom from his woman. That's why we revere them."

Dal found his philosophy inspiring and another part inside her relaxed toward him. "And yet you aren't weak or soft like a woman."

He laughed deeply. "Each gender has something to give to the other. As our woman gives us emotional strength, we give her our ability to hunt and protect her and her children."

Children… Dal closed her eyes tightly for a second. God, how she had ached to have children. She loved them so much and had wanted one for so long. But Jack never wanted to be tied down with a family. And when he had wanted her in bed, he had always made sure he was protected from the risk of impregnating her. The last two of those six years had been spent in a desert without warmth…without real feeling, and now, Jim Tremain had quietly entered her life and was giving her new hope, renewing needs she thought had died within her.

"I like your outlook on life, Jim," she admitted, stopping at the bottom of the wooden stairs that led up to the rear door of the ranch house. She was about to say something else when she heard the distant sounds of helicopter blades puncturing the late-morning air.

Jim had heard it too, and turned toward the noise.

"Rafe's back," Dal told him, pointing to a helicopter coming rapidly out of the blue of the sky. She gave him a grim smile. "And you'd better hope he's in a good mood or he'll probably turn down your plan."

"Was he supposed to return in a bad mood?"

Dal shrugged. "His wife died in childbirth a year ago, Jim, and he hasn't gotten over it yet. Rafe is normally on top of things business-wise, but he's let a lot slide since then." She looked up at him. "I came here six months ago for two reasons. One was to escape from Jack's influence after the divorce, and the other was to try and help Rafe through this awful period. I try to keep up the accounting records and our investments that keep the Triple K solvent. But I don't have Rafe's business acumen. And he's been too mired in grief to do his normal good job." Her mouth tightened as she watched the helicopter hover over a circular concrete slab in the distance. "Rafe went to Denver to borrow some money from a bank. And I don't know if he got the loan or not. If we didn't get it, things are going to go from bad to worse…." She gnawed on her lower lip, her eyes dark with worry.

Jim squeezed her arm and then allowed his hand to drop to his side as he watched the helicopter land, the blades slowly swinging to a halt. "He got the loan," he told her.

Dal gave him a perplexed look. "How could you know that?"

"A feeling," he said with a grin.

She gave him a disgruntled glance. "You run on your gut like a woman does."

"Do you?"

"No, and I should. Jack wore me down so far that it's a wonder I survived crawling out of that marriage from him," she admitted.

"That's over now, Dal, and you've got back your identity. Soon you'll be back on your feet," he promised huskily.

Now it was her turn to smile. But it wasn't a happy one. "Is that your gut speaking?" she asked as she began to walk toward the helicopter where Rafe was disembarking.

Jim joined her, meeting her smile. "Yes, it is."

Chapter 4

Jim decided that the Kincaid family was indeed a horse of another color. Rafe Kincaid was a typical rancher in that the Rocky Mountains appeared to have molded him from their craggy, granite cliffs. There was a power radiating from the tall rancher, Jim noted as he rapidly assessed the man when he and Dal walked out to meet him on the helicopter pad. Dal's brother possessed a square, uncompromising face, unfathomable dark blue eyes and raven-black hair. Jim wouldn't have needed Dal to tell him that Rafe had suffered a tragedy; the marks were too clearly etched in the slashes at the corners of his mouth and in the dark recesses of his large, intelligent eyes. His shoulders, although broad and capable, seemed broken.

Jim stood back as Dal ran to her older brother, cried out his name and threw her arms around him, giving him a welcoming hug. For an instant, Jim was envious of Rafe Kincaid. Dal's face lit up, her mouth free of tension and blossoming into a smile as she greeted Rafe. Dressed in a blue chambray shirt, jeans and well-worn boots, Rafe hugged Dal, but his gaze remained solidly on Jim. Jim stood calmly beneath the rancher's intense inspection, sensing Rafe's immediate wariness. Was it inbred in all of the Kincaid children to show a natural distrust of strangers? Part of it, he knew, was due to the harsh and demanding conditions of ranch life where there were few people other than close family members. Strangers were to be eyeballed until they could be accurately cataloged by the ranchers.

Standing on tiptoe, Dal gave Rafe a quick peck on his cheek. "Well," she whispered breathlessly, standing back, "was it successful?"

Rafe nodded, his gaze remaining on the lean man standing ten feet away from them. "It was," he rumbled, giving his sister one of his few smiles. "And who's this?"

"Jim Tremain."

Rafe placed the leather attaché case in his left hand and moved toward him. "Oh yeah, the guy from the Department of the Interior."

Dal gave him a stunned look. "You know him?"

"His secretary called here a couple of days ago. I left the message for you on the desk."

She gave Rafe a patient look. It wasn't the first time he thought he had done something and hadn't. And she didn't have the heart to tell him that she had found no such message. "Right. Come on over and meet him. He has some business he wants to discuss with you, too."

The rancher looked sharply down at his sister, as if

trying to figure out the sudden lightness in her voice. "I thought it involved only you."

Slipping her arm through Rafe's, Dal chided, "Come on, big brother, quit giving me that look. Meet Jim and then we'll all go to the dining room for lunch. I'm starved!"

Rafe gave her another shocked look and then quickly veiled it as he halted in front of Jim Tremain. Introductions were made by Dal, and when the two men clasped hands, each monitored the firm strength of the other's grip. Saying little, Rafe then led both of them to the ranch house.

Dal stole occasional looks at her brother. She and Jim sat at each other's elbow, with Rafe at the head of the oak table. Sun poured through the floor-to-ceiling cedar-framed windows, enhancing the reddish cast of the highly polished floor. Millie had clucked over Rafe like a broody hen when he had first come in and then had sent them into the dining room. For the first time in a long while Dal found herself ravenously hungry, and she cleaned up every bit of Millie's tuna casserole, a garden salad and thick slices of homemade bread. Rafe crooked one eyebrow in her direction from time to time, but said nothing about her dramatically improved appetite.

The housekeeper took their emptied plates and silverware away, then poured freshly perked coffee and left them in the returning silence of the dining room. Thanking her, Rafe leaned back and studied Jim.

"Dal said you needed to talk to me about something."

Jim nodded, cradling his white mug between his hands. "That's right, Mr. Kincaid."

"Your secretary said it concerned Dal, here. She made no mention of me becoming involved."

"Well," Jim said, hedging and glancing across the table at Dal, "I needed to speak with Dal first to see if she would agree to help us. If she did, then I needed to get your permission, also."

Rafe scowled and hunkered forward, resting his elbows on the table. "For what?"

Dal found herself gripping her mug until it might have broken. Why, all of a sudden, did she care whether Jim persuaded Rafe to allow him to initiate his plan to nab the poachers? As Jim explained his proposal to Rafe, she tried to assimilate her changing feelings toward Jim and to understand why she was siding with him. When had she had decided to work with him? she wondered. Then, poignantly, the memory of him holding her while she cried out her anguish and fear came back to her. She cast Jim a look, finding the gentleness present even though his face was serious. The way he lifted the corners of his mouth, his eyes narrowing or widening, and the soothing balm of his voice were all the reasons why he had won her support.

She flicked a glance to her brother, watching a scowl darken his features. Rafe didn't like Jim's explanation; that was easy to see. She was about to step in and defend Jim when her brother's gaze swung to her.

"Gordon's in on this? Did you know that, Dal?"

Dal pursed her lips. "Yes, Jim told me," she admitted quietly, unable to hold her brother's stare of disbelief.

"Dammit, Mr. Tremain, there's no way in hell I'm going to let her anywhere near Gordon."

Jim held the rancher's implacable glare. He didn't blame Rafe for trying to protect his sister from Gordon. "Dal isn't going to be anywhere near the action, Mr. Kincaid. I'd like her to come down to Denver in two weeks and work with me on locating where all the aeries are on your ranch and the one adjoining wildlife refuge that butts up against your property. Then, two weeks later, we'll go on horseback and locate each one of them. After that, I'll have my men staked out at certain points waiting for Gordon's gang to show up. They'll radio in to me and we'll send in a helicopter crew that's specially trained to deal with situations like this."

Rafe stared at him. "What if Gordon shows up early, while you're locating these aeries, Mr. Tremain?" He suddenly got to his feet, his nostrils flared. "Gordon's a dead man if he so much as sets foot on Kincaid property, and he knows it. The reasons are personal and of a family nature, but I'll kill the bastard with my bare hands if I get the chance. I don't think he'll try and steal from the Triple K aeries. If he does, Gordon's a bigger fool than I ever gave him credit for." Shoving his hands in his pockets, Rafe turned and paced the perimeter of the dining room.

Dal stole a look across the table at Jim. He seemed totally unperturbed at Rafe's outburst. And yet she saw the compassion in Jim's face, and it made her heart twist in her breast. Rafe had a rough kindness about him that had become even harsher since the tragedy. As Dal watched Jim, she came to understand that kindness and affection simmered just beneath the surface, and the discovery gave her a euphoric sensation that made her dizzy. She had never known that type of man—someone so sensitive and attuned to other people—and she found herself wanting the chance to explore him.

"Rafe, if we don't help Jim, then the FBI will step in.

Do you want greenhorns from the East on our ranch? They'd be here during calving and when the herds are moving to the northern pastures. You know what a helicopter would do to the cows and their young calves." Dal looked up at Jim and saw him quietly watching her. Twenty-four hours before she had turned down his proposal; now she was siding with him. She twisted in the chair, keeping her gaze level with Rafe's black stare. "The FBI could come in here with helicopters and trucks. At least Jim is suggesting horseback, something that won't disturb either the calving or the birds and their aeries."

Rafe glared past her to Jim. "I'll think about it," he rumbled, then added, "Mr. Tremain, you come with me."

Dal rose. What was Rafe up to? "What—"

"This is between men, Dal," he warned.

She set her lips, realizing that Rafe was going to play overlord, as he did so well, anyway. It would be no use trying to argue with him when he dug his heels in, and she gave Jim a look of apology. "All right," she muttered. "I'll be out in the barn working with Liss."

"Now look, that black devil hasn't been ridden for five days now, Dal."

"For God's sakes, Rafe! I can do some things on my own!"

"That stud is mean by nature."

Dal glared at her brother. "I can take care of myself!" With that, she stormed out of the dining room.

Jim watched her go and then turned to Kincaid. "Was that the black Arabian I saw earlier?"

Rafe snorted vehemently, turning on his heel and heading toward the study. "Yeah. I bought him just a little over a year ago as a four-year-old. Liss is Arabic for thief and that stud will steal your life if he gets a chance. Damn," he growled, running his long, spare fingers through his hair. "Sometimes I think Dal tries fate. Sometimes I think she wants to kill herself...."

Jim walked at his shoulder, several inches shorter than Rafe. "I saw her handle the horse she rode this morning like a pro."

"Humph."

"Not to mention that eagle. Not many women have that kind of courage to deal with a bird of that savagery and size."

Rafe pushed open the door to the study, going around the desk to the liquor cabinet. "In some ways, all the Kincaids are crazier than hell. We were raised to take chances," he said, rummaging around in the cabinet and finding two shot glasses. He pulled out a bottle of sipping whiskey. "Want some?"

Jim shook his head and sat down on the leather sofa, placing one booted foot across his thigh. "No, you go ahead."

After pouring some of the whiskey, Rafe sat down at the desk. His eyes narrowed speculatively on Tremain. "In some ways, Dal is the weakest of the three Kincaid children. Cat, the middle sister, has a spine made out of pure steel like I do. She's a globe-trotting trouble-shooter on all kinds of mining problems. She risks her life on almost a daily basis." He took a sip of the whiskey and leaned back in the chair, some of the tension easing from his face. "Dal's the youngest. As children, Cat and I would let her tag along with us and we always had to kind of watch out for her. She didn't have the gumption it took to jump a horse over a chasm or swim one across a river that was flooding its banks."

Jim nodded and smiled to himself. Jumping a chasm on a horse or swimming a violent river on horseback wasn't prudent. "What are you saying? That Dal's less able to handle herself under certain circumstances?"

"She's the baby of our family, Mr. Tremain. The one who cried easily for an injured animal, or for Cat or me when we'd break an arm or get into trouble." Rafe's scowl deepened. "She's fragile in comparison to us. That's what I'm trying to say. Now, if you wanted Cat or me to help you, I'd say fine. But you're dealing with Dal."

"Meaning?" Jim's eyes met and held Rafe's.

"Just how much do you know about Dal's personal life, Tremain?"

"Not much. She's recently divorced from Gordon, that's all I know."

Rafe downed the rest of the whiskey then set the shot glass down on the cherry desk. "Ordinarily, family business is no one's business," he began. "You don't know what you're asking of Dal. I doubt if she realizes the potential of your plan to hurt her progress."

"Go on."

"In my opinion, Gordon married her for one reason: her expertise as an ornithologist. He dragged her all over the damn globe, squeezing every ounce of Dal's lifeblood out of her. She wasn't made for that kind of life, Mr. Tremain. Thanks to Gordon, she caught malaria three different times, hunting for rare birds in the jungles of Asia." His eyes grew flat and hard. "The third time Dal damn near died of it. I flew over to Hong Kong where they had put her in a hospital. Gordon was off in Thailand and had left her alone to struggle for her life."

Jim sat up, clasping his hands between his thighs, his features hardening. "I see."

"No, you don't. Not yet," Rafe growled. "I was an army helicopter pilot in the closing days of the Vietnam conflict. I knew what it was like to get malaria and dysentery. Everyone got it over there sooner or later. When we found out Dal was near death in Hong Kong, I left the Triple K and flew over there. I'd seen men wasted and ravaged by disease, Tremain, but never a woman." He took a deep breath, trying to control the anger that burned in his eyes. "Dal's tall and can easily carry a hundred and thirty pounds on her frame. When I arrived in Hong Kong, she was down to ninety pounds, Tremain. Ninety goddamn pounds. She was skin and bone. I found out from the doctor who was caring for her that Gordon had kept her in the jungle for three weeks before he decided she might need medical help. As it was, Dal contracted blackwater fever on top of the malaria. I spent a week in her room, praying she'd pull through it. She damned near didn't."

Anger began to uncoil deep within Jim and he inhaled slowly in an effort to calm down. Dal had been through so much...so much.... "And then what happened?"

Rafe's eyes glittered. "I had Dal flown stateside and brought her here to the Triple K to recover. And all that time, Gordon contacted her twice. Once by phone and the other with a postcard. Not even a damned letter. A lousy postcard. He used her like I'd never have believed. Even to this day I don't understand why Dal stuck it out so long with him."

"We all make mistakes, Kincaid. Maybe ours are a little less noticeable on the surface than Dal's, that's all."

Rafe nodded and rubbed his face. "There's more. The only reason I'm telling you this is to get you to understand that Dal's not ready for anything yet. She's so damn fragile. After she recovered from that last bout of malaria, Gordon miraculously showed up at the right moment to come and take her back overseas. The minute he came, I took him out back and beat the hell out of him." Rafe allowed a savage smile of satisfaction to cross his chiseled mouth. "He got a broken nose out of the deal and I busted up my knuckles. It was worth it. I warned him that if he ever did anything like that again, I'd finish the job."

"What was Dal's view of Gordon leaving her like that?"

"By that time, Dal was finally accepting the fact that Gordon didn't love her and only wanted her knowledge. They had a big fight here one night. But the next morning Dal had her bag packed and was leaving with Gordon, telling me everything was going to be fine. They kissed and made up, I guess. I don't know what that bastard promised her, but she actually seemed happy when she left with him."

"How long ago was this?"

"A year ago." Rafe got up, moving restlessly around the study. "And then, six months ago, I got this hysterical phone call from Dal. She was in San Francisco at the time. She and Gordon had just come back from Indonesia." He stopped, his features suddenly mirroring his exhaustion, his eyes bleak as he stared at Jim.

"She was sobbing so hard I could barely understand her. It took me a good ten minutes to get her to settle down and speak coherently." His mouth thinned into a hard line. "I'd never heard Dal like that before or since...."

Jim rose to his feet, tension vibrating through him

as he watched the rancher closely. His mouth was dry and he heard the anger in Rafe's voice. "What happened to her?" he demanded, remembering all too well Dal's reaction that morning and her screams.

Rafe dropped his gaze to his dusty boots. "Just lately the courts and society in general are recognizing the fact that some husbands rape their wives...."

His throat constricted and Jim stared hard at Rafe. The silence thickened between them. Unconsciously, Jim closed his hands into fists. Anger flowed to the surface with bitterness as he cataloged each of Dal's reactions to him. Rape. The word left a cold anger inside him. He had no mercy for any man who would violate a woman in such a way. He saw Rafe wrestling with very real hatred in those moments.

"That's why Gordon knows if he ever comes anywhere near Dal again, I'll kill him." He looked toward Jim. "You haven't been here to hear her screams and nightmares. I can't tell you how many times I've awakened and she was out there on the living room couch caught up in that nightmare," he whispered harshly. "Six months. Six months of pure hell for her." He shrugged tiredly. "And Dal's just starting to come out of it on her own. She won't talk about it to me, my parents or even Millie. However brutal it was on her is something only Dal knows. She's trying to combat this by herself and it isn't working."

"She needs some help," Jim agreed quietly.

Rafe snorted and poured himself another shot of whiskey. "Typical of all Kincaids, they don't ever ask for help. We were taught to hold our own, take care of ourselves and survive. Well, Dal isn't surviving very well. She's brittle, Mr. Tremain. Like a fine china cup, she'll break if you put too much pressure on her. I know her. I know her limits. And I've watched her for six months here at the ranch. The only thing that brings her out of that shell of depression and humiliation is working with that golden eagle and riding." He shook his head. "That's why you coming here and dumping your plan at her feet isn't what she needs. Maybe you can understand why I won't agree to go along with it now. I'd rather deal with the FBI instead and protect her from what it might cost her in emotional terms."

Jim nodded, moving over to the cabinet and pouring himself a shot, then downing it in one gulp. The fiery liquid burned all the way down, blotting out some of the anguish that was rising inside of him for Dal's sake. "Okay, Mr. Kincaid, I'll back off. I don't want to see her break any more than you do. She's too special...."

Rafe managed a one-cornered smile. "You see it in her, too, don't you?"

"What?"

"There's a cleanness to Dal. A part of her is so child-like and untouched even yet by that world we all have to crawl through and survive on a daily basis."

Nodding sadly, Jim softly replied, "Yeah, I sense that about her." He offered his hand. "I'd better get going. Thanks for your help on this, Kincaid."

"Call me Rafe."

Jim shook his hand firmly. "I'll pack my bag and say goodbye to Dal. I'll be in touch with you and coordinate the FBI's plan with you shortly."

"Fine. The Kincaids and conservationists go back a long way, Jim."

Jim had just shut the door on the Blazer when Dal rounded the house. She looked incredibly beautiful on the spirited black Arabian stallion that danced beneath her sensitive hands. He smiled up at her, thinking how happy she looked in that moment and feeling his body tighten with want of her. Despite her terror and the trauma she had endured at Gordon's hands, Dal Kincaid was a woman in all ways to his mind and heart. He shared her warming smile as she pulled the stallion to a stop a few feet from the Blazer.

"Where are you going?"

"Back to Denver. Your brother and I concluded our business."

Dal brushed the hair from her eyes, frowning. "I don't understand. Is Rafe going to let you work with me on this poaching project?"

"Since when did you change your mind?" he teased. She had heart, Jim would give her that. And he thought Rafe was wrong about her courage and that Kincaid backbone of steel. No, Dal possessed it, even if Rafe was blind because of his love and concern for her.

She dismounted and walked up to him, her smile dissolving as she studied his face. Jim felt her inspection just as sharply as if she had reached out and caressed him. "Since early this morning. What's wrong? Didn't Rafe agree to your plan? I thought you realized over the lunch table that I'd work with you. I know we didn't discuss it before Rafe demanded you to talk to him in the study."

Jim leaned against the Blazer, crossing his arms, studying her. "Rafe is concerned for your welfare in this, Dal."

She grimaced. "Oh, yes, my overprotective brother. Don't tell me he said no?"

Jim hesitated, his voice lowering. "We both felt it

would be best if you stay clear of this entire situation, Dal."

Anger leaped to her sapphire eyes and she squared her shoulders. "Since when do either of you run my life? You damn men are all alike, thinking you can boss a woman around!"

"Now, look, Dal, we didn't just decide on a whim to scratch the plan."

She planted her fists on her hips, her eyes blazing and color rushed to her cheeks. "You said yourself that all I have to do is locate the aeries first on the map in your office and then go out to the mountains and find them. Jack isn't going to be around. So how is this going to hurt me? I fail to see the connection. If you ask me, Rafe is going overboard on this."

"Like you did when I first talked to you about it, Dal?" he reminded her.

"Well," she said, "that was different."

"How is it different?" he probed, holding her furious gaze.

"Well—it's you," she stammered, crossing her arms.

"I'm the same person today as yesterday. What changed your mind?"

She licked her lower lip. "I trust you, dammit. Now will you let it go at that, Jim?"

A slow grin pulled at his mouth. "You trust me?"

"Don't be such a peacock about it."

Jim swallowed his smile, his honey-brown eyes remaining serious. "Okay, I won't ask you anything else about your decision."

She colored prettily. "Let me go in and talk to Rafe. Doesn't he realize it's a pack trip we'll be going on? Nothing more?"

"I outlined the plan to him in detail." Jim put a hand on her bare arm, feeling the sun's warmth on her firm flesh. "He feels the chances of us running into Gordon are too high to risk your involvement, Dal. And I can't guarantee your brother that we won't accidentally be up there finding those aeries at the same time Gordon and his gang show up. We'll be going up about two weeks before they should arrive. The nestlings probably won't be mature enough until then."

Dal handed him the reins to Liss. "Here, walk him back to the stable and have one of the hands unsaddle him, Jim. And then come back in. I think once Rafe realizes I want to do this, he'll relax his stance...."

Dal's heart began to pound heavily in her breast as she quietly approached the study where Rafe was working. As she saw the exhaustion on her brother's lined face, compassion flooded her. Life hadn't been kind to him in his thirty-four years. And then she looked grimly at herself; her life was nothing to brag about, either.

The instant Rafe heard her, an unreadable mask dropped over his face, effectively erasing his fatigue.

"Is something wrong?" he asked, looking up from the sheaf of papers beneath his hands.

Dal smiled softly. "No. I just met Jim out at his Blazer. He was packing to leave."

"Yeah."

"I want to work on this project with him, Rafe," she began, holding her brother's stare. Dal raised her hand. "Yes, I know he can't guarantee that Jack or any of the poachers won't be up there while we're locating those aeries."

"Dammit, Dal, it's too dangerous!" He got to his feet.

A new calmness invaded her. Dal was astonished as

the feeling flowed through her like a serene river, soothing her raw and exposed emotions. Had her belief in
Jim been the reason for the sensation? Dal savored the
feeling for several seconds, all the while holding Rafe's
angry gaze. "I believe in what Jim is trying to do for
all of us. His plan is workable with a minimal disrup-
tion to the wildlife on the ranch. I don't want a bunch
of government agents crawling all over the Triple K,
and I know you don't, either." Her voice grew husky.
"I understand why you tried to talk Jim out of it, Rafe.
And I love you dearly for it. But let me stand on my own
two feet. Don't keep trying to protect me from that big,
bad world. I'm ready to go out there."

Rafe's brows rose, a faint flicker of shock readable
in his expression as he studied her. And then his eyes
narrowed. "You're in no shape for this, Dal."

"And I never will get over this trauma unless I reach
out and start trying to live. I can't hide on the Triple K
forever, Rafe. I have to feed back into life again and learn
how to roll with the punches, just like everyone else."

He raked his fingers through his coal-black hair.
"Dammit, you're too fragile yet, Dal!"

She nodded. "Yes, I'm fragile. And hurting. And so
are you." Her voice thickened. "We both have to go on,
Rafe. I—I think this plan will be good for me. It's going
to force me out of the mountains and to go to Denver. I
need to get back and integrate with society." Then she
added, "And so do you. We've both been like ostriches
sticking our heads in the sand, trying to avoid our own
personal grief and pain."

Rafe grimaced and stared down at her, his large
hands splayed out on the desk in front of him. "It's
him, isn't it?"

Color fled up into her cheeks, but Dal didn't avoid Rafe's piercing look. "Jim?"

"Yeah. There's something between you two. I can feel it."

Her blue eyes softened. "Early this morning he woke up when I started screaming, Rafe. He heard me clear down by Millie's room and came out and held me."

"I see...."

"It's not what you think. And even if it was, it wouldn't be any of your business."

A slight grin creased his features. "You're right. What you do with your life is your business, not mine."

"I trust him, Rafe."

"You? Trust a man? Any man?" He snorted and walked around the desk, halting inches from her, trying to understand the change in her.

"I didn't trust any man until he walked into my life," Dal admitted.

Rafe rested his hands on his hips. "He's different," he growled.

She tilted her head, meeting her brother's indecipherable gaze. "I trust him. That's all that matters, Rafe. And I want to work with him in capturing those poachers."

"All right, little sister, have it your way. I just don't want to see you getting hurt again, that's all."

Dal gave him a wry look. "Since when did a Kincaid ever back down from pain?"

He nodded. "Dad always said we had heads full of rocks. Now I believe him." He put his arm around her shoulder and drew her to him. "Just take it slow and easy, Dal...you aren't ready for another emotional blow. This last one crippled you."

She slipped her arms around his huge form, giving him a hug. "Neither of us can," she murmured, her voice cracking.

Rafe patted her awkwardly on the shoulder and then released her. "So, what's on the agenda?"

"Jim's coming to the house after putting Liss away. We'll make some plans to meet in two weeks in his Denver office."

He went back to his office chair, sitting down. "Two weeks?"

"Yes. Why?"

Rafe flipped through his appointment book. "I'll be flying to New York to spend that week tying up contracts with three restaurants that want to use our beef."

Perching on the edge of the desk, she smiled. "Don't feel like you have to stay here because I'll be gone, too, mother hen."

He managed a sour smile, getting back to the paperwork that begged for his attention. "Just stay out of trouble," he growled.

Her laugh was silvery and infectious. "Rafe Kincaid! When are you going to let me grow up, and see me as a thirty-year-old woman instead of a little brat of five?"

"Probably never, Dal…."

Dal's hands were damp and clammy as she gripped the wheel of her small silver Mazda. She chewed on her lower lip, conscious of the butterflies that were alive and well in her stomach. Two weeks… In some respects, they had dragged by with almost unbelievable sluglike slowness. In other ways, those fourteen days had passed too quickly for her.

Denver looked clean and pristine as she guided her

car down out of the Rockies on the large eight-lane interstate. The late-morning sun sent mid-May rays over the plain, and Dal enjoyed the splendor of light dancing off the modern skyscrapers in the distance.

She swallowed convulsively, her hand moving to the purse resting next to her on the leather seat. In it was a short letter from Jim, along with a map of how to get to the hotel in downtown Denver where he would meet her. The letter had arrived four days after he left and she had found herself absorbing each word and studying his handwriting. Like a lovesick eighteen-year-old girl, she had memorized that letter.

Dear Dal:
Today I sat in my office and found myself wishing I was back up in the mountains sharing the day with you. I thought about riding Flight and how beautiful you looked as we raced across that meadow. You're a fine horsewoman; but then, I'd expect that of you. You're like that eagle who owns you. There's a refreshing gift of life within you. With time I think you'll become more like that glint I see lingering in those big, doelike eyes of yours.

When you come to Denver, we're going to mix business with pleasure if you want. I'd like to take you out for dinner afterward. I've got a hotel reservation for you at the Westin. Give me a call after you check in and I'll come by and take you to my office.

Dinner. Did she want to go to dinner with Jim? A part of her did, the part that was inexplicably blossoming beneath his gentle persuasion. The other part of her reared back in abject terror. She felt vulnerable with any man, especially someone like Jim, who she knew could influence her emotionally. She wasn't ready to reach out again...she just wasn't. And yet, Dal found herself needing Jim's quiet presence, his husky words, which soothed her chaotic state, and the physical stability of his touch.

Her heart was beginning a heavy pounding in her breast as she stood a short while later in the spacious marble lobby of the Westin Hotel, waiting for Jim to pull up outside the front doors. Dal smoothed her white linen suit, which was set off by an orange silk blouse. The color brought out the spice-colored highlights of her hair and emphasized the flush on her cheeks. Her hands were damp, and she wished she had a handkerchief in her leather purse. She touched her small gold earrings, and smoothed several strands of hair from her cheek. Dal was conscious of men taking a long moment to stare at her. Nervously she moved around the lobby, feeling suffocated by their male interest. Perhaps Rafe was right, she still hadn't healed sufficiently from Jack's savage attack upon her. Men scared her.

"Dal?"

Dal turned swiftly, her face draining of color. She stood, eyes large and luminous as she saw Jim smile and saunter toward her. As she swallowed convulsively, her heart rate soared like a snared rabbit's. Jim looked so good. Immediately Dal felt safer in his presence, and her knees went watery with relief. He was wearing a long-sleeved white business shirt, the collar open to display the strong column of his throat and the dark hair nestled at the vee. The walnut-colored slacks outlined his lower body to perfection and Dal felt dizziness sweep through her. She was experiencing such a clash of emotional reactions that she couldn't sort them all out.

Jim smiled warmly as he approached. "I've got to tell you, Dal, you're the best-looking woman here in the lobby."

"Th-thanks." She looked up...up into his golden eyes that said so much to her in the ensuing silence. Dal was achingly aware of just how much she had missed him and wanted to simply step into the haven of his arms as she had done that morning of her nightmare when he had held her. Shoring up her broken defenses, Dal mustered a weak smile.

"Are you all right?" he asked, slipping his hand beneath her elbow.

"I'm fine." *Liar.* She felt euphoric. Miserable. Up and down. If this was what coming alive was all about after the trauma, Dal didn't find it very pleasant. Only Jim's presence gave her any measure of solace.

"I thought we might go up to the top of the hotel to have lunch. They've got a fine restaurant and we can grab a bite to eat before we go over to the office."

"I'm not very hungry. But if you are, I'll join you for a cup of coffee."

He gave her a sidelong glance, guiding her toward the bank of elevators. "You were supposed to gain ten pounds after I left. What happened?" he asked teasingly.

Dal shrugged, grateful that he didn't release his hold on her elbow as they took the elevator up to the restaurant. "I don't know...." That was another lie. She was finally sleeping better at night, but her appetite had all but deserted her. Millie had been waving her wooden spoon, threatening to use it on her if she didn't start eating decent meals again. And then, the housekeeper had blandly pointed out that while Jim was around, Dal had eaten like a horse.

Now she stole a look up at him, mesmerized by the tender flame burning in his eyes as he met her gaze. Her lips parted as she read the intent in his eyes and felt his fingers tighten perceptibly upon her elbow. His mouth… so strong and competent looking… Dal dragged in a deep breath, wondering wildly what it would feel like to be kissed by him. She had wondered often. She was beginning to live again, and she weakly accepted that fact by wanting to be kissed by Jim Tremain.

Jim forced himself to relax his hold on Dal's arm. He felt her tremble, her eyes wide with trust as he hungrily looked at her. He wanted to kiss her, to feel the velvet softness of her full lips against his mouth…. Groaning inwardly, Jim placed an ironclad control over himself. Two weeks…two of the longest damn weeks of his life had passed before he could see Dal again, and God, she looked so good to him. He wanted to tell her all of that, but knew if he did he would frighten her away.

The elevator doors slid open and Jim escorted Dal through the plush lobby to the restaurant, which was enclosed in glass and heavy forest green drapes. He glanced down at Dal, aware that she needed his physical support. She was so damn pale, he thought. Was it a reaction to seeing him? Or coming down to Denver? There were so many questions that couldn't be asked, so Jim switched fully to his internal sensing system to feel Dal out, to find out how to handle her correctly instead of scaring her away from him.

He was hungry only for Dal, as she sat opposite him at a table covered with a pale linen cloth that matched the flush of her cheeks. He had ordered coffee and she Scotch on the rocks. Jim laughed at himself; he had spent his nights dreaming of Dal, of the conversations they would have, and his dreams had been nothing like their present predicament with each other. He sensed her discomfort, saw it in the way her deep-blue eyes were veiled with uncertainty. And he felt helpless. Mentally giving himself a shake, Jim decided to hell with it, and instinctively reached across the table, his hand covering her tightly clasped fingers in front of her.

"Let's talk," he urged huskily, holding her frightened gaze.

Dal closed her eyes, allowing the strong warmth of his fingers to seep through her fragmented state. "You're healing," she whispered. "Just your touch…" And then she reopened her eyes, meeting his understanding gaze. "I'm scared, Jim."

"Of what? Me?"

She watched as his other hand gently pried hers apart, cradling them between his. A soothing balm spread through her and Dal's lips trembled. "No, not of you." She looked around the restaurant, which was slowly beginning to fill with the noontime trade. "People…men…"

"Look," Jim began slowly, "Rafe told me what happened to you, Dal." His hands tightened by degrees on her cool, damp flesh.

Her heart banged away in her throat. "He did?"

"Yes. He wanted to protect you from what I was asking of you. He didn't feel you were ready to take life by the horns yet." Jim's mouth twisted into a grimace. "And maybe he's right. You're pale and I can feel you trembling…. Maybe it wasn't a good time for you to come down here. You've been out of the flow of life for six months, Dal, trying to lick your own wounds and heal yourself from that trauma." Jim managed a sad smile. "And in my own selfishness, I pushed you into working on this project. I was wrong, I—"

"No! Don't you understand, Jim? I've got to do it sometime. I've got to get over my fear of men in general. I can't keep running from life."

He slowly rubbed the backs of her hands with his thumbs. "You also shouldn't jump back in and shock the hell out of yourself, either." Impatience tinged his tone, but it was directed at himself. "I shouldn't have asked you down here. I should have driven back up to the ranch to discuss the aerie sites."

Dal felt the hotness of tears rimming her eyes, though a soft smile touched her lips. A powerful wave of emotion lifted her high above her present fear. At that moment, she wanted to reach out, slide her arms around Jim's shoulders and melt against him. Hold him and kiss him. Thank him for his concern, because she'd never experienced this kind of depth of care from Jack. And knowing that gave her a new kind of courage she hadn't been aware she possessed. "Don't be angry with yourself, Jim."

He lifted his chin, meeting her luminous eyes, eyes that he could drown his soul within and know that he had held heaven in his arms. "Someone has to be," he said wryly.

A smile curved her lips. "No."

He picked up one of her hands and leaned forward, pressing a kiss to her velvet flesh. She smelled of fresh pine, of mountain air mingling with the special scent of her. "Talk to me, then. Tell me what is comfortable for you," he urged quietly, allowing her to reclaim her hands.

Dal's hands and arm tingled wildly beneath his brief, fleeting kiss. She had melted inwardly as his mouth brushed her hand. And she was hotly aware of a shaft of fiery longing igniting within her, despite the chaos inside. "To sit here and enjoy our lunch. I need to eat more."

He nodded his head. "You do. And then?"

"Take me to your office and we'll go over the aerie sites."

"You have a lot of courage, Dal."

She shrugged and picked up the drink, the ice soothing against the hotness of her flesh. "Maybe it's a Kincaid trait."

"What is?"

"Meeting trouble head-on. We don't have enough sense to approach it carefully or with constraint." Dal's features relaxed as she thought about the family trait. "Rafe suggested that I get therapy for what Jack had done to me, but I couldn't.... At first, I just couldn't speak to anyone about it."

Jim heard the pain in her voice and wanted to take it away. And yet, he was a man. Someone she had learned to fear. "Everyone has their own way of dealing with traumatic situations, Dal. When you feel stronger, you might find someone here in Denver who's a specialist in that area to help you."

She nodded, sliding her slender fingers around the coolness of the tumbler that sat before her. "I can't believe this, Jim. You're a stranger who walked into my life and I'm talking about it to you. I couldn't even talk to my parents after it happened. And Rafe had to drag it out of me when I asked him to let me stay at the ranch to get myself together again." She raised her head, confusion in her eyes. "I've tried to understand why I trust you like I do. You're a man and you're just as capable of hurting me, and yet, I'm here with you."

"Are you sorry you've come?"

Dal dragged in a deep breath. "No, Jim, I'm not. All the way down to Denver I kept wanting to turn back, to run home. The only thing that kept me going was remembering how you took care of me that morning when I woke up from that nightmare." She stole a look at him through her thick lashes. "You could have handled that situation a lot of different ways than you did. You could have taken advantage of me...but you didn't. And I guess that surprised me. I thought all men were out for themselves.

"You—" she lifted her chin, her eyes sparkling with tears "—took care of me and gave to me. You somehow knew I needed to be held, to be rocked like a hurt child in your arms. How did you know? Rafe never did. My dad never held me if I was hurting. Kincaids are tough. They're supposed to be able to take it on the chin without crying about it."

Jim swallowed hard against the lump forming in his throat. Right then he wanted to be in the privacy of his home, not having a conversation of that weight and magnitude with Dal in a restaurant. But it didn't really matter. What was important was that Dal was finally talking about it.

"My mother raised me, Dal. I grew up in the company of women more than men. Although I had uncles around me all the time, the women taught me about emotional issues." He traded a gentle smile with her. "My father died when I was only eight, and I can still remember my mother's courage through that time in our lives. She's still a schoolteacher on the Navaho reservation in New Mexico."

"I'm sorry about your father. You sound as if you were close to him."

Jim nodded. "I was."

"What did he do for a living?"

"He worked for the Bureau of Indian Affairs."

A wistful note crept into her husky voice. "And he met and fell in love with your mother? I think that's wonderful."

"They loved each other very much. My mother's three brothers taught me Navaho ways when I was very young, and my father approved of it." He smiled fondly in remembrance. "In some ways, my father was more Indian by philosophy than by blood. He adopted Navaho customs, to the joy of my mother's family, and most of the time we lived in a hogan on the red desert in New Mexico near Fort Wingate rather than live in the government housing."

Dal smiled gently, resting her chin on her hands. Just listening to Jim's low timbre relaxed her to the point where all of the former chaos dissolved. "I don't know much about the Navaho other than what you've shared with me, but if you're the rule and not the exception to them, then I think our men could take a lesson or two from you," she said ruefully.

The waiter came and apologetically interrupted their conversation. Jim ordered for them, handing the waiter the menus afterward. Inwardly, he breathed a sigh of relief as he noticed color coming back to Dal's face. Her eyes held less fear in their cobalt depths. "The Navaho man reveres his wife. My mother's family was typically close and communal even though we lived many miles away from each other," he continued. "When my father died of a heart attack, my mother's older brother moved his family next to our hogan. He took on the responsibility of raising me to be a man."

Dal shared a warmth-filled look with Jim. "Do you have any idea of how special you really are?"

Jim picked up the cup and took a sip of coffee, all the while holding her gaze. "No. I'm just a man, Dal. I've made my share of mistakes in the past and I've got feet of clay. I'm far from perfect."

"Not in my eyes," she whispered.

"Careful," Jim warned her, "don't put me up on any pedestals, Dal." His mouth quirked into a smile. "I manage to fall off them pretty easily."

A smile touched her lips and she held his amused look. "Okay, I've been fairly warned. Still... I'm glad I came. And I hope my personal problems don't overshadow what we want to accomplish on this poaching project."

Jim shook his head. "Dal, you've never been a problem to me. I'm glad Rafe told me what happened. Otherwise, I'm sure I'd have pressured you too much and ended up hurting you."

"For better or worse, I'm seeing this through. I know if I can tackle it and meet it halfway, I can begin to live again, Jim. Don't ask me how I know that, I just do...."

He picked up her hand, cradling it between his own. "I think part of it has to do with facing Gordon again. Not that we'll physically face him, but the fact that you are addressing your past with him." He squeezed her hand, which was now warm like his own. "And I'll be there to help you, if you want...."

Chapter 5

Dal smiled to herself when Jim took her to his office on the fifteenth floor of the federal building. Although he was dressed in business clothes, his coat and tie hung inconspicuously on a coatrack behind the door of his light, airy office. Two large umbrella plants towered more than six feet tall in each corner near the plate-glass windows. A small planter sat on his elegant walnut desk, overflowing with greenery and tendrils of grape ivy. If Jim couldn't be outdoors all the time, he brought the world of nature with him. Dal slid him a tender look as he walked around his desk, scooping up a batch of papers. With his shirt sleeves rolled up on his forearms and his shirt collar open, he epitomized the Westerner's casual attitude toward formality.

"Have a seat," he invited, rummaging through his phone messages as he sat down.

Dal enjoyed the opportunity to observe Jim while he was engaged in other activity. She longed to run her fingers through his black hair that shone with blue highlights. Was it as soft and thick as it appeared? And, as always, her gaze settled on his well-shaped mouth—a mouth that could give orders or drop into a husky whisper and make her feel as if she were being physically caressed by him. Taking a long breath, Dal tried to control her rampant thoughts and keep her mind on the business at hand.

Lunch had been anything but business. But then, Dal had hoped it wouldn't be. In that short hour she had learned a great deal about him. And, as she looked around his spacious office, she saw Indian artifacts and several prints by Indian artists hanging on the three ivory walls. Beneath her feet lay a rug beautifully handwoven in earth tones; she was sure it had been created by some Navaho woman. Green plants, earth colors and the sun spilling through the venetian blinds all combined to relax Dal.

Jim frowned and sat up, buzzing for his secretary. "Hold on just one more second," he told Dal.

"Okay," she said with a nod. She heard the door to the office open and looked up. Her heart sank. An elegant young woman sporting shoulder-length blond hair entered the office. In Dal's eyes, she was fresh, exuberant with life and devastatingly beautiful. A shaft of jealousy shot through Dal and she blinked, assimilating the unaccustomed emotion. When had she ever been jealous? The emotion was foreign to her. Until now.

"Yes, Jim?"

"Mandy, get me those aerie site maps on the Triple K ranch and the wildlife refuge, will you?"

Mandy smiled pertly. "Right away. Would you or Dr. Kincaid like coffee?"

Dal shook her head, forcing a smile. "Not for me, thanks."

"Me neither."

Dal's hands had grown damp and cold. She envied Mandy's youth and vitality. At this point in her life she had neither, and she felt as if she were coming out of a long, dark tunnel. In all fairness to Mandy, it wasn't her fault that she looked so—untouched.

Jim glanced up at Dal. "That's my right-hand assistant, Mandy Prigozen. She pinch-hits for me when the paper pushing gets to be too much and I want to escape out into the field for a few days."

"She's very pretty," Dal commented in a low voice.

Jim held her unsure gaze, aware of the tenor of her soft voice. "But you're beautiful."

Heat swept up Dal's neck and into her cheeks and she avoided his warming golden gaze, which sought to reassure her. Was she that transparent that Jim could see her jealousy of Mandy? Before Dal could think of anything to say, Mandy swept back into the office with several large rolls of paper. She placed them on the drafting board at one end of the office and unrolled them.

"Thanks, Mandy," Jim said, rising.

"If you two need anything else, just let me know. I'll hold all your calls, Jim."

Jim nodded and placed his hand on Dal's arm. "Ready to go to work?" he asked with a slight smile.

A tremor flowed through Dal at his look and touch. "Ready."

A headache was lapping at Dal's temples as they completed the task. Looking down at her watch, she realized it was 6:00 p.m. Time had melted into nothingness as she and Jim had stood shoulder to shoulder, going over each site on the series of maps.

"I didn't realize it was so late," she said, straightening up. Hours ago she had shed her blazer and seemed unaware of how the orange color of her silk blouse complemented her natural skin tone.

Jim rolled down his sleeves, buttoning the cuffs. "I didn't think it would take this long, either," he apologized. "However, I intend to make up for it by making you dinner tonight."

Dal's head snapped up. "What?"

"I asked you out for dinner in that note I sent to you a couple of weeks ago. I never got an answer, so I figured you were agreeable."

Her eyes widened. "But—"

Sauntering across the office, Jim picked up her blazer and his coat jacket. "But what?"

Dal looked down at her watch again. "It's so late. And I've got a four-hour drive home."

"Home?" Jim echoed as he shrugged into his jacket. "I had Mandy make that hotel reservation for you so that you could stay overnight and go back to the ranch tomorrow morning."

Gnawing on her lower lip, Dal avoided his inspection. She slid off the stool and took her blazer. To the west of them over the mountains the sky was turning dark and threatening. Another spring storm was brewing and was sure to come sliding down off the Rockies and strike Denver. "Well, it's just that..." Her voice ebbed away. Dal touched her temple, all too aware that her fingers were trembling. "God, you're going to think I'm crazy...."

Jim walked over, taking her blazer and holding it for

her while she slipped into it. "Try me," he urged quietly. "You're upset about something."

Dal sat down again, afraid to look up and meet his eyes. She nervously folded her hands in the lap of her linen skirt. "This is going to sound childish and immature," she muttered in a strained voice.

Jim reached out and placed his finger beneath her chin. "When an animal has been abused by a human, do you lose patience with it because it reacts to you out of fear?" he posed softly, forcing her to meet his gaze.

A lump formed in her throat and Dal couldn't speak. She merely shook her head. She watched as Jim drew over the other stool and sat down, their knees almost touching.

"What's bothering you, Dal?"

A tremor of anguish soared through her as his low voice stroked her like a lover's caress. Every time Jim whispered her name like an endearment her heart automatically opened and responded to him of its own volition. Taking a deep, steadying breath, Dal whispered, "Ever since it happened, I haven't been able to sleep in a bedroom at night, Jim. That's why I sleep out on the couch. The living room is more open. I can see someone coming. It's not so dark or suffocating."

"I see. And a hotel room?"

She shut her eyes. "It's just a larger bedroom. I—I couldn't stand being cooped up in one all night. I'd go crazy. I know my fears sound infantile, and I know I have to deal with them one day. But not now. I'm not ready to confront them yet."

He reached out, gently taking her cold hands into his. "I'd say you've taken a major step forward by working on this project, plus driving down here. You're right, it's enough for now."

Dal felt the heat of her tears and tried to blink them away as she lifted her head to study Jim. She drowned in the honey color of his thickly lashed eyes. A ribbon of calm soothed her exposed nerves and she managed a broken smile. "Do you know how it feels to have all these stupid fears ruling me? In my head I know better, Jim. I know my bedroom at the Triple K isn't the same one where it took place. But if I step into it, I start tearing loose emotionally and I begin to lose control."

He squeezed her hands. "I have something I want to share with you. When I was ten, I crawled into an old, abandoned mine shaft. Part of it caved in on me and I was trapped in the darkness for almost five hours. Somehow, the hatali, the old medicine man of our tribe, found me. To this day, I'll never know how he knew I was slowly suffocating to death in that blocked mine passage. I was unconscious when they dug through the debris and rescued me, Dal. For years after that, I had one hell of a time going into any place that was dark or cramped." He managed a self-deprecating smile. "You should have seen me in college that first year as a freshman. Some of the seniors threw me into a dark closet as a joke and then locked it. I sat in there for three hours, coming face-to-face with the horror of that mine cave-in."

Dal's eyes widened with compassion. "Oh, Jim, that was awful!"

He shrugged. "I can't say it's recommended therapy for everyone in coming to grips with fear, but it did the trick for me. The first hour in there I sat frozen, just trying to control my hysteria. The second hour the fear had me by the throat and I cried and screamed. By the third hour, I had experienced all those emotions I had withheld over the years and was cleansed. I had accepted them. And in reality, I was accepting that I could have died. That was the bottom line. Fear of dying." He gave her a sober look. "And what Gordon did to you was to almost kill some vital essence of your selfhood. Of you, as a human being. It takes time to confront those terrors and come to grips with them."

She hung her head, fighting back the tears. Tears for him. For the horror he had had to face by himself without any help or support. What would she have done without Jim's understanding? His strength was her strength at the moment. And he had had no one in his hour of need. "Thank you for sharing that with me," she murmured thickly.

"We're all walking wounded, honey. Just remember that. You. Me. Rafe. Everyone."

Dal managed a slight laugh. "All except your pretty assistant. She's so untouched."

"Ah, do I detect a bit of jealousy in your tone, Dr. Kincaid?" he asked with a grin.

"I think you do, and I'm not very proud of myself for it. I don't wish Mandy any rotten experiences in life."

"I know you don't. You couldn't hurt a fly if your life depended on it," Jim said dryly, rising to his feet. Reluctantly he released her fingers. "And as for jealousy, well, I think that's a backhanded compliment to me."

She grimaced and met his amused expression. "I should find a more positive way to admit that I enjoy your company."

"I happen to like the way I found out that you like

hanging around me," he countered softly. He glanced out the window. "I have an idea, Dal."

"What?"

"Originally, I was going to take you home and fix us a meal. It's twenty after six. Even if you left now and headed home, you'd run into that storm front that's approaching. I heard the weather forecast this morning and they're calling for severe storm warnings tonight." He glanced down at her. "And you know as well as I do that storms this time of year are hazardous in the higher reaches of the Rockies. So—" Jim reached out, gripping her arm to help her stand "—how about if I offer you a home-cooked meal and the couch in my living room for the night? You can leave tomorrow morning after the storm's passed."

The offer sounded good. And logical. But her heart and emotions had a life of their own in her breast. "I don't know, Jim."

He lightly rested his hands on her shoulders. "No strings attached, Dal. I just want to know you're safe and not out driving in that hellish weather."

"But… I didn't bring a nightgown or anything…."

"You can wear one of my shirts to bed. I've got an extra toothbrush in the medicine cabinet, too."

"I'll have to call Millie when we get there. She's expecting me home tonight."

"No problem."

The sky was darkening as they drove into Jim's driveway. Dal's eyes widened in appreciation of his home. It was a large two-story A-frame complete with sun decks on the first and second floors. Both decks faced a small lake no more than a hundred feet from the house, which was surrounded with quaking aspen and white-barked birch trees interspersed with blue spruce.

"It's lovely," she whispered, sharing a look with him.

"It's a forty-five minute drive out of Denver, but worth it," he agreed, shutting off the engine of the Blazer. He rested his hands on the steering wheel for a moment. "When I got transferred up here three years ago, I didn't want to live in the city."

"You can almost fish off your sun deck for dinner," she said, laughing.

"Almost. I have a small wooden wharf where we can do that. Come on. I don't know about you, but I'm starved."

Jim made her comfortable in the living room and then went upstairs to change. The highly polished reddish cedar floors and walls lent a warm atmosphere to the room, as did the many Navaho rugs scattered here and there. The rugs had simple designs in brilliant shades of blue, yellow, white and black. The field-stone fireplace was complemented by the huge, thick sheepskin rug in front of it. The rustic furniture was fashioned from cherry wood, with dark, forest-green cushions, reminding her of the pines outside the sliding glass doors.

"You have any other clothes to climb into?" Jim asked, coming up behind her.

Dal turned, stunned again by his rugged good looks as he rolled up the sleeves of his blue plaid shirt. He was wearing worn jeans and scuffed cowboy boots.

"I always carry a pair of sneakers with me if I have to walk any distance."

"You look uncomfortable in those heels."

She smiled. "Is it that obvious?"

He matched her smile, coming to a halt a few feet from her. "That obvious. You're like me, you want to be comfortable and not trussed up like a Christmas goose in modern-day business fashion."

Her heart was buoyed by his teasing. "What do you suggest?"

"I've got a pair of jeans that might halfway fit you. Then you can get out of the skirt and heels. If you want to change, they're lying at the foot of my bed upstairs."

"I'd like that."

"Meet me in the kitchen when you're done. If you want, you can help me."

Suddenly the evening was turning into magic. All the annihilating weight Dal had been carrying slipped free of her shoulders as she walked up the stairs and into the master bedroom. She stood at the doorway, stunned by the beauty of the view. The lake was surrounded by aspen, pine and oak trees. The orange of the sunset blended with the murky darkness of the approaching storm. Her gaze moved back to the four-poster brass bed. She reached out, caressing the brass footboard with her slender fingers. The brass was in dire need of a polishing. Colorful Navaho designs had been woven into the wool blanket that served as a spread for the massive bed. Again, she was aware of the simplicity and spareness of Jim Tremain, which shored up her own complicated and fluctuating world.

By the time Dal had slipped out of her suit and donned the jeans, she could see forks of lightning on the far horizon. Tucking in the tails of her orange blouse, she padded down the cedar stairs in her sneakers and into the living room, where she picked up the phone and called Millie.

A few minutes later, Jim turned, drinking in Dal's slender figure as she quietly entered the small kitchen. He smiled in welcome as his gaze moved from her hair, which was still captured tightly in a chignon at the nape of her slender neck, down to her feet. He dried his hands on a towel and turned around as she approached.

"You're a dichotomy, Dal," he told her in a low, vibrating voice as he slowly raised his arms and encircled her.

Dal took a swift breath, wildly aware of his maleness as his arms settled lightly on her shoulders. One look into his honey-colored eyes and she relaxed as he stood inches from her. "Wh-what do you mean?" Her voice was almost a whisper.

"Your hair," he murmured, gently easing the pins from the chignon. "Here you are looking gorgeous and natural in jeans." His mouth curved as he looked down into her shadowed sapphire eyes while he collected the pins, urging the silken mass of hair from its captivity. "And you come out here without your hair down or loose.... There," he said, pleased as he coaxed the thick, entangled strands in place around her shoulders, "now you look like the woman I know—relaxed and free."

A nerve-jangling tingle flared from wherever his strong fingers brushed the nape of her neck or shoulders as he freed her hair from the severe chignon. Jim's touch was feather light, and it made her achingly aware of the hungry chemistry that throbbed palpably between them. He was so close...so excruciatingly male in a way she had never before encountered. In his arms, Dal felt no fear. She felt safe and loved. Loved? Her eyes widened as she stared up into his serious face and melted beneath his golden gaze, which caressed her in those moments afterward. He was a man. And yet, she ached to merely reach up on tiptoe and place her lips against his strong mouth and feel of him.

Tremors of longing moved through Dal in earthquake proportion. Was she beginning to fall in love with Jim? How was that possible? The feelings that were evoked by merely the thought of him or by his presence weren't what she had experienced with Jack. Dal licked her lower lip, waging a war within herself. Was this love? Real love? Was it merely the feeling of being respected by Jim as an equal? Or the sense of total care and protection that radiated so strongly from him toward her?

The giddy sense that he cherished her, man to woman, almost overwhelmed Dal. Her lashes lifted and met his hooded expression. Jim was so close...so pulverizingly male that her heart began a slow pounding of expectation. She wanted him to kiss her. But how could she tell him that? What would he think of her inexperienced efforts to share? Was it wrong to want him to simply touch her mouth so that she could taste the heated warmth of him and absorb his strength into her dark, cold soul?

Jim read all of her thoughts in her transparent expressions. He had to control the hunger of his own body. He wanted to lean down and brush those parted lips that were begging to be caressed by him. The patience of his Indian heritage curbed his need, and instead Jim allowed his hand to barely caress her shining spice-colored hair.

"Come on, I want you to meet a friend of mine. He's out back."

Shaken, Dal allowed him to take her arm and lead her out the sliding glass door to a large fenced area. Her heady euphoria was ripped away and she pressed herself against Jim, eyes wide with sudden terror.

"It's all right," Jim said. He watched her cheeks lose their flushed quality. A huge eighty-pound gray dog came loping happily from the far end of the yard, which was protected by pine and aspen trees.

"My God," Dal whispered, "that's a wolf!"

Jim smiled and raised his hand, signaling the dog to sit. Obediently, the amber-eyed dog sat a good ten feet in front of them, whining in greeting and thumping his full, brushlike tail on the grass. "We share a similar calling with wild animals," he told her. "You have your golden eagle and I have Raider. Relax, he won't hurt you. He's a big, overgrown puppy."

"Sure. You bet he is," Dal muttered, eyeing the animal.

Jim laughed softly, walked over to Raider and petted his large head. "He's half wolf and half Alaskan malamute."

"That's quite a combination."

"It's not uncommon for malamutes or huskies who escape their sledding traces to turn wild and mate with wolves up in Alaska."

"And you were lucky enough to get one of these... these..."

"Half-breeds? Yeah, I think I'm lucky." Jim smiled, meeting her guarded expression. "Come on over here. Let me introduce you to Raider and then you'll be friends. I promise you, he's nothing more than a big puppy. Especially around a beautiful woman."

Dal flushed hotly over the inference in his low, vibrating voice and stood there, trusting Jim, yet wary of the wild-looking animal. "I don't know much about wolves," she began hesitantly, taking small steps toward them.

Jim offered her his hand and pulled her down beside him. "Wolves are communal animals who respect one leader. The alpha male, in this case, is me. I'm imprinted on Raider as his boss. As long as I show strength, he'll never turn on me. Give me your hand."

Her throat tightened with fear, but Dal allowed Jim to take her hand. "Well, I'm certainly not a leader or strong appearing," she muttered, wondering if she was going to lose one or all of her fingers as Jim guided her hand forward for Raider to smell.

"No, but you're my woman and Raider will know to respect you as he does me."

Dal's breath caught over his softly spoken words. She felt Raider's pink tongue on her fingers but was more stunned by Jim's admission. When he lifted his head and turned toward her, she melted beneath his golden gaze. "Y-your woman?"

"In the world of wolves, the mate of the leader is just as powerful as the male is." A careless grin pulled at his mouth. "Does it bother you to be my mate while you're here?"

He was teasing her now. Dal returned her attention to Raider, who had inched closer, wagging his tail happily. "Which is more dangerous. You or this wolf?"

Jim's grin blossomed into a smile. "We're both big puppies if you'll just give us some of your attention and a pat on the head." He stood up, leaving Dal in a kneeling position with Raider. The wolf thumped his tail and then lay down in front of Dal, rolling over on his back and exposing his belly to her.

"He's posturing to you," he told her. "That's a sign

of obeisance on his part in recognizing you as superior or as the leader."

"I've seen dogs do that, too," Dal noted, taken with Raider's joyous display. The wolf returned to his feet and approached her, whining and lowering his head. Dal laughed and began to pet him. "His fur...it's so soft and beautiful...."

"Typical of a wolf," Jim agreed, placing his hands on his hips, watching Dal and the wolf. In a sense, he thought, they were both wild animals. Raider's natural instincts were those of a wolf with a cloak of domesticity thrown about it through the genes of its malamute mother. Dal was domesticated but fearful of men, with a cloak of distrust that bordered on a wild animal's reactions.

Delighted with Raider's doglike responses, Dal sank to her knees and allowed him to come into her arms while she lavished pats of affection on him. "He's wonderful!"

"He's a typical male," Jim returned dryly, matching her smile. In that crystalline moment, Jim saw the real Dal Kincaid. Not the embattled woman fighting for survival, but the relaxed child within her. It took his breath away. He knelt beside her, wanting to share the moment with her. Raider rolled on his back between them, thumping his tail happily.

"When did you get him?" Dal asked, wildly aware of Jim's closeness. Sharing of something as small as this shook her. When had she laughed or felt so delighted over anything so simple? Not for a long, long time. Her eyes softened as she watched Jim play with Raider.

"Ten years ago. I had a friend of mine who was stationed up in Alaska with the Department of the Interior. Ray stumbled on the puppies after a hunter had killed their mother, thinking she was a wolf." He shook his head. "Typical hunter from the lower forty-eight, I guess. He couldn't tell the difference between a malamute's coat and a wolf's. Anyway, Ray found the pups. He was born in Alaska and knew about local dogs mating with wolves."

"So he called you up and asked you to take one of the pups?"

Jim nodded, giving Raider a final pat before standing. "Yeah. I had done quite a bit of research on wolves and he knew of my interest in them."

Dal stood, brushing her hands off on the sides of her jeans. "You have eyes like a wolf yourself."

He turned and studied her, a slight smile on his mouth. "I've been accused of that a number of times. My mother has golden brown eyes, too."

"When I first met you, I thought you had Nar's eyes. His are amber, too."

"Maybe I'm an animal in the guise of a man."

A shiver of yearning threaded through her. In many ways, Jim reminded her of an animal, but only in a positive sense. "I think you are," she admitted.

"Oh?"

"Well, I mean…" Dal gave a nervous laugh.

"No, I'd like to know how you see me."

Heat crept up her neck and into her face. She twined her fingers nervously in front of her. The air stirred with a slight breeze. "You'll laugh… I have such an overactive imagination. Rafe used to laugh at me when I'd sit out in a meadow and tell him about the clouds in the sky. I could see shapes and things in them."

Jim nodded, remaining serious. "I used to do the

same thing, only no one accused me of being a day-dreamer."

Dal felt another defensive wall slip free of her, releasing even more of the tension she had been carrying around with her. She turned, looking out across the small lake that was now ruffled by the sporadic breeze. "I see you as a hunter in the guise of a man." And then she added quickly, "You have extraordinary hearing. And as I said, the color of your eyes reminds me of Nar's. You walk so quietly that I sometimes think you're a cougar padding around." Dal avoided his tender gaze. "I'm sure you think I'm crazy. Jack always said I was an immature child who needed to grow up."

Jim reached out, taming several strands of hair from her cheek as she lifted her chin to meet his gaze. "That's one of the many things I like about you. You are a child." His mouth flattened slightly. "Maybe it's my Indian blood, but I've seen too many adults of all races lose their wonder toward life. I think when you do that, you've lost half your soul." He allowed his hand to rest lightly on her shoulder, watching Dal for reaction. "For instance, Raider brought out the child in you. You were down there on your hands and knees playing with him. Did you hear your laughter? How free it was? Did you know all the tension around your mouth disappeared for those few magical moments?" He brushed one corner of her lips, watching them part beneath his caress. God, he thought, to lean down and touch them with his mouth...

Dal read the intent in his golden eyes, which burned with desire as he touched her lips with his thumb. A heated bolt of fire leaped down through her and she felt her nipples hardening against the confining softness of her bra. A slight gasp escaped her as she felt his fingers slide beneath her jaw, tipping her head up…up to meet his strong, masculine mouth. Automatically, her lashes dropped closed, brushing her flaming pink cheeks as she felt the hot moistness of his breath against her flesh. She froze inwardly waiting…waiting…wanting him. The instant his mouth brushed her lips, she melted from the heat of his tentative exploration of her. Explosions rippled through her as his mouth worshiped her with slow, gentle pressure, asking her to part her lips. A moan rose in her throat as she felt his fingers splay against her jaw, cradling her within his hands.

Fire throbbed achingly throughout her and her breath caught as she shyly returned the coaxing kiss. Mindless, Dal felt herself becoming a willow, bending beneath his strong but controlled direction as he sipped hungrily from her mouth.

"Honey," he murmured thickly against her, "you're pure, sweet honey."

A quiver raced through her as his tongue traced her lips. Never had she felt so adored or so cherished. Her fingers rested tensely against his taut chest and Dal capitulated to the throbbing heat building between them, her thighs molding against his. She entrusted herself utterly to Jim's arms as his mouth moved slowly across her lips.

A thrill arced through Dal's dazed mind as she realized Jim was giving back to her, not plundering from her as her previous experience had taught. She found herself a neophyte in his arms, starved for the kind of love that he offered to her. His male scent filled her flared nostrils and her fingers came to rest in the thick silk of black hair at the nape of his corded neck. Each nip of his mouth was as if a butterfly were lightly touching her.... Each teasing stroke of his tongue sent a fiery shudder of longing coursing hotly through her. She wanted Jim. In every way. He gave as much as she took in offering from him. How did he know she needed his love? she wondered. His care? So much had been stripped from her that Dal discovered in that moment just how badly she needed the care of another man. Only one man. One who could heal her. And that was Jim.

All those precious seconds of discovery entangled in the fire of his tender exploration. She felt bereft as Jim dragged his mouth from her lips, her lashes barely rising to meet his burning amber gaze. A shiver of expectancy sizzled through her as she read the message in his eyes. Dal wavered unsteadily, her knees threatening to give way, but steadied by his arms holding her captive against his strong, powerful body. How could she tell him how vulnerable and fragile she felt inside at that moment? How his kiss had torn away all her defenses? Dal was emotionally naked and knew it. Jim could wound her in such a way that she would never recover, and that thought paralyzed her. As she drowned in his gaze, it was as if he knew that, too, as if he were in some sort of telepathic union with her.

Jim eased one hand from her waist and caressed her cheek. "Neither of us was expecting that," he said thickly, apology in his tone. His eyes darkened as he looked deeply into her sapphire ones. "You're beautiful, Dal. All the way to your heart and your frightened soul." His voice lowered into a chanting tone. "The shadow I see in your eyes is fear. Fear of what another man did to you. And fear that I have the same capacity to hurt you also. Whatever you do, don't fear me. I would never do anything to harm you, Dal. I'd rather injure myself, instead." His thumb traced the outlines of her full, glistening lips which had rested so softly beneath his mouth moments before. His body hardened with the longing to bring her into complete union with himself, to heal her as she was healing him.

"I trust you," she admitted softly in a strained tone.

Jim groaned and slowly released her, noticing how shaky she had become. One small, shared kiss had devastated them equally. Would she smile if she knew his own knees felt hardly more solid than water in a stream? "Don't fear me, honey. But trust?" He groaned and a self-deprecating smile stretched the corners of his mouth. "Better to trust a wild animal at this point than me."

Dal managed a broken smile of her own, relieved he kept one hand around her waist while she reoriented herself. "To me, you are a wild animal under the veneer of a man's form."

"In some ways, I guess I am," he admitted. "I was raised out on the desert and herded sheep and goats as a kid. I had to use the cries of a crow to alert me to the eagles that flew around the flock, looking to snatch a newborn lamb. With my eyes, I had to ferret out a stalking coyote waiting in the camouflage of brush to snare a straggling ewe from the herd. I can smell a rattler downwind by a good twenty feet." He gave her an intimate look laced with amusement. "You're probably right; I am more wild animal than human."

Unconsciously, Dal touched her lips, which still tingled wildly from his caressing exploration. "The wild animals have a code they live by, Jim. I feel far safer with you than I do with any other human." Her brow furrowed. "People have lost so much of the code that animals live by. You never see murder, greed or hatred among animals." She rubbed her arms, trying to get rid of the sudden goose pimples she got when she thought of Jack Gordon.

He nodded, watching the purple and steel-gray clouds continue to build from one horizon to another. The sun had long ago been swallowed up by the approaching storm front, and there was just the lingering orange of dusk now. "Animals respect one another," he agreed. "It's like Raider; he knows who's boss and would never challenge me unless I was incapacitated or too old to be leader."

Dal looked up, drowning in Jim's features, which were now softened. Had her returning his kiss done that? A thrill of discovery spiraled through her. How easily touched Jim was. Or was it just with her? And then an icy avalanche of despair cloaked her. Jim had said he had never met a woman right for him, yet. Where in his life did that leave her?

"Did you call Millie and tell her you'd be staying overnight?"

Dal blinked, tearing herself away from her own internal anguish. "Yes. I called her earlier."

"Did she threaten you with a broom if you didn't come home tonight?" he teased, leading her toward the rear of the yard and through a gate to the lakefront.

"She was a bit surprised, but seemed to take it in stride. I don't think I'll get swatted with the broom when I go home tomorrow morning."

Torn by the realization that she might be less of a woman than what he wanted, Dal knew she had to make a decision. If she allowed herself to continue to open and blossom in his presence, she might still be opening herself up to hurt. And if she withdrew from Jim, what was left? Nothing but darkness and cold in her heart. Dal had agonized over her lack of boyfriends during her college years. Yes, she had had many dates, but nothing so serious as to get her to climb into bed with them. Jack had been her first and only lover. Dal looked up at Jim through her thick lashes as they walked down by the grassy bank of the lake. Her instincts screamed that she had little control over herself when it came to Jim. She wanted him in all ways, understanding intuitively that he could heal the scarred parts of her soul. She was able to give herself to him, but he wouldn't do the same to her. Or only up to a point. He could give her emotional support, physical love, but not his heart. No, she wasn't strong enough, woman enough. Dal wanted to cry, to release the scream slowly uncoiling deep within her.

As they stood on the wooden wharf that jutted out into the blue-green water of the lake, Dal made a decision. It might not be the best one, she told herself, but at least I'm capable of choosing now. Six months ago, Rafe and Millie had had to make even the smallest of decisions for her. Jim had given her back the sense of being in control of her own life once again. And for that she was grateful. Dal rested against Jim, his arm around her shoulders as they stared out over the lake.

"I never knew what kind of courage it took to live," she began softly, staring at the muddy horizon. "Now I understand what my favorite writer, Antoine de Saint-Exupéry, meant."

Jim looked down at her, his hand automatically tightening around her shoulder. She was warm, soft and vulnerable with him since their kiss. "Ah, the French aviator who turned writer. And what words of wisdom did he have to say?"

Dal's eyes grew as dark as the thunderclouds approaching them. "He said, 'A single event can awaken within us a stranger totally unknown to us. To live is to be slowly born.' I feel like a stranger to myself, Jim…as if I'm slowly being reborn and trying to find the courage to live again. To take life by the horns and make my own decisions."

"There's a stranger in everyone, Dal," he agreed. "I like to think of them as facets. Diamondlike facets in all of us. You're like that, a gem of such quality."

Her smile was tender as she regarded him. "I'm a rough, unpolished diamond, then."

"Life has a way of polishing those facets in all of us. And you're not unpolished. You've just started to grow and find out all about yourself, that's all."

"That's all?" she muttered. "That's enough."

Jim grinned. "Some people remain rough-cut rocks all their life, but you won't. I've a feeling that all the Kincaids enjoy pitting themselves against life, determined to come out the winner. And when you do that, you're bound to get a polishing through many experiences."

"Well," she murmured, "I've been polished enough. All I want to do is heal myself, Jim."

He leaned down, placing a kiss on her hair, and then allowed her to step away from him. "You will," he promised huskily. "You're strong even if you don't realize it yet. Come on, I don't know about you, but I'm hungry."

They walked back side by side, Raider padding along behind them. Jim shut the gate to the fence and then they sauntered to the sun deck. A bed of hot coals glowed in the grill and in no time, Jim was barbecuing two thick porterhouse steaks. Dal lounged on a nearby cedar chair with a glass of wine. The wind came in sporadic gusts.

"That storm is going to hit in about another hour," she told him.

Jim looked to the west as he turned the juicy steaks. "And it looks like a bad one. I'm glad you're staying."

Dal took another sip of the fruity red wine. Was it wise for her to stay? The storm that was coming surely couldn't compare to the one inside her. She ran her fingers idly around the beaded coolness of the glass. Funny, she'd never have believed she was a risk-taker like the rest of the Kincaids. But she had made a decision to risk her heart and place it in Jim's hands.

Dal closed her eyes. What was she doing? she asked herself. She felt confused and unable to explain why she was going to allow the relationship between her and Jim to continue to develop. She had everything to lose. *And everything to gain,* a small voice added. He was teaching her there was give and take in a relationship and that all men weren't takers as Jack had been. Right now, Dal decided, she needed emotionally what Jim gave to her—regardless of the cost to herself in the long run.

After taking a deep, unsteady breath, Dal opened her eyes. She watched Jim as he efficiently worked over the grill. A tender smile touched her lips and she felt her fears melting away. Above her, the rolling clouds were beginning to blot out the apricot dusk. A storm was coming and this time, she welcomed it with open arms and an open heart....

Chapter 6

"Have you given any thought to our pack trip two weeks from now?" Jim asked, clearing the dishes away. He put them in the sink and then pulled a freshly baked cherry pie from the refrigerator.

Dal blotted her mouth with a napkin, feeling comfortably full after having eaten a healthy portion of the delicious steak. "A little. Jim, I can't eat another crumb!"

He looked up from slicing the pie. "Sure? I made this myself last night."

Just the way he said it made Dal feel guilty. "All right. Just a sliver of a piece, though. It's a good thing I don't eat here all the time, or I'd get fat."

With a grin, he handed her the plate, poured them freshly brewed coffee and sat opposite her. "You need the weight," he remonstrated.

A sharp crack of thunder shattered overhead and Dal looked out the kitchen window. The sky was a bruised purple color, promise of a vicious storm. "Looks like we're in for it," she murmured, taking a bite of the pie.

Jim turned and watched the storm through the sliding glass doors that led out to the sun deck. "Don't worry. We've weathered a lot of nasty stuff here. Haven't we, Raider?"

Raider lifted his head from his crossed paws. The wolf had lain down near Dal's chair earlier.

"I think he likes you," Jim said, motioning to the animal. "He usually doesn't take too well to strangers."

"I'm your mate, remember?" Dal said with a sour smile. "Or at least Raider remembers it."

"I haven't forgotten," he told her, holding her amused gaze. He saw the sudden turmoil in her sapphire eyes and decided to steer away from the topic of their burgeoning relationship. "Back to business. About the pack trip. Do you want to supply two saddles, horses and a pack animal?"

"Sure."

Jim finished off his pie, set the plate aside and reached for his mug of coffee. More wind pelted furiously against the window and another streak of lightning tore jaggedly through the gathering darkness outside the house. "The color of the horse is important."

"Oh?"

"Gray, black or brown horses. Nothing palomino or white."

Dal's eyes narrowed and she set her fork down. "Colors that blend in with the forest and meadows and would be hard to spot. Is that it?"

"Yes," Jim replied. "White stands out like a sore thumb to anyone with a pair of binoculars."

Dal placed her half-eaten pie to one side and folded her hands on the table. "You're expecting trouble, aren't you?"

"It's just a precaution, that's all."

Unsettled by the conversation, Dal tried to mask her discomfort by sipping her coffee. "Do you want rifle cases on the saddles, too?"

He nodded, his eyes hooded. "I have my own that I'll bring. But you should have one, too."

"If Rafe finds out, he's going to hit the ceiling, Jim. The only reason he's not fighting me on this is because he thinks that what we'll be doing is safe."

Jim turned the mug slowly around in his hands. "It should be. The hawks and falcons should have just laid their eggs when we arrive. If Gordon learned anything from you, it's that nestlings are easier to keep alive than eggs. I don't think he'll try for these babies until after they've been hatched in early June."

The first sharp, stinging splatters of rain sounded against the window as Dal replied, "With him, you never know, Jim. If he had ample means of keeping those eggs protected and warm, he might come early."

"Only if he has a helicopter. There's no way he could get those eggs out of there by horseback. He'd end up breaking a lot of them. Plus, he'd have the added problem of trying to keep them warm without killing the embryo."

"That's true. But Jack might try anything to make some money, regardless of the risk."

Jim nodded and rose. "Come on, let's go to the living room and enjoy this storm."

In the living room Dal curled up on the couch beside Jim, her bare feet tucked beneath her. She cradled her coffee mug between her hands, allowing it to rest on her thigh. The floor-to-ceiling windows faced west and provided a spectacular view of the fury of the storm breaking. She could hear the wind whistling through the damper in the chimney of the large fireplace. Raider ambled in and lay on a Navaho rug in front of the couch, content.

"He's just like a dog, isn't he?"

"In some ways," Jim agreed. "He's highly trained. When I'm out in the field, I can't afford to have him go ahead of me, scaring wildlife or people. When Raider was old enough to learn, I taught him eight hand signals. I can make him lie down, crawl or come to me with no sound. That way, whenever we ride into the mountains, he doesn't disturb the environment."

Admiration was apparent in Dal's eyes. "Try training a dog to do all that."

"It's done all the time with animals that work on television and movies." Jim smiled and sipped his coffee. "Raider has a keen intelligence, though."

She warmed beneath his smile. Jim was sitting near her, but hadn't made any movement toward her; part of her was relieved, yet another part wanted his continued closeness. "So he goes out on your field trips?"

"Every chance I get." His brows knit momentarily and he traded a glance with Dal. "How would your eagle respond if Raider went with us?"

"Rafe has dogs and Nar leaves them alone."

"Golden eagles are used in some countries to hunt wolves and foxes. I was just wondering if Nar had developed a taste for them."

She smiled. "He loves his rabbits. I think Raider would be safe."

Jim nodded, inwardly relieved. He had tried to soft-pedal the potential threat of running into Jack Gordon, so as not to alarm Dal. If Raider went with them, with his animal instinct operating, like a sophisticated radar system, he could warn them well in advance if other humans were in a given area. "Good. How long has it been since you went on any pack trips?"

Dal sat back, a wistful expression on her face. "A long time. When we were kids, we'd ride with the wranglers for weeks on end and during the summer." She sobered. "Ever since I married Jack, I've done nothing but live in tents in the middle of jungles."

Jim said nothing as anger stirred deep within him. He couldn't believe that Dal had nearly died from malaria. "How about if I do the cooking, then? I'm out on week-long pack trips two or three weeks a year."

"Great! I'm not the world's best cook, anyway."

A bolt of lightning zigzagged blindingly across the window and the entire house shuddered as the bolt struck a tree not far away. Dal winced, throwing up her hand to protect her eyes from the glare. She felt Jim's hand on her shoulder and relaxed.

"It's a long time since I've been around thunderstorms like this," she said. "In the jungles of the Far East, we'd get monsoon rains. But not a good old Colorado thunderstorm."

"They can be vicious," he agreed quietly. The wind pounded against the house and Jim could feel the temperature dropping. "Cold?"

"A little," Dal said with a nod.

"Stay put," he told her, rising. "I'll get a fire started in the fireplace."

The evening passed quickly. The bright warmth of a good oak fire chased away the dampness brought on by the storm. Rain continued to come and go with each thunderstorm and lightning danced across the sky without relief. At one point the electricity went out. The darkness was almost complete except for the fire in the fireplace. Jim's presence allayed any fear that Dal had of the darkness. He found a candle, placed it on the floor next to the maps and lay on his belly. She joined him and they began to make plans for the pack trip.

Raider got up and walked over to where Dal lay on her stomach. The wolf plunked down no more than six inches from her, thumping his tail in friendly fashion. She reached out and petted the animal affectionately. When Dal returned her attention to Jim, she saw an unfathomable flame in his dark-golden eyes. A warmth spun between them and she felt as if she were wrapped in a cocoon woven with his caress.

Dal got to her knees only inches from him. Her eyes focused on his mouth and she tingled hotly, recalling his feather-light kiss. She wanted him to kiss her again. With a conscious effort she marshaled her thoughts to the task at hand and pointed to the map. "Rafe had a series of line shacks built about seven years ago. They've saved a couple of our wranglers' lives when they were caught up there in early snowstorms."

"And one of them could save ours if we get a late snow up at that elevation," Jim said, writing down the information.

"Rafe said he'd fly the helicopter up to each cabin

and stock it with food and other necessities before we go on our trip."

"Good. Although," he drawled with a grin, "I'm a pretty fair cook and don't need to rely on canned goods."

Dal hooted, sitting up and resting her hands on her thighs. "I see. You're one of those outdoor cooks who believes in trapping dinner each day."

"Ordinarily, I am. Raider is good at scaring up a quail or rabbit."

Her eyes gleamed with a challenge. "So is Nar."

Jim met and matched her fiery gaze. "Is that a bet, Dr. Kincaid?" he asked softly.

"That Nar can provide us with the food we need?"

"Yes. Or that Raider can do a better job of hunting than Nar. You know, we aren't going to be able to fire a rifle to bring down our meals. I don't want any undue noise to scare the birds or announce that we're in an area. That was another reason why I wanted Raider along. If I send him to hunt game, he'll do it. And he'll bring it back to me. I can't help wondering if Nar will release anything he's caught to you."

Dal leaned back against the couch, putting her arms around her drawn up legs. "He will if he's eaten first. Rafe always has a jack rabbit problem on the ranch and I've flown Nar against them. He's caught as many as eight in one day. And once he's had his fill, he gives up the rest of his quarry to me."

Jim pursed his lips. "Impressive."

"Still want to bet who will provide us with food?"

He held out his hand toward her. "Yeah, I do."

Dal gripped his hand and smiled. "What do I get if we win?"

"You don't have to do dishes after I finish cooking."

She laughed delightedly. "Done!"

"And what if I win?"

"Then I'll do the dishes after we eat."

He scowled. "You were going to do them anyway. You know the rule of the trail: what the cook fixes, he doesn't clean up."

"Male chauvinist! Let me sleep on it, Jim. I'll come up with something," she said with a laugh.

He had a few answers to her question, but kept silent. None of them was appropriate right then. He contented himself with completing the outline of the two-week trip. Dal looked more relaxed than he had ever seen her, a glint of excitement dancing in her dark blue eyes.

"If I didn't know better, I'd say you were really looking forward to this."

Dal smiled softly, relaxing in Jim's aura and that of the warming fire. "Mmm, I am. I love the mountains and I've missed them so much since I left six years ago. I like sleeping out under the stars and feeling the earth beneath me. There's nothing like the fresh scent of pine mixed with the smell of perked coffee when you wake up in the morning," she said with a sigh.

"No," he agreed, getting up, "there isn't. It's almost eleven. Let's get ready for bed."

While Dal showered and donned one of Jim's shirts to sleep in, as well as the robe he had lent her, he made up her bed on the couch. The fire had been built up, throwing off adequate heat and light by the time she padded softly down the stairs. Jim smiled, watching as she descended.

"Somehow, you make my robe look good," he said. Jim hungrily drank in her image—her hair was in damp disarray about her heart-shaped face, softening her high cheekbones; the terry-cloth robe was wrapped lovingly about her slender form, emphasizing the ivory color of her skin; and a rose flush stained her cheeks as she shyly met his gaze. Quickly Jim veiled the feelings apparent in his eyes.

"It's a warm robe," Dal admitted, running her fingers up the loose, bulky folds of the sleeves. Wearing Jim's robe was almost as if he were holding her, Dal thought, feeling a pleasant sense of tiredness overtaking her.

"You mean I might find it gone when you leave tomorrow morning?" Jim queried as he motioned to the makeshift bed.

"You might," she said, halting at the couch. Her eyes grew tender as she turned and met his darkened gaze. The electricity was still off, and only the firelight caught the shadowed planes of his face. "You didn't have to go to all this trouble," she protested. "A blanket or two would have been fine."

He shook his head. "I wanted you to feel as if you were home on your own couch," he confided.

Dal felt the intensity of his gaze and shivered beneath it as she leaned down and pulled back the covers to reveal a set of flower-patterned sheets. "Thank you, Jim."

"I'll see you in the morning. Oh, Raider will probably be going up and down the stairs tonight, so don't let it frighten you."

She turned toward him. Raider lay on the rug before the fire, his amber eyes partly open, as if listening to their conversation. "Oh?"

"He'll be checking on you. To make sure you're all right."

Dal smiled down at the wolf. "I'm impressed."

"Just don't let it scare you. Good night."

In that moment, Dal wanted to walk those few steps to where Jim stood and kiss him. A chaste kiss for his thoughtfulness under the circumstances. Instead, Dal lowered her lashes, her voice barely above a whisper. "Good night, Jim. And thanks...for everything...."

"Only good dreams, tonight, honey," he returned huskily, and slowly mounted the stairs, disappearing into the gloom.

Dal saw Raider lift his head to watch his master ascend the stairs. "You can go with him," she told the wolf, shedding the terry-cloth robe.

Raider tilted his head, his intelligent amber eyes resting on her, then thumped his tail, and remained where he was. Dal smiled and gave him a pat on the head before retiring to the comfortable couch. The moment she closed her eyes, she spiraled into sleep. Even the rising howl of the wind didn't keep her from slipping over into the abyss. Somehow, she knew she was safe, and for the first time in six months Dal slept deeply.

The thump, thump, thump continued and Dal frowned, slowly pulling away from the fingers of sleep. What was that sound? She had been lying on her back and now slowly rolled onto her side and forced her eyes open. It took her long seconds to realize Jim was leaning over the fireplace and quietly adding a few more logs to the coals. Raider was directly parallel to the couch, his tail thumping happily as he watched his master. Warmth spread throughout Dal as she realized Jim didn't want the fire to die because it represented light to her darkness.

Her heartbeat picked up speed as she hungrily gazed at his partially clad body. He wore only drawstring pajama bottoms, the light blue color setting off the burnished quality of his skin. Dal keenly recalled resting against his chest, dark with soft black curling hair, his deep, soothing voice falling over her while he rocked her gently in his arms. A pang of need surged through her, an almost tangible hunger to know more about him.

"Jim?" Her voice was thick with sleep.

He turned. "Go back to sleep. Everything's all right," he said softly.

Dal struggled to rise and the blanket fell away, revealing the wrinkled shirt, top button open, with the shadowed cleft of her breasts visible beneath the material. "What time is it?"

Replacing the grate across the fire, Jim brushed his hands and replied, "Almost four. Why don't you lie back down?" He walked over, his face shadowed.

"I guess Raider thumping his tail woke me," she said huskily, looking up into his dark, unreadable eyes. She saw the slight upward curve of his mouth and thought how devastatingly handsome he looked.

"He's been down here with you all night." Jim longed to reach out and remove several tendrils of hair from her cheek. She looked like a gloriously beautiful child: lips slightly parted, eyes half-open and filled with the remnants of sleep, and her voice…a soft, vulnerable huskiness that tremored through him. His gaze moved from the slender expanse of her neck to her exposed collarbone to the slight fullness of her breasts covered by his shirt. He crouched down in front of her, lost in the awakening sapphire of her eyes.

"Looks like a cup of hot chocolate is in order," he murmured, smiling softly.

Dal rubbed her eyes. "That would be wonderful."

"Stay put," he told her, rising. "And I'll make it."

A blanket of languor captured her and she nodded. "Are you sure? I mean, I could get up and make it...."

Jim turned at the door. "I kind of like our habit, Dal. Just sit there and rest."

The soft snap and pop of the fire mesmerized Dal. She had sat up and tucked her long legs beneath her. With the blankets across her lap, she was reasonably warm. The storm had passed and she could feel the chill in the air that had followed on its heels. Raider began thumping his tail again and she looked up to see Jim coming. It never ceased to amaze her how silently he trod. She reached out, taking the ceramic mug.

"Oh, whipped cream this time," she teased, smiling.

"Couldn't find any in Millie's kitchen," Jim returned, sitting down on the rug and resting his back against the couch inches from where she sat.

Dal took a cautious sip, closing her eyes. "Mmm, you make the best chocolate. Even better than my mother and she's pretty good at it."

"Am I hired, then?"

Her laughter was low. "You're spoiling me rotten, Jim Tremain. Chocolate at the ranch and now here."

Leaning his arm on the couch, he turned and looked up at her. "You need a little spoiling," he said softly. And then the smile in his eyes spread across his mouth. "And you also don't know how to drink chocolate, I see."

Dal tilted her head and rested the mug in her lap, her fingers wrapped around it. "What are you talking about?"

Amusement was in Jim's eyes as he rose to his knees. He set aside his mug and reached over. "This," he murmured, cupping his hands about her face. His thumbs moved lightly across her upper lip. "You have a whipped cream mustache," he said huskily. "Might look great on a man, but it does only one thing for you...."

He was so close and so incredibly male that Dal automatically held her breath as he gently removed the whipped cream. Her lips parted and she raised her eyes, meeting...melting beneath his fiery inspection. She saw his eyes narrow slightly and was aware of the prickling sensation where he had moved his thumbs across her upper lip. "What?" she barely whispered.

"It makes a man want to lick it off you," he growled softly.

Her lashes drew closed and she waited. "Yes..."

The instant his mouth claimed hers, a shock jolted through Dal. This time he wasn't testing or teasing. No, this time, Jim was claiming her as his own. His mouth moved masterfully across her lips, parting them, hungrily taking her, feeding the fuels of her own desires until they burst into explosive life. He tasted of the rich chocolate, of the sweet whipped cream and his own maleness. She gloried in those branding seconds as his mouth worshiped hers, drugging her, coaxing her to become his. A moan of pleasure vibrated within her throat as his tongue traced each curve and hollow of her mouth, and Dal trembled violently, seeking further contact with him. His fingers moved through her hair, gently massaging her scalp, sending hundreds of tingling sensations downward. Her nipples hardened as she came to rest against the wall of his chest and her breathing became as ragged as his.

Jim reluctantly broke their kiss, taking small sips from each corner of her parted lips, licking off the last of the whipped cream. He felt her quiver as he held her by the arms. "You're so feminine and beautiful," he whispered, kissing each of her closed eyes. His nostrils flared and he drank in her special female scent. "And you smell so sweet to me. You're so much a woman in every way...."

A growing ache uncoiled deep within Dal and she felt reality slipping away. Her heart was pounding erratically and her breathing was ragged as she relaxed within his web of love. She felt lost as his mouth left hers a final time, and she opened her eyes. His amber gaze burned with a fire that stunned her, and Dal could only stare, realizing in those precious seconds his need of her. She saw him reach down and steady the mug on her lap, which threatened to spill because she was barely able to hold it. Dal gave him a helpless look as his dark, powerful hand wrapped around the mug and her hands.

"You make me feel again," she said unsteadily. "I never realized a man could make me feel—" she groped for the correct word, her mind scattered beneath his passionate campaign "—wanted."

Jim reached up, caressing her flushed cheek. "Cherished," he corrected huskily. "As a woman should be by her man."

Tears blurred her vision and Dal hung her head, her voice an aching whisper. "Ever since...since it happened, I've felt anything but whole. Or wanted." Tears dribbled down her cheeks, silvery paths in the firelight. "I've felt so dirty...so humiliated by what happened.... I don't see how you could want me after...after—"

Jim slid his hand across her cheek, feeling the heat of her tears between his fingers as he sought to ease the pain so evident in her wobbly voice. "I think I've wanted you ever since I met you three years ago," he

began. "Look at me, Dal. Come on, there's nothing for
you to be ashamed of. Come on…" he coaxed.

It hurt to lift her lashes and to meet his clear, calm
eyes filled with compassion. She sniffed. "Three years?
What are you talking about?"

Lifting the mug from her hands he placed it on the
table beside the couch. He got up and sat down beside
her, taking her into his arms. Dal came without hesitation, her smaller body fitting against the harder planes
of his own. Like a hurt child, she curled up, head on his
chest, hands pressed against her breast. He smoothed
her hair with his trembling hand. "Three years ago I
saw you, Dal. I was attending a conference where you
were speaking on predatory birds." He closed his eyes,
recalling that day with vivid clarity. "You were wearing a peach-colored suit made of linen and I thought
you were the most beautiful woman there. Previously, I
had heard of you, but never met you. And men flocked
around you. They saw what I saw: a flower of rare
beauty. At the time you were thin, like you are now,
and you looked exhausted."

Dal nuzzled into the heated warmth of his chest,
content as never before. "I was. I'd just gotten out of a
South American jungle and away from Jack for a while.
That was after our first big fight. I'd spent almost three
years in that green hell and I was desperate to get back
to civilization, Jim. I craved just talking to people. As
it turned out, the conference president invited me to
speak on my favorite topic and I accepted."

Jim pressed a kiss into her hair, inhaling the apricot
fragrance. "I'm glad you did."

The steady beat of his heart soothed her ragged composure and Dal found herself smiling. "When I first saw

you at the ranch, I was positive I had seen you before... but I couldn't place where."

"I came up and introduced myself at the conference. Although," he drawled, amusement lacing his voice, "five other men were also vying for your attention at the same time. I don't blame you for not remembering me." And then he took a long, unsteady breath. "Three years, Dal. I didn't know what it was, but I never forgot you. And then, when I met you again at the ranch..."

She slowly sat up, her hands resting on his arms. "You met me three years ago. I can't believe it. I mean..."

Jim ran his thumb across her lips; they were soft and full and beckoned him to kiss them again. He resisted. Barely. "I think it's our destiny—you were meant to be my woman."

His woman... Dal rested her cheek against his palm. "I can't believe any of this," she began in a strained voice. "I don't know what to think of it, Jim. Of you. Or myself."

He nodded, his eyes darkening. "I know, honey. We'll take it slow and easy. There's no need to hurry. Open wounds need time to heal first."

Dal gave him a trembling smile; her lashes were strewn with tears. "I wish I could show you how much you mean to me. You've given me so much already, Jim. And I've given you nothing."

"You've given me your trust. And with trust comes a blossoming of feelings. Don't be sad. Everything will work out for us."

A vague sense of foreboding stalked Dal and she tried to fight off the feeling. "You're so patient."

With a smile he gently disengaged from her. He didn't want to, but he knew it was best under the circumstances. Dal wasn't ready to share any more of herself than she had in what had already passed between them. Jim urged her to lie back down and then tucked her in. "Patient with you," he agreed. Leaning down, he caressed her hair. "I'll see you when you wake up. No bad dreams..."

Sunlight lanced through the wall of windows, bathing Dal with brilliance as she slowly woke up. Her nostrils flared as the scent of bacon wafted through the living room and made her mouth water. Her stomach growled, and she realized she was starved. A delicious ribbon of happiness threaded through her as she languidly stretched her arms above her head. Dal heard a thump, thump, thump and knew Raider was nearby. Opening her eyes she saw Raider sitting next to the couch, his pink tongue lolling from his mouth in welcome, his amber eyes wide and alert as he watched her rise.

"Good morning," she told the wolf, petting him. After struggling out from beneath the covers, Dal grabbed the terry-cloth robe at the bottom of her bed and shrugged it on. The rich smell of coffee spurred her into action. She pushed her fingers through her hair hurriedly; a real brushing could wait—the coffee and bacon smelled wonderful!

Jim was at the stove, dressed in his familiar blue jeans and a cranberry-colored cowboy shirt with the sleeves rolled carelessly up on his forearms. Dal leaned against the door frame, a soft smile lingering on her lips and in her eyes. Sun spilled through the curtained window, lending radiance to the breakfast nook. Outside the sliding glass doors, the world looked washed clean by the storm—the azure sky bright and clear, the lake calm and crystalline.

"Good morning," she called.

Jim turned and greeted her with a heart-stopping smile. "It is. Make yourself at home. The biscuits are ready to come out of the oven and the eggs are done."

She returned his smile and sat down. He had set the table with pink linen napkins and a handful of wildflowers in a small vase. Dal gently touched the petal of one white daisy. "They're beautiful, Jim," she told him as he came over and put eggs and bacon on her plate.

"Found them this morning by the lake when I took Raider for his morning walk." He met her wide, vulnerable gaze. "They reminded me of you, so I decided to pick some of them." And then his grin widened as he put the rest of the fare on his own plate. "They don't smell half as good as you do, though."

Dal flushed, trembling at his nearness. He hadn't shaved yet and the darkness of the day-old beard did nothing but emphasize the lean planes of his face, a face that was forever imprinted in her heart and in her mind. She gave Jim a grimace as he piled four hot biscuits on her already loaded plate.

"That's too much!" she protested lamely.

"No, it's not," he said as he sat down. "Come on, hurry up and eat. We've got a busy day ahead of us."

Dal gave him a dumbfounded look. "Day? Us?"

Pausing between bites, Jim said, "I didn't wake up until nine this morning, so I was late for work. I decided to call in and take a vacation day." He smiled. "Besides, you were sleeping so well, I didn't have the heart to leave you here by yourself."

"What time is it?"

"Almost ten-thirty."

Dal pressed her fingers to the base of her throat. "My God, I slept a long time."

"You needed it. Now, come on, eat before the food gets cold."

Obediently, she did as he coaxed. "I need to tell Millie—"

"I already called in and checked with your guard dog."

Dal smothered a smile, and felt an urge to reach across the table and tousle Jim's slightly curly hair. He was such a little boy at that moment. "Guard dog? You mean Millie?"

"One and the same," Jim agreed, meeting her smiling eyes. She looked incredibly well rested to him. Had it been the kisses they'd shared, he wondered, or was the time they had spent together healing her wounds? Jim wasn't sure. What he was sure of, was that Dal wasn't going to retreat back up to the Triple K. Right now, she needed some fun. And some laughter. He had awakened earlier, knowing that he would take the day off and that they would share it.

Dal laughed delightedly, spooning some honey onto her third biscuit. "Is that what she reminds you of?"

"Millie and your brother Rafe."

She lost her smile. "What did he say?"

"Not much." Jim shrugged nonchalantly. "I assured him you were okay and that we were going to spend the day hiking in the hills."

"Hiking?" Dal bit into the biscuit, happiness soaring through her at the thought of spending more time with Jim.

Nodding, Jim tackled a fifth biscuit himself, spreading homemade strawberry jam across it. "Every spring

I gather a number of herbs that I keep for medicinal purposes or for cooking. I want to go hike in the hills behind us and see what's coming up so I can make a note on my map. Later on, probably in June, I'll begin picking and drying the flowers. Roots are pulled up in the fall, and bark stripped in the spring."

"You collect herbs. That's amazing," she murmured, shaking her head. "Is there anything you don't do? You seem so self-sufficient."

He smiled, gathered up their plates and put them in the sink. "One of my uncles is the hatali or medicine man for our tribe. I can remember tailing him around when I was six or seven. He taught me a lot about herbs and how to use them." He put the plates in hot, soapy water and began washing them. A strong flood of contentment swept over him. He loved Dal, loved seeing how she looked when she first woke in the morning. But if she ever realized the extent of his love for her, it might frighten her away from him. He heaved a silent sigh.

Dal looked wistfully outside. "It's so beautiful here."

"So you're going to go hiking with me?"

She smiled. "I don't think you had any doubts, Mr. Tremain, or you wouldn't have called Millie or my over-protective brother."

His teeth flashed white and even against the bronze color of his skin. "I think you're right, Dr. Kincaid."

"What am I going to do for clothes, though?"

"Wear your sneakers and the jeans I loaned you last night. I've got a clean shirt up on the bed. It's a little chilly out there, so I'll loan you one of my coats."

Dal got up, feeling like a stuffed Christmas goose. It was a good sign. Raising one eyebrow at Jim, she took her leave with Raider padding silently behind her.

* * *

The air was crisp with the perfume of spring as Dal stepped off the sun deck. She looked over her shoulder, watching as Jim shrugged on a small pack. He had donned a pair of sturdy hiking boots and a padded vest of dark blue. Dal buttoned the goose-down coat he had loaned to her, and she tried in vain to roll up the thick sleeves.

"Here," Jim said, coming down the steps, "let me help you with that."

Dal watched as his strong dark fingers quickly made a cuff on each sleeve. The wind tousled her bare head and Dal lifted her face to the warmth of the sun. "This is wonderful," she said, closing her eyes and smiling. "I'm glad you decided to keep me captive for one more day."

Not able to resist the temptation of her smiling lips, Jim leaned down and lightly brushed her mouth. She tasted of honey. "Come on," he urged huskily, taking her hand, "let's get back into the woods."

Raider followed obediently at their heels as they climbed slowly out of the small meadow that surrounded the A-frame and the lake. The storm had washed the newly formed leaves on the oak, ash and elder trees and the wet greenery glinted in the sunlight like emeralds. They crossed the road and Jim led her up the gently sloping meadow to a stand of pine at the top of the hill, where they paused before descending the other side. It seemed so natural to Dal that they would hold hands. Although Jim had long legs, he had kept his pace moderate so she wouldn't have to run to keep up with him.

"Does Raider always follow behind?" she asked, brushing strands of hair from her face.

"Yes. Why?"

"Why don't you let him run ahead of us? He looks like he wants to."

Jim tossed a look back at Raider and gave him a hand signal. The animal leaped ahead of them, nose to the ground, following whatever scents he came upon as he moved down the slope. "You're a real softie," Jim taunted, squeezing her hand.

"And you aren't?"

He grinned. "Only toward you." Pointing to the right toward a clump of ash trees he said, "We'll stop there for a minute."

"Why?"

"These ash trees have matured enough this year to be put on my map."

Dal followed him through the lush buffalo grass, which was peppered with a multitude of wildflowers that would bloom shortly. "Do you use ash for something?"

"Yes. I'll shave some of the bark off and I'll use it for a tincture."

"And these herbal remedies really work?"

He nodded. "I never saw a doctor as I grew up. My uncle, the hatali, always had an herb that would get me over whatever sickness I had."

"Amazing," Dal murmured, impressed.

"I make the bark, roots and flowers into tinctures, or dry them for my uncle. When I take a week off to visit my mother and her family on the reservation near Gallup, New Mexico, I give my uncle the herbs."

The grass was still wet from the previous night's storm, and Dal's pant legs got wet. It didn't matter because the chill of the morning was being replaced with warmer air, and she began sweating beneath the jacket.

"Tell me about your growing-up years, Jim. You said you herded sheep?"

"And goats," he added. "I don't like goats. They eat anything and everything. Including my shirt or jacket if they could get hold of them and if I stood still long enough to let them nibble on me."

Dal's laughter was silvery. "Goats?"

"Sure. The Navaho keep goats and sheep, usually. The goats gave us milk and two kids a year. Not to mention meat. The sheep gave us wool to weave our rugs, a lamb a year and meat."

"Didn't you ever hunt, though?"

"Sometimes. There's hardly any game at all left on the reservation. About all you'll see when you're out herding is coyotes, rattlesnakes and jackrabbits."

"That seems like a stark way of living," she murmured.

Jim slowed as they approached the ash trees. He relinquished her hand and shrugged out of his pack. From his belt he took a small hatchet. Running his fingers over the bark of several ash, he found one to his liking. "You don't often see a fat Navaho," he said dryly. "I suppose it was stark in one sense, but we always had enough to eat. Get me that one jar from the pack, will you? We'll put the bark shavings in it."

Dal knelt down, unsnapping the red canvas pack. Curious, she lifted the quart mason jar and held it up to inspect it. "What's in this?"

"Alcohol. It will pull out and suspend the chemicals found in the bark that my uncle can use for a tincture."

"Fascinating." She rose and went over to watch him carefully shave bark from the ash. Each smooth stroke with the hatchet spoke of Jim's experience as a forester.

He took only a bit of bark from each of five trees, not wanting to damage any of them permanently.

"My uncle taught me to talk to whatever I had to take something from," he went on. "For instance, I had to ask these ash trees for permission to take some of their bark. We were taught everything has a spirit and if we don't explain what we're going to do, then we can bring the wrath of the spirits down upon us."

Dal smiled. "How much of that do you believe?"

He grinned, a sheen of sweat visible on his broad brow, and shrugged out of his vest, letting it fall to the ground at his feet. "Well, let's put it this way, the Navaho respects everything around him. He's taught to never take without asking."

"Tell me about the Navaho. They seem so different from white men in their philosophy toward life."

Jim put the hatchet back in his belt and reached for the jar. Kneeling down, he unscrewed the lid and carefully packed the damp bark into it. "We are considered a gentle-natured people," he said. "But that's because we're taught from early on to revere everything around us. Everything has life, a spirit, and therefore should be respected and never taken advantage of." He twisted the lid back on the jar, a satisfied look on his face. "For instance, on the reservation I could hunt only certain animals and then the hunt had to be preceded by a proper ceremony. We rose with the sun, our life-giver, every morning. Our hogan always faced east, for the rays of the sun to awaken us. Navaho sand paintings and ceremonies celebrate life in every way from the four points of the compass to the four seasons of the year. When we bless anything, we always begin the ceremony on the eastern side. And when the sun sets, we go to sleep. We're a people ruled by the sun."

Dal sat down, her back against one of the ash trees, and watched as Jim gently shook the jar. "When I met you, you seemed so in tune with everything," she murmured. "You were lucky that you were taught such reverence for nature."

He smiled at her. "For people, too. You'll never hear a Navaho say anything bad or evil about anyone else. For instance, on the reservation we greet one another differently than white men do."

"How?"

"Is that a pun?"

Dal colored, embarrassed by her unconscious pun. "No. I'm sorry."

His laughter was deep and rolling. "Don't be. I don't take offense to it."

"Well, how do you greet one another, then?"

"When we first meet, we say nothing for probably a minute or so. It's our way of giving respect to those we meet. And then we begin to talk. We never mention the name of the person present because it's considered an offense."

Dal gave Jim a wistful look as he placed the filled jar back into the pack. Then, getting to her feet, she said, "That would drive whites crazy. They'd think something was wrong if you didn't come up and start talking immediately."

Jim agreed, shrugging back into the pack after placing his coat in it. "My mother said the first time she met my father, he was totally distraught when she greeted him in silence. My father was fresh out of college and all fired up to be a good agent working with the Indians on the reservation. My mother was a schoolteacher who rode from hogan to hogan giving classes to the children. My father tried out the few words of Navaho that he knew and finally blushed a beet red when my mother just stood there looking at him." He laughed, capturing Dal's hand, and led her up and out of the ash grove.

"Did he realize his gaffe?" Dal asked.

"Finally. The next day, as a matter of fact. My mother said he brought her flowers in apology and that's when their relationship began. A year later, they married."

"That sounds so romantic," she said with a sigh.

As they walked on they found themselves in an oval meadow that stretched half a mile in front of them, and gently rolled down to a small stream. Dal was still thinking about Jim's Navaho heritage. "But what about you? How did your mother's people accept you?"

"My mother's family accepted me as Navaho. It was only when I went to high school that I ran into the half-breed label and the prejudice that went along with it."

Dal chewed on her lower lip, feeling guilty for having called him a half-breed on their initial meeting. "That doesn't say much for us whites, does it? Your people made no distinction of your parentage, and yet we did."

He released her hand and slid his arm around her waist, drawing her close. "That's in the past," he said in a soothing voice.

"No, it's not. Not really, Jim. Even in your position now, I imagine you run into some prejudice from time to time."

"Not often." His eyes crinkled with amusement as he looked down at her. "Now tell me, where did you get a first name like Dahlia? I've been wanting to know how you got christened with that."

Dal laughed, sliding her arm around his lean waist. "My mother's idea. It's her favorite flower, and originally I guess she wanted to name all her kids after flowers. My dad wouldn't hear of it, so they struck a bargain. Dad promised Mom if they had a third child, she could name it. So, I came along and Mom called me Dahlia. Dad hated it, and for as long as I can remember he's always called me Dal."

"Much to your mother's consternation, no doubt," Jim said with a chuckle.

"When I was around age ten, she finally gave in and started calling me Dal, too."

"I think your mother's right—you're fresh, clean and beautiful like a hardy meadow flower." He leaned down, inhaling her feminine scent. "And you smell sweet like one," he murmured huskily.

Following her instincts, Dal looked up and pressed her lips shyly against his smiling mouth. For her, it was an incredibly risk-laden action. The rape had made her retreat from her normal reflex of sharing how she felt; it had robbed her of her natural spontaneity to show her affection openly and without hesitation. This was one of those times she wanted to share; her lashes fell softly against her cheeks as she leaned forward, her breasts barely grazing Jim's chest as she told him in a silent language how much he had come to mean to her. He was freeing her to feel again without reprisal; as frightened as she was, Dal deepened the kiss.

Jim froze momentarily as her lips sought and tentatively found his mouth. An explosion of aching need arced like wildfire through him as he willingly brought her into his embrace. Surprised at her boldness, he recognized Dal's unexpected action for what it was. And in that tender moment, he loved her more than he'd ever thought possible. A rush of fierce protectiveness welled up inside of him, mingling with his desire, and he held on to her fiercely as he shared her tender gift.

Chapter 7

Nar's scream echoed through the small valley as he swept up past where Dal sat on her gray gelding. She smiled in awe, as she always did, at the eagle's beauty. This morning Nar was exceptionally playful. The sun was barely edging the mountains, sending streamers across the lush green meadow where she sat quietly on her horse. Dal was unable to still another kind of excitement threading through her. In another hour, Jim would arrive in his black Blazer, and their two-week odyssey into the back country would begin. She took an unsteady breath, recalling how alive she felt.

Dal's gaze followed the graceful wheeling of Nar far above her, the eagle's feathers a bronze color as sunlight struck him. That was how Jim illuminated her dark and distrustful heart. He touched her with life, she thought, resting her arm on one leg, which she had thrown around the saddle horn. Closing her eyes, Dal relaxed as the sun's strong mid-May rays struck her, enveloping her in a warm blanket. After her return from Denver to the Triple K, she had had two weeks to mull over her burgeoning relationship with Jim. Two weeks…so long and yet, so short. Even Rafe had noticed the change in her as one of their conversations flowed back into her wandering mind.

"What are you doing?" Rafe had asked as he stood in the hall outside Dal's unused bedroom.

Dal fluffed the pillow and threw the pink bedspread over it. "I'm going to try and start sleeping in my own room again." She straightened up, pushing a few strands of hair away from her eyes.

Rafe leaned against the doorjamb, his arms crossed against his massive chest, a scowl on his features. "Is it time to push yourself like that?" he asked in a voice deep with concern.

Dal looked around her neat, feminine bedroom. She had been raised in this sunlit room, which had several windows on the eastern side of the house. It brought back Jim's comment that all hogans faced east to welcome the sun. Well, she was going to welcome the light back into her life by trying to sleep once again in a darkened bedroom each night. And each morning, the life-giver of light would steal into her room to soothe away any remnants of her life with Jack. Tucking her lower lip between her teeth, Dal studied her brother. "Is there ever any good time to face something painful?"

Rafe grimaced. "You're asking the wrong person. Life's a pain."

Dal sat on the edge of her bed, giving Rafe a compassionate look. "Eventually, that pain eases," she whispered, wanting to help him somehow in his grief and loss. But Rafe allowed no one to help him.

"I suppose this experiment is Tremain's idea?"

"He doesn't know anything about it."

Rafe's mouth thinned. "He's having one hell of an effect on you in a short amount of time."

Dal ran her fingers across the organdy fabric of the spread. "Yes, he is." She lifted her chin and met Rafe's dark stare. "And I'm going to continue to allow him to help me."

"Look, the last time you fell like a ton of bricks for someone, it ended in disaster, Dal. For God's sake, don't make that same mistake again."

Anger stirred in Dal as she unflinchingly met his accusing gaze. "Jim is nothing like Jack."

"But you're allowing him to influence you."

"Jim's a good influence on me, Rafe. And Jack wasn't always a negative influence." She spread her hands, her voice lowering. "Give me some credit; I'm older now. And hopefully, wiser. I might have made a mistake, but I'm not repeating it."

Rafe scowled and shifted on his feet, his features stubborn. "He's not your type, Dal."

She almost laughed, but had the good grace to maintain her sober expression. "My type?"

"Yeah," Rafe said, shifting again uncomfortably.

"What's 'my type,' big brother?"

"You need a man who's successful in business and wants to settle down. You need that element in your life, Dal. You survive best when there's a rut to follow. Not by getting dragged here and there like Gordon did to you."

She almost smiled. Rafe, in his own way, was trying

to protect her again. "Jim is extremely successful at his job, Rafe. He's the head of an entire region."

"He's a wrangler underneath that veneer," he warned her.

Wranglers were usually single men who punched cows for a living and preferred the range to being tied down to one woman, or worse yet, to a family. "I see. Are you saying that because he's a knowledgeable horseman and is familiar with ranching?"

Rafe's mouth quirked. "You said yourself he was raised on a reservation," he defended darkly.

"Is that it, Rafe? Are you saying he didn't come from the right side of the tracks like we did?"

"Dammit, don't go getting defensive on me, Dal. I'm just trying to get you to see some things you might be blinded to because you like him."

Like him? She loved him. And Jim knew that. Dal could hide nothing from him and never wanted to. "He was raised with the Navaho," she admitted. "In my eyes, that doesn't make him less of a man, Rafe. It makes him more of one."

"Yeah, well maybe in your eyes…"

Dal rose, her eyes narrowing on her brother. "Would it make Jim more acceptable in your eyes if I told you he graduated from Princeton with honors, Rafe?" she asked in a dangerously low voice. "He earned a scholarship and then worked his way through that university. You and I had our education paid for by Mom and Dad. We didn't have to worry about getting a scholarship to help pay part of our tuition. And we certainly didn't have to take two or three part-time jobs to pay for our tuition or our housing or the food we put in our mouth." Her voice rose as she walked toward Rafe. "Jim has more drive and assertiveness in the business sense than you. And that's saying something, Rafe."

"Okay, okay, I was wrong. I'm sorry."

"And as for him being half-Navaho… I wish he was full blooded. The way he respects me as a person and as a woman, would make you and every other red-blooded American macho male turn green with jealousy!"

Rafe winced and held out his hands. "Look, I was wrong, Dal. It's just that you're falling hard for him and I'm worried. Worried for your sake. I don't want to see you get hurt again. You aren't even over Gordon, yet."

The anger drained from her voice and she reached out, resting her hand on Rafe's hard-muscled arm. "I know that. Consider this: for four of those six years, I received love from Jack. The last two years were empty for me in the emotional sense. Maybe I am starved to be touched and held again. What you need to understand, Rafe, is that this isn't some whim that suddenly cropped up in me. Everyone needs someone. Jack decided money was more important and he didn't need anyone to supply normal human requirements such as respect, interest or affection. Jim gives me all of those. And yes, I'm soaking them up. We're both adults and we know what we're doing and why. Please, don't hate him. Be happy for us. I've finally found someone who gives instead of takes from me all the time."

Grudgingly, Rafe nodded. "Okay, Dal. I am happy for you. It just seems sort of sudden, that's all."

Dal reached out, throwing her arms around her brother's broad shoulders. "I love you, you silly macho male," she said, planting a kiss on his cheek before releasing him. She stood back, watching Rafe's face flush beneath his tan. He never could deal with her effusive displays of kissing and hugging.

"Well," he said gruffly, "just go in with both eyes open with Jim Tremain, that's all."

She laughed softly, watching him throw the black felt cowboy hat back on his head. "My eyes are open," she promised. *And so is my heart....*

Dal released a sigh now and squinted up into the sky. Smokey stamped his foot. Nar's angry screech startled Dal out of her reverie. She saw the eagle circling above the road that led to the ranch headquarters. It was Jim. She could feel it. She swung her leg over the horse and settled her foot into the stirrup, urging Smokey into an easy, rocking-chair canter and headed back toward the ranch. Looking over her shoulder, she could see Nar was following her, wafting on unseen currents of air high above.

By the time she arrived at the ranch house, Jim was already there. Rafe was with him and another wrangler near the barn where the pack and trail horses were being given a final check. Breathless from the long canter, Dal dismounted outside the barn, handing Smokey to a waiting wrangler. Her heart was beating fast, but only partly from the exertion of the ride. Unconsciously, she smoothed her hair from around her face, taming the thick strands across her shoulders.

Jim looked up, watching as Dal walked toward them. Even in the dim light provided in the aisleway of the barn, he thought she had grown more beautiful. His eye missed nothing as she approached—the apricot western shirt and dark orange goose-down vest brought out the highlights of her flushed complexion, the jeans lovingly outlined every contour of her lower body. He felt himself tighten in reaction.

He wanted her. All of her. At his house, he had tapped into that fiery, vibrant life that smoldered just beneath the surface of Dal. It had surprised him as much as it had her, he thought wryly, smiling. She looked as if she had gained back the lost ten pounds; her cheeks were rounded and filled out now as they should be.

"Good morning," she said, coming up and standing between him and Rafe.

Jim smiled, drowning in the happiness he saw lingering in her sapphire eyes. "It is," he agreed huskily. Out of the corner of his eye, he saw Rafe's brows draw downward. And he saw Dal notice it, too. "It looks like we're about ready. How about you and that eagle of yours?"

"We're more than ready." Dal looked around. "Where's Raider?"

"In the Blazer. I didn't want anyone to panic if I brought him out too soon. We'll let him go when we're ready to mount up."

She nodded, excitement throbbing through her. Jim looked so good! Two lonely weeks without him made her ache to reach out and touch his smiling mouth, to feel the strength of his kiss against her lips once again. But that could all wait. There was no sense in upsetting Rafe any more than necessary. With time, he'd adjust to the idea that Jim was a part of her life now.

"We've checked that radio over," Rafe told Jim, moving to a horse that was loaded down with pack gear. "It's here in a watertight plastic bag."

Jim checked out the harness and pack on the bay quarter horse gelding. "Good idea."

"If you get in trouble, give us a call. But remember, you'll be too far out of range to contact us when you hit the last two line shacks and move from our property into the wilderness refuge." Rafe rested his hand on the carefully tied heavy canvas that provided shelter for the tent, cooking equipment and food stored beneath it. "Once you get back into range, give us a call and let us know you're all right."

"That will be on the tenth day," Jim agreed. Short-range radios were often used by ranchers to stay in contact with their wranglers, but even the radios had a limited range. And in the mountains, particularly, radio communication was difficult under optimum conditions.

"Millie has packed us chicken for lunch," Dal said, as she brought out her bay gelding.

"Sounds good," Jim agreed. He took the reins of a large Arabian gelding that was gunmetal-gray in color. It was taller and had much heavier bones than most of its breed. Jim held out his hand to Rafe.

"Thanks," he said.

Rafe gripped his hand. "Just be damn careful out there." And then he threw a look over at Dal as she mounted up. "And you, too. You haven't been packing for a long time. There's a lot of different dangers out there you've got to be on the lookout for, Dal."

She gave him a patient look filled with love. "I am rusty," she admitted. "And I'll try to be very careful, Rafe. We'll see you in two weeks...."

They were off! Nar's scream drifted high above them as they moved out into the meadow that led up into the ash-and-aspen-clad hills. Raider panted happily, always at Jim's side, but never ahead of them. From time to time, Dal would look over at Jim and exchange a silent look of happiness with him. A golden flame burned in the depths of his eyes each time she met his gaze, and she melted a little more with each visual caress.

The day was chilly at first, but by the time they got to the first foothills, Dal was shedding her vest and tying it to the back of her saddle. She rolled up the sleeves of her shirt to her forearms and kept her brown felt cowboy hat in place; at seven thousand feet, sunburn could occur quickly.

She automatically looked to the packhorse, an old quarter horse called Jake that weighed close to twelve hundred pounds. He had been the main pack animal for many an expedition since Dal was a teenager. The lead rope from Jake's halter was tied onto a special D-ring Rafe had devised at the back of Jim's saddle, rather than being attached to the saddle horn where it could chafe Jim's thigh.

Pushing up the brim of his hat, Jim studied the golden eagle in the distance. "Is he hunting?"

Dal rode up alongside of him, their legs barely touching. "He caught a jackrabbit early this morning, so I don't think so." She smiled. "Probably just out inspecting his territory."

Jim shed his vest and tied it to the back of his saddle and rolled up the sleeves of his shirt. Like all wranglers, he wore a pair of thin leather gloves to protect his hands. Dal had a pair, but she elected to keep them stored in her saddlebag for now. She warmed beneath Jim's inspection.

"I'm surprised Millie wasn't out there giving you the devil, too, before we left," he teased.

"I got it earlier when she was packing the chicken for our lunch," she admitted, grinning. "Once the baby of the family, always the baby, I guess."

"You're hardly a baby," he stated huskily, reaching out to capture her free hand, and giving it a squeeze.

A thrill of pleasure prickled through her fingers at his touch. "Tell Rafe that. He's getting more protective toward me than ever before."

"Maybe that's because of me being around."

She nodded, reluctantly releasing his hand as the horses began their climb in earnest through the spindly white birch and aspen. "I know it is."

Jim took the easiest path up the wooded and rocky hill. Far above them, the magnificent mountains were still clothed in their winter raiment of snow, and towered over them like silent guardians. It would be up there, along the cliffs, that Dal and Jim would begin locating the aeries. The nests would be built out on craggy lips of the cliffs, large sticks comprising each fortress that would hold one or more eggs.

Jim and Dal crested the first series of hills, the sun beating down on them in earnest as they reined in their horses at the edge of another meadow. Wildflowers bloomed in profusion; white-petaled daisies waved gently in the inconstant breeze that caressed the hillside. Jim glanced at his wristwatch; they had been traveling for four hours and it was nearly noon. The high, thin mountain air made him feel exhilarated and famished. Spotting a stream at the other end of the meadow he said, "Let's take our lunch down there."

Dal nodded. "Good. I'm ready."

"So am I."

Like a good pack-team member, Dal loosened the

cinches on the horses, hobbled them and took off their bridles so they could eat their fill of the succulent grass and sip water from the icy spring that gurgled nearby. A sense of contentment sang through her as she hung the bridles on a nearby broken branch of a pine tree and walked back to the camp. Jim was hunkered down, putting the finishing touches on a small fire. He had taken out an iron rod, placed it in the ground and suspended a pot to boil water in. She rubbed her hands.

"Coffee? I'm impressed," she teased, going to the plastic container next to him.

"Can't live without it," Jim admitted, meeting her smile. Something magical was occurring, he thought. He felt it. Perhaps it was the mixture of being back in the wilderness and mountains again with the woman he had waited a lifetime for. Jim saw the happiness in her dancing eyes and the soft upward curve of her lips. The day was beautiful. And so was she. He asked nothing more of life than what he shared with Dal right now.

She sat cross-legged next to him, against a hollow log, and unwrapped the chicken sandwiches and potato salad Millie had fixed for them. "You can't blame that on your Navaho blood. Even we white people have a penchant for coffee."

He added a few more twigs to the fire. "That's two things the Navaho took from traders—coffee and tobacco. Kids start drinking coffee as young as two years old, did you know that? The Navaho like their coffee."

Dal shook her head and handed him a sandwich. "Well, so do I."

Raider circled the small camp and finally came to rest next to Jim, his pink tongue lolling from the side of his mouth. Jim pinched off a piece of his sandwich and gave it to the animal. At that moment, Nar swooped down into the meadow.

"Oh, God!" Dal muttered, pushing to her feet and dropping her sandwich. She grabbed for the gauntlet she always carried in the belt at her waist and shoved it on. "Look out, Nar's coming in!"

Jim had little time to do anything. He had seen the giant eagle suddenly dip from above the trees and drop like a rock into the meadow. He watched, open mouthed, as the raptor skimmed the meadow, the speed of his approach startling. Grass and flowers twisted and flattened wherever he skimmed. Raider remained at Jim's side, his ears against his skull. Automatically, Jim reached out, gripping the wolf's heavy leather collar just in case. Neither Nar nor Raider had been introduced to the other, and Jim didn't want to take any chances.

Nar braked at the last possible second, his wings a blur of back beats, his claws stretched outward as he aimed for Dal's arm, which was held high above her head. Jim watched in awe as Dal bent her knees deeply, bracing herself for the eagle's thunderous approach. The wind whipped her hair across her eyes as the eagle's claws made contact around the kidskin of the glove protecting her arm. Jim saw pain register on Dal's face as the raptor's blue-black claws wrapped around her arm. Nar then folded his wings with aristocratic grace and delivered a series of scolding chirps at Dal.

Jim tensed as Nar turned his head. He saw the eagle's feathers stand on his head, a sign that Nar was upset. And then Jim saw how tightly Nar's feet, armed with the black talons, were gripping Dal's arm. His bronzed back was broad and his chest deep and filled with his recent kill. Jim saw the raptor's eyes change to a smoky gray, but was unable to interpret what that meant. Raider, in the meantime, sat quietly, his yellow eyes pinned on the eagle.

"What do you think?" he asked Dal quietly. "Is Nar angry?"

Dal grimaced, inwardly wishing Nar would quit gripping her arm so tightly. She'd have huge bruises there before the hour was out. "I think he's confused by you and Raider. I've never gone anywhere with someone else. I think he's trying to figure out if you're friend or foe."

"Tell him we're friends," Jim all but growled.

"He doesn't understand English."

"Fine time to tell us that."

Dal managed a sour grin. "Bring me that chicken sandwich I threw down, Jim. And no fast movements."

He did as he was instructed.

"Okay," she said quietly, reaching up to stroke Nar's breast, "hold it up to him."

"Hold it up? You see the beak on that thing? He could take my hand off if he wanted to."

Dal licked her lips. "He won't. I don't think. But the only way to show him you're a friend is by feeding him."

"I don't mind giving him the sandwich, but I want to keep my fingers." Jim grimaced.

"I'm sorry about this...."

He steeled himself, sweating beneath the bird's piercing amber eyes. "So am I.... Well, here goes nothing."

Nar's head feathers smoothed down as Jim lifted the morsel up to him. For a long second, the raptor studied him and the food. With all the delicacy of a ballet dancer, Nar lifted one foot and wrapped his claws about the peace offering. Jim slowly lowered his hand, amazed that the eagle hadn't even touched his fingers.

"Now just stand there," Dal instructed quietly. She watched Nar, noting that the tightened feathers around his body were beginning to fluff out once again. She gave a little sigh. "It's okay. He's relaxing now. Everything is going to be all right."

Nar finished the sandwich, his claws in a gentler grasp around her arm. He chirped contentedly, leaning down and riffling Dal's hair with his beak, as if to lovingly scold her.

"He's a big baby," Jim muttered, still feeling uncomfortable at being so close to the eagle.

Dal grinned. "Aren't all males? Never mind, don't answer that. Okay, step away. I'm going to launch him so he can find a vacant tree limb to sit on. I can't hold him much longer."

Stepping aside, Jim watched as Dal flexed her knees once again and twisted her body to the left. The eagle opened its bronze wings, preparing for flight. It was a concert of coordination, beauty and grace as Jim watched Dal throw all of her strength into a smooth forward motion of her arm, shoulder and body. An eagle as large as Nar would have a hard time lifting off from a standing position or the ground. By hurling him with the full forward thrust of her arm, Dal gave Nar an easier launch, and he was airborne instantly in a flurry of powerful flaps of his wings. Dal had carried through with the motion, coming to rest on her right knee, head bowed to escape the chance of getting sliced by Nar's long, deadly primary feathers.

Jim went to her, reaching out, lifting her back to her feet. Worriedly, he pulled the glove off her left hand.

Dal winced as he gently pushed up the sleeve on her forearm. His mouth pursed when he saw the white and bloodless flesh where Nar had gripped her with his talons.

"It's okay," Dal said. "One of the benefits of having an eagle own you."

Reluctantly, Jim released her arm. They both turned and saw Nar land on the stout branch of a pine, about fifty feet off the ground. "I'd never want that eagle angry with me," Jim muttered, returning his attention to her. "You sure you're all right?"

Dal flushed beneath his concern. "Fine. Nar was just doing his duty as watch bird," she explained, tucking the gauntlet back into her belt.

Taking her arm, Jim led her back to the fire. "You're surrounded by watchdogs of all kinds," he noted wryly. He knelt down, added coffee grounds to the now boiling water and put the lid on the kettle.

"Nar normally doesn't come charging in like that. I think he's just curious about what's going on. Look at him now. See how he's watching us?"

It made the hair on the back of Jim's neck rise. The golden eagle was watching them intently. "He reminds me of a cartoon where two buzzards are talking to each other as they sit in this dead tree. One turns to the other and says, 'Patience hell, I'm hungry.' Will he stay there or is he going to attack me?"

"He'll probably get bored in a while and take off again," Dal assured him with a laugh. Her arm ached as the blood slowly recirculated into the area where Nar had gripped her. She knew he had the strength to literally rip the flesh from her bone if he chose. It wasn't a pleasant thought.

Jim gingerly poured the coffee into two tin mugs and handed her one. "What does he do at night? Sleep with you?" He made himself comfortable on the log next to Dal, keeping one eye on the eagle.

Dal added cream and sugar, stirring it with a twig of pine before sipping it. "I've never been anywhere overnight with him, so I don't know." She shot him a wry look. "Why?"

Jim grinned, holding the tin cup between his gloved fingers. "Because I'm going to be sleeping beside you at night. And I don't intend to share that privilege with Nar, that's why."

A tremor of longing raced through Dal as she held his honey-colored gaze. There was amusement in his tone, but she saw he was serious when she looked into his eyes. Dal had had two weeks to think about their relationship. She was afraid. She was aching to share herself with Jim, but she was confused. A vulnerable smile fled across her lips. "I think Nar will probably be more comfortable sleeping up on a tree limb tonight."

"I know I wouldn't be."

Laughing, Dal rested her arm on Jim's long, hard thigh. Since the day they had hiked in the hills to get the herbs, she felt an unspoken closeness to Jim and suspected he felt the same. And frequent touching was welcomed by Dal; a part of her giving nature. When Jim's hand settled on hers, a spiral of joy uncoiled through her. "The only one spending nights in a tree will be Nar," she promised.

"Does he get jealous?"

She shrugged. "I hope not."

"He's seven years old. Does he have a mate?"

"I don't know, Jim. The first year he was with me,

he was too young to search for a mate. Rafe mentioned that sometimes, after that, Nar would bring another eagle over the ranch." Her eyes grew shadowed. "But if he did have a mate, she isn't alive now."

"Why do you say that?"

"Because it's breeding season and Nar would be with her and not me."

Jim nodded. "Will eagles pair again if their mate is killed?"

"Evidence points in that direction," Dal murmured. "I have a feeling Nar did have a mate. But you know what it's like for a bird that size to survive. If ranchers don't shoot at them, the sheepmen do. Some people lay out poisoned meat for them to consume. It's awful."

Before they set out for the afternoon ride, Jim interrupted Dal as she tightened the cinches on their saddle horses. His deerskin-gloved hand reached down, capturing her fingers as she pulled at the cinch, and he gently drew her around to face him. The startled look in her sapphire eyes turned to smoldering desire as he cupped her chin and drew her against him.

"I've waited too long," he said huskily, framing her face with his hands.

A raw jolt of pleasure sped through her as his mouth molded possessively against her lips, parting them, sipping the sweet nectar from her depths. Dal pressed herself against his hard, lean length, glorying in the movement of his mouth against hers. He was so much a man, and yet, so giving. He nipped hungrily at her lower lip, soothing her with the warmth of his tongue, tasting her, goading her into reveling in their mutual joy.

Jim tangled her hair between his fingers, tilting her head slightly to drink more deeply of her. She tasted of honey and coffee. The velvet pliancy of her lips fit perfectly beneath his onslaught. He had to have her… all of her. His hands slipped from her face down across her shoulders and he gently brushed the fullness of her breasts. A groan reverberated through him as he felt their lush firmness. Slowly he trailed a series of wet, nipping kisses down the slender expanse of her exposed neck, tasting the saltiness of her flesh.

"You taste so good," he murmured raggedly as he followed the graceful contour of her collarbone and pushed her shirt aside to continue his exploration.

Dal's knees nearly buckled as his tongue dipped to caress the valley between her aching breasts. A small cry of need tore from her lips and she clung to him, gulping for breath. Never had any man made her feel so wanton! Just the mere touch of his mouth upon her flesh and the light caress of his fingers cradling her breasts had kindled all the smoldering coals of desire to brilliant life within her. She felt his arms sweeping around her to steady her against his strong body. Breathing hard, Dal rested her head against his shoulder, aware of the thunderous pounding of his heart within his tightly muscled chest.

"I can't stand…"

"I know."

Dal heard the amusement in his voice and smiled. "You affect me so strongly," she whispered.

"I noticed," Jim said as he caressed her shoulder and curved back. "If I didn't have you to lean against, I wouldn't be standing either…."

By late afternoon the sun's rays had brought a heat wave in the eighties to the upper hills. As they traversed another meadow on their way up to the cliffs, the dry wind moved the long-stalked buffalo grass as if it were wheat bending before an invisible hand. The mountains loomed closer and Dal could see where the timberline stopped near the nine-thousand-foot level and the bare rock and snow claimed the rest of the rocky crags. Spring in the Rockies was incongruous, she thought, as she rode at Jim's side. A mere two thousand feet could separate snow or ice from the sweat-producing heat of the sun burning down across the meadows.

Nar's screeching cry tore at Dal's dreamy state and she raised her head. She saw the golden eagle stoop into a hard dive, his wings folded back against his hurtling body.

"What's going on?" Jim asked. He glanced at Raider. The wolf had his nose in the air, testing it.

Frowning, Dal squeezed her gelding. "I don't know, but I'll find out. That's not like Nar. He sounds angry."

"Hey! Be careful," Jim called.

She turned and gave him a smile. "Don't worry, I will."

Frowning, Jim watched the eagle suddenly flare at the last minute, his legs extended with those deadly talons wide to catch some unseen prey in the knee-deep grass. And then Jim's gaze moved back to Dal as she cantered her bay horse toward the eagle. He clucked to his mount, unable to move out at top speed because of the packhorse in tow. The gelding broke into a slow trot.

Jim's immediate urge was to send Raider ahead to protect Dal, but he didn't dare. Nar could turn on the wolf and it would be a fight to the death. He couldn't risk it. Frustration curdled in his throat and he pulled the hat down more tightly on his head, urging his horse to move at a faster pace.

Dal cantered easily across the flower-strewn meadow. The sun was blinding her and she stood up in the stirrups to see what Nar had attacked. The eagle had almost disappeared in the tall grass; only his hackled head was occasionally visible. She heard Nar screaming and shrilling and then saw him flapping around. What on earth had he attacked? she wondered uneasily.

Her gelding suddenly began to slow, fighting her guiding hand. Dal scowled and clapped her heels against the balking horse's flanks. This was no time for the horse to start acting up! Only fifteen more feet and she would be close enough to see if Nar needed help. The eagle flapped wildly upward, screaming. The horse leaped sideways, nearly unseating Dal. She had barely gotten her balance back when her eyes widened in horror.

There, all around them, were gopher-size holes in the ground. Only they weren't gophers. A cold sweat drenched Dal as she realized the dangerous error she had just committed. No matter where she looked beneath the dancing feet of her wild-eyed Arabian, there were angry, hissing rattlesnakes coiling and ready to strike at the unwelcome intruders. Dal was barely aware of Nar twisting the head off the rattler he had attacked. The eagle dropped the lifeless body and dived for another one.

The gelding snorted violently, dancing. Snakes hissed. Another rose into a coil, striking savagely at the legs of the horse. Dal jerked hard on the bit, the powerful stench of rattlers filling her flared nostrils. Fangs flashed, yellow and dripping with clear venom.

A scream rose in her throat as the gelding reared high into the air, trying to dodge the nest of striking rattlers.

The horse landed and then humped his back, leaping with all four feet off the ground, hurling Dal off. The scream of the eagle melded with the scream of the panicked gelding. Dal flew through the air, terror filling her as rattler infested ground flashed under her. Then she struck the earth and darkness swallowed her up.

Jim had seen the eagle rise with the snake twisting violently between his claws. In one deft movement, he jerked the slip knot loose, freeing himself from the pack horse. Leaning forward, he urged the Arabian into a pounding gallop, jerking his rifle out of its sheath and holding it ready. His heart slammed into his throat as he watched the unfolding drama, realizing Dal had ridden her shying horse into a nest of snakes. What were they? Rattlers? Copperheads? It didn't matter. Both were deadly. His mouth thinned into a single line as he gave Raider a signal to surge ahead and pulled his horse to a skidding stop yards from the barely visible nest. The wolf circled like a silent ghost, staying clear of the eagle, which was tackling a second snake.

Dal lay limp and unconscious only a few feet from the main nest. Jim shouldered the rifle, firing again and again, taking aim at the angry snakes with deadly accuracy. The gunshots shattered the screams of the eagle and Nar angrily took to the air, flapping to gain altitude. Jim felt his horse balk and looked down. A rattler was coiling no more than six inches from the trembling animal. But like a good mountain horse, the gelding knew to stand when someone was firing a gun from his back. Jim aimed, firing at point-blank range. The horse jerked and flinched, but didn't move. Dal! He saw Raider with a snake in his fangs, shaking it savagely scarcely a foot from where she lay.

He couldn't risk getting off the horse to rescue her. The grass was high and he had no way of knowing how many more snakes lay in wait. No, better the horse than him. Jim slapped the horse on the rump with the barrel of the rifle. Startled, the animal leaped forward, jumping over the slight mound of earth that contained the community. Jim saw no snakes near Dal and he dismounted. With little wasted motion, he put her limp form across the saddle and remounted. The horse was mettlesome; sweat lathered his neck and hindquarters when Jim finally brought him out of the canter and to a halt beneath the shade of a towering pine a good quarter of a mile away from the snakes.

His heart was pounding heavily in his chest as he gently pulled Dal from the saddle and eased her to the ground. Tearing off his gloves he threw them aside and examined her bleeding head wound. Her color was waxen, her flesh almost transparent, showing the blue of her veins beneath her eyes. Fingers trembling, he placed them against her wrist; her pulse was slow and strong. *Thank God.* But had she been bitten? There was only one way to find out. He took the hunting knife from the sheath on his belt. With quick, sure strokes he slit open the thin fabric of Dal's shirt and pulled it off her, looking for the two puncture holes that a poisonous snake would leave on her skin if it had sunk its fangs into her. Sweat dripped down his temples as he anxiously scoured every square inch of her skin, both front and back and even up to the hairline on her neck.

Moving down, Jim yanked the boots off her feet. The jeans came next. With the eye of a surgeon, he examined her hips, thighs and her boots. A bruise was appearing on her left shoulder where she had originally hit the ground, but there was no evidence she had been bitten. Shakily, Jim began to breathe a little easier. He felt her pulse once again; it was remaining stable. Snakebite made the pulse rapid and erratic, and so far, that wasn't happening. Still kneeling over her, he checked her scalp for a wound. Dal had a cut on her left temple, but had escaped being bitten.

Jake, the packhorse, ambled up, trailing the rope attached to his halter. Jim stood and went over to the horse, untying the canvas flap of the pack. He jerked several blankets from it and came back, stooping to wrap Dal tightly within them. She was showing all the signs of mild shock, and treatment to stop her spiral into it had to be taken immediately. Raider came up, wagging his tail. His gray muzzle was stained with blood.

"Guard," Jim commanded, pointing at Dal.

The wolf obediently lay at her side.

Jim rose in time to see the gelding Dal had ridden into the nest of snakes fall to its knees and then lie there, nose touching the ground. Grimly, Jim knew the horse would die. More than man died at the fangs of a rattler.

Worried, he looked down at Dal. Had her head struck a rock? he wondered. If she had only suffered a mild blow to the head she should regain consciousness soon. He reached for the radio, pulling it out of the pack and its protective plastic covering. If Dal didn't wake in another ten minutes, he would call Rafe and tell him to fly in by helicopter and pick them up.

Chapter 8

The sharp report of a rifle being fired at close range jerked Dal to consciousness. Her lashes fluttered against her pale cheeks and she tried to lift her hand only to realize she was wrapped tightly within a blanket. She heard the thump of Raider's tail and his panting very close to her head. With difficulty, Dal forced her eyes open. The light streaming through the pine branches overhead blinded her momentarily and she shut them again. Then she heard another sound—the soft shush of feet moving through grass nearby. Pain lanced intermittently through her left temple and her mouth felt gummy.

The instant Jim's hand fell upon her blanketed shoulder, Dal opened her eyes again. She winced as light and pain combined to make her squint. She felt Jim's hand tighten.

"Don't try to move," he told her in a low voice, "you've been unconscious for almost fifteen minutes."

Her heart began an erratic pounding as her vision gradually cleared and she saw the naked terror written across his sun darkened features. And then, like puzzle pieces slowly being put together in her shorted-out memory, the entire episode congealed. Jim knelt over her, pressing a thick dressing to her temple, and expertly encircling her head with gauze to keep the bandage in place. Dal closed her eyes.

"Oh, God," she muttered thickly, "I could have been killed."

"I know. Just lie there, honey. You didn't get bitten, but you've got a good inch-long cut on your left temple. It isn't deep, but it's bleeding heavily. How do you feel? Dizzy? Pain?"

Just the quietness of his voice falling across her hot, sweaty body like a cool waterfall soothed her. Then humiliation surged through her. She had acted like a dude from the East, riding into that snake nest. She should have listened to her horse's warning, but had ignored it. The horse had smelled the snakes. Through her self-recrimination, she realized there was no anger over her stupid mistake in Jim's voice or his touch as he ministered to her head wound. If Jack had been present, he would have been screaming at her. Rafe would have been angry, too.

"Dal? What's wrong?"

Hot, scalding tears stung her closed eyes. When she opened them, the tears dribbled from their corners. "Oh, Jim, what I did was so stupid. My horse? Is he—"

Jim's mouth tightened slightly as he gently knotted the bandage around her head. "I shot him. He had been bitten too many times. I'm sorry. I couldn't let him suffer."

A sob rose in Dal's throat and she managed to pull her arms free of the blanket and cover her face with her hands. "No… Oh, no… I killed him."

Whispering her name, Jim slid his arm beneath Dal's shoulders, drawing her up against him so that he could cradle and hold her while she cried. The afternoon heat was stifling and her skin was damp with perspiration as he ran a trembling hand across her naked back, trying to ease her pain. Jim rested his head lightly against hers, inhaling the scent of her hair, aware of its silken quality.

"It's all right, Dal," he whispered thickly. "I don't care about the horse. My God, if you had been bitten or—" He couldn't finish, the terror was still too fresh within him. Dal could easily have been killed. If she had fallen two feet closer to the nest, she would have been bitten as many times as her horse—or more. And no matter how fast a helicopter had come to take her to a hospital, Jim knew her chances of survival would have been slim to none. She would have died in his arms. Before his eyes. The sting of tears blinded him and he buried his head against her, holding her tightly. Holding her forever. "I can't lose you," he said hoarsely, near her ear. "I won't. I love you too much. Too much…"

The words were out and there was no way to take them back. He had spoken from his heart, as was the way of his people. He recognized no games when the feelings he carried for Dal were invovled. He felt her sobs lessen after his admission and swallowed hard. Had he just destroyed all that he had wanted to share with Dal, by that moment of admission? he wondered. Jim caressed her hair, taming it beneath his trembling fingers, soothing the ragged edges of her shattered composure.

He felt the shy, tentative movement of her hand up across the sweat-soaked shirt that clung to his chest, her fingers curling about his neck. Jim was wildly aware of her hammering heart and the roundness of her breasts pressed against him. It was sweet agony; a mere blanket lay like a thin barrier between them. She was naked and his fingers splayed against the damp flesh of her back, pressing her hard against him. He sensed a change, not daring to believe it. As Dal lifted her tearstained face to meet his descending mouth, an incredible surge of joy fused through him.

He tasted the salt of her spent tears mingled with the utter sweetness of her soft, velvet lips, which molded to his mouth. Dal had heard his whispered words and she wasn't shrinking from him. Her other arm came around his shoulder and a low groan was torn from him as she drew herself completely against him. He warred with the violent joy that wanted to be expressed by loving her totally. Completely. Dal was his! She was offering herself on the altar of his spoken love and it took every last bit of control he had to stop what they both wanted to share with each other. He dragged his mouth from her now swollen, glistening lips. His breath was ragged.

"You taste so good," he said thickly. "You're a flower. A rare, beautiful flower filled with the honey of goodness. Of life…" He pressed his mouth to her lashes, which were beaded with spent tears, taking the bitter salt of her anguish away beneath his kisses.

"Hold me, Jim…just hold me. I need you so much…."

"I know," he whispered raggedly, embracing her, but not so tightly as to hurt her. He wanted to crush her in his arms, to show her just how powerful his love for her was. Time…they had time, and right now, Dal was still feeling the effects of her fall. He could wait, he told himself. They would know when it was time to walk into each other's arms and complete their destiny.

As Jim stroked her back, Dal felt her heartbeat begin to return to normal. She was more content than she could ever recall being, lying in his arms, head resting against his powerful chest. The blue chambray fabric beneath her cheek was soaked with her tears and his sweat. She inhaled his musky male scent, which helped to stabilize her tattered emotional state. Closing her eyes, Dal allowed herself to draw strength from Jim in every way. The buzzing of the bees, the raucous call of a bluejay and the soft snort of a horse all served, too, to help her regain her lost composure.

As she lay there in his arms, only one phrase kept pounding through Dal's aching head. Jim's voice had been like an anguished rasp against her ear when he'd told her of his love. Her heart wrenched with the idea. He loved her. Dal's lashes lifted, and she stared through the fringe at the peaceful meadow that stretched out before them. She loved Jim, but… Dal allowed herself to admit it, she was afraid. Her heart thundered in un-fettered happiness, but her wary and scarred mind re-acted differently.

"How do you feel?"

Dal closed her eyes, wanting to hang on to the beautiful discovery of Jim's love for her. But his voice was low with concern. She felt him shift and gently press her back down on the pine needle carpet beneath the blanket. "I'm okay. Just a little shaken." *Liar.* She was devastated by the idiocy of her error. And she was trembling inwardly with a euphoria that threatened to deluge her with such happiness that Dal didn't know what to do, having never experienced such a pure rush of joy in her life. She forced herself to meet Jim's gaze. His eyes were almost a raw umber color, revealing his uncertainty. She reached across the inches, her fingers covering his hand as it rested on the hard curve of his thigh. "Really."

Jim watched her closely, twining her fingers between his own. "Headache?"

"Yes."

"Bad?"

"It hurts."

He smiled. "Do you want me to drag the information out of you?"

Dal closed her eyes, the sun dappling light and shadow across her. "I'm sorry. I don't mean to be like that. It's just that..."

"What?"

The corners of her mouth drew in. "Jack hated anyone who complained about a little pain or a cut." Opening her eyes, she stared up through the branches of the pine. "I guess I'm conditioned to keep everything to myself."

Grimly, Jim removed one of the two blankets from her. "That's what almost got you killed with malaria." He folded the blanket and placed it beneath her feet to elevate her legs a bit more.

"You're right." She managed a small smile of appreciation as he moved back to her side. "I've got a horrible headache, I'm dying of thirst and I'm sweating to death."

A slight grin creased the corners of his harshly planed face. "Dizzy?"

"I don't think so."

"That's a good sign, then. Your pupils aren't dilated, either. I think you probably rattled your brain, but there's no sign of a concussion." He got to his feet. "Stay lying down," he warned.

Dal followed him with her eyes as he went to the packhorse and lifted the canteen from the pommel. His black hair was ruffled and she longed to thread her fingers through it and feel the thick silk of it. She noticed the effects of the trauma on Jim—his eyes were dark, his mouth thinned. A bolt of shock rippled through her as she began to realize the extent of his love for her. It was another new experience for her, because Jack had never treated her this way when she had been ill with malaria.

She welcomed Jim's arms around her when he raised her just enough so that she could drink freely from the canteen. A trickle of water fled from her chin down the curve of her jaw and it felt heavenly. After he laid her back down, Dal gave him a look of desperation.

"Can't I get out from under this wool blanket? I'm going to die from heat prostration."

A smile glimmered in his eyes as he stood. "Sure. But before you fling it off, you'd better let me get you a fresh set of clothes."

Dal's lips parted as the question of *how* she got undressed finally arose in her mind.

"What? I mean, how?"

Jim sauntered to the packhorse, putting the canteen away. "I had to see if a snake had bitten you," he said over his shoulder as he searched for clothes in the pack.

"And I couldn't do it with your clothes on." Regret came to his voice. "I had to slit the shirt off you. I'm afraid it's destroyed."

Dal lay there, completely at odds with her turmoil of feelings. Jim had seen her naked. Totally naked. And he was treating the situation as if it happened every day. As hot as it was, Dal felt a fiery flush settle in her face as Jim turned around with a fresh shirt in hand and a set of her lingerie. Dal searched his face for some sign that he was enjoying her discomfort, but she could find none.

He knelt, depositing the clothes next to Dal. "Listen, I'm going to ride a ways to see if I can find a good place to camp." He glanced back toward the nest in the distance. "I don't want to stay here. With those rattlers riled, there's a good chance they'll be active tonight and I don't want one crawling into the sleeping bag with us."

Dal shivered at the thought. More than one cowboy had awakened in the morning to find a snake curled up in the warmth of his sleeping bag. It wasn't the best start to one's day, to say the least. She saw Jim reach above her head and place a rifle next to her.

"I won't be gone more than half an hour, but you keep this nearby just in case a rattler comes close. Raider will stand guard and alert you if one is near." He gave her an intense look. "Will you be all right here by yourself?"

Dal nodded, lost in the gold of his eyes. She wanted to reach out and tell him how wonderful it felt to be cared for. To be more important than an exotic bird or a business deal. "Yes, I'll be fine," she murmured, her voice unsteady. "There should be a small lake no more than five miles north of here. It would be a good campsite."

Jim cocked his head, hearing the strain in her voice. "Feel like riding that far if I can locate it?"

She gave him a tremulous smile. "Yes."

Reaching over, he caressed her cheek. "If anything happens, fire two shots with that rifle and I'll be back before you know it."

Tears ached in her throat and Dal could only nod. His love for her was overwhelming to her shredded state and she felt like a little girl instead of a grown woman. She watched as he walked to his gelding and mounted in one lithe motion. He was a wrangler by breeding, his body lean and sculpted by the elements that he pitted himself against regularly. And she loved him just that much more.

When Jim returned Dal was dressed in a pale pink cowboy shirt with the sleeves rolled up and her clean pair of jeans. She had gone down to a small stream on the other side of the pine tree and washed herself as best she could. If only that lake were near enough, she'd thought, she could wash the sweat and dirt of the day from herself. And the smell of rattler. The odor clung to her skin and Dal wrinkled her nose, wishing mightily for a tub of hot water and some fragrant salts. Raider never left her side, always stiffly alert, his yellow eyes large and constantly roving any area where she walked. A sense of safety blanketed Dal as she began to relax from her experience.

Now, Jim dismounted and smiled. He removed his hat, wiping his brow with the back of his sleeve as he walked over to where she was sitting.

"You look better," he said, squatting in front of her.

"If I could just get a bath or anything to wash up in,

I'd feel a hundred percent better," she said. "Did you find the lake?" He was so incredibly breathtaking, Dal thought, aware that her pulse rate was rising. She stared at his mouth, heatedly aware of enjoying the sensual pleasures of it earlier and wanting to enjoy him again.

His smile deepened as he studied her. "You've got your wish, then," he said. "About twenty minutes from here is the lake, plenty of grass for the horses and a small clearing for a camp. If you feel up to it, we can leave now and get you settled."

Dal's eyes widened with delight. "That's wonderful!" She struggled to stand. Jim stood and leaned over, helping her to her feet. He watched her steadily for a sign that she might be dizzy. Her eyes were clear now and he saw happiness flecked within them. Breathing easier, Jim noted color returning to her flesh. There was such a thin line between suffering disaster and walking away from disaster, between life and death, or love and hate... He gently put all those feelings and thoughts away for later inspection and guided Dal to the horse.

He placed his hands around her narrow waist, lifting her into the saddle before she could protest. Dal turned and gave him a grateful look.

"You're spoiling me rotten. I want you to know that."

He picked up the packhorse's lead and put his foot in the stirrup of the horse Dal sat upon. In one easy motion, he sat behind her, their bodies inches from each other. "You deserve to be spoiled, honey," he told her softly, near her ear. He clipped the lead to the D-ring at the rear of the saddle and picked up the reins, but not before placing a protective arm around Dal. He didn't want her to get suddenly dizzy and fall.

Dal savored his nearness and the slow plodding fall

of hoofs beneath her. Her head ached and the stabbing light of the sun forced her to close her eyes. "Lean against me," Jim coaxed, pulling back and allowing her to use his body as support.

She acquiesced, melting against the hardness of his seemingly inexhaustible body. Heaven! She was in heaven. Or as close as she would ever get, she thought. Just the gentle motion of the horse beneath them, Jim's steadying arm around her and the heat of the sun hanging low on the western horizon lulled her almost to sleep.

"Dal?"

The words roused her from the edges of sleep. She felt the sandpapery quality of Jim's jaw as she rested her brow against him. Dal was too comfortable; she wanted to stay forever in Jim's embrace. The horse came to a halt that broke the wonderful rhythm that held her and she forced herself to sit up and open her eyes.

"We're here?"

Jim pressed a kiss to her hair, retaining an arm around her waist. "Yes. What do you think?" he asked. "Does it look like the Garden of Eden?"

He had brought the horse to a halt on a small knoll that overlooked an oblong blue lake. A gasp of pleasure came from Dal as she surveyed the small glade near the lake. "It's perfect."

There was a smile in his voice. "Like you."

Dal quivered beneath his sensual caress. He hadn't touched her, but his voice had a lover's touch. "I'm far from perfect."

"There's more beauty in imperfection than perfection."

She smiled and leaned back against him, her head

resting on his neck and shoulder. "I like your philosophy more and more. It doesn't make me feel so small or...worthless."

Jim scowled and unconsciously tightened his arm around her waist momentarily. "Every facet of you is worth more than money could ever buy, Dal. Never forget that." He urged the horse down the grassy knoll.

The glade was carpeted with yellow buttercups and white daisies. Several mallard ducks rose from the glassy surface of the dark blue lake, taking wing. Dal wondered if Nar was nearby. If he was and was still hungry, he could easily pluck a bird from the sky. She found herself wishing that the golden eagle was full, wanting nothing to mar the peace that embraced them as they descended to the lush clearing. The sun was slipping behind the peaks that surrounded them on all sides, shadows of the trees deepening where they stopped. The spindly trunk of a pine wove with a white-barked birch.

"Still have a headache?" Jim asked, slowly dismounting. He turned and lifted her from the saddle, gently setting her on the ground.

Dal nodded, carefully touching the dressing on her head. She was hotly aware of Jim's gloved hands resting around her waist and looked up at him. "Some. I think if I take some aspirin that will help."

Reluctantly, he released her. "You can do one of two things while I set up camp and get the horses hobbled. Go swim or sit there and look beautiful."

She smiled, giving the lake a look of longing. "I need to bathe."

"All right. There's a small cul-de-sac about halfway around the lake, that's protected with those aspens over there. Should be enough room to stretch out in the grass afterward if you want, and relax. The bottom is sandy there. Right here it's rocky."

Dal took the proffered towel, soap and washcloth from him. Before Jim let her leave, he handed her the canteen and a couple of aspirin. Murmuring her thanks, Dal wandered around the small lake, Raider at her side. She felt guilty about Jim having to set up camp by himself, but one look into his set features and she knew her arguments would be in vain. Right now, all she wanted was the feeling of water on her body.

She relaxed afterward on the grassy bank, combing her wet, tangled hair free of the snarls. Dusk was setting in quickly after the sun had dipped behind the mountains and finally, Dal forced herself to dress and go back to camp. The campfire was blazing with two kettles suspended over it, and the delicious odor of venison permeated the air. Jim had removed his chaps, cowboy hat and gloves, and was busy preparing their dinner.

Dal dropped beside him on an old log he had pulled close to the fire. "It smells wonderful."

"Figured you could use the strength venison has in it," he commented, handing her a cup of freshly brewed coffee.

"Dried venison?" she asked, nodding her thanks for the coffee.

"Yeah. There were times on the reservation when I'd be out for weeks at a time with venison jerky and dried corn for food, and that was it. I'd use the juice of a prickly pear cactus for liquid. I always carry venison jerky with me whenever I pack into an interior."

She watched his economical movements as he made bannock, a pan bread that had been an Indian specialty for hundreds of years and was welcome at any camp.

Her mouth began to water as he added chopped nuts and raisins to the batter.

"I have trouble with the idea that your mother would let you herd sheep out in the desert for weeks at a time without checking up on you."

He smiled and gave her an intent look. Did Dal realize how lovely she was with her hair drying in soft waves about her face? She looked almost as good as new, he thought thankfully. She had taken the bandage off her head and the cut was no longer bleeding and only slightly swollen from the blow she had taken earlier.

"It wasn't child neglect," he said dryly, pouring the batter into a skillet that contained hot bacon grease. With a deft movement, he held the skillet over the hot coals, allowing the pan bread to bake. "When you consider how sparse grass was for our sheep and goats, you can understand we had to travel ten or so miles a day just to let them find enough to stay alive on. My uncles had taught me where the watering holes were and I'd take my old spotted mustang and follow the herd. About every ten days, I'd bring the herd back toward our hogan. By that time the grass the herd had sheared off previously had grown back up, and the cycle would start all over again."

Dal grimaced. "Still, isn't that a lot of responsibility for a ten-year-old boy?"

"Maybe for a white child it would be," he answered, expertly flipping the pan bread in the skillet so the other side would bake to a golden brown. "But Navaho children are raised to behave responsibly at any age, whether it be two or a hundred." He smiled at her, the corners of his eyes crinkling. "I'll always love those growing-up days on the reservation with my people.

I learned to survive on little, defend the herd with my staff and sleep so light that I could hear a coyote approaching the flock at night."

Dal watched as Jim set aside the skillet with the cooked pan bread and stirred the kettle that contained the venison stew. "You know so much about nature. And people," she murmured softly. "I envy you in some ways, Jim."

"Don't. We each have talents. For instance, I could never handle that fierce eagle of yours. Nor do I have your knowledge of birds. We each give something to the other from our life experiences. It's a good trade, honey."

Dal slowly turned the coffee mug between her hands. "Rafe is going to kill me when he finds out the mistake I made today."

Finished with tending the stew, Jim sat back on the log with her, his arms resting on his drawn-up knees as the kettle's contents began to slowly bubble. "I think your brother will be more happy to see you alive than angry over what happened. Which," he said, sliding a look at her, "also means we have something else to discuss."

"What?"

"We've only got one riding horse now."

Chewing on her lower lip, Dal mulled over the problem. "We'll be at the elevation to start looking for the aeries tomorrow and it won't be that much of a strain on the horse."

"I wasn't too concerned about the horse, Dal. We'll be riding double the rest of the trip. I can do it, but do you want to?"

The idea of being that close to Jim all of that time

sent a thrill through Dal. And then she felt a hot flush accompany her thoughts, and knew full well Jim saw it, too. "It won't bother me," she said quietly, holding his warm golden gaze.

He rose, a slight smile curving his mouth. "Good. At this point, I don't think there's any sense in radioing your brother to tell him what happened. He'd get needlessly upset."

Dal raised her eyes heavenward. "Rafe would come zipping in here with that helicopter he flies like he's still a pilot in Vietnam, and drag me back to the ranch. He's so damned arrogant sometimes. A throwback to the macho male type that believes in dragging a woman off to his cave by her hair."

Jim ladled a healthy portion of stew into a tin bowl and handed it to her. "I think part of it is a sham," he murmured, dishing up stew for himself and sitting back on the log with Dal.

"He's so protective. But he's always been that way, Jim."

"Let's face it, he had two younger sisters to be responsible for," Jim said with a smile. "And I get the feeling you two weren't exactly angels all the time."

Laughing, Dal began to eat the stew. "I was, but Cat wasn't. She was always in hot water. I just got blamed for it because I happened to be in the general vicinity when Dad or Mom would catch us."

Jim's eyes twinkled, but he said nothing. The camp was quiet as the golden dusk gave way to darkness. As hot as it had been during the day, dampness seeped into the area, cooling the earth. The firelight created a dancing shadow around them, pushing back the darkness. Jim shared the warm bannock bread with Dal, supplying honey for it, and they consumed it between them. Then, stretching out on a sleeping bag that he had placed near the fire, he sipped his second cup of coffee.

Dal poured herself another cup, too, and walked over to him. As if knowing in advance what she was going to do, Jim patted the surface of the sleeping bag.

"Sit with me," he said huskily, meeting her questioning gaze.

Without a word, Dal sat with her legs crossed, using his body as a brace for her back. His arm went around her waist and she was content. They sat in silence, watching the fire die down to glowing, heated embers. Dal lifted her face, drinking in the diamond droplets of stars that had become a carpet in the heavens above. "I love this time of night," she began softly. "The stars are so close I feel like I could reach out and touch them."

He smiled, staring into the dancing, changing coals of the fire. That was how Dal affected him—she was hot-blooded, and as changeable as quicksilver. "The fruit of the sky gods to be plucked," he murmured as he caressed her ribs in slow, circular motions. Jim noticed that Dal hadn't put on her bra since the accident. He watched her nipples harden against the soft cotton of her shirt as he continued to absently stroke her.

She turned, meeting and melting beneath his hooded inspection. Even by firelight his eyes were amber, reminding her of Nar's fierce, intelligent gaze. A tremble passed through her and Dal felt herself giving way beneath his assault. Jim was barely touching her, but just his closeness created a throbbing ache deep in her body and within her healing heart. "Do the Navaho have sky gods?" she asked in a hushed voice, setting her coffee cup aside.

"A god or goddess for every occasion and reason," he answered, reaching up and removing several strands of hair near her eyebrow. "You're like Estanathlehi or Changing Woman. She changes like the seasons each year and is immortal. The mineral turquoise, relates to her and is therefore related to the land. She is the dispenser of corn, seeds, plants, precious stones and medicines. In our eyes, she is fruitful, promising abundance and care." Jim rose into a sitting position and brought Dal closer, his arm around her shoulder.

"I don't see the comparison," she said quietly, closing her eyes and relaxing completely in Jim's embrace.

He kissed her uninjured temple, inhaling the scent of the lake water with the natural perfume of her skin. "You're like the earth, honey. There is a simplicity to you. One of richness of care linked with the warmth that flows outward to others." Jim trailed a series of small kisses down her cheek and the delicate line of her jaw until his mouth met her lips. "You are changeable and allow me to see those many facets of yourself," he whispered, running his tongue across the corner of her lips. He felt her inhale sharply, her fingers dig reflexively into his chest. An inner tremble shook him. "I want you, Dal...all of you...but you have to want me, too. It has to be mutual, my frightened, beautiful deer...."

A swell of powerful need swept through Dal as she turned her head to fully meet his mouth. Her lashes swept downward as her heart began a wild pounding in her chest. "Yes," she whispered against his mouth, "yes, love me, Jim. Please, I want...need you so much. So badly..." She curved her arm around his shoulder, fingers entwining in the rich thickness of his ebony hair at the nape of his neck to show him of her need.

Gently, Jim eased her back on the downy sleeping bag. He lay beside her, propped up on his elbow. Worry conflicted with hunger within his golden eyes as he met her vulnerable blue gaze. "Are you sure?" he asked softly, caressing her now dry hair, which reminded him of ripe corn silk as he touched it. "It's not your fall this afternoon or the trauma from it that's making you want my nearness?"

Reaching out, she allowed her fingers to outline the harsh planes of his face, and saw her effect on him. "I'm sure," she whispered. "I'm ready now, Jim. I wasn't before, but I am now. The accident told me that each second, each minute is precious to us." Her voice grew tremulous. "I've wanted you, but I was so frightened because of what had happened before. But I'm all right now. You've helped me heal myself. I don't know how, but you have."

Leaning down, he barely brushed her full, waiting lips. "Love is the greatest healer of them all, my woman," he said thickly, lightly tasting the texture of her. She was soft velvet beneath his heated exploration and he felt his body hardening like molten steel against her feminine length.

Dal closed her eyes and gently eased her fingers through his hair, glorying in the sensation of his nearness, his heated body. "Hate tore me apart and your love has put me back together. Jim," she whispered, matching his urgent kisses, "love me. Make me whole again. Please…"

He drew in a deep, ragged breath, his heart pounding like a sledgehammer in his chest as he drew away. With ruthless honesty, he searched her sultry face, taking in her half-closed eyes and glistening lips, which were parted and begging to be worshiped once again. He had waited so long for this moment; dreamed of it during his hours of darkness and thought of her during his days at work. Dal had never left the home of his heart during all that time. He skimmed her cheek with trembling fingers. If he hurt her…if he gave her more pain because of his starving, driving need of her, he couldn't stand the torture of knowing he had added to her anguish and not taken some of it away from her. She had suffered cruelly at the hands of one man. Was he any different? Didn't he want to fulfill his need within the loving vessel of her warm body that now lay pressed to his? Was he any less an animal than any other male was with a female? No.

As he slowly released the buttons of her shirt and pulled the folds back to expose her beautifully curved breasts, he knew the answer to all his turmoil. He loved her. And if he allowed all of those tightly withheld feelings ease from the haven of his heart, he could never give her more pain. He bent his head, running his tongue the length of her slender collarbones, feeling her press urgently against him. "Our love for each other will set us both free, my woman," he told her in a low, gritty tone. He cupped her breast, feeling the flesh tighten in his hand. "Like eagles, we'll soar to the limits of the sky together. You and I. We'll fall earthward in union just as eagles grip each other by the talons and cartwheel downward. Free me as I will you…love me in return with all that you feel in your beating heart…."

Dal gasped as his mouth pulled one peak into the heated depths of his mouth. A jagged bolt of pleasure tore through her from deep within her body and all she could do was arch into his waiting arms, straining to be one with him in all ways. His mouth wove wet patterns around each of her breasts, tantalizing her, driving her to the edge of oblivion before he gently teethed her erect and hardened nipples, which were begging to be touched and tamed by him.

A cry of pleasure tore from her lips as his hand slipped beneath the waistband of her jeans, his hand finding the soft triangle, parting her damp thighs to discover the delight of her as a woman. She was trembling with need of him. Somewhere in her fragmented, hazy mind, Dal had never felt so alive, hot or hungry for any man as she did for Jim. The violent reaction he evoked each time he stroked her with his tongue or pressed the heel of his hand against her swollen, waiting core were new sensations and discoveries about herself.

Love. Love was the only thing that could make her feel this strongly about Jim. Dal wanted to please him as much as he was pleasing her, but she was a helpless slave to what her body wanted and was receiving from his continued touch. And as he raised his head after sucking gently on her breast, Dal realized that this time it was her turn to please him. Tears shimmered in her eyes and she saw a momentary darkness in his. She felt him remove his hand and cried out in protest, but he smothered the sound with his mouth capturing her lips. Her tears dribbled down, meeting and touching where their mouths were joined.

Jim licked the last of her tears from her lips. "Tears?" he asked thickly, concerned.

Dal took a shaky breath, cradling his face between her hands. "Of happiness, darling. Not pain. Never pain from you…" He kissed her again, only this time it was with such tender reverence that more tears fell and became part of their sweet hunger for each other.

She shrugged out of her jeans and boots, lying naked within the welcome of his embrace. Every juncture where her body touched his felt branded. Jim drank deeply of her, his hand skimming the velvet surface of her form, caressing her breast, following the roundness of her rib cage to the flat of her belly. Woman. She was all woman. Warm and fertile in his hands, to be molded, savored and loved.

A tremor quaked through her as his hand slid between her straining thighs. And another cry softly broke the darkness as he worshiped her aching core, sending shafts of excruciating pleasure rolling through her in wave after consuming wave. Her skin glistened with damp luster as she gasped for breath, clinging to him mindlessly, pleasantly weak from the fire he had ignited by simply stroking her. He kissed away the sheen on her brow, brushed her closed lashes and finally placed his mouth across her parted lips, drinking deeply of her offered love that she gave so effortlessly in return to him.

"Now you've flown free," he whispered raggedly near her ear, his voice unsteady as he covered her with his body. "Now you know what it's like…." Sliding his hand beneath her hips he said thickly, "Share the fruits of your body with me. Let us be free together and give the other the gift of ourself…forever…."

Her breath caught in her slender throat and she threw her head back as she arched to meet him. She was free… free and floating within the white-hot molten lava that coursed through her as they met and melded into one. He filled her with his power and male strength and the last shackles of the past were broken. She was an eagle flying free from the captive jesses of life in his arms, moving in higher and higher circles of light, glorying in the joy of their union that could come only through the fiery need of love. Each movement, each glorious stroke drove her closer and closer to the edge of an unnamed universe that throbbed with the pounding rhythm of life. And just as she reached that unknown area between the darkness of space and the limits of the blue sky, she shattered into a million golden fragments that were kissed by the sun as she fell earthward back into the safety of his arms.

Chapter 9

Dal lay satiated and exhausted within Jim's embrace. Her heart slowly began to settle back to its normal rhythm as she rested her head in the crook of his shoulder, breathing in his warm musky scent. Weakly, she moved her fingers across his chest, his hair tangled and damp from their union. She felt his lips across her brow, upon her cheeks and nose, worshiping her, loving her.

"I never knew…" she uttered brokenly.

Jim half rose, placing her beside him, his one arm a pillow for her head and his other hand resting protectively against her hip. "Knew what?" he asked huskily. His heart swelled with such an intense feeling of love as she lay naked and vulnerable in his arms. Her spice-colored hair was like a tangled halo about her head, flowing across his arm, several strands clinging damply to her temples and cheeks. And her eyes…

Jim felt himself hardening again as he drowned in the unveiled beauty of her luminous sapphire eyes, which were languorous with sated desire.

His gaze traveled to her kiss-swollen mouth and he didn't fight the urge to tenderly stroke her lower lip to soothe away any pain she might have experienced from their urgent need of each other. Her response was still shy and he began to understand why. She had known only one other man in her life, one who had obviously never given back to her, only taken. And Dal had so much to give that he groaned softly as she returned the tender kiss they were sharing. Her lips were warm velvet molding and pressing to his mouth, telling him of her unfettered love for him. His hand ranged down her form and he gathered her tightly against him, burying his head in the thick strands of her pine-scented hair.

"I love you, Dal," he said in a low gritty voice. "You've always been mine, sweet wildflower."

Her throat constricted with tears and all she was capable of was holding him tightly, their hearts pounding in strong unison against each other. "You've given me so much," she finally whispered, kissing his jaw, his cheek and finally his mouth.

His smile was shadowed with tenderness as he stroked her hair. "And you've always been taken from," he told her in a hushed voice that was absorbed into the darkness of the night surrounding them. "Love, real love, is giving and taking." His fingers trembled as he gently untangled strands of her shoulder-length hair.

"You've just shown me that, Jim. I never knew..." Her voice clogged with tears as she stared up at him. "Before, Jack would take. There was never any holding afterward. No, nothing..." Dal looked away, humiliation flowing through her. "I'm sure you knew that. I'm not very skilled...."

His laughter was low as he sat up and took her into his arms. The coals of the fire were bright and warming as Jim allowed her to nestle against him. "You have nothing to apologize for or feel badly about," he began. "I loved your response to me. In all ways. Skill doesn't make what we shared better. How you loved me was what counted." He caressed her cheek, lost in the dark sapphire quality of her large eyes. "You gave me your heart, honey. Could any man ask for more than that?" His eyes burned with a golden flame as he absorbed her expression in those telling moments. "No man could ask more of his woman than for her to give freely from her heart. That is the greatest gift shared by any two people. No amount of money, skill or persuasion can buy the heart or soul of a woman or man." He leaned down, caressing her lips. "We've freed each other with our love. Nothing else matters. Just come to me with your heart. That's all I'll ever need from you."

"You have my heart," she whispered against his mouth, and she felt the coals of her body rekindle into burning life once again.

Jim held her for a long time before getting up to throw more wood on the fire. He unzipped their sleeping bags and put them together. Dal snuggled between the downy folds, watching as he put on a kettle to boil water. Her heart blossomed with happiness when he brought her a cup of hot chocolate laced with tiny marshmallows, so that she thought she might cry. They sipped their chocolate together, watching the flames dance and disappear into the blackness of the star-filled night, the soothing sound of the lap of water only a few feet away from them. Later, as Dal snuggled back into Jim's arms to sleep, she thought she might die from happiness. What a wonderful way to go, she thought as the fingers of sleep pulled her over the abyss, to die from such euphoria....

The twittering chirp of Nar awoke Dal the next morning. She jerked up, her eyes wide as she looked around for the eagle.

"It's all right," Jim told her quietly, working over the fire while he fixed them breakfast. "He's been here since dawn." He pointed to the log they had sat upon last night.

Dal stared in disbelief and then managed a slight laugh. There, no more than a few feet from Jim, the golden eagle sat majestically, one leg tucked up beneath his feathers, watching her. And then she realized the sleeping bag had fallen to her lap, exposing her naked form. Jim gave her a heated look that spoke volumes, and he got up, handing her a clean shirt.

"Nar flew in when I started making breakfast about an hour ago."

Dal shrugged into the shirt, running her fingers through her disheveled hair. "Is he hungry?"

Jim made his way back to the fire where he cracked six eggs into the hot skillet. "Not anymore."

Struggling out of the sleeping bag, she searched for her jeans. "What do you mean?"

"That buzzard ate almost half a pound of our bacon earlier."

Dal blinked once and then began to laugh, a silvery laughter that filled the glade with joy. Jim looked up, enjoying her response. Did she know how lovely and fulfilled she looked this morning? he wondered. He knew he must look the same.

Nar mantled, lifting his wings, and chirped scoldingly at Dal. She grinned and went over to him, squatting down in front of him, and ran her fingers lightly across his bulging crop and breast feathers. "You're such a pig, Nar," she said, laughing, enjoying the eagle's display. The bird's amber eyes were sharp and intelligent and Dal could tell he was supremely happy. She turned to Jim and sat down cross-legged near him and the warmth of the fire. The sun was barely edging the horizon and a chill remained.

"I think Nar likes you."

"Only because I feed him," Jim said wryly, meeting her smiling eyes. He reached over, touching the smooth velvet of her flushed cheek. "How are you this morning?"

Dal trembled beneath his inspection, resting her cheek against his palm for a moment. "Happy. Happier than I can ever recall." She met his gaze and remembered with aching clarity how he had loved her the night before. "I feel as if I'm in this wonderful dream that I never want to end. Your loving me…what we shared last night went beyond my wildest imagining."

Jim nodded and dropped his hand, returning his attention to the eggs sizzling in the pan. "Dreams are reality coming into being," he told her, pulling over two tin plates.

"Is that Indian philosophy?" she asked as she poured them both coffee and sat back down.

"In a sense," he said, putting two eggs on her plate and four on his. "When you dream of something, you are pulling energy from the unseen and form the wish.

And if you want it long enough and hard enough, it will manifest into the physical state." He put two thick slices of pan bread and a rasher of bacon on her plate, and then joined her. "When I met you, you were a dream coming true for me."

Dal dug hungrily into her food, relishing the salty taste of the bacon. "In what way?"

"My uncle, the hatali, told me as a youngster that I would meet the woman of my life who had the heart of an eagle." He smiled fondly in memory. "Of course, that didn't make any sense to me at the time, but I believed in what he had to say. He said she would rise from the great mountains of the north and that I would meet her in two and a half cycles of the moon. The moon has eighteen year cycles, so that would make me thirty-five years old when it would happen. And I'm thirty-five now."

"That's amazing," she whispered, confounded by how an Indian medicine man could have predicted such an event so far into the future, much less, have it come true!

Jim shrugged, cut off another slice of pan bread and offered her some. Dal shook her head and he placed it on his plate. "Most Navaho hatalis are in touch with the unseen side of our world. Just because we can't see it, doesn't mean it can't exist. My uncle often said he talked with the plants and trees, and they told him of such things."

Dal smiled warmly. "I'm glad he was right, no matter who told him."

He met her smile with one of his own. "I am too."

They cleared camp within another hour, just as the sun was edging over the peaks, sending long, slanting rays snaking across the steep valleys and the crags that overlooked them at every turn. Dal was content to ride behind Jim, her arms loosely hooked around his waist as they climbed slowly out of the glade. She pressed her cheek against his back, closing her eyes for a moment.

"That was our Garden of Eden back there," she murmured.

"It was," he agreed huskily, placing his gloved hand over hers. "A place where we gave of our hearts to each other."

The morning was one unfolding magical moment after another to Dal. Was it that she saw everything differently because she had cast off her past the previous night and felt reborn that morning? The weight she had carried on her shoulders was no longer there, and she felt like laughing and dancing in praise of the glorious sun, the heavy dew on the thick stalks of buffalo grass and the just-opening petals of the fragile yellow buttercups. Heaven. This was heaven for her, and the man with whom she rode was responsible for it. Even Nar, who could be pesky, was the epitome of good manners. The golden eagle never once dive-bombed them. Instead, he flew high above, wings outstretched and floating on invisible air currents, performing a graceful ballet for them to admire and share. Raider trotted steadily at their side, forever alert. Yes, it was heaven—their kind of heaven—and Dal smiled in utter contentment as she rested against Jim.

By midafternoon, she had spotted and confirmed the nests of a red-tailed hawk family and a goshawk. The red-tailed hawk had placed its nest in a huge pine tree, while the goshawk had chosen the rocky side of a cliff. After placing notations on the map Dal added other comments in her notebook and then put the map and log on the packhorse. She wiped her brow with the back of her hand feeling the effects of the sun beating down.

"We're making progress," Jim said, mounting and then holding out his hand to help her aboard.

Alighting on the back of the horse, Dal settled next to him. "As we move up above the timberline, we'll spot more," she promised.

"First things first, though. I don't know about you, but I'm ready to take on a snow-fed lake and cool down," he said, pointing below them toward the west.

Dal was always amazed at Jim's keen eyesight. She squinted, following where he had pointed. There, barely visible, was a piece of blue lake hidden by the forest of pine trees. "You mean you'd brave hypothermia?" she teased. At this time of year, the snow melting off the high reaches would make the water icy at best.

"Are you game? A quick dip?" He urged the horse down the rocky incline and they began to weave between the pines.

"If you are. Frankly, I'd rather dip a washcloth in that lake than swim."

He grinned and gave her a glance across his shoulder. "Where's your Kincaid sense of adventure?"

Dal laughed. "If I freeze to death, Jim Tremain, it will be on your conscience. Just remember that!"

"I won't let you freeze, honey," he promised in a gritty tone.

The crescent-shaped lake reminded her of a half moon's curve. It had a rocky shore, composed of small granite pebbles, but at one end there was a sliver of a grassy bank, which provided them with a place to put their towels. Dal's heart quickened as she watched Jim discard his clothes. His body was beautiful—hard and masculine—and the sun bathed his bronzed flesh in a wash of golden light. There was no apparent shyness in him as he stood naked before her, and she managed a small smile of apology as she slowly released the buttons on her blouse.

"Are you always so at ease without clothes?" she asked breathlessly when Jim came to her and took over the task of unbuttoning her blouse. His hair was black with blue highlights, and she ran her fingers through the strands, delighting in the texture.

"Indians are taught not to be ashamed of their bodies the way most white people are," he murmured, easing the blouse off her shoulders. She had worn no bra and his gaze followed the proud curve of her breasts with their hardened nipples. Cupping them gently in his long, brown hands, he drew her forward against him, slanting his mouth hungrily across her lips. "You taste of the sun," he said in a raspy voice, moving his tongue across her full lower lip, "and wildflower honey." Slowly he probed between her teeth, seeking the moist sweetness of her depths. Jim felt her shudder as he grazed her nipples with his thumbs. "You're so sensitive and vulnerable," he whispered huskily, nibbling down the expanse of her slender neck, feeling her knees buckle.

Easing the jeans and then the panties from her lower body, he picked Dal up in his arms. If he hadn't, she would have fallen. As he walked to the edge of the lake his heart soared with the knowledge that he affected her so greatly. To his surprise, the water was warmer than he'd expected. The pebbles turned to a grainy sand as he waded into the shallow water.

"You're going to like this lake," he murmured, setting her on her feet, although he still kept an arm around her for support. Her eyes widened in surprise and he met her smile. "Come on, let's go swimming!"

Dal frolicked like a lazy seal around the edge of the small lake, dog-paddling at times, rolling over on her back and floating at others. The combination of sun and coolness coupled with the sensuous water around her made her feel pleasantly languorous. The water was warmer near the banks of the lake, growing cooler with depth. At one point Dal sat on the bank, watching Raider and Jim play. Jim would toss a stick and Raider would leap from the shore into the water, retrieve the stick and swim back to Jim, dropping it into his waiting hand. She wasn't sure who enjoyed the game more.

During that half hour, Dal discovered that she loved watching Jim move. He was tightly muscled and lean like a mountain lion; each group of muscles moved in blended precision, bunching and relaxing. His bronzed flesh gleamed from the water and she found herself hungry for him all over again. Was it the laughter contained in his eyes, or the generous curve of his mouth that enticed her the most? she wondered. She couldn't decide. When he stood in the waist-deep water and gave her a heated, intense look, Dal felt an ache uncoiling deep within her. As if in telepathic communication with him, she slid into the water, the coolness lapping around her as she took sure, steady strokes to meet him halfway.

Dal wasn't disappointed as Jim slid his long, tapered fingers up the length of her rib cage, teasing her firm nipples beneath the water. A gasp of pleasure broke from her parted lips as she brought her arms around his powerful shoulders. He groaned as she pressed herself against his male hardness, and his hands tightened around her body.

"I want you," he growled, nipping playfully at her jawline and neck and teething her nipples gently as he lifted her partially from the water.

Dal threw back her head, arching like a drawn bow into his arms, as shocks of pleasure radiated from her breasts. Her fingers dug convulsively into the thickly bunched muscles of his shoulders, and a small cry of pleasure was torn from her lips. The cool water lapped at them as their bodies reacted like heated metal, trying to fuse and meld into each other. Dal gave herself entirely to Jim as his hand moved down across her hip, easing her thighs apart to seek the center of her throbbing core. They floated in the shallows, the fingers of water laving like a cool caress in and around them. Her breathing became ragged gasps as she collapsed against him. Before Dal could gather her scattered senses, she felt Jim lift her, allowing her to slide down upon him.

She welcomed him into the heated moistness of her body, clinging to him, feeling him shudder as he gripped her hard to him. Feverishly she kissed his thick, black lashes, ran her tongue down across his wet cheekbone and, following the curve, nibbled at the corner of his mouth. They were one, as they should be—as the sun, the playful breeze and the cool water had ordained. She reveled in the strength of his mouth and the power of him sheathed within her. Moving slowly, Dal was filled with a sense of her own feminine power as she felt his groan reverberate through her. Her fingers tangled in his wet hair and a smile formed on her parted, kiss-swollen lips as she exercised her right as the female half to her male counterpart, and felt him slowly melt beneath her gentle, exploratory assault. His flesh became heated, the friction of their bodies moving against each other with the coolness of the water providing the slippage, until she heard him breathing in great, ragged gasps. Joy, keen and euphoric, shattered her as he gripped her hard, stiffening against her, burying his head against her waiting breast. And then Dal allowed herself to give the gift of herself to him, a small cry bubbling up in her throat as she clung to him.

Slowly, ever so slowly, she drifted back down to earth in his arms. They stood in the warming shallows, the water absorbing their fused heat, resting against each other, fearful they would collapse like rag dolls if they tried to move.

Jim kissed the tangled hair that framed her joyous face. "You bring heaven and earth together in me," he whispered thickly, caressing her lips.

She sighed, resting her head on his chest. "You shake my world apart. I feel like a hundred happy, fragmented pieces of sunlight showered before you, darling."

Gently, he lifted her into his arms, carried her to shore and set her down on the lush grass. Taking one of the towels, he began to dry her hair. He leaned down, nipping one shoulder, then soothed it with the moist warmth of his tongue.

"You are Changing Woman," he told her in a chanting voice. "The warmth of the sun, the fertileness of the earth and the healing coolness of the water. You bring the fire of life in my body and make me burn until I'm consumed by your heat." Gently he pushed her backward so that she lay before him, beads of water sparkling across her naked form. Dal relaxed as he began to sip the moisture from her skin, luxuriating in the

heat of his tongue and mouth. Each velvet caress made
her skin tighten with tiny prickles radiating outward,
sending wild tingles throughout her. She found herself
wanting him all over again.

Her fingers threaded through his hair, bringing his
head to rest on her breast as he lay on her. She closed
her eyes, feeling the heat of the sun warming them, the
breeze drying what little water was left on them. His
hand moved up her body, cupping her breast, and she
felt like the most desired woman in the world. "You
make me feel so special," she said softly. "As if I were
the most priceless possession in the world. Is this what
real love is about, Jim? The difference between you and
Jack is frightening, and what you give so effortlessly
in return to me makes me starved for more. I don't understand it."

Rising on one elbow, he met her troubled eyes. He
cupped her cheek, lightly tracing the bone. "You're like
any other human or animal that has been denied love
and affection, Dal. The way I treat you, love you, is
to be expected between a man and his woman. You
were on an emotional desert, and it's understandable
that right now, you're like a sponge. You drink every
touch, every kiss from me as if it will be the last." He
shared a tender smile with her. "It won't be, I promise
you. At some point later on, once you've gotten your
fill and are no longer starved, you'll begin to give back
to me. A vessel that's been robbed of emotions cannot
give back before it's filled, honey. Don't worry that you
aren't giving what you think you should in return. You
are. And it's enough for me. For now, let me fill you.
Just take from me, drink from me until you're sated."

He caressed her trembling lower lip. "Remember,"

he said thickly, leaning down to kiss her, "love heals all of us. This is your healing time and I have enough love for both of us. So erase that little frown between your brows. What you're feeling isn't wrong. Nor is what you need wrong." His mouth molded gently against her lips. "You're mine...and I want to give to you...."

The next four days passed too quickly for Dal. Sunlit days were spent logging in all the various nesting sites, and darkness embraced them in a lovers' cradle in each other's arms. She began to understand what Jim had meant about her being emotionally deprived. In those four days he had given and given, and in turn, she was learning to reciprocate. When the sun rose on the fifth day, Dal eased from sleep, having been thoroughly loved the night before, knowing she could never stand waking again without Jim at her side. He was sleeping soundly, his head nuzzled against her breast, arm thrown across her hip as she lay on her side.

Dal's eyes darkened as she thought about the past week. Jim had professed his love to her, and never once had she uttered those words in return. Why? She knew she loved him more than any man in her life. He had given her rebirth into a world of nonstop joy. They were a team in every sense of the word, whether it came to finding the aeries, setting up camp or doing the cooking. And how she loved when he would reach out and touch her hand or shoulder, needing that wonderful contact. How did he know she valued his touch? Jack had never touched her unless he wanted something from her. For Jim, touching was simply another beautiful form of communication that they shared between them. He wanted nothing except to let her know that he loved her through those small, but oh, so important moments.

The sun was touching the pines with a golden crown when Jim roused from sleep. Dal drew away slightly and watched him awaken, a tender light burning in her blue eyes. Oh God, she thought, her heart ached with so much love for him. And it was so easy to follow her heart where Jim was concerned. Lovingly she caressed his stubbled face, watching his lashes slowly open.

"Good morning," she whispered, leaning over and pressing her lips to his strong mouth. His hands slid around her, drawing her on top of him as he lay on his back. She smiled, resting on top of him, planting her chin on her hands, which lay upon his chest.

"It is," Jim said in a voice still thick with sleep. He caressed her back and hips. "You're so smooth and soft. Like expensive velvet."

Dal closed her eyes, content as he continued to map the contours of her form. "I woke this morning knowing I never want to be apart from you."

Jim's hands stilled. He studied her serene features in the silence that wove between them. When she opened her eyes, he saw tears shimmering in their blue depths. Wordlessly, he cupped her face. "Frightened?"

She nodded, swallowing hard. "I—I've never said I love you—"

"I understand why."

"But you said it so easily. And I know you mean it." She blinked back her tears, his face wavering before her. "Every time I try to say it, a fear grips me. I feel as if a hand is squeezing the life out of my heart. I know you want to hear me say it. You deserve to hear it from me." Anguish bled through her strained tone. "Oh, Jim, I'm so happy I'm scared. I'm scared that it won't last. That it's too quick. Like before. With Jack. I'd barely known him three months and I was agreeing to marry him."

Gently, Jim eased her off him and helped her sit up. He held her hands in his. "We're in no hurry, honey. I was wrong to admit I loved you so soon, but when I saw you almost die out there, it was torn from deep within me." He brushed the tears from her cheeks with his thumbs. "I'm sorry it came out. Originally, all I had wanted was for us to continue to slowly get to know each other. I knew we had the time. And I had the patience to wait." Jim gave her a wry smile, meeting her pained expression.

She sniffed. "Did—did you know I was divorced when you came to see me?"

"Yes. The FBI had a file on both you and Jack. I can't say I wasn't happy to see you had divorced him. It gave me a chance with you, Dal. To see if in some way you might be interested in me the way I had been with you."

"Interested? The first time I saw you at the ranch, I felt like someone had unlocked all these guarded feelings I'd kept in my heart for so long."

He nodded, his eyes dark with her pain as he continued to hold her hands. "There was something there," he agreed quietly. "And I had sensed it at the conference when I first met you."

"I don't even remember that meeting," she said apologetically.

"You were having problems in your marriage, Dal. You were trying to save something that needed to be dissolved."

"I wish I had known it then," she said bitterly, lifting her head.

"There's a time for everything, Dal. My uncle taught me that there are many cycles to life. The key is recognizing when one cycle has ended and a new one is beginning."

"This is a new cycle for both of us, then."

He nodded. "Yes, and that's why we have all the time we want, to be all that we can be to each other." His voice lowered. "You'll know when the time is right to tell me of your love. Until then, don't put extra pressure on yourself. You show me your love with the way you look at me, or—" he reached out, touching the corner of her lips "—when you smile for me. Or when you come willingly into my arms each night."

Dal managed a broken smile, her heart mushrooming with such a fierce rush of love that it nearly smothered her. "I think your uncle was a wise old medicine man, and I'm glad you listened to him."

"Our people are taught to listen first to their hearts, and not their heads," he murmured, running his finger down between her breasts to where her heart rested. "Your heart loves me, Dal. It's only your wary head that tells you differently. There will be incidents that will persuade your frightened head that, at some point, it will be all right to say verbally all that you show and hold for me here...."

Dal mounted the gray gelding, looking across her shoulder at Jim. He was rearranging the pack on the quarter horse, which was in need of some adjustment. A soft smile crossed her lips as she watched him. With his worn chaps, black felt hat pulled low over his sweat-covered face, he was more wrangler than anything else. She wondered if he would like to return to ranching and leave the four walls of his paper-pushing job behind. Then, aware of stifling heat and the waning sun, she decided to make herself useful.

"That's going to take you a good half hour," Dal called. "I'll ride ahead and see if I can find us a good campsite for tonight."

Jim's scowl eased as he lifted his head. His heart wrenched in his chest as he saw how happy Dal had become. She was like a flower unfolding the petals of herself before him, and the happiness within was evident in the sparkle in her sapphire eyes. "Okay. And from the looks of the slippage, it's going to mean a total repack. I won't be done for about an hour."

"Good, that will give me more time to scout around for another Garden of Eden," she teased, lifting her hand in farewell.

"Take Raider with you," he called, sending the wolf after her.

Dal nodded and urged the gelding into a slow trot between the timberline and the rocky cliffs that brooded above them. Within ten minutes, they had rounded one granite escarpment, and then the land dipped steeply toward what looked like only a carpet of pine for as far as she could see. Deciding to follow the rocky timberline to try to spot another small lake, Dal urged her horse around the base of the gray and black promontory. Out of habit, she scanned the skies for telltale signs of falcons or hawks that were hunting.

The shadow of the mountain was cooling as Dal pulled the animal to a halt, standing in the stirrups. She had traveled a good half hour one way, the extent of her foray. Squinting, she thought she spotted a thin ribbon of blue between the pines in the distance. Above her, she heard the unmistakable screech of an eagle. Frowning, Dal twisted in the saddle, looking skyward. The call was not like Nar's throaty cry, and she searched for the source. Her eyes widened in disbelief and she grabbed for the binoculars that were strapped to the side of the saddle in a carrying case. No, it couldn't be. It was a total impossibility.

Fumbling with the binoculars, she watched as an eagle slowly circled above her, no more than a thousand feet higher than where she stood. Her heart began a slow pounding as she adjusted the glasses. No...impossible... And yet... It was a harpy eagle, a gloriously beautiful white eagle that inhabited only the jungles of Central and South America. Dal's mouth went dry as she watched what was considered the most powerful bird of prey in the world move lazily upon the updrafts provided by the mountain. The body of the eagle was a creamy white with a few darker-tipped feathers, giving the broad breast and feathered legs of the predator an aristocratic look. She vividly recalled tracking the feared killer of monkeys, macaws and three-toed sloths through the jungles of Central America.

Dal was mesmerized by the terrible beauty of the eagle. She could see the group of head feathers that could rise like a dais about the eagle's head when it was upset and angry. Even the people who lived in the jungle feared the harpy. They had told her and Jack many stories of how the bird would stoop just above the top of the thick, vine-laden jungle and explode through the trees, branches and vines, twisting and turning like a ballet dancer to grip its fleeing prey with its deadly black talons. The harpy was one of the most exotic birds that a falconer could own. Dal had heard more than one story about the vicious, unstable temperament of a captive harpy, which often turned on its master with its yellow beak curved like a scimitar and its flashing, knife-sharp talons. The harpy was an unsuitable bird for falconry, and yet, falconers wanted to own such a magnificent hunter.

Dal could clearly remember one time when she and Jack had been tracking down a pair of harpy eagles for a German zoo, when she had seen what the bird was capable of as a hunter. She had risen early in the morning, and was drinking her coffee while standing on the jungle floor with an umbrella of trees above her. The denizens of the jungle always chattered, called and yelped to one another, but as she stood there, a terrible hush had spread over the entire area. Knowing a predator was near, Dal had unsnapped the holster of the pistol she always carried, not knowing if it was a jaguar going home after hunting all night or a deadly snake slithering nearby.

She would never forget seeing at least fifteen monkeys suddenly scatter like leaves before the wind from the very tops of two trees. There was an eruption of small tree limbs snapping, leaves torn and heavier branches breaking, and she stood openmouthed as a large female harpy eagle attacked the scurrying prey. Like a bolt of white lightning, the harpy's incredible diving speed sawed off twigs and leaves with her powerful wings. Monkeys screamed, hurling themselves three hundred feet to their death on the rotting jungle floor below, instead of being caught between her murderous talons. A shriek that sent a blood chill through the forest ripped through the area as the eagle twisted and turned to catch a fleeing monkey. Dal stood frozen, awed by the power of the eagle and her attack. The harpy snagged a male monkey that was easily three feet in length, not including the tail, and lifted him skyward with snapping flaps of her wings. As the harpy broke free from the jungle covering in another explosion of leaves and twigs, she screeched in triumph, her cry hurting Dal's ears.

And now, Dal was watching what she was sure was a female of the species. How could it be? And then, as she fine-tuned the binoculars, she knew how. There, wrapped around each yellow scaled leg and trailing behind, were jesses, thin leather straps showing that a falconer owned the bird. Here? Impossible. Had the harpy decided to leave its owner and fly south toward its homeland in Central America? That would be possible she concluded. More than one captive predator had taken flight and never returned to the falconer who had stolen it from its habitat. A rush of excitement flowed through Dal as she sat watching the magnificent eagle, until it suddenly went into a stoop, folding its wings and disappearing in a dive behind the craggy cliffs.

Dal turned the gelding around, calling to Raider to follow as she kicked the horse into a canter. Guiding the horse between the rocky ground and the pine-needled expanse, Dal followed the curve of the mountain, wanting to see if she could find the eagle. She heard its screech in a wooded area below them and urged her Arabian to a faster pace, winding in and out of the stands of pine, Raider loping easily at her side. The wolf was just as excited as she was about finding the eagle.

She broke out of the heavily wooded area into a small meadow, and horror swept over her like an icy hand squeezing her pounding heart. Before she could rein her horse to a halt she was almost on top of a party of three men. And the one who held the mantling harpy eagle on his left arm turned. It was her ex-husband, Jack Gordon.

Dal heard Raider snarl, the wolf surging past her as she jerked the horse to a stop. Before Dal could call back the wolf, she saw a heavyset man raise his rifle at Jack's snapped order and take aim.

"No!" she screamed, throwing out her hand to stop him. Her plea echoed with the firing of the rifle. A cry tore from Dal as she saw Raider crumple and roll lifelessly into the grass before her horse's feet. Sobbing, she threw herself off the horse and ran to the gray wolf, sinking to her knees and calling his name over and over again.

As she gathered the limp wolf into her arms, sobbing against his silky gray fur, Dal could think of nothing else in her shock, swept away on a tidal wave of anguish over the death of the wolf who had done nothing more than run ahead to protect her.

"Foss, get her up," Jack ordered sharply. "Pete, grab the horse."

Tears ran hotly down Dal's cheeks, blurring her vision as she felt a hand settle like an eagle's talon on her shoulder, jerking her to her feet. She stumbled backward, off balance, as the man's fingers dug cruelly into her flesh. Dal's shock was replaced with anger as she was shoved toward her ex-husband. Jack stood supremely confident, with the harpy eagle settling proudly on his gloved left arm. He hadn't changed one bit since she left him, she noticed, although now his blond good looks were marred by the obvious displeasure visible on his mouth under the thick mustache.

Dal raised her arm, wiping the tears from her eyes as the man named Foss yanked her to a halt before him. Jack's green eyes narrowed upon her and so did the amber eyes of the harpy eagle.

"You bastard," she cried, "you didn't have to kill Raider. You—"

"What the hell are you doing here, Dal?"

Stunned by the steeliness in his deep voice, she took a step back, only to run into Foss. Dal cringed away, looking first at Foss, who was built like a huge bull, and then back at Jack. She tried to think coherently. Oh, why wasn't she like Rafe and Cat? They were always so calm and collected in any emergency. Right now, all she could feel tearing through her was grief over Raider's unexpected murder and the terror of meeting Jack again. Somewhere in her brain, though, a warning bell was screaming at her to watch what she said.

"This is Kincaid land!" she cried hoarsely. "What are *you* doing on it? If Rafe finds you're here, he'll kill you."

Jack's mouth curled upward and he reached out, stroking the white-and-brown-speckled breast of the eagle. "Is he with you, Dal?"

Dal choked back her tears, standing tensely, her hands clenched at her sides. They were in a small meadow ringed by pine with the cliffs towering above them. Ideal country for falcons, hawks and eagles to nest in. She tried desperately to think, to piece things together. "No one's with me!"

Jack pursed his lips, giving her a branding look, one that said he didn't believe her. He walked over and allowed the eagle to hop onto a roughly fashioned bow perch three feet above the ground. Then he slowly peeled off the heavy leather gauntlet and walked toward her. He was tall, almost six foot three, and heavily muscled. But on Jack, Dal thought, the weight made him look like a prizefighter. Her stomach curled in remembrance of what he could do if pushed too far. Jack rarely lost his temper, but when he did, it was as if he were no longer in possession of himself. And on that one fateful night, Dal had pushed him too far and tasted his maniacal side. She licked her lower lip, tasting the salt of her tears as she backed away from him. Foss reached out and gripped her upper arm hard, bringing her to a halt.

"Don't hurt her, Foss." And then Jack looked down at her. "You never did lie well, Dal," he continued in a sharp tone. "Did I ever tell you that I could read every emotion in that lovely face of yours? You never could hide how you were feeling. And you can't now." He stopped a foot from her. "Now, who's with you? And why are you up here?"

Dal swallowed hard, her eyes widening as she watched Jack slowly begin to work the soft kidskin of the gloves between his large-knuckled fingers—fingers that had once closed around her throat and nearly caused her to black out as he attacked her. Sweat stood out on her upper lip and brow as she considered her options. "I'm here to check on nesting sites, that's all," she said in a scratchy voice.

His green eyes mocked her and his mouth twitched into a thin smile. "All by yourself, Dal? You're a good five days from the ranch." He raised his head, looking over at the gray gelding. "I don't see any pack. No gear. No food." He returned his gaze to her. "I want the truth. Is Rafe with you?"

She shook her head, her heart aching in her throat. Foss's meaty hand pinched her arm and pain shot up through her shoulder. Dal uttered a small cry, trying to jerk free of him. It was no use. "No one's with me! I swear it. I—"

"Hey, boss," said Pete, a smaller man with red hair. "The leather sheath carrying this rifle on the saddle says 'Jim Tremain, Department of the Interior,' on it." Pete withdrew the rifle, appraising it with a knowing eye, and then brought it to where Jack was standing and handed it to him.

Dal's breathing grew ragged. None of the three men had an honest face between them. Foss seemed to enjoy hurting her. Pete, the smallest of the three, had a narrow face and merciless gray eyes. They were all dressed in dark-colored long-sleeved shirts, jeans and mountain-climbing boots meant to blend into the cover of the environment surrounding them. Of course, they were locating the nests and removing the eggs.

Sweat dribbled into Dal's eyes, making them sting. She blinked, trying to think coherently. Jim was in danger. He would have heard the rifle being fired and know something was wrong. Would he walk into the trap? she wondered. Only if she told Jack he was near. She closed her eyes, feeling faintness sweeping through her, making her knees watery. She couldn't faint! Not now. Jim.... She loved him. Oh, God, why hadn't she told him she loved him? Jack wouldn't let her go. And he was capable of killing Jim if he discovered him. She had seen her ex-husband's competitiveness against other bird hunters. Jack would use any dirty trick to outsmart another hunter, to find an exotic bird first. But would he kill?

Her heart was thundering in her breast, blood pulsing like a sledgehammer through her head. Jack had nearly killed her emotionally and had taken her by force. Just now he had ordered Raider murdered. And Jim would stand in his way of gathering the eggs, becoming his next target.

Dal broke out in a cold sweat, although the afternoon temperature was close to eighty degrees. She turned her head with a jerk, staring over at Raider sprawled out in death. That could have been Jim instead. It still could be... Suddenly, she cared nothing for her own life or for what Jack might do to her. The knowledge that Jim was near would never be torn from her. Trembling, Dal looked back to Jack and saw the hatred flickering in the depths of his sea-green eyes. He hated her for running away from him. She had caused him to lose a great deal of prestigious business when she had left. And as a result, to keep up his expensive life-style, he had stooped to stealing valuable eggs and nestlings to keep him in his jet-setting ways. During the bitter divorce proceedings Jack had blamed her for the loss of his clientele, and now, Dal knew, he would show her no mercy. Internally, she tried to find strength to prepare herself for any eventuality at Jack's hands. She knew he would even that invisible score with her one way or another....

Chapter 10

"If you're out here by yourself, what are you doing with this rifle?" Jack asked, tossing it back to Pete. And then his mouth lifted in a snarl. "Or is Jim Tremain a new boyfriend? Really, Dal, aren't you starting a little soon after our divorce?"

Dal jerked free of Foss's grip, glaring up at the meaty man. He had tiny eyes for such a massive head, and they narrowed upon her. Her thought that she might run away was squashed. If Foss had used the rifle on Raider, he could just as easily turn it on her. "You know the Kincaids have always worked closely with the Department of the Interior," she spat.

Jack lifted his head, scanning the darkness of the forest. The sun would be setting soon. "You didn't answer my question."

"It doesn't deserve an answer, Jack. Now look, just let me get on my horse. I've—"

"You're going nowhere. Foss, tie her hands."

Dal's voice sounded strangled as she said, "Why, Jack? Why are you doing this?"

His smile was cutting as he walked back over to the harpy eagle. "Because, my sweet ex-wife, you're up to something. I can feel it. Someone's out there. And until we call his bluff and find out just who he is, you're going to be like the lure we train magnificent eagles such as this with. You'll lure him to us." He held his gloved hand out and the harpy spread her wings, once, twice, and landed on Jack's arm. Jack smiled at Dal. "What do you think of her, Dal? Isn't she a prime specimen?"

Foss lumbered over, a thin nylon rope in his hands. He jerked Dal around, methodically tying her hands behind her. She winced as the nylon cut deeply into her wrists.

"Ow! Dammit, Jack, he's hurting me! I've got to have circulation in my hands."

Gordon gave Foss a slight nod. "I don't want her lovely fingers to drop off, Foss. Tie her just enough so she can't wriggle out of it."

Dal moved her fingers, feeling the binding cord eased slightly.

"I call her Shiva. After the Hindu god of destruction," Jack told her in a pleasant tone. "Got her on my last trip to Central America."

"It's illegal to have her, and you know it."

Jack stroked the massive breast of the eagle, which eyed him with disdain. The plumage on her head had risen slightly, indicating she was getting upset. He al-

lowed his hand to drop back at his side and smiled at
Dal. "Shiva's got special talents even you'd appreciate."

After finishing the job, Foss stepped away from Dal.
She licked her lower lip, trying to unobtrusively scan the
periphery of the meadow. She knew Jim would come.
But when? "Such as what?" she asked, deciding to try
to keep Jack occupied.

Jack held out his hand toward her. "Come on, you're
going back to camp with us."

Warily, Dal walked toward him. She would rather
have trusted the temperamental, savage harpy than Jack.
"What about this eagle?" she demanded, walking at
his shoulder.

"I fly Shiva at other falcons, hawks or eagles. She
keeps Mama and Papa busy while we steal the eggs or
nestlings from the nests, so we don't get attacked." Jack
smiled, amusement in his eyes. "Although I can't say
Shiva leaves them in very good shape afterward, if they
decide to tangle with her. Maybe you'll get a chance to
see her fly against a hawk. Or, if we're lucky, perhaps
a golden eagle. You know those two weigh the same.
Pete, who's our ornithology expert, seems to feel Shiva
would destroy a golden eagle in a fight. What's your
opinion, doctor?"

They left the meadow for the thick pine forest. Dal
tried to steady her own fear of an uncertain future by
keeping Jack on an even keel. She had no wish to invite
his terrible anger. "I don't have an opinion. I think it's
terrible you'd fly a harpy against anything. You know
they're vicious."

Jack held up his right hand. "Take a look at my
thumb. Shiva took it off to the first knuckle when I
was training her to bend to my will."

Dal stared at the disfigured thumb and swallowed hard. The beak on Shiva was a lethal instrument just like the talons that lightly gripped Jack's left arm.

"You're lucky she hasn't tried to rip your face off." If there was one thing Jack prided himself on, it was his good looks. In her mind, Dal wondered how she had ever fallen for Jack. Now that he was forty, his baby-faced look was slowly turning to plump jowls, despite his hard life trekking through jungles. Jim's dark, rugged face danced before Dal and she clung to the intense feeling for him that flowed through her. He was the diametric opposite of Jack in every possible way. What would he do when he found out that Raider was dead? She shivered.

The group came to a halt at the edge of a campsite. Three large tents had been set up in a triangle. Dal saw a small portable gasoline generator beside one tent. How had they gotten all this equipment packed into here? The generator alone weighed at least fifty pounds. It would have been hard even for a packhorse to handle its bulky weight.

"Go sit down over there, where Foss can keep an eye on you while he fixes us dinner," Jack said, pointing to a log near the camp fire. "Pete, I want you to walk the perimeter and keep an eye out for Dal's friend. He's bound to show up sooner or later."

Dal sat, watching as Jack placed the harpy eagle on another bow perch just outside the large tent. His tent. Again, an icy hand crept up her spine. What would Jack do with her? What did he want? Right now, he was being his usual suave, unruffled self. She watched as Pete tied her gelding to a tree and took a rifle, becoming a vigilant guard. There were no signs of other horses around. As Jack came over and poured himself some coffee into a tin cup, she gathered what remained of her courage.

"Where are your horses?"

Jack smiled, joining her on the log. "Who said we needed horses?"

She twisted the ropes carefully, trying to loosen them. "Didn't you pack in?"

He sipped the coffee, watching the darkening forest. Long shadows filled the area as the sun eased down in back of the mountains. "Are you playing twenty questions?"

Dal scowled. "Look Jack, this is stupid! Why tie me up? What have I done? You're being awfully suspicious. Don't you think I have a right to know?"

He swung his head toward her, his eyes glazed. "You have no rights," he snarled softly. "You lost all of them when you decided to run out on me."

"I didn't run out on you!" she cried. "There was nothing left of our marriage. Nothing!"

Jack jerked his head away, stonily drinking his coffee, every muscle of his body tense. "Nothing? I thought it was pretty damn good. You were the one who was complaining."

Breathing hard, Dal hung her head, trying to find a way to reason with him instead of angering him. She felt an aura of violence around Jack and automatically cringed as if he were going to hit her. "Look," she pleaded in a strained voice, "I don't want to discuss our marriage, or its ending." Her tone turned softer. "It isn't necessary to tie me up, Jack. What are you afraid of?"

"Not you, that's for damn sure. It's your boyfriend I'm worried about—Tremain. That his name?"

"I told you, I'm alone."

His eyes mocked her. "Okay, let's hear how you were out here in the middle of nowhere without a pack."

"I—I told you before, I'm logging in the nests around the ranch."

"You're supposed to be teaching in Denver."

Her eyes hardened. "I took six months off."

His smile was cruel. "Because I worked you too hard, Dal?"

"Yes," she whispered tautly. "I told Rafe I'd check out the nesting sites for the Department of the Interior. That's why I'm up here."

"Without a pack?"

"I have a rifle. I was eating what I shot."

"Funny, we've been up here three days and I've never heard a shot fired. And the crack of a rifle carries a long, long way, sweetheart."

Dal stiffened when he called her sweetheart. He had always teased her with that endearment sarcastically, making a mockery of her love and their doomed marriage. "I was raised on this land. It's easy enough for me to get by on plants if I need to. I've been eating arrowhead root the last couple of days. I found some down by a lake," she lied, praying he'd believe her.

"So much for being a good shot," he muttered. "You'll starve on stuff like that."

Jack threw the last few drops of coffee from his battered tin cup into the roaring fire. Foss was busy frying steaks, the odor mixing with that of the whitish smoke that rose from the flame. "Okay, game time's over, Dal. I don't want to have to force the truth out of you. You'd better come clean now." He gave her a heated look, his gaze roving across her tense form. "You're still just as desirable to me."

A tremor of fear strangled her and Dal's eyes widened in terror. Automatically, she tried to stretch the nylon cord that bound her wrists. Realizing the futility of her situation, she gathered her courage and took the offensive. "You're robbing the nests of eggs, aren't you?" she attacked. "Don't look so surprised, Jack. Everyone knows what you're up to, including the FBI."

In one lithe movement, he reached over, jerking Dal to her feet by the collar of her shirt. The fabric gave way, the ripping sound making her cry out as she stumbled backward out of his grasp.

Jack's face turned white with terror over her statements as he reached out, slamming Dal hard against the trunk of a pine. The bark bit savagely into her tender back and she sobbed, watching his eyes narrow like a cougar's.

"What do you mean, the FBI?" he whispered against her face, his knuckles whitening as he pressed her shoulders against the trunk.

A small cry of terror tore from Dal and she squeezed her eyes shut. "They know!" she screamed. "You won't get away with the poaching! You won't!"

His nostrils flared as he gave her a savage jerk. "You bitch! This is the second time you've hurt me!" His lips drew away from his teeth, his breathing was labored. "Let me tell you something. You ruined me! You ran out and destroyed my business. This time…this time you aren't going to ruin anything for me, Dal. I've got fifty orders to fill. Fifty! Do you know how much that's worth to me? It's enough to set me up again like before.

Before you ran out on me. And no one…not even you, is going to stop me."

Abruptly, he eased his grip and shook his head, remorse filling his strained voice. "God, Dal, why did we end up like this? We loved each other at one time." The fury in his features disappeared and he eased his hold even more. "I'm sorry. I didn't mean to hurt you. Sometimes you push me too hard, Dal."

She braced herself against the trunk, unable to say anything. Tears filled her eyes. "I'm sorry, too, Jack. What you're doing is wrong. We both know that."

"Freeze! All of you!"

Dal jerked in a breath, opening her eyes. Jim's voice was deadly quiet as he held the rifle on the three men. He stood near one pine tree, legs slightly spread to give him maximum balance, a fighter's stance in case he had to move fast. His face was hard as the granite that rose above them, his eyes a chilling thundercloud-black as they swung to Jack. Sweat made the taut planes of his face glisten.

"Let her go."

Hatred suddenly filled Jack's once saddened features. "Who the hell are you?" he snarled.

"Doesn't matter. Back away from her. Now."

Dal felt Jack's fingers slowly relax. Her knees went wobbly, but she pulled out of his grip, stumbling away from him.

"Dal. Over here."

Slowly Jack turned, his face draining of color. "You're making a big mistake, cowboy." And then he leveled his glare on Dal. "One of your ranch hands, or is this Tremain?"

Jim kept his eyes on the three men who stood tensely

before him. He didn't dare look at Dal as she staggered between them. Anger simmered like scalding liquid just beneath his veneer. Her shirt had been torn at the shoulder and he had seen one man slam her up against the tree. He had wanted to shoot the bastard, but he might have hit Dal instead. His finger squeezed the trigger a little more firmly.

"The only mistake that's been made is taking her prisoner," he warned, slowly unsnapping the leather case holding his knife on his belt. Out of the corner of his eye, he saw Dal come up to him. "Put your back to me, Dal, and hold your hands away from your body."

She tried to stop from sobbing with relief and did as Jim instructed. He risked one glance down and deftly sliced the nylon, freeing her. He saw the blond-haired man tense.

"You move and you're dead."

Jack eyed the rifle only two feet from him, near the tent entrance.

Dal rubbed her wrists, her fingers numb. "Jim, that's Jack Gordon. These others are Foss and Pete. They're here to take the eggs—"

Jim put out a hand, bringing her behind him, out of the line of fire. "Are you all right?"

"Y-yes."

"Where's their horses? I didn't see any."

She wiped her eyes free of the tears. "I don't think they have any. I—I saw a radio, like ours, inside his tent."

"Go get it."

"Now just a damn minute!" Jack growled, flexing his hands into fists.

Jim held the barrel of the rifle steady on Jack. "One

step…" he warned him softly. "Just take one because that's all the excuse I'll need, Gordon."

Dal returned with the rectangular black radio in hand. Jim's sensitive hearing picked up the familiar sound of a helicopter in the distance. And then he saw Jack begin to smile. "Friends, Gordon?"

Jack grinned, relaxing slightly. "That's right, cowboy. Too many for you to take care of. In another ten minutes, you're dead meat. I got four men coming in on that chopper, and they're all armed. If I don't signal them on that radio she's holding, they're going to know something's wrong. And that's when they'll come walking into this camp with their M-16s on semiautomatic." His smile broadened. "Ahh, I see that made an impact on you. Good, at least you know when you're outsmarted." He glared at Dal, who was partially hidden behind him. "Tough luck, sweetheart. Looks like you're going to be spending the night. With me."

Jim's gaze never wavered. "Dal, go get our horse. Now."

Jack laughed. "Don't be stupid, cowboy! Those boys in that chopper can run down an elk and fire at him in three hundred yards with their rifles. If you're smart, you'll put down that rifle and give up. Don't make this hard on yourself. You try and leave and we'll hunt you down like I did that wolf of Dal's."

"That was my wolf, Gordon," Jim said in a cold voice. "And one way or another, you're going to pay for killing him. And for hurting her." He glanced over as Dal rode up on the gelding. She was white-faced, her large eyes filled with terror. But they had no choice, Jim decided, they had to make a run for it. One man and one rifle against seven men armed to the teeth didn't make sense. And Dal would be caught in the middle of it. No, he thought quickly, if they could melt back into the forest under the cover of the coming night and ride for help, that was the best they could do.

"All of you," Jim ordered, "on your bellies. Now!"

Grudgingly, the three men obeyed. Jack smiled broadly before he lay down on the dusty earth. "You're dead, Tremain. I won't let you live long enough to get help."

Jim leaped on the back of the horse and slung the radio over his shoulder. "Let's go, Dal," he told her, his voice barely above a growl.

She kicked the gelding hard and the horse leaped forward, startled. Within moments, they were over the small rise, weaving in and out of the pines, on their way down the hill. The horse slipped a number of times, the pine needles slick beneath his shod hooves. The sound of the helicopter grew louder and louder. Dal hugged the horse, urging him on at a breakneck speed down the steep incline. If he stumbled, they could easily fly over his head, slamming into a tree that brushed by them or onto the earth. The wind whipped past her face, making her eyes water, and she squinted into the murky gray light that would turn to blackness in a matter of minutes. All that time, she felt Jim's arm around her waist, holding her against him, both of them moving as one while the horse wove right and then left in his pounding gallop through the forest.

Darkness fell like a curtain and Dal reined in after a few close calls with trees. She was sobbing for breath, thankful for Jim's arm around her.

"Here, you guide him," she panted, "I can't see that well." She slid off, allowing him to move forward and slip into the saddle. In one motion, Jim gripped her arm, helping her up behind him.

"Quiet," he said, pulling the heavily breathing horse to a halt.

Dal tried to steady her breathing, terror leaking into her veins, making her shake. Suddenly the forest was silent except for her thudding heart in her breast. She gripped Jim's arm, straining to hear anything.

"What is it?"

Automatically, he put his hand on her thigh to reassure her. "The chopper's landed."

"And?"

"They can't hunt us on foot. A horse is faster."

Sweat dribbled down her temple. "That means they can't chase us now?"

Jim's hand tightened momentarily on her thigh. "They've got lights on the bottom of that helicopter," he told her in a husky tone, "and they'll probably be up after us as soon as Gordon has told them what's happened."

Terror seized Dal and she rested her head against his shoulder. "Oh, God, will they?"

Grimly, Jim turned the horse, heading back down the slope of the valley. "Count on it. Hang on, I'm going to push him hard to put distance between us. Will you be all right? Did Gordon hurt you?"

Tears scalded her eyes and Dal slipped her arms around his rock-hard stomach. Jim felt so strong and steady, while she was crumbling apart inside. "He scared me to death, but I'm okay."

"He didn't touch you?"

"No. But he would have, Jim," Dal said with a sob. "Oh, God, he's unstable. Worse than before—"

"I know," came the clipped answer. "Hang on, Dal. We're going to do some dangerous riding."

She shut her eyes tightly, clinging to his tall, lithe frame, moving in sync with him and the laboring horse. The pitch-blackness surrounded them like a suffocating embrace and Dal could only pray that they would remain hidden. They had made it down to the narrow V-shaped valley floor before she heard the helicopter blades far above them. Jim was right—Gordon was going to hunt them down like animals. The rough snorting of the Arabian horse made short, explosive sounds through the forest as Jim forced the animal to continue to weave and thread through the woods. Dal could smell the raw odor of Jim's sweat mingled with that of the foam-flecked horse. And she could smell her own fear.

For a while the helicopter moved to the west of them. Occasionally, Dal could see the stark stab of the white light moving slowly one way and then the other, hunting for them. The Arab suddenly stumbled and Dal bit back a cry, gripping Jim hard to keep from falling off. He pulled the horse to a stop, the animal trembling with exertion.

"Slide off," he ordered, helping her down.

Dal felt her legs wobble and rested against the panting horse while Jim dismounted. He slid his arm around her waist, drawing her upright.

"Come on."

She didn't have time to ask what he was doing after he tied the horse beneath heavy undergrowth that was protected by the pine trees overhead. She stumbled along and would have fallen several times if Jim hadn't had his arm around her. As much as she tried, Dal could barely see anything, but trusted herself to Jim's uncanny night vision; he had the eyes of an owl. Finally, after running along a slippery pine-needled-covered slope, Jim pulled her down a bank beside a small, trickling stream. Thick ferns on the bank hung over the ribbon of water and he drew her beneath the scratchy leaves. Her fear subsided slightly as he brought her protectively against him, encircling her with his arms.

Exhausted, Dal laid her head on Jim's damp chest, and heard his heart thundering beneath her ear. Weakly, she slid her arms around his middle, allowing the over-whelming danger of their situation to finally wash over her. She felt the roughness of his leather-gloved finger against her bare shoulder and his hard, punctuated breathing.

"Just rest," he rasped, and felt her begin to relax in his arms. All the while, he kept watching and listening for the helicopter. Slowly Jack was moving the chop-per toward the area where they were hidden. Reflex-ively, Jim increased his grip on Dal as he felt her begin to tremble. He pressed a kiss to her tangled hair. "It's going to be all right," he murmured. But was it? He wasn't sure. Without the packhorse, which he had un-loaded and ridden to where he'd found Raider's body, they were in trouble. The gelding was tired from being ridden double the past five days, without their trying to push any more out of him in this emergency. Even if they both had a horse, they were two days out of range to radio Rafe at the Triple K. But with its double load the gelding was going to move more slowly, and that made them three days out of contact, instead of two. And he knew that Jack wouldn't stop hunting them until he found them.

Mentally, Jim went over the situation. They had one

rifle and only six bullets, which he had pulled from the pack when he heard the echo of the rifle shot and went riding to find out what had happened. Six bullets were not enough to stop seven men armed with ultramodern weapons. A horse could never outrun a helicopter. But Jack Gordon had a fuel supply problem to worry about, which meant that if he were going to try to recapture them, it had to be soon. Tonight or tomorrow at best, Jim figured. He shut his eyes, sweat running down the sides of his jaw.

After a while, Dal raised her head from his soaked shirt. She could barely see his dark eyes. "Do you think they'll come this way?" Her voice was hoarse and strained.

"Yes."

"I never realized what an effect the divorce had on Jack. He blames me for his business losses. He said I pushed him into poaching so he could make back the losses."

Jim turned, studying her upturned face. He touched her cheek. She looked so fragile—as if at any moment, she would shatter like fine crystal. Frustration curled through him. He wanted to protect Dal and instead they were having to run for their lives. Dammit, he should have listened to Rafe about Gordon being up here at the same time as they were. "None of it's your fault, Dal. Don't buy that. Gordon does exactly what he wants to do for monetary reasons. He's just taking his anger out on you, that's all."

She closed her eyes, resting her cheek against his open palm, the smell of damp leather from his glove encircling her nostrils. "I was so scared, Jim," she whispered. She opened her eyes. "Foss shot Raider on Jack's orders. Raider hadn't done anything. He just ran ahead of me when he saw the men. I'm sorry...."

He took a deep breath and pulled her back against him, needing her warmth. Her softness. She gave him strength by simply being with him. "He looks like a wolf, and Gordon probably thought he was going to attack him," he muttered near her ear.

Tears streamed down her cheeks and she gripped the fabric of his shirt. "He's so cruel!" she cried hoarsely. "Everything happened so fast...."

Jim glanced up, watching as the light from the helicopter moved closer and closer. Did they have enough cover to hide them completely? What if they could be spotted from the air? The thought of four M-16 rifles opening up on them made him hold Dal even more tightly.

"You can tell me what happened as soon as they leave," he said huskily, releasing her. He crawled a few inches on his hands and knees, scooping up mud from the bank in his gloves, then smeared it over Dal's exposed arms, neck and face. He did the same for himself, and then huddled her tightly against him as the roar of the helicopter moved upon them.

Jim's breath was hot and moist against her as he spoke in a low, growling tone. "Whatever happens, don't move unless I tell you to. All right?"

Dal barely nodded, knotting her body up as tightly as possible against his own. The thick overhang of ferns hid them completely. Her mind knew that, but her shredded, terrorized emotions didn't. As the sound of the helicopter blades grew louder, the urge to run nearly strangled her. The roar serrated the night as the chopper hovered almost directly over them, the stabbing light from beneath the belly moving slowly back and forth, trying to ferret them out. She cringed, a small cry caught in her throat. Jim's hand moved across her mouth. Tears squeezed from beneath her lids as she allowed him to crush her tightly against him. The light snaked over the stream, coming back and blinding them. Dal muffled a cry, ducking instinctively. Jim froze. The light fanned across the ferns on the bank. And then it moved on....

Dal felt Jim's hand loosen against her mouth and she suddenly went faint with relief. The helicopter flew in a southerly direction, leaving them alone in the darkness once again. How long they stayed in that crouched position, Dal didn't know. When the helicopter was finally out of sight, she felt Jim slowly unwind from his position, freeing her. She got to her knees and sat back on her heels before the stream.

"Get a drink of water," he said, rising.

"Where are you going?"

"To see if the horse is still tied to that tree. I'll be right back. Don't wash the mud off, Dal. We need all the camouflage we can get."

It seemed like hours before Jim came back, leading the gelding. He allowed the animal to drink its fill while he took mud and slathered it thickly across the white stockings on two legs of the gray horse. The sounds of the helicopter had faded completely and Dal wondered if it had returned to the base camp. She tested her legs, standing and finding herself stiff. Jim knelt by the stream, drinking the icy cold water and then got up. By now, Dal's night vision was as good as it was going to get and she saw the grimness on Jim's face. Only his eyes shone like cold flint in the starlit heavens that lay carpeted above them. She shivered, suddenly cold to her soul.

As if sensing her need to be held, Jim walked over, sliding his arm around her shoulder. She came immediately to him, resting against him, burying her head beneath his chin.

"What now?" she asked hoarsely.

"We'll push the Arab all night. When dawn breaks, we'll find a good place to hole up for the day. We can't afford to travel in broad daylight because Gordon can spot us more easily. We'll let the gelding rest a couple of hours and if we've got heavy cover, we'll start riding again around noon."

"Can we try the radio now? Maybe it has more range than ours."

Jim gave her a squeeze. She was thinking despite the trauma. "I already did. It's too dark to read the range on it. All I got was static, so I know Rafe couldn't receive us. We'll keep trying every few hours, but we have to conserve its energy. It's only battery powered."

Hope gave way to fear within her. "Jack won't stop hunting us, Jim. I know him too well."

He kissed her hair. "I know. Come on, honey, we've got a lot of miles to cover tonight."

The grayness of dawn was pushing back the night when Jim finally allowed the stumbling horse to come to a wobbly stop. The horse had to splay all four feet to keep from falling. Dal felt similarly dazed with exhaustion as well as from the emotional expenditure of the evening before. Every muscle in her body screamed in protest as Jim lifted her from the saddle. Her fear had been replaced with grogginess as Jim put his arm around her waist and led her up to the side of a small hill. She swayed unsteadily as he came to a halt in front of a large hole that had been dug out of the hillock.

"What is it?" she mumbled.

"Bear lair more than likely. Stay here. I'll see if it's been vacated."

Dal felt a stirring of adrenaline as Jim cautiously approached the lair, rifle in hand. If a black bear, or worse, a grizzly, was still using it... She rose to her feet, waiting. If there was a bear in there, it could come charging out at them. She held her breath, stifling the urge to call out to Jim to be careful; he knew what he was doing. He picked up a few small rocks and stood to one side of the lair, throwing them in. Nothing happened. Dal's fingers went to the base of her throat as he got down on his hands and knees to make a thorough search of the darkened hole. It was impossible to make out anything in the semidarkness of dawn. Her mouth grew dry as she saw him slowly enter the lair. If there was a bear in there...

How many minutes she stood there, wavering unsteadily, Dal couldn't recall. Jim finally emerged, his face less tense. He gave her a slight smile as he settled the hat back on his head.

"It's empty."

She sat down before she fell down. "Thank God."

He gave her the rifle and then went over to the horse. Above them was a thick canopy of dense pine along with sufficient brush all around them. The area abounded in bearberry bushes that stood two to three inches off the ground, alive with small pink flowers that would later yield red berries that bears foraged for. Highbush cranberry provided their brush cover, stand-

ing nearly eight feet tall around the lair and hillside. Dal
blinked, remembering the survival training her father
had taught her. While Jim unsaddled the horse and hobbled it close to a tiny stream, she began to search for any
of the dried berries that might still be around from the
season before. The berries were a rich food source, and
Dal realized she and Jim hadn't eaten for a long time.

"Come on," Jim called. He stood below her with rifle
and saddle blanket in hand. "The birds probably got any
berries that were left during the winter."

Dal turned, watching her step as she walked the
few feet to where he stood. Despite the grueling ride,
Jim looked tired, but not exhausted. Was it his Indian
blood that gave him that extra stamina, that hardness
she didn't possess?

"I was hoping we could find a few. They're good
for energy."

He nodded, leading her to the lair. "I saw some arrowhead down by the stream. Let me get you settled
and I'll see what I can find in the way of food for us."

Dal didn't have the energy to even nod. Jim smoothed
out the damp horse blanket in the lair and then motioned
her to crawl into the hole. She was too tired to hesitate
and disappeared into the yawning cavern. The blanket
was damp, but the lair was dry. The powerful odor of
bear permeated her nostrils, along with the sweet smell
of the earth and the acridness of the sweaty horse blanket. The pitch-blackness was only relieved by the gray
light seeping into the hole. Dal curled up into a fetal
position, and had just closed her eyes and was drifting
off to sleep when Jim joined her.

"Here," he said, carefully turning around and lying

on his belly. "Arrowhead roots. They're small, but edible. Eat your fill."

The tuberous root of the arrowhead had been washed free of mud and Dal chewed on the crunchy, starchy root, the flavor and texture reminding her of water chestnuts. The root turned sweet in her mouth and she discovered she was hungrier than she had thought. With her stomach slightly filled, she allowed Jim to bring her into his arms. Tiredly, she rested her head in the crook of his shoulder. The soothing beat of his heart further reduced her level of fear.

"Are you all right?" she asked.

"Yeah. You?"

"Whipped. I don't know how you do it. I would have fallen off at least four times if you hadn't caught me."

There was a smile in his voice when he answered. "Fear kept me awake."

She nuzzled beneath his chin, needing the strength he offered to her by simply holding her. "How far do you think we traveled?"

"Probably twenty-five miles or so."

"We're lucky the gelding hasn't pulled up lame. He stumbled so many times."

Jim nodded, closing his eyes. "He's Arab. That says it all. Remind me to thank Rafe personally for buying that breed. If the packhorse hadn't pulled up lame earlier when I rode him to find you, he'd never have been able to keep up with the Arab anyway."

"Rafe'll be glad to hear that. Dad's given him a lot of grief about using Arabs instead of quarter horses on the ranch."

He kissed her hair. "Try to sleep."

She slipped her hand across his damp chest, feeling

the powerful breadth of his muscles. "Jim?" Her speech was slurring now.

"What?"

"I love you...."

He gave her a gentle squeeze. "I know you do."

Sunlight spilled blindingly into the hole. Dal jerked awake, a scream on her lips, dragged from the nightmare. The instant she felt Jim react, pulling her tightly to him, she uttered a small cry of relief.

"Dal?"

"It's all right...just a nightmare. About Jack. Oh, God," she groaned, her voice muffled as she buried her head beneath Jim's jaw. Hot tears filled her eyes, spilling over and trickling down her cheeks to soak into the fabric of his shirt.

He got up on one elbow, keeping her next to him protectively. The light from the opening illuminated the depths of the hole and he could see the tension in Dal's face. Most of the mud had worn off, leaving her skin smudged with dirt. His voice was low and thickened with sleep. "I shouldn't have brought you up here. I should have listened to Rafe about the possibility of Gordon being up here at the same time." He stroked her tangled, disheveled hair awkwardly.

"It's not your fault," she mumbled, trying to dry her tears. She looked out of the hole. "Can we get out of here?"

"Yeah, let me go first. I want to make sure it's safe."

Dal had never been so glad to get out and stand up. Her body protested each movement as she slowly stretched to bring blood back into her cramped muscles. The sunlight lanced through the canopy of pine, although most of the area below the branches remained in shadow. While Jim stood and listened, she walked to the stream, took off her torn shirt and knelt down. Scooping handfuls of icy water to her face, neck and arms, she tried to clean herself up. Jim joined her a few moments later. She looked up, water dripping from her face.

"Anything?"

He hunkered down beside her, splashing water over his face, head and neck. "I don't hear the helicopter," he said.

Resting back on her heels, she watched the sparkling droplets of water soak into his thick black hair. She reached out, running her fingers through the silken strands. He caught her hand, his brown eyes taking on those familiar honey-colored highlights as he hungrily drank in her features. Dal's heart beat wildly as he turned, taking her into his arms. The moment her breasts touched the coarse fabric of his shirt, she inhaled sharply. His fingers, rough and callused, slid teasingly down across her shoulders. A tremor of longing swept through her and she closed her eyes, lifting her lips to meet his descending mouth.

A sweet, hot fire uncoiled deep within her as his mouth captured hers, worshiping her lips, parting them and stroking them. His breath was moist against her face and she felt the prickle of his day-old beard on her tender skin. All of it served to heighten the emotions she'd withheld since her capture by Jack. Dal returned his achingly tender kiss, drinking deeply of his offering, wanting him, needing him in ways she had ever needed anyone before. A cry tore from her as he dragged his mouth from her.

"No," she sobbed softly, "love me, Jim. Now. Please, I want you…need you…." Her heart was fluttering wildly in her chest as she gripped his shirtfront. How could she explain what she felt in those volcanic moments? All her fear of being raped again by Jack, of possibly being killed or of Jim dying, avalanched upon her. She anxiously searched his eyes, sensing his hesitation. Amid her world gone awry, the only person Dal wanted was Jim.

Without waiting, she leaned upward, her lips pressed to the grim line of his mouth. Dal saw that the hunger in his eyes for her was shadowed by darkness. They were safe here. She knew it on some instinctual level. She fumbled with the snaps on his shirt, freeing them until she could run her fingers over the length of his magnificent chest. She felt him shudder as she worked his jeans open at the waistband. And then he gripped her, easing her down on the pine needle carpet, his eyes narrowed with gold.

"Dal…" he groaned, covering her waiting lips, smothering her with the fire of his longing.

This time, there was only a consuming hunger ignited by the knowledge that either of them could have been killed at any time during the past twelve harrowing hours. After undressing, Dal arched against Jim's now naked form, inviting him to take her, to love her and to satiate the driving need throbbing achingly within her. His hand caressed the curve of her firm breast, and she cried out in pleasure when his heated, moist mouth caressed her hardened nipples. Her fingers clenched and unclenched against his back and a whimper of need escaped from her as Jim trailed a series of kisses down the flat of her belly to the silken carpet below. As he cradled her hips, caressing the swollen core of her, she became moldable clay within his knowing hands, stiffening against him, cries of pure pleasure bubbling up within her exposed throat. A series of explosions tore through her and her world became gauzy with a shower of golden, blinding light.

Her breath came in ragged sobs as she felt Jim ease her thighs apart, and she closed her eyes, her lips parting as she used what little was left of her strength to arch and meet him. He filled her with his strength, his power, and it rocked her. He brought her into rhythm with himself, giving, taking the offered sweetness of her body, and she joined him as heaven fused with the earth beneath them in that instant of culmination. She heard Jim groan, his fingers tightening upon her shoulders, and she knew victory. The victory of loving her man completely. Totally. Never before had she felt so euphoric as he collapsed against her, holding her tightly to him, his heart a sledgehammer beat against her yielding breasts.

Words weren't necessary as Dal kissed his dampened cheek and ran her fingers through his thick black hair. Her body sang with fulfillment and she relaxed beneath his weight, glorying in those stolen moments. As if conscious of his weight being too much for her, Jim moved to lie beside her, keeping her close.

He ran his hand over her damp, beautifully curved side, drowning in the blueness of her luminous eyes. His heart twisted in his chest as he remembered Jack slamming her up against the trunk of the tree, and he slowly rose on one elbow. "Turn around," he urged.

Dal did as he asked. She winced as he lightly touched

one of several scrapes on her back. "It's nothing," she murmured.

"Nothing?" Jim leaned over, kissing her shoulder gently. "I almost raised the rifle to shoot him when he did that to you."

Dal brought up her knees, resting her head against them, content to be in his embrace. "Worse could have happened, Jim."

He nodded, worry in his eyes as he got to his knees. Not only was she heavily bruised, but her skin was scraped and lacerated from her ex-husband's savage attack. "Come on," he coaxed, "let's get washed up, and then we're going to have to leave."

Turning, Dal held out her hand. She felt no embarrassment standing naked with him in the small stream. Jim cupped water in his hands, allowing it to run over her body. She gave him a tender look and reached up, sliding her arms around his shoulders to kiss him. Happiness thrilled through her as he groaned, bringing her tightly against him; the heat of their flesh meeting was as shocking as the icy water they stood in.

"God, I love you," he whispered harshly.

"As much as I love you, Jim," Dal whispered, her voice strained with tears. She held him more tightly, wanting to block out their dangerous situation. "When Jack had me tied up, I kept asking myself why I hadn't told you I loved you." Tears glimmered in her eyes as she pulled back, looking at him. "I knew he was capable of killing you if he found you. And I didn't want to lose you. I was so worried, Jim." She sniffed, cradling his face between her hands. "I haven't made very many good decisions in my life. But as I sat there tied up, I promised myself that I'd never tell Jack where you were."

Jim nodded, his face grim. "I know you wouldn't have. We've all made mistakes, honey. Stop believing you make more than the rest of us." He caressed her trembling lips, tasting the salt of her tears beneath his mouth. "I shouldn't have brought you up here. That was my mistake."

"No...it was the best thing you could have done. I discovered my love for you, Jim. That far outweighs everything else."

"My woman with the heart of an eagle," he said, shaking his head. "You don't even realize your own bravery, do you? I know Gordon was threatening you. And I know you weren't going to give me away to them." He brushed her pale cheeks tenderly with his thumbs. "Your kind of strength far outweighs what your brother or sister possess. You didn't crumple when most would have. And last night, as we rode, you never cried out once, complained or asked me to stop." He caressed her lips one more time, reveling in the softness of her flesh. "You're an eagle. Never forget that. And I love you...."

She gave him a tremulous smile, her eyes shining with love for him. "Then I'm your mate, darling. We're both eagles. We both have a courageous heart when the chips are down."

He swept her hard against him, holding her so tightly that he thought he might crush her. His chest was bursting with so much pride in Dal's strength and unexpressed emotion that he wanted to cry. "They say that courage is either born through the fire or it dies," he told her thickly. "My uncle would tell us that we were both reborn this day."

Dal was content to be held by him, absorbing the strength he gave her so effortlessly. "My life began when I came into your arms," she whispered.

He sought her lips and found them, worshiping them tenderly. As Jim drew away, he stared intently into her upturned face. "My life has no meaning without you in it, Dal." With an effort, he addressed more immediate concerns. "Let's wash up, and then we've got to try and get within radio range to contact Rafe."

Chapter 11

Dal was gathering another meal of arrowhead roots from the muddy bank of the stream when Nar's call shrilled above her. She stood in the ankle-deep water watching as the golden eagle tunneled through the crown of pincs and came to rest on a branch not far from where she stood. The eagle's amber eyes were large as he looked at her, chirping and talking to her as if he were out near the garage waiting for a late-morning meal.

Jim walked over, leading the saddled horse, and exchanging a glance with her. He grinned. "Tell him all we have today is some roots."

She returned his smile, wading out and dividing the roots between them. "Somehow, I don't think Nar will be excited about our vegetarian meal."

As he chewed on the crunchy fare Jim watched the eagle. "Will he get angry and fly at us, then?"

"I doubt it. From the looks of his craw, he's already eaten this morning."

"I'm surprised he found us."

Dal shook her head, washing her hands and drying them on the thighs of her jeans. "I'd be surprised if he didn't. Eagles have fabulous vision."

Jim gave the horse a well-earned pat on the neck and then looked at her. "You carry the radio."

She slung it over her back and then waited until Jim was in the saddle before she got on board. Groaning, she placed her arm around his waist. "God, I feel like I got hit by a Mack truck."

Chuckling, Jim said, "Makes two of us." He urged the horse out at a slow trot through the level expanse that unrolled before them. It was nearly 1:00 p.m. and the sun was overhead. Gradually, all of Dal's sore muscles loosened up with the long, elastic trot of the horse, and they settled into a pattern of trotting several miles and then walking a few more before trotting again, staying beneath the heavier growth of pine. Sometimes Jim would stop, read the compass, try the radio to no avail and then they'd be off again at a slow trot. And all the while, Nar would sail overhead, occasionally breaking through the pines and sweeping past them. Dal would hold her breath, watching as the bronze eagle awkwardly turned and twisted between the pines in order not to hit the branches. Unlike Shiva, who was more compact, had a smaller wingspread and was aerodynamically more agile because of her conformation, Nar was built for open-country flying only. As they rode, she told Jim about the harpy eagle and what Jack was using the bird for.

Jim pulled the gelding to a halt beside a small stream.

A vast, rolling meadow spread five miles in length and two miles in width before them. After traveling a good three hours they were ready to dismount. As soon as she was off the horse, Dal took the radio off her back and set it on the ground. The meadow was knee-high with rich buffalo grass, blooming buttercups and pasture brake. Dal pointed to a spindly six-inch plant.

"Fiddleheads. What luck! Think I can stay along the edge of the meadow and collect enough for us to eat?"

He removed his hat and wiped his brow with the back of his sleeve. He knew fiddleheads were sweet and delicious when they were still in the curled-up stage of growth. As they uncurled and straightened, they became poisonous to both cattle and humans alike. In the spring, however, the plant was ripe and safe to consume. "Go ahead, but be careful. And watch for rattlers."

Dal didn't need a second warning on that account. The fiddlehead thrived in sunny, dry locations, unlike its fern cousins who demanded moist, shadowed areas. They grew in huge clumps, the uncurled portions covered with silver hair that rubbed off easily beneath Dal's gentle massage. She popped a few in her mouth and collected the rest in the tails of her shirt. So engrossed was she in her hunt for the fiddleheads, Dal didn't realize until she looked up that she had wandered too far out in the meadow. The sudden challenging shriek of Nar caused her to look up into the azure sky. Her heart thumped hard. There was the white harpy eagle, Shiva, lazily circling. A scream rose in her and Dal twisted around.

"Jim!" Her voice carried strongly across the meadow. She saw him, half a mile away, as he jerked the rifle from its sheath on the saddle. She pointed skyward, wanting him to see the eagle. Her mind spun with questions. How had Shiva gotten this far south? Had she escaped from Jack? Was it possible that the eagle was leading Jack and his party to where they were hiding? She could see the jesses trailing behind the eagle as she glided past, several thousand feet above them. This was Nar's territory, and the golden eagle wouldn't tolerate another eagle of any species invading his territory.

Jim mounted the gelding, spurring it forward around the edge of the meadow just as she heard the dreaded sound of helicopter blades. Dropping her treasure of fiddleheads, Dal turned toward the sound, terror in her eyes as she looked skyward. Like an unraveling nightmare, she watched a dark green helicopter suddenly roar down upon her. The peace of the meadow was shattered by a cacophony of sound—the thunder of a horse fast approaching from her left, the shrill scream of Shiva and the whump-whump-whump of the chopper. Dal ran toward the edge of the meadow in full view of the approaching aircraft. She had barely turned to try to make it to the forest when Jim's arm went around her like a steel band, lifting her up into the saddle behind him.

The Arab spooked sideways as gunfire erupted from the approaching helicopter. Bullets angrily stung through the air, lifting geysers of dirt and grass in their wake as they followed the horse. Dal bit back a scream as Jim wrenched the frightened animal around, spurring it toward the forest. She clung to him, feeling the horse slipping beneath them. And then, as the helicopter roared overhead, the animal, in its panic, stumbled. She heard the horse grunt as it slammed into the ground. In the next instant, she was flung through the air. Dal hit the ground hard, the breath momentarily knocked out of her. She lay stunned, watching as Jim rolled from his fall and then leaped to his feet. His face was devoid of emotion, his eyes thundercloud-black as he sprinted to her side.

The helicopter banked steeply, barely a thousand feet above them as it came roaring back across the meadow. Dal saw the horse scramble to its feet, galloping wildly away from them. She crawled to her knees only to be pushed back down by Jim. He positioned himself in front of her, down on one knee, steadying the rifle against his shoulder, aiming for the chopper bearing down on them. Sweat stood out on his face as he squinted and aimed.

Dal covered her head as another spate of bullets began chewing up the ground around them. Jim was a perfect target! She reached out to jerk him down. Just as she touched his arm, he squeezed off a shot. And then another. She heard him curse, his teeth clenched as he aimed again. The third shot barked and his shoulder took the recoil of the weapon. Dal's eyes widened as she heard the helicopter suddenly sputter and go out of control. Jerking her to her feet, Jim pulled her along as fast as she could run. She saw the chopper begin to wobble around and around, dropping rapidly toward the meadow. Jim's grip tightened on her arm as he dragged her through the woods, heading toward a rocky outcrop far ahead of them.

"Come on!" he yelled.

Dal's breath came in ragged gasps as they attacked the small hill. She heard the change in pitch of the helicopter blades and, suddenly, the screeching of metal torn apart on impact. But that didn't stop Jim or the pace he had set for them. She barely had time to look back to see smoke rising thinly from the meadow. And then her blood chilled. Voices! Angry male voices. A sob tore from her as they hit the slippery shale and began their climb. Jim had crippled the chopper, but whoever had survived the crash was coming after them!

Sweat trickled into her eyes as she reached for the sharp granite of the outcrop. The promontory rose steeply and Dal ignored her bleeding fingers and scraped hands as they moved quickly toward the summit. The first bullets exploded around them. Jim pulled her up, forcing her in front of him to give her more protection. Dal sobbed, realizing she wasn't as strong or fast as he was. She was slowing them down. If only they could make it over the crest, they would have some protection! Another spate of gunfire erupted and shards of rock exploded as the bullets bit into the boulders and ricocheted off them. Dal heard Jim grunt and turned. A cry tore from her as she saw Jim stagger and spin around, slamming into the rock face. His upper left arm was bloodied and the rifle dropped from his hand.

Without thinking, Dal scrambled back to him. She saw Jack and three other men coming out of the woods. Picking up the rifle, she gripped Jim's good arm, dragging him upward with her. Tears blurred Dal's vision as she pulled, pushed and helped Jim up and over the summit. Blood was trickling through his gloved fingers and down the length of his left arm. His lips were drawn back from his clenched teeth as he fell to his knees, holding his wounded arm tightly.

"My necktie," he gasped, sucking air in between his teeth, trying to control the white-hot pain soaring up through his shoulder, rendering him almost faint.

Dal raised her head, watching Jack's progress up the

mountain. He and his men were slipping, falling and cursing on the loose shale. She unfastened Jim's red neckerchief and tied it tightly around his arm above the wound to staunch the bleeding. She was bruised and bloodied by the climb, her breath coming in panting gasps as she crawled back to her lookout position. Jim joined her, bringing up the rifle. From their vantage point, Dal could see in all directions. They sat on a small promontory that rose above the forest, and from what she could discern in one sweeping look, they guarded the only way to the top of it. All the other sides of the rocky point were sheer cliffs, impossible to scale. Anxiously, she looked over at Jim. His face was pale beneath the bronze tint of his skin, his eyes narrowed to slits as he watched Jack below.

"Dal," he gasped, "take the rifle. I can't fire it. I can't flex my fingers at all on my left hand."

Shakily she took the rifle. "How many bullets do we have?"

"Two."

Her heart sank. She wasn't a sniper. She hated guns and had always turned a deaf ear to her father's suggestion that, like Rafe and Cat, she learn to use a rifle and shotgun. "I'm not a very good shot."

Jim fought against the waves of pain radiating up into his shoulder and neck. "Then don't shoot. Just save the bullets."

An idea came to her and she placed the rifle aside and got to her knees. Picking up boulders the size of cantaloupe and watermelon, she began to hurl them down on the men trying to climb the rocky trail. Satisfaction soared through her when she heard them shout and then saw them duck for cover as the rocks gathered speed, bouncing down the incline, creating other small avalanches. Each time Jack tried to make progress, she would pick up rocks and pelt the men, driving them back down to the loose shale skirting the base.

Jim squinted against the lowering sun in the crimson-red sky. Thirst clawed at his throat. His back rested against a huge boulder, and some of his pain was finally beginning to abate. He watched Dal systematically gather rocks, waiting for Jack's next charge.

"I think they're quitting," Dal panted, on her hands and knees watching the group below. Sweat stained her features, her hair was in disarray around her face. The wind was cooling up on the promontory and she drew in a thankful breath.

Jim twisted around to look. Jack was backing off, disappearing into the forest. A man with an M-16 stood guard, rifle poised, watching them. Wearily Jim sat back, closing his eyes.

"For now they are," he said. "They'll be back."

Dal rose, careful not to expose herself to any possible rifle fire and went to Jim's side. Her hands trembled as she gently laid them on his arm. "I know," she whispered. "Let me see the wound, Jim."

He was amazed at the coolness in her voice, but barely opened his eyes, feeling suddenly drained and tired. Had he lost that much blood? he wondered. Frustration curled through him. They were stranded on a rock with no water and no food. And no communication. He had tried the radio one last time before Dal had called to him in the meadow. And as always, there was static, indicating they were still too far out of range. "It's a flesh wound," he mumbled.

Dal leaned over him, unsnapped his hunting knife

and used the point of it to rip his sleeve cleanly away from the wound. He winced and stiffened, but said nothing. Tears came to her eyes as she realized she'd caused him more pain by removing the sleeve. The bullet had entered the fleshy part of his upper arm, passing cleanly through the other side without touching the bone. The arm was beginning to swell and she gently loosened the neckerchief. The wound oozed a little blood, but for the most part, the bleeding had ceased.

"How does it look?" he asked, his voice thick.

She glanced up at him. "Awful."

Jim managed a grimace that was supposed to pass as a smile. "I'm not bleeding?"

"Just a little, thank God. You're right, the bullet passed through."

"Good. Why don't you wrap that tie right around the wound? I don't want any dirt in it if I can help it."

Licking her lower lip, tasting the salt of her own perspiration, Dal did as she was instructed. After fastening the tie, she got up to keep watch, to make sure Jack wasn't coming back to try to scale the cliff. "It's quiet down there."

Jim slowly sat up. The world around them was beautiful in the early evening, the red of the horizon meeting and melding with the blue of the sky, creating a ribbon of lavender in its wake. A peaceful world met his eyes. And then he looked at Dal. She resembled a broken rag doll, her clothes frayed and torn, bruises on her lower arms, fingernails broken and bleeding. He studied her face, his heart swelling with love for her. With painful slowness he got up and went to her side. "Come here," he said.

A cascade of warmth flowed through Dal as Jim slid

his good arm around her shoulder, drawing her against him. He kissed her damp temple and then her hair.

"You were brave, my woman," he whispered.

"It's the company I'm keeping."

Jim managed a broken smile, the pain in his arm now abated to a hot, throbbing ache. "I love you. And I'm proud of you."

Dal raised her head, meeting his golden brown eyes that were now marred with pain in their depths. Her lips parted and she wanted to cry, but she fought back the tears. Right now, Jim needed her strength. "I'm so scared, Jim…. I reacted out of fear, not courage, believe me."

He tipped her chin up, placing a warm, molding kiss on her lips. "When it came down to it, you kept your head on and saved both of us."

Tears made her blue eyes luminous as she met and held his tender gaze. "Well then, we're even. You saved my life the day you met me, Jim. You didn't judge me, but allowed me to be myself. You helped heal me…and I love you so much that I ache inside."

Caressing her flaming red cheek, he nodded, his eyes fraught with conflicting emotions. "Come on, let's keep watch," he urged. "Sooner or later they're going to try again."

Dal sat next to Jim for two hours. Finally, she urged him to lie down and rest, promising to keep watch. Neither had spoken of the possible outcome. There was only one way off the promontory and that was guarded down below by Foss with an M-16. Jack could easily wait them out; sooner or later they would need water or food. And if they did give up… Dal shut her eyes, rubbing them tiredly.

It was almost dark when Nar flew in unexpectedly. The flap of the golden eagle's long wings woke Jim. The bird perched on a low stone opposite where Jim lay. In a scolding chatter that was interspersed with little high-pitched chirps, Nar talked to them.

Smiling, Dal left her post and went over to Nar. She squatted in front of the eagle, gently stroking his breast feathers, and then she devoted her attention to Jim as he stiffly sat up. She saw the pain in his eyes and the sheen of sweat covering his face. Putting her hand on his wrinkled brow, she felt the fever.

"You've got to be thirsty," she said in a low voice, gently checking the wound. The neckerchief was damp, but the bleeding had halted.

He grunted and looked up at the darkening sky. "I am. How about you?"

"The same."

"How long was I out?"

"About two hours. It's been quiet all that time."

Jim reached out, steadying himself, and slowly got to his feet. Dizziness washed over him and he stood wavering until Dal came to his side. "They're probably trying to repair that chopper."

Dal helped him over to the lookout and allowed him to sit down, remaining nearby. "What did you do? I mean, how did you know what to hit to make that helicopter crash?"

"I was a helicopter mechanic in the marine corps. Your brother may have flown them, but I was the one who fixed them." He allowed a semblance of a grin to ease the tense planes of his face. "One good shot to the tail rotor and that bird was out of control."

"Thank God you knew what to do. I've never been so scared."

"Right now, I've got to think Gordon is more worried about getting that chopper fixed. If he can't, he's stranded like us."

"He's got a radio in the helicopter, though, and can call for help."

Jim nodded to her flawless logic. "Depends. I saw smoke coming from the meadow when the bird autorotated down. It could mean electrical failure. And if that's the case, he doesn't have the means to call anyone."

A cold shiver attacked Dal and she hugged herself. Night was falling swiftly, and the temperature with it. She slid a look over to Jim. He looked incredibly haggard. "What are we going to do? What can we do?"

Jim slowly moved his left shoulder, his mouth thinning. He had to see how much movement he had left. "We can either sit up here and let them eventually capture us, or go down."

Her throat constricted. "Down? There, you mean?"

He nodded, studying the gray light and the darkened forest. "Yes."

"But your arm...you're wounded."

"We don't have much choice, Dal. Up here, we'll faint from thirst and then we'll be staring down Gordon's gun barrel." His eyes narrowed. "He's not going to lay a hand on you if I can help it. Never again."

The chill in Jim's voice sent a warning prickle up her spine. "All right, what can I do to help?"

Jim looked over at Nar as he sat preening himself. "Tell me, will Nar fly against something you've pointed out?"

"Well…yes, he will. I trained him to attack a lure no matter where I threw it."

"Would he fly at something if you threw a rock at it?"

She gave him a confused look. "A rock?"

"Yes, instead of a lure. Could you make him think the rock you threw was a lure?"

"I don't know. He flies best when he's hungry."

"Is his crop empty?"

"Yes."

"All right, here's the plan," he said in a low voice laced with pain.

A sickle shaped moon rose over the darkened horizon, lending a thin wash of light to the forest below them. Dal had taken Jim's shirt off him and wrapped it tightly around her left arm in replacement of the glove that she would normally wear. They had waited past midnight, watching the changing of the guard below. The flicker of a campfire could be seen through the timber in the meadow. Dal was amazed at Jim's patience. He had sat at the lookout, staring into the darkness, trying to penetrate it. Even she could pick up male voices from the meadow every once in a while…heated voices that were raised in argument. Glancing back at Nar, Dal wondered if the eagle would follow her command. Normally, eagles did not fly at night. Would he? Her heart began to pound.

Jim rose stiffly, giving her a nod of his head. As she looked at him in the moonlight, only parts of his angular features were visible, which made his appearance terrifying.

Dal walked over to Nar, bending down and holding

out her arm. The eagle, who had been resting with one leg drawn up beneath him, stepped onto her arm without question. Dal gave a relieved breath, glad that Nar was barely gripping her arm. He was relaxed and happy.

"Okay?" Jim called softly.

"Okay." Without another word, Dal followed Jim down over the promontory, watching each step she took down the steep, graveled path. They were safe until the path twisted down to the right, exposing them to the guard standing a hundred yards away, just within the tree line. Jim stopped and flattened himself against the cliff face, hugging it as he slowly rounded the edge of the path. He could see a man standing near a tree, smoking a cigarette, the butt glowing in the darkness. Obviously, he wasn't expecting any trouble. Jim motioned Dal to bring Nar forward.

The eagle suddenly became alert as Dal drew out a yellow-colored rock the size of her hand. He chirped softly, lifting his wings, preparing to fly. She handed the rock to Jim, who could throw it farther and more accurately than she could. Dal's mouth went dry as she tried to gauge the distance between her and where Jim was pointing. Her heart rate climbed, adrenaline soared through her. Muscles in her shoulder were beginning to cramp from the weight of the eagle, and she gritted her teeth, pulling back her arm as Jim threw the rock.

By having the eagle distract the guard's attention, Jim hoped to be able to slip down the shadowed cliff and fade into the forest. He knew Dal was worried that Nar might get shot at. Hopefully, the guard wouldn't see the eagle's swift approach out of the darkness, and Nar would be able to pass overhead and disappear before the man had a chance to react. Still, it was a large risk.

The golden eagle suddenly took flight, his wings snapping to gain altitude as he followed the trajectory of the aimed rock. At the same time, Jim ran like a silent ghost down the trail, gripping the rifle in his right hand. The golden eagle stretched his wings, a ghostlike apparition out of the darkness, as his eye caught the red glow of the cigarette. Ignoring the rock as it clumped into the shale making a shattering noise, the eagle fixed his sight upon the movement just at the tree line.

The sudden cry of the eagle shrilled through the night as he stooped at the top of the pines, bent his wings and plummeted earthward. Jim slipped on the shale, taking a jarring fall. He heard the guard utter a small cry as the eagle passed within a few feet of his face, and heard a round being slammed into the chamber of the rifle. Sweeping high above the trees, Nar melted back into the night when he saw his quarry was much larger than he. Controlling his need to breathe deeply, Jim skirted the jumpy guard, whom Dal had identified as Pete, and then stepped up behind him. He punched the barrel of the rifle into Pete's rib cage.

"Don't move," Jim growled softly. "Lay the rifle down. Now."

Pete dropped the rifle, holding his hands high over his head. "Don't shoot—"

"Shut up. Get down. On your belly."

Once the guard was down and disarmed, Jim gave a low whistle. He heard Dal return the call and waited for her. Twisting around, Jim listened. The same murmuring as before was going on around the camp fire in the distance. Dal arrived, her face taut and eyes large.

"Take his belt off him and tie his hands behind him, Dal," he ordered.

Fingers trembling, Dal made sure the belt bound the guard's hands securely.

"Now, pick up the M-16 and hand it to me."

She did so, handling the weapon with great care. Jim gave her his rifle. "If he so much as makes a sound, pull the trigger. Understand?"

The guard stiffened. Dal stared at Jim. He meant it. Could she pull the trigger? She knew she couldn't. And so did Jim.

"If he so much as moves an inch or breathes hard, he's dead," she promised in a husky voice, watching the effect of her lie on Pete. Sweat had popped out and beaded his forehead.

Jim gave her a slight smile that said volumes. "This won't take long."

"Be careful…."

She stood in the darkness and saw her eagle land nearby in a pine tree. Nar came to roost, scolding her loudly, and Dal cringed. Would Jack hear the commotion and be alerted? Dal signaled the bird to be silent but it did no good, Nar's chirps continuing sharp and sustained with anger. He had expected a piece of meat and not a rock. He had a right to be upset, she realized. But right then, she could have throttled him by his short, feathered neck. It seemed as if Jim was gone for hours and she strained to hear any unusual sounds. Nothing. God, had something gone wrong? she wondered frantically. Had Jim fainted from loss of blood? Had they captured him instead?

A short, sharp whistle made her knees go wobbly with relief. That was Jim's signal telling her to come into the camp. Gingerly nudging the prisoner to his feet, Dal made Pete move ahead of her. As they broke out of the woods into the meadow where the helicopter had been forced down, she saw the other three men lying down with their hands on the backs of their heads. Jim was leaning against the helicopter, his face taut and ashen.

"Over here," Jim ordered Pete.

Dal joined him, worriedly searching his face. "Jim?"

"There's plenty of nylon rope in the chopper, Dal. Get it and tie their hands behind them and tie their feet together." With trembling hands, Dal divided her attention between her task and Jim. He looked as if he were going to faint at any moment. Jack twisted his head to one side as she tied him, and glared up at her, but said nothing.

She rose, walking back to Jim. "Now what?"

He sat down on the edge of the open helicopter deck, the M-16 lay across his lap. "I've tripped the emergency signal that this bird's down. That means someone will be sent to investigate."

Dal sat down beside him, realizing she was exhausted. Wearily, she brushed a fallen strand of hair away from her eyes. "And the electrical system? Is it up, so we can call Rafe?"

Jim shook his head, glancing over at her. She felt warm sitting so close to him. And he felt so cold from the loss of blood. "The entire system is out of operation. Someone with the F.A.A. will pick up that other signal that keeps sending out for help every few seconds. It's battery powered so it doesn't need an electrical system." He managed a semblance of a smile. "We're as good as rescued. All we have to do is wait and keep our eye on them," he said, pointing at the four prisoners.

The shock of the past few hours was beginning to

make Dal shaky, and she rubbed her arms, suddenly cold. She got up, rummaged around in the helicopter and found Jim a goose-down vest. Then she donned a coat many sizes too big for her.

"Where are the rest of Jack's men? Do you know?" she asked, setting between them a small first-aid kit she had found.

Jim leaned against the frame of the chopper, tipping his head back and closing his eyes. He felt incredibly drained and tired. Part of his exhaustion was caused by his wound. But a larger part came from the realization that he had nearly lost Dal because of his being so sure that the poachers wouldn't be in the area so early. He had taken a bullet that had come within inches of possibly killing her. That knowledge left him badly shaken. There was so much he wanted to tell her. To share with her. All their tomorrows had almost been torn from them before they could experience them. A bitter taste coated his mouth and the prick of tears beneath his closed eyes underscored the powerful sensations exploding within him. Then he pulled himself together to answer Dal's question.

"The rest of the men are up at that base camp waiting for him. Or so he says. We'll take turns sleeping and the other will guard through the night," he mumbled thickly.

"This is going to hurt, Jim," she warned him softly, unknotting the necktie. "I want to try and wash the wound and put antiseptic on it."

"There's hot water on the fire," he said, his voice slurring.

Dal watched as the rifle started to slip through his long, tapered fingers, realizing Jim was going to faint.

She got the weapon from him and got him to lie down on the metal deck of the helicopter. Glancing around, Dal fought the terror that suddenly rose in her. With Jim unconscious, she was the only one to watch the four men who were tied up near the fire. Could she do it? Rafe and Cat would have said it was an impossibility, because she was always the most frightened of the world around her. All she could do was try.

Grimly, Dal placed the M-16 within easy reaching distance and then quickly cleaned Jim's wound. At least in unconsciousness, he would feel no pain, she thought.

It was Nar's friendly chirps that jerked Dal awake from her slumped position near the helicopter skid. She had sat on the grass, rifle in hand and using the skid as a back support to stand guard throughout the night. At some point, she had dozed off. Now the horizon was a pale apricot color and she greeted it with bloodshot eyes. All four men were still tied and sleeping around the dying camp fire.

Stiffly Dal rose, going over and checking on Jim. She had found several warm blankets and had covered him with them earlier while he slept deeply on the floor of the helicopter. Placing her hand against his brow to feel his temperature, she was alarmed by how hot and fevered he felt. He had to get to a hospital soon or infection and blood poisoning could threaten his life. She lifted her head to see the golden eagle sitting contentedly on one of the helicopter blades, and couldn't help but smile. On the opposite blade was the powerful white harpy eagle, glaring steadily at Nar.

Would they fight? For a moment she watched the two magnificent eagles. If they hadn't fought already,

chances were they wouldn't now. Nar seemed far more
gregarious than the wary Shiva. Perhaps their being of
different sexes explained their lack of aggression toward
each other. Dal threw a few pieces of wood on the fire.

The sound of helicopter blades broke the peacefulness of the surrounding forest. Dal jerked her gaze skyward, her heart pumping strongly in her chest. In the
predawn light, she could make out the bright blue and
white of Rafe's helicopter. With a sob, Dal put her hand
against her mouth. Saved! They were saved! Fighting
back tears of relief, she picked up the rifle and waited
for Rafe to land.

The puncturing sound of the helicopter landing sent
both eagles skyward. Dal watched briefly as Nar rose
swiftly, with the white harpy following him, both eventually disappearing over the trees. She returned her
attention to the helicopter, watching three sheriff's dep-
uties emerging from the aircraft along with her brother.
Rafe's face was set and hard, but softened immediately
when he saw her come around the end of the downed
helicopter. And in four long strides he was there, taking her into his arms, crushing her tightly against him.
It was then that Dal knew they were finally safe, and
she clung to Rafe.

They stood aside, allowing the sheriff and his depu-
ties to place the four poachers in handcuffs and read
them their rights. Another helicopter landed a few minutes later, bearing a paramedic. Dal hovered near as the
woman stabilized Jim.

"Look." Rafe pointed.

Dal turned to see Nar coming back, with Shiva following him. The golden eagle landed on his new perch,
the helicopter blade. This time, the harpy landed on

her bow perch, the jesses trailing her. Dal's heart went out to the beautiful, snowy eagle, and she reached inside the helicopter, donning Jack's falconer's glove on her left hand.

"What are you going to do?" Rafe demanded, scowling.

"Free the harpy," she said quietly.

Jim groaned, weakly lifting his right hand. Dal turned, watching as he slowly became conscious. She leaned over, pressing a kiss to his fevered brow. "Everything's fine, Jim. Rafe's here with the sheriff."

Feeling as if there were weights on his eyes, Jim finally forced them open. Dal's heart-shaped face gradually sharpened and he stared hungrily up at her. She was smiling and there was happiness in the depths of her large, lovely eyes. "Rafe?"

Rafe came over. "Yeah, we picked up your emergency call. I got the sheriff and a paramedic and came. Figured something was up."

Jim nodded, watching as the paramedic suspended an IV above him. "You were right, Kincaid—"

"We'll talk about that later," Rafe said. "Right now, you're in no shape for anything except a flight to a Denver hospital. Dal and I will be taking you there just as soon as the paramedic gives us the go-ahead."

The dark-haired woman smiled. "A few more minutes, Mr. Kincaid."

Jim turned his attention back to Dal. He noticed the glove she wore on her left arm. "Is Nar around?" he asked with some effort.

She smiled, gently pushing a lock of ebony hair off his brow. "Yes. And so is Shiva. I'm going to try and get the jesses off and free her."

Rafe's black brows drew down as he studied her. "You see that bird? She looks pissed off at everything. Don't risk it, Dal. She doesn't know you. You can't trust her."

Dal traded a silent glance with Jim, realizing that he did understand why she had to try to free the harpy. "I'll be okay, Rafe."

Both men watched as she crossed the camp to where the harpy sat on the bow perch a few feet above the ground. Rafe looked up, wondering if Nar was going to become jealous. The golden eagle was equally rapt with his attention on Dal, but his head feathers were down, indicating he wasn't perturbed in the least.

"Damn her," Rafe growled under his breath, trading a look with Jim, "she shouldn't be doing that."

"I think you need to change your view of Dal," Jim told him, holding the rancher's black stare. "If it weren't for Dal, we wouldn't be here. She's got real courage when it counts."

Rafe rubbed his jaw. "Maybe you're right. Maybe my baby sister has grown up."

Dal clucked softly to Shiva as she squatted down in front of the bird. The eagle's head feathers hackled, her yellow eyes blazing as Dal slowly reached down, gently loosening the soft, thin leather of the jesses around first one yellow scaled leg and then the other. She knew the eagle could strike like lightning with one of her taloned feet or simply lean over and slash the side of her face open with her murderous beak. In the background, she heard Nar's scolding chirps. The first jess came off, and Dal allowed it to drop to the ground. And then Shiva's freed leg shot out, her talons sinking deeply into her gloved hand.

Biting back a cry, Dal froze, allowing the eagle to hold her protected arm captive as she mantled in fury, her wings spread and flapping. Dal heard Rafe yell.

"Stay there!" she cried, not daring to look away from Shiva. Jolts of pain shot up her left arm as she felt Shiva's talons tighten. And then she saw the eagle's hackles begin to lie back down and felt the claws gradually release her. Breathing in shakily, Dal waited until the eagle had totally removed her talons from her arm before gently working the jess free from the other leg. As the leather dropped to the ground, Dal gradually backed away from the harpy. She got to her feet, stripping off the falconer's glove.

"You're free," she told the eagle softly. "Just like I am, now...."

Dal sat in the quiet lobby on the surgical floor of the hospital. Rafe sat next to her, his cowboy hat dangling between his fingers. On the flight out of the mountains to the hospital in Denver, Dal had remained on the deck of the helicopter, holding Jim's uninjured hand. She hadn't realized how dirty or disheveled she was until the stares of nurses and doctors made her aware of the fact. She hadn't cared, concerned only for Jim.

Now, an hour later, she was beginning to get worried. The doctors in the trauma unit had examined Jim's wound and told her he'd have to be placed under general anesthesia. She had thought they'd simply give him a local painkiller and clean up the wound.

Worriedly, she rested her face in her hands. Rafe's hand came to rest on her shoulder and she was grateful for his presence.

"How much longer do you think?" she asked hollowly.

"Can't be much longer, Dal. Look, why don't I find us a hotel and we can go get cleaned up? You look like hell. You haven't slept in thirty-six hours."

She shook her head. "I want to wait for Jim to come out of surgery. If you want to make reservations, go ahead. You don't have to wait here, too."

His hand stilled on her shoulder, where the sleeve had been ripped away. "He's special to you, isn't he?"

Dal looked up and met his unreadable eyes. "I love him, Rafe."

"You haven't known him long."

"I didn't have to," Dal shrugged tiredly. "Besides, we have the time now to explore our relationship."

"I just don't want you jumping from the frying pan into the fire like you did with Jack, that's all, Dal," Rafe explained. "I like Jim. He's got substance. And integrity."

Dal managed a wan smile. "Two things Jack certainly didn't have."

"True."

"But I was too young then to know that, Rafe. I'm older now. And wiser. Jim has the qualities I need. He's fair and honest with me. I've never met a man who was so forthright about his thoughts and feelings. I never knew any man could communicate like he does."

Rafe grimaced, dodging her gaze. "Must be the Indian in him then, because I'm sure as hell not like that."

A gentle smile pulled at her lips. "It's a learned trait, Rafe. You wait, someday a woman will get you to come out of that tough nutshell you've built around yourself."

He shook his head. "That will never happen, baby

sister. It didn't happen when I married before, it won't in the future."

Dal didn't agree, but said nothing. She looked forlornly toward the operating room doors at the end of the pale white hall. Her heart skipped a beat when she saw the doctor emerge, pulling the green surgical cap off his balding head, and walk toward them. She rose, clenching her hands in front of her.

The doctor's thin face broke into a pleasant smile as he stopped before her and Rafe. "He's going to be just fine, Ms. Kincaid."

Dal put her hand to her breast, suddenly weak. She felt Rafe's arm go around her. "Thank God. When can I see him, doctor?"

"He's in recovery right now. I'd say in about an hour, as soon as the anesthesia wears off."

"And his arm?"

Walters loosened the ties of his green gown from around his neck. "There was some muscle damage and we sewed him back together. Plus infection. With luck, he won't have sustained any nerve damage. We'll know more about that after he regains consciousness and we put him through a few preliminary tests."

"But Jim's going to be all right?"

With a broad smile, the doctor nodded. "Why don't you see for yourself?"

By the time Jim was transferred to a private room, he was fully conscious. His heart pulsed strongly in his chest as he saw Dal quietly open the door and step inside. A slight smile stretched his mouth as she came to his side. "I'm okay," he whispered.

Dal leaned over the steel tubing of the bed, placing a light, lingering kiss to his taut mouth. He was cool be-

neath her warmth and she felt him respond to her kiss.
A flow of relief moved through her as she reluctantly
ended their kiss, studying him beneath her thick lashes.
"You don't look okay," she said in a scratchy voice.

"I am now," he reassured her, sliding his fingers be
tween hers as they rested on his gowned chest.

"Are you thirsty?"

He nodded. "I'm dying of thirst."

Dal got a glass from the bedside table and poured
some water from the nearby jug. Gently she slid her
arm beneath his shoulders, lifting him slightly. He nois-
ily drank the entire glass, asking for more. After two
glasses, he lay back, closing his eyes.

"You're looking tired," Jim noted, holding her hand
tightly in his.

"I'll be okay. Rafe's going to get us a hotel room
nearby. I'll wash up and get some sleep then."

A slight smile brightened his waxen face. He forced
open his eyes, warming beneath the brilliance of her
gaze. "We've both been through hell."

"And back," she agreed softly. Dal squeezed his
hand. "Rafe's going to fly up to the base camp and
find Raider. I told him what happened, Jim, and he's
going to bring him down off the mountain."

His eyes, already dark with the remnants of pain,
grew even darker as he held her wavering stare. "He
doesn't have to do that...."

"Rafe knows how much Raider meant to you." She
cleared her throat of the tears clogging it. "And to me...."

Jim dragged in a ragged breath, closing his eyes, feeling tiredness sweeping through him. "Tell him thanks
for me."

She leaned over, kissing his cool, damp brow. "Get

some sleep. As soon as I get some rest, I'll be back," she promised softly.

When Dal left, the lobby was empty except for hospital personnel. Exhaustion numbed her mind and emotions. Luckily, Rafe met her outside the doors of the hospital and drove her to a nearby hotel. Dal soaked in a tub of fragrant bath salts, allowing the hot water to ease the stiffness out of her bruised and punished muscles. After washing her hair, she didn't even have the energy to comb it out, opting instead to wrap it in a towel and lie down...down to sleep off six years of her life and shed the past once and for all. As her lashes rested softly against her skin, she hugged the pillow to her and dreamed of Jim.

Chapter 12

Dal sat on her gray gelding, watching as the strong October sunlight glanced off the molten bronze feathers of Nar as he slowly circled the small valley. The splashes of gold, orange and red contrasted sharply with the silvery radiance of the blue spruce, the darker green of the pine and yellow-needled tamarack that surrounded them. A smile pulled at her full lips as she shaded her eyes from the sun that stood almost directly overhead as Nar glided with the grace of a ballerina. His screeching call broke the peace of the noontime languidness that embraced the valley.

Dal turned, realizing Nar had called in warning to her. Her smile broadened to one of unabashed joy as she saw Jim riding Liss, the black Arab stallion, out to where she was. He had been gone two weeks to Washington, D.C., finishing up the details of the poaching case, and how she had missed him! Turning her horse around, she cantered down the length of the narrow valley to meet him.

She was always breathless over Jim's quiet masculinity, even more so now because they had been separated for two long, lonely weeks. He was wearing typical wrangler gear, the black felt hat drawn low across his eyes, the sun making sharp divisions between shadow and light on his angular features. The sleeves of his red plaid shirt were carelessly rolled up on his sun-darkened forearms, and he rode with the easy grace of having been born to a horse and saddle. The smile he gave her quickened her already pounding heart as she pulled Smokey to a halt, dismounting.

Jim slid from the saddle, landing lightly on both feet, and opened his arms to welcome Dal into them. With a cry, she threw her arms around his neck, pressing herself against him. He groaned, burying his face in the silken fragrance of her hair, inhaling her scent, holding her roughly to him.

"Oh, Jim," she whispered, hugging him, "I didn't expect you back so soon."

He tilted her smiling face upward, drinking in the joy that rested in her gold-flecked eyes. "Come here," he growled, "I've missed you so much...." He slanted his mouth demandingly across her full, yielding lips. She tasted of sunlight and a meadow flower sweetness. She was all soft, womanly curves in his arms as he pressed her to him. "I'm starved for you," he said in a low, vibrating voice against her wet, velvety lips.

Dal moaned softly as she pressed her lips to his strong mouth, reveling in his masculinity and his gentleness. He kissed her long and hard, but controlled the amount of pressure he placed against her. In the months since she'd met him, Dal had been led into a realm where she was taught that a man could be just as strong as the situation demanded, but also, just as tender as the feelings that were blossoming in her heart for him. A shadow of regret came to her eyes as Jim dragged his mouth from hers. She rested against him, wildly aware of his hardened arousal where their hips met and melded.

"I just happen to have packed a picnic lunch if you're hungry," she teased, running her fingers up across his chest.

Smiling, Jim released her, although he still kept one arm around her waist. "I'm starved for one thing, and that's you, my woman."

She colored prettily beneath his husky compliment, feeling cherished and utterly loved. "Well, if you don't eat the chicken sandwich, Nar will."

Jim lifted his head, watching as the golden eagle slowly glided across the valley toward them. "That bird is a pig with wings," he complained good-naturedly, leading her to a small grove of pine nearby. "I'll eat the sandwich. It will do him good to go hunt for his own game instead of mooching off you for once."

Dal laughed, took the saddlebags off the horse and brought them with her to the shade of the pine. Nar called shrilly, gracefully alighting on a branch only a few feet above where they sat down. He cocked his head, his amber eyes on the saddlebag that Dal was opening.

"Go hunt, Big Bird," Jim told him, grinning over at Dal. God, she looked beautiful, he thought. He reached out, lightly touching her spice-colored hair, which had taken on red and gold tones through the summer. She raised her head, meeting his smile, and handed him a sandwich.

Nar chut-chut-chutted as Jim bit into the thick, juicy portion. The eagle moved from one end of the branch to the other, making it bend dangerously with his weight. Dal laughed, moving to one side to watch the raptor's antics.

"He wants your sandwich, Jim."

"He's not getting it," he growled, keeping one eye on the eagle.

Nar sprang from the branch, dropping like a rock to the pine-needled ground, his wings causing a flurry of wind around them. Jim stared in disbelief as the eagle gingerly lumbered over to him, his wings half-open, and scolded him with twits and chuts.

Dal stifled a giggle, resting her back against the tree, watching Nar trying to beg a piece of Jim's sandwich from him. The eagle was three feet tall and stood eyeball to eyeball with Jim in his sitting position.

"This isn't funny," Jim said, ever watchful of the raptor, transferring the sandwich to his left hand away from the amber-eyed beggar.

"I think it is. Come on, don't be so hard-hearted. Nar's being nice about this. He could have gotten angry and landed on your head, tearing it out of your hand. Instead, he's being a real gentleman about it and asking you nicely."

"A threat is a threat," Jim muttered, holding the eagle's expectant gaze. "I don't care if he asks nicely or not. He knows I'm afraid of him. He's just pushing his weight around."

Her laughter got the best of her and Dal held her

sides. She saw Jim raise one eyebrow, and his look sent her into another fit of laughter. "You two," she choked out, "are so much alike. Both male, both pushy on occasion, and both of you think you're so wonderful that we can't turn you down."

A grudging grin broke on Jim's features. "So, that's how you see me?"

She wiped the tears from her eyes and wrapped her arms around her drawn-up knees. "Since when have I ever told you 'no' to anything you asked of me?"

Jim shrugged, trying to look properly chastened. "Well...none that I can think of...."

"Ever since you got out of the hospital, I've been down in Denver more than here on the ranch."

He slid her a warm glance. "Any regrets?"

Dal shook her head, a dreamy look coming to her half-closed eyes. "None."

Jim glared at the eagle which was only a foot away from him now, giving him the Mexican standoff routine. "What's he going to do if I don't give him the rest of my sandwich?"

"Ever seen an eagle have a temper tantrum?"

"That's not even funny, Dal, so quit laughing."

"You've seen him when he misses a quarry."

Jim's mouth turned downward and he glanced first at his sandwich and then up the eagle. "Yeah, he gets really angry and goes around dive-bombing the chickens and Goodyear."

She stifled another giggle. "He'll probably dive-bomb you if you don't at least give him some of it."

"How much is some? I haven't eaten all day. I just flew in, picked up some clothes from the house and came out here."

"Give him at least half if you want him to be happy."

"Half? Why that fat, overfed—"

Nar tilted his head, making scolding sounds, and opened his wings, taking another step toward Jim.

Jim drew back, distrust evident in every feature of his face. "You're getting away with murder, Nar," he growled in disgust, throwing the rest of his sandwich at the feet of the eagle and getting up.

Nar cocked his head as Jim rose and walked over to where Dal was sitting. Then the bird looked down at the sandwich, delicately picking it up in one foot to disassemble it over the ground. Daintily, he picked up the scraps of chicken, making pleased sounds as he gulped them down.

Dal snuggled under Jim's arm as he sat down with her, smiling. "Boy, your feathers are bent out of shape, aren't they?"

He grudgingly nodded. "Nar knows I'm wary of him," he muttered, holding her close. "And he takes advantage of that knowledge."

"Want part of my sandwich?" she teased, holding it up under his nose.

"Sure. Thanks."

Dal watched as the two males in her life satisfied themselves on the chicken sandwiches, a smile playing on her lips. The warm, dry autumn breeze lifted strands of her hair and then settled them back on her shoulders. Gradually, the laziness of the early afternoon filtered around them and she tipped her head back, content to lie on Jim's broad shoulder.

"How did it go in Washington?" she wanted to know.

"Good," he murmured, wiping his mouth with the napkin. "The Royal Canadian Mounted Police caught up with the other poachers who were linked with the U.S. ring. Twenty people were involved."

"What's next," Dal asked, barely opening her eyes. "The trial?"

"Yes. Government lawyers from both Canada and the U.S. are working jointly on presenting the case. I talked to one and he said the poachers will all get prison sentences if they're convicted. Canada's tough on them. The U.S. may give the Americans a lighter sentence." His embrace tightened slightly. "And with Gordon trying to kill us, he and his men are up on other, more serious charges."

Dal sat up, worry in her eyes as she turned to Jim. "And that means testifying before a jury, doesn't it?"

He reached over, caressing the velvet slope of her now tanned, golden cheek. "Yes. But I'll be there, Dal."

Closing her eyes, she nuzzled his callused palm. "I keep trying to get Jack out of my life and out of my mind, Jim. And like a bad penny, he keeps coming back. That part of my life is a closed chapter." Frustration laced her soft voice. "I'm happy now, with you, and with what we share. I never thought this kind of happiness was obtainable or even existed."

Jim cradled her face between his hands. "After the trial, you won't have anything more to do with Gordon," he promised her quietly, searching her eyes. His gaze grew tender. "Come on. I've got a surprise for you."

"A surprise?"

He got to his feet, holding out his hand to her. "Yes. Come on, it's a good surprise, honey."

Nar flew ahead of them, sweeping down like a dive-bomber between the ranch house and barns, scattering the squawking chickens in fifty different directions. Millie was out hanging clothes when Nar swooped by on his way toward the coop. With a shout, she ran for an old broom she always kept handy for just such emergencies. As Dal and Jim rounded the barn, Goodyear streaked by as fast as his twenty pounds of blubber would carry him, with Nar in hot pursuit.

Dal saw Millie chasing the eagle, waving her broom, hollering at the top of her lungs at him. Goodyear squalled like a scalded cat, making a beeline for the open chicken coop door. Feathers flew.

Goodyear got going so fast that he was unable to keep his feet under him and rolled, like a rubber ball, right through the coop door. Nar swept up sharply and landed on top of the coop, shrilling triumphantly and mantling his wings. Millie stood below, calling the eagle every name in the book and a few more to boot, waving her broom above her head. Nar ruffled his feathers and then folded his wings, calmly eyeing the squawking chickens and Millie. He chirped loudly as Dal and Jim rode up, as if to ask why everyone was so upset.

Millie turned, her eyes blazing. "I swear, Dal! That bird of yours is chasing Goodyear on purpose! You ought to make him stop it!"

Dal had the wisdom not to smile and shot a glance at Jim. He was trying to hide a smile, too. She dismounted with Jim and they stood looking up at the roof where Nar sat with a smug look on his feathered face.

"I'll try to get him to come down and follow me to the garage, Millie. I think he's hungry."

"Humph! Look at poor Goodyear!" she said, pointing as the yellow and white cat poked his head cautiously out of the coop door. Just at that moment, the rooster, who had had the good sense to hide when the eagle first flew over, decided to let the cat know that he was trespassing on his territory. The big red rooster landed on Goodyear's back. The cat squalled, leaped a foot out the coop door and shot back into the yard like a fired cannonball.

Jim broke into gales of laughter. Dal couldn't hold her smile in any longer and she, too, turned away, her laughter silvery. Millie glared at them both imperiously, her hands on her hips.

"How would you like to be in Goodyear's place? Chased by an eagle and then landed on by that no-account rooster?"

Jim wiped the tears from his eyes. "I'd say he needed to lose a little weight. Nar's just helping him stay away from the fat farm, that's all."

Dal groaned and led her horse back toward the barn, knowing that Millie wasn't going to take kindly to Jim's comment. She loved that cat of hers and spoiled it by overfeeding it. Jim joined Dal, still grinning.

"I don't think I'll be welcome to stay for dinner tonight," he said with a chuckle.

"Yeah, if you do stay, you'd better watch that Millie doesn't poison your food."

They unsaddled their horses, brushed them down and then put them into their individual stalls. Jim removed his hat as they walked out toward the front of the ranch house. "Now, you have to close your eyes. I'll lead you to the Blazer from here." He smiled down at her. "Trust me?"

Dal sobered. "With my life. Okay, my eyes are closed."

"Sure? This has to be a surprise."

Anxiously, Dal gripped his hand as he carefully led

her around the side of the house to the gravel drive-way. "What is it, Jim? You never said anything about any surprises when you left for Washington. Oh, tell me! What is it?"

He gave her a patient smile, swept up in her childlike enthusiasm. He brought her to a halt at the back of the Blazer. "Let's just say I've been planning this surprise for quite a while," he told her enigmatically, lifting up the hatch door of the Blazer. "All right, hold out both your hands in front of you...."

Odd noises were coming from the truck, but Dal was unable to distinguish what they were. She did as Jim asked, holding out her hands. The instant a warm, wriggling mass of fur was placed in her hands, she opened her eyes and gasped. She was holding a puppy that could only be described as a miniature copy of Raider. Dal looked up, her eyes luminous with tears. Jim had sat on the bumper and was holding a second wriggling puppy that was licking his hand. He smiled up at her.

"Come on, sit down with me," he urged.

Dal sat, completely taken with her puppy. The little gray ball of fur had two amber button eyes and it whined, wriggling its small tail and avidly licking Dal's fingers. "Oh, Jim! They're beautiful!"

He slid his one arm around her shoulder and allowed the puppies to play happily on their laps. "Do you like them? I know you didn't have a chance to know Raider for long, but he was taken with you. Like I was." He shared a tender smile with her, noticing tears streaking down her flushed cheeks as she held the puppy with a pink ribbon around its neck. His throat constricted, but he went on. "I contacted my friend up in Anchorage in

June and told him what had happened. He had a wolf bitch who was pregnant by his malamute sled dog and asked if I wanted one of the puppies when they were born. I said yes, I wanted two." He hesitated, his heart beginning a slow, agonizing pounding in his chest.

The half-wolf puppy licked Dal's face, whined happily and wriggled. "Why two, Jim?"

He avoided her searching blue eyes, his mouth growing dry. And then, gathering his courage, he said in a low voice, "I wanted one for each of us. You and the animals share a common spirit. I saw that first between you and Nar. And then Raider fell under your spell." He managed a slight smile, gently wrestling with his puppy which had a blue ribbon tied around its neck. And then he looked up, meeting her luminous gaze. "And I think I fell under your spell many years ago, Dal. I never forgot you. And I love you even more now that you've allowed me to share your life." He ruffled the male puppy's fur. "I flew up to Alaska to bring the puppies back, Dal. I was in Washington until three days ago. One's a female. She's for you. And this one's a male, for me." He held her tender gaze. "You told me once how much you loved babies of all kinds…. Well, I thought you might want to practice on these two until we have some of our own." His gaze wavered and he swallowed hard. "What do you think?"

Touched beyond words, Dal placed her puppy on the floor of the Blazer and slid her arms around Jim's neck. She saw the uncertainty in the depths of his honey-colored eyes. They had spent all summer and early fall getting to know each other better. Often, she had spent weekends at his house where they would hike, fish or simply share each other's company. And it had all been sheer heaven. She rested her brow against his, their lips barely touching. "I think it's a wonderful idea, darling."

Jim stared at her, as if not believing his ears. His hands tightened on her shoulders. "Keeping the puppy, or marrying me?" he asked hoarsely.

Dal laughed softly, hugging him hard. "Both," she murmured, kissing his sandpapery cheek and nuzzling her face into the thickness of his black hair. "I love you so much, Jim...so much...."

Tears squeezed from beneath his tightly shut eyes as he crushed Dal to him. A soaring joy moved through him with such fierceness that it took his breath away. He had wanted her for so long and had known that it could be right between them. "I love you," he told her thickly, smothering her eyes, nose and lips with kisses. "You're mine...you've always been mine, my woman."

Dal sobbed and held Jim tightly, vaguely aware that both puppies had climbed back into their laps to play. She eased away, realizing his cheeks were damp with spent tears, and her hands automatically moved to dry them. And then her anguish fled when she realized they were tears of joy, and she reached over, kissing away the dampness beneath her lips. "You're an eagle," she told him softly, resting her cheek against his, "one mate for a lifetime."

Jim claimed her lips gently, tasting the salt upon them. His amber eyes burned with the joy and knowledge that she was going to be his partner for the rest of their lives. Tenderly, he framed her face between his long, tapered fingers. "We've both got the heart of an eagle...the courage to face whatever odds are thrown in our path and to surmount them regardless of how frightened we become. And we'll face our future together the same way, honey. You and I. We're one. Forever…"

* * * * *

Joan Johnston is the *New York Times* and *USA TODAY* bestselling author of more than fifty novels with more than fifteen million copies of her books in print. She has been a director of theater, drama critic, newspaper editor, college professor and attorney on her way to becoming a full-time writer. You can find out more about Joan at joanjohnston.com or on Facebook at Joan Johnston Author.

Books by Joan Johnston

Hawk's Way: Jesse
Hawk's Way: Adam
Hawk's Way: Faron
Hawk's Way: Garth
Hawk's Way: Carter
Hawk's Way: Falcon
Hawk's Way: Zach
Hawk's Way: Billy
Hawk's Way: Mac
Hawk's Way: Colt

Visit the Author Profile page
at Harlequin.com for more titles.

HAWK'S WAY: ADAM

Joan Johnston

Chapter 1

"May I kiss you good night, Tate?"

"Of course you can, Hank."

"Your brothers—"

"Forget about them! I'm a grown woman. I certainly don't need permission from Faron or Garth to give you a simple little good-night kiss." Tate Whitelaw stepped closer to the tall cowboy and slipped her arms around his neck. The bright light over the front door didn't quite reach to the corner of the railed porch where she was standing with Hank.

Hank took advantage of Tate's invitation, drawing her into his arms behind one of the massive fluted columns that graced the front of the house and aligning their bodies from breast to hip. She was uncomfortably aware of his arousal, since only two layers of denim—her jeans and his—separated their warm flesh.

His mouth sought hers, and his tongue thrust inside. It was more than a simple good-night kiss, and Tate suddenly found herself wishing she hadn't been quite so encouraging.

"Hank—" she gasped, pulling her head back and trying to escape his ardor. "I don't think—"

Hank's arms tightened around her, and Tate found herself in a wrestling match. She struggled to get the heels of her hands to his shoulders to push him away. He gripped her short black hair with one hand and angled her face for his kiss.

"Hank! S-stop it!" she hissed.

Caught up in his lust, Hank was oblivious to Tate's urgently whispered entreaties. Tate had already decided it was time to take desperate action when the issue was taken out of her hands. Literally.

Tate knew someone had arrived on the scene when Hank gave a grunt of surprise as he was jerked away from her. Her brother Faron had a handful of Hank's Western shirt in his grasp and was holding the young man at arm's length.

"What the hell do you think you're doing with my sister?" Faron demanded.

Hank blinked owlishly. "Kissing her?"

"Who the hell gave you permission to kiss her?"

"I did!" Tate said through gritted teeth. Fisted hands on hips, chin up, she faced her brother defiantly. "Who gave *you* permission to interfere!"

"When I see my kid sister getting mauled—"

"I can take care of myself!"

Faron arched a brow, and Tate knew it was because she hadn't denied the fact she was being mauled. Hank had just been a little exuberant, that was all. She could have escaped her predicament without her brother's interference.

To Tate's horror, Garth shoved open the front screen door and asked, "What in blue blazes is going on out here?"

"I found this coyote forcing his attentions on Tate," Faron said.

Garth stepped onto the porch, and if the sheer size of him didn't intimidate, the fierce scowl on his face surely would have. "That true?" Garth demanded of Hank.

Hank gulped. Perspiration dripped at his temple. The color left his face. "Well, sir..." He looked to Tate for rescue.

Tate watched Garth's lips flatten into a grim line as he exchanged a decisive look with Faron. Hank had been tried and convicted. All that was left was sentencing.

"Get your butt out of here," Garth said to Hank. "And don't come back."

Faron gave Hank a pretty good shove in the right direction, and Garth's boot finished the job. Hank stumbled down the porch steps to his pickup, dragged open the door, gunned the engine and departed in a swirl of gravel and choking dust.

There was a moment of awful silence while the dust settled. Tate fought the tears that threatened. She would *never* let her brothers know how humiliated she felt! But there was nothing wrong with giving them the lash of her tongue. She turned and stared first into Garth's stern, deep brown eyes, and then into Faron's more concerned gray-green ones.

"I hope you're both happy!" she snapped. "That's the fourth man in a month you've run off the ranch."

"Now, Tate," Faron began. "Any man who won't stand up to the two of us isn't worth having for a beau."

"Don't patronize me!" she raged. "I won't be placated like a baby with a rattle. I'm not three. I'm not even thirteen. I'm twenty-three. I'm a woman, and I have a woman's needs."

"You don't need to be manhandled," Garth said. "And I won't stand by and let it happen."

"Me neither," Faron said.

Tate hung her head. When she raised it again, her eyes were glistening with tears that blurred her vision. "I could have handled Hank myself," she said in a quiet voice. "You have to trust me to make my own decisions, my own mistakes."

"We don't want to see you hurt," Faron said, laying a hand on Tate's shoulder.

Tate stiffened. "And you think I wasn't hurt by what happened here tonight?"

Garth and Faron exchanged another look. Then Faron said, "Maybe your pride was pricked a little, but—"

"A *little!*" Tate jerked herself from Faron's grasp. "You're impossible! Both of you! You don't know the first thing about what I want or need. You can't imagine what it's like to have every step you take watched to make sure you don't fall down. Maybe it made sense when I was a baby, but I'm grown-up now. I don't need you standing guard over me."

"Like you didn't need our help tonight?" Garth asked in a cold voice.

"I didn't!" Tate insisted.

Garth grabbed her chin and forced her face up to his. "You have no idea what a man's passions can lead him to do, little sister. I have no intention of letting you find out. Until the right man comes along—"

"There's no man who'll come within a hundred miles of this place now," Tate retorted bitterly. "My loving brothers have seen to that! You're going to keep me a virgin until I dry up and—"

Garth's fingers tightened painfully on her jaw, forcing her to silence. She saw the flash of fury in his dark eyes. A muscle flexed in his jaw. At last he said, "You'd better go to your room and think about what happened here tonight. We'll talk more about this tomorrow."

"You're not my father!" Tate spat. "I won't be sent to my room like a naughty child!"

"You'll go, or I'll take you there," Garth threatened.

"She can't go anywhere until you let go of her chin," Faron pointed out.

Garth shot a rueful look at his brother, then released Tate. "Good night, Tate," he said.

Tate had learned there were only two sides to Garth's arguments: his and the wrong one. Her stomach was churning. Her chest felt so tight it was hard to breathe, and her throat had a lump in it that made swallowing painful. Her eyes burned with tears that she would be *damned* if she'd shed!

She looked from Garth to Faron and back again. Garth's face was a granite mask of disapproval, while Faron's bore a look of sympathetic understanding. Tate knew they loved her. It was hard to fight their good intentions. Yet their love was smothering her. They would not let her *live!*

Her mother had died when she was born, and she had been raised by her father and her three brothers, Garth, Faron and Jesse. Their father had died when Tate was eight. Jesse had left home then, and Garth and Faron had been responsible for her ever since. It was a responsibility they had taken very seriously. She had been kept cloistered at Hawk's Way, more closely guarded than a novice in a convent. If she went anywhere off the ranch, one of her brothers came along.

When Tate was younger she'd had girlfriends to share her troubles with. As she got older, she discovered that the females she met were more interested in getting an introduction to her brothers than in being her friend. Eventually, she had simply stopped inviting them.

Tate hadn't even been allowed to go away to college. Instead she had taken correspondence courses to get her degree in business. She had missed the social interaction with her peers, the experience of being out on her own, that would have prepared her to deal with the Hanks of the world.

However, Garth and Faron had taught her every job that had to be done on a ranch, from branding and castrating to vaccinating and breeding. She wasn't naive. No one could be raised on a ranch and remain totally innocent. She had seen the quarter horse stallions they raised at Hawk's Way mount mares. But she could not translate that violent act into what happened between a man and a woman in bed.

So far, she had found the fumbling kisses of her swains more annoying than anything else. Yet Tate had read enough to know there was more to the male-female relationship than she had experienced so far. If her brothers had their way, she would never unravel the mysteries of love.

She had come to the dire conclusion over the past few

months that no man would ever pass muster with her brothers. If she continued living with them, she would die an old maid. They had given her no choice. In order to escape her brothers' overprotectiveness, she would have to leave Hawk's Way.

This latest incident was the final straw. But then, kicking a man when he's down is sometimes the only way to make him get up. Tate took one long, last look at each of her brothers. She would be gone from Hawk's Way before morning.

When the front door closed behind Tate, Faron settled a hip on the porch rail, and Garth leaned his shoulder against the doorjamb.

"She's too damn beautiful for her own good," Garth muttered.

"Hard to believe a woman can look so sexy in a man's T-shirt and a pair of jeans," Faron agreed with a shake of his head.

Garth's eyes were bleak. "What're we going to do about her?"

"Don't know that there's anything we can do except what we're already doing."

"I don't want to see her get hurt," Garth said.

Faron felt a tightness in his chest. "Yeah, I know. But she's all grown up, Garth. We're going to have to let go sometime."

Garth frowned. "Not yet."

"When?"

"I don't know. Just not yet."

The next morning, Garth and Faron met in the kitchen, as they always did, just before dawn. Charlie One Horse, the part-Indian codger who had been chief cook and bottle washer at Hawk's Way since their mother had died, had coffee perking and breakfast on the table. Only this morning there was something—someone—missing.

"Where's Tate?" Garth asked as he sat down at the head of the table.

"Ain't seen her," Charlie said.

Garth grimaced. "I suppose she's sulking in her room."

"You drink your coffee, and I'll go upstairs and check on her," Faron offered.

A moment later Faron came bounding into the kitchen. "She's not there! She's gone!"

Garth sprang up from his chair so fast it fell over backward. "What? Gone where?"

Faron grabbed Garth by the shoulders and said in a fierce voice, "She's not in her room. Her bed hasn't been slept in!"

Garth freed himself and took the stairs two at a time to see for himself. Sure enough, the antique brass double bed was made up with its nubby-weave spread. That alone was an ominous sign. Tate wasn't known for her neatness, and if she had made up the bed, she had done it to make a statement.

Garth headed for the closet, his heart in his throat. He heaved a sigh of relief when he saw Tate's few dresses still hanging there. Surely she wouldn't have left Hawk's Way for good without them.

Garth turned and found Faron standing in the doorway to Tate's room. "She probably spent the night sleeping out somewhere on the ranch. She'll turn up when she gets hungry."

"I'm going looking for her," Faron said.

Garth shoved a hand through his hair, making it

stand on end. "Hell and the devil! I guess there'll be no peace around here until we find her. When I get hold of her, I'll—"

"When we find her, I'll do the talking," Faron said. "You've caused enough trouble."

"Me? This isn't my fault!"

"Like hell! You're the one who told her to go to her room and stay there."

"Looks like she didn't pay a whole helluva lot of attention to me, did she?" Garth retorted.

At that moment Charlie arrived, puffing from exertion, and said, "You two gonna go look for that girl, or stand here arguin'?"

Faron and Garth glared at each other for another moment before Faron turned and pressed his way past Charlie and down the stairs.

Charlie put a hand out to stop Garth. "Don't think you're gonna find her, boy. Knew this was bound to happen sooner or later."

"What do you mean, old man?"

"Knew you had too tight a rein on that little filly. Figured she had too much spirit to stay in them fences you set up to hold her in."

"It was for her own good!"

Charlie shook his head. "Did it as much for yourself as for her. Knowin' your ma like you did, it's no wonder you'd want to keep your sister close. Prob'ly fearful she'd take after your ma, steppin' out on your pa like she did and—"

"Leave Mother out of this. What she did has nothing to do with the way I've treated Tate."

Charlie tightened the beaded rawhide thong that held one of his long braids, but said nothing.

Garth scowled. "I can see there's no sense arguing with a stone wall. I'm going after Tate, and I'm going to bring her back. This time she'll stay put!"

Garth and Faron searched canyons and mesas, ridges and gullies on their northwest Texas ranch, but not a sign did they find of their sister on Hawk's Way.

It was Charlie One Horse who discovered that the old '51 Chevy pickup, the one with the rusty radiator and the skipping carburetor, was missing from the barn where it was stored.

Another check of Tate's room revealed that her underwear drawer was empty, that her brush and comb and toothpaste were gone, and that several of her favorite T-shirts and jeans had also been packed.

By sunset, the truth could not be denied. At the age of twenty-three, Tate Whitelaw had run away from home.

Chapter 2

Adam Philips normally didn't stop to pick up hitchhikers. But there was no way he could drive past the woman sitting on the front fender of a '51 Chevy pickup, its hood raised and its radiator steaming, her thumb outstretched to bum a ride. He pulled his late-model truck up behind her and put on his Stetson as he stepped out into the heat of a south Texas midsummer afternoon.

She was wearing form-fitting jeans and an off-the-shoulder peasant blouse that exposed a lush female figure. But the heart-shaped face, with its huge hazel eyes and wide mouth framed by breeze-ruffled, short-cropped black hair, was innocence itself. He was stunned by her beauty and appalled at her youth. What was this female doing all alone on an isolated stretch of southwest Texas highway in an old rattletrap truck?

She beamed a trusting smile at him, and he felt his

heart do a flipflop. She slipped off the rusty fender and lazily sauntered toward him. He felt his groin tighten with desire and scowled. She stopped in her tracks. About time she thought to be wary! Adam was all too conscious of the dangers a stranger presented to a young woman alone. Grim-lipped, he strode the short distance between the two vehicles.

Tate had been so relieved to see *someone* show up on the deserted rural route that the danger of the situation didn't immediately occur to her. She got only a glimpse of wavy blond hair and striking blue eyes before her rescuer had slipped on a Stetson that put his face in shadow.

He was broad-shouldered and lean-hipped, with a stride that ate up the distance between the two trucks. It was a fair assumption, from his dusty boots, worn jeans and sweat-stained Western shirt, that he was a working cowboy. Tate saw no reason to suspect he meant her any harm.

But instead of a pleasant "May I help you?" the first words out of his mouth were, "What the hell do you think you're doing?"

Tate was alarmed by the animosity in the stranger's voice and frightened by the intensity of his stare. But his attitude was so similar to what she had recently gone through with her brothers that she lifted her chin and retorted, "Hitching a ride back to the nearest gas station. In case you hadn't noticed, my truck's broken down."

The scowl deepened but he said, "Get in my pickup."

Tate had only taken two steps when the tall cowboy grabbed her arm and pulled her up short.

"Aren't you going to ask anything about me? Don't you want to know who I am?"

By now Tate was more irritated than frightened. "A Good Samaritan with a bad temper!" she retorted. "Do I need to know more?"

Adam opened his mouth to make a retort, took one look at the mutinous expression on the young woman's face, and shut it again. Instead he dragged her unceremoniously to the passenger's side of his long-bed pickup, opened the door, shoved her inside, and slammed it closed after her.

"My bag! It's in the back end of the Chevy," Tate yelped.

Adam stalked back to the rattletrap Chevy, snagged the duffel bag from the rusted-out truck bed and slung it into the back of his pickup.

Woman was too damned trusting for her own good! he thought. Her acid tongue wouldn't have been much help to her if he had been the kind of villain who preyed on stranded women. Which he wasn't. Lucky for her!

Tate didn't consider herself at all lucky. She recognized the flat-lipped expression on her Good Samaritan's face. He might have rescued her, all right, but he wasn't happy about it. The deep crevices formed around his mouth by his frown and the webbed lines at the edges of his eyes had her guessing his age at thirty-five or thirty-six—the same as her eldest brother Garth. The last thing she needed was another keeper!

She sat back with her arms crossed and stared out the window as they drove past rolling prairie. She thought back to the night two weeks ago when she had decided to leave Hawk's Way.

Her escape from her brothers, while apparently sudden, hadn't been completely without direction. She had taken several ranch journals containing advertisements from outfits all over Texas looking for expert help and headed south. However, Tate soon discovered that not one rancher was interested in hiring a woman, especially one without references, as either foreman or ranch manager.

To confound her problems, the ancient pickup she had taken from the barn was in worse shape than she had thought. It had left her stranded miles from the Lazy S—the last ranch on her list and her last hope for a job in ranch management.

"Do you know where the Lazy S is?" she asked.

Adam started at the sound of her voice. "I expect I could find it. Why?"

"I understand they're looking for a ranch manager. I intend to apply for the job."

"You're just a kid!"

The cowboy could have said nothing more likely to raise Tate's neck hairs. "For your information, I'm twenty-three and a fully grown woman!"

Adam couldn't argue with that. He had a pretty good view of the creamy rise of her breasts at the frilly gathered edge of her blouse. "What do you know about ranching?" he asked.

"I was raised on a ranch, Hawk's Way, and—" She stopped abruptly, realizing that she had revealed more than she had intended to this stranger. Tate hadn't used her own last name to apply for any jobs, knowing that if she did her brothers would be able to hunt her down and drag her back home. "I hope you'll keep that to yourself," she said.

Adam raised an inquiring brow that met such a gamine smile that his heart did that disturbing flipflop again.

"You see," Tate said, "the truth is, I've run away from home."

Adam snorted. "Aren't you a little old for that?"

Tate's lips curled ruefully. "I suppose so. But my brothers just wouldn't let me *live!* I mean, they watched every breath in and out of my body."

Adam found the thought rather intriguing himself.

"My brothers are a little overprotective, you see. I had to run away if I was ever going to meet the right man and fall in love and have children."

"Sounds like you could do that better at home than traipsing around the countryside," Adam observed.

"You don't know my older brothers! They want to wrap me in cotton batting and keep me safe. Safe, ha! What they mean is, they want to keep me a virgin forever."

Adam choked at this unbelievable revelation and coughed to clear his throat.

"It's true! They've chased away every single beau I've ever had. Which is only a waste of time and energy because, you know, a man who's born to drown can manage to drown in a desert."

Adam eyed her askance.

"I mean, if something is destined to happen, it'll happen no matter what."

Tate waited for Adam to say something, but when he remained silent, she continued, "My older brother, Jesse, left home, too, when I was just eight. It was right after my father died. We haven't seen him for years and years. I don't plan to stay away for years, of course, but then, who knows how long it will take to find my Prince Charming. Not that I have to marry a prince of a man."

Tate grinned and shrugged. "But it would be nice,

you know, to just once kiss a man good night, without having my brothers send him packing because he's not good enough for me."

Tate realized she was talking to fill the silence and forced herself to shut up.

Behind the young woman's bravado Adam saw the desperation that had sent her fleeing from the safe haven her brothers had provided for her. He felt sick inside. Was this the way his younger sister had felt? Had Melanie seen him as an oppressive tyrant, the same way this young woman perceived her brothers?

Tate held her breath as the stranger looked into her eyes. There was an awful sadness there she felt constrained to dispel. So she began talking again.

"I've been looking everywhere for a job," she said. "I must have been to fifteen different spreads in the past two weeks. But I haven't had so much as a nibble of interest.

"What I find so frustrating is the fact that most owners don't treat me seriously. I mean, I know I'm young, but there isn't anything I don't know about running a ranch."

"Do you know how to figure the amount of feed you need for each head of stock?" Adam asked.

"Depends on whether you plan to keep the stock penned or let it graze," Tate said. "Now if it's penned—"

Adam interrupted with, "Give me some symptoms of colic."

"A horse might have colic if he won't eat, or if he starts pawing, or gets up and down a lot. Generally an animal that can't get comfortable has a problem."

"Can you keep books on a computer?"

Tate snorted inelegantly. "Boy can I ever! I got stuck

with all the bookkeeping at Hawk's Way. So, if you were hiring at the Lazy S, would I get the job?"

"What will you do if you *don't* get the job?" Adam asked instead.

Tate shrugged, not realizing how revealing the gesture was of the fact she wasn't the least bit nonchalant about that distressing possibility. "I don't know. I only know I *won't* go back home."

"And if your brothers find you?"

Her chin took on a mulish tilt. "I'll just run away again."

Adam wondered if his sister was so forthright and disarmingly honest with the man who had picked her up the night she ran away from home. Had that stranger known all about the young woman he had raped and murdered and left lying in a ditch on the side of the road?

Adam's teeth clenched in determination. If he had anything to say about it, the innocent young woman in his pickup would not become another such statistic. And he, of all people, was in a perfect position to help her. Because he owned the Lazy S Ranch.

However, in the months since Adam had put his advertisement in the ranch journal, he had changed his mind about needing a foreman. He had decided to place his country medical practice on hold and put the Lazy S Ranch back in the black himself.

But if he told this young woman he had no job for her, where would she go? What would she do? And how would he feel if he sent her away and she ended up dead somewhere on the side of the road?

"Say, there's the Lazy S Ranch!" Tate pointed at a wrought-iron sign that bridged a dirt road off the main thoroughfare. To her surprise, the cowboy turned and drove across a cattle guard onto the Lazy S.

"I thought you were going to take me into town!" she said.

"I thought you wanted to interview for a job!" he retorted.

Tate eyed the cowboy. She was perplexed. Many western men were the strong, silent type, but the stranger who had picked her up was something more. Aloof. The more distant he was, the more intrigued she became. It was a surprise to find out he had been kind enough to take her directly to the Lazy S.

She could have kicked herself for telling him so much personal information without finding out anything about him—not even his name. When he dropped her off, she might never see him again. Tate suddenly realized she wanted to see him again. Very much.

As the cowboy stopped his pickup in front of an impressive adobe ranch house, she said, "I can't tell you how much I appreciate your giving me a ride here. I'd like to thank you, but I don't even know your name!"

Adam turned to look at her and felt a tightening in his gut as she smiled up at him. Well, it was now or never. "My name is Adam Philips," he said. "I own the Lazy S. Come on inside, and you can interview for that job."

Chapter 3

Tate was stunned when the mysterious cowboy revealed his identity, but buoyant with hope, as well. She scrambled out of the pickup after Adam, certain that he wouldn't have bothered bringing her here if he didn't intend to at least consider her for the job of ranch foreman.

"Follow me," he said, heading into the house.

Tate stopped only long enough to grab her duffel bag and sling it over her shoulder before scampering up the three steps after him.

Adam's living room was masculine through and through, filled with massive Spanish furniture of natural leather studded with brass. There was not another frill or a furbelow to soften the room. *No woman has lived here in a long time—if ever,* Tate decided.

She discovered that the adobe hacienda formed a U shape. The two wings enclosed a garden shaded by immense moss-laden live oaks and bright with blooming bougainvillea. A central tile fountain splashed with cascading water.

They finally arrived at Adam's office, which was located at the tip of one wing of the house. The thick adobe walls and the barrel-tile roof kept the inside of the house dark and cool, reminiscent of days gone by when everyone took an afternoon siesta.

Tate saw from the immaculate condition of the office that Adam must be an organized person. Everything had a place and everything was in its place. Tate felt her heart sink. She wasn't averse to order, she just refused to be bound by it. That had been one small rebellion she was capable of in the space in which her brothers confined her.

Instead of sitting on the leather chair in front of the desk, she seated herself on a corner of the antique oak desk itself. Adam refused to sit at all, instead pacing the room like a caged tiger.

"Before we go any further, I want to know your real name," he said.

Tate frowned. "I need a promise from you first that you won't contact my brothers."

Adam stopped pacing and stared at her.

Tate stared right back.

"All right," he said. "You've got it."

Tate took a deep breath and said, "My last name is Whitelaw."

Adam swore under his breath and began pacing again. The Whitelaws were known all over Texas for the excellent quarter horses they bred and trained. He had once met Garth Whitelaw at a quarter horse sale. And he was intimately acquainted with Jesse Whitelaw.

Tate's brother Jesse, the one she hadn't seen in years, had recently married Honey Farrell—the woman Adam loved.

Honey's ranch, the Flying Diamond, bordered the Lazy S. Fortunately, with the strained relations between Adam and Jesse Whitelaw, Tate's brother wasn't likely to be visiting the Lazy S anytime soon.

Adam turned his attention to the young woman he had rescued from the side of the road. Her short black hair was windblown around her face, and her cheeks were flushed with excitement. She was gnawing worriedly on her lower lip—something he thought he might like to do himself.

Adam felt that telltale tightening in his groin. He tucked his thumbs into his jeans to keep from reaching out to touch her.

Tate crossed her legs and clutched her knee with laced fingers. She could feel the tension in Adam. A muscle worked in his jaw, and his expression was forbidding. A shiver ran down her spine. But it wasn't fear she felt, it was anticipation.

She was so nervous her voice cracked when she tried to speak. She cleared her throat and asked, "So, do I get the job?"

"I haven't made up my mind yet."

Tate was on her feet and at Adam's side in an instant. "I'd be good at it," she argued. "You wouldn't be sorry you hired me."

Adam had his doubts about that. His blood thrummed as he caught the faint scent of lilacs from her hair. He was already sorry he had stopped to pick her up. He couldn't be anywhere near her without feeling as randy as a teenager. That was a fine state of affairs when he had appointed himself her guardian in her brothers' stead. But he believed Tate when she had said she would just run away again if her brothers tried taking her home. Surely she would be better off here where he could keep a close eye on her.

He carefully stepped away from her and went around to sit behind his desk. Perhaps it would provide a more comfortable barrier between himself and the uncontrollable urges that struck him when he got within touching distance of this engaging runaway.

He steepled his fingers and said, "The job I have available isn't the same one that was advertised."

She braced her palms on the desk and leaned toward him. "Oh? Why not?"

Adam took one look at what her careless posture in the peasant blouse revealed and forced his gaze upward to her wide hazel eyes. "It's complicated."

"How?"

Why didn't she move? He had the irresistible urge to reach out and— He jumped up from behind his desk and started pacing again. "You'd have to know a little bit about what's happened on the Lazy S over the past couple of months."

Tate draped herself sideways across the chair in front of the desk, one leg swinging to release the tension, and said, "I'm listening."

"My previous ranch manager was a crook. He's in prison now, but besides stealing other people's cattle, he embezzled from me. He left my affairs in a mess. Originally, I'd intended to hire someone else to try to straighten things out. Lately I've decided to put my medical practice on hold—"

"Wait a minute!"

Tate sat up and her feet dropped to the floor, depriving Adam of the delicious view he'd had of her derriere.

"Do you mean to tell me you're a doctor?" she asked incredulously.

He shrugged sheepishly. "Afraid so. Over the past few months I've been transferring my practice to another physician who's moved into the area, Dr. Susan Kowalski. Now I have time to supervise the work on the Lazy S myself. What I really need is someone I can trust to organize the paperwork and do the bookkeeping."

Adam pointed to the computer on a stand near his desk. "That thing and I don't get along. I can't pay much," Adam admitted, "but the job includes room and board." That would keep her from sleeping in her truck, which was about all Adam suspected she could afford right now.

Tate wrinkled her nose. She had cut her teeth on the computer at Hawk's Way, and what she didn't know about bookkeeping hadn't been discovered. But it was the kind of work she liked least of everything she'd done at Hawk's Way. Still, a job was a job. And this was the best offer she had gotten.

"All right. I accept."

Tate stood and held a hand out to Adam to shake on the deal.

When Adam touched her flesh he was appalled by the electricity that streaked between them. He had suspected his attraction to Tate, all the while warning himself not to get involved. His powerful, instantaneous reaction to her still caught him by surprise. He blamed it on the fact that it had been too damn long since he'd had a woman. There were plenty who would willingly satisfy his needs, women who knew the score.

He absolutely, positively, was not going to get involved with a twenty-three-year-old virgin. Especially not some virgin who wanted a husband and a family. For Adam Philips wouldn't give her one—and couldn't give her the other.

Tate was astonished by the jolt she received simply from the clasp of Adam's hand. She looked up into his blue eyes and saw a flash of desire quickly banked. She jerked her hand away, said, "I'm sure we're both going to enjoy this relationship," then flushed at the more intimate interpretation that could be put on her words.

Adam's lips curled in a cynical smile. She was a lamb, all right, and a wily old wolf like himself would be smart to keep his distance. He didn't intend to tell her brothers where she was. But he was betting that sooner or later word of her presence on the Lazy S would leak out, and they would find her. When they did, all hell was going to break loose.

Adam shook his head when he thought of what he was getting himself into. Tate Whitelaw was Trouble with a capital *T.*

"Where do I bunk in?" Tate asked.

Adam dragged his Stetson off and ruffled his blond hair where the sweat had matted it down. He hadn't thought about where he would put her. His previous foreman had occupied a separate room at one end of the bunkhouse. That obviously wouldn't do for Tate.

"I suppose you'll have to stay here in the house," he said. "There's a guest bedroom in the other wing. Come along and I'll show you where it is."

He walked her back through the house, describing the layout of things as they went along. "My bedroom is next to the office. The living room, family room and kitchen are in the center of the house. The last bedroom down the hall on this other wing was set up for medical emergencies, and I haven't had time to refurnish it. The first bedroom on this wing will be your room."

Adam opened the door to a room that had a distinctively southwestern flavor. The furniture was antique Americana, with woven rugs on the floor, a rocker, a dry sink, a wardrobe and a large maple four-poster covered with a brightly patterned quilt. The room felt light and airy. That image was helped by the large sliding glass door that opened onto the courtyard.

Tate sat down on the bed and bounced a couple of times. "Feels plenty comfortable." She turned and smiled her thanks up at Adam.

The smile froze on her face.

His look was avid, his nostrils flared. She was suddenly aware of the softness of the bed. The fact that they were alone. And that she didn't know Adam Philips...from Adam.

However, the part of Tate that was alive to the danger of the situation was squelched by the part of her that was exhilarated to discover she could have such a profound effect on this man. Adam was quite unlike the men her brothers had so peremptorily ejected from Hawk's Way. In some way she could not explain, he was different. She knew instinctively that his kiss, his touch, would be unlike anything she had ever experienced.

Nor did she feel the same person when she was near him. With this man, she was different. She was no longer her brothers' little sister. She was a woman, with a woman's need to be loved by one special man.

Instead of scooting quickly off the bed, she stayed right where she was. She tried her feminine wings just a bit by languidly turning on her side and propping her head up with her hand. She pulled one leg up slightly, mimicking the sexy poses she had seen in some of her brothers' magazines—the ones they thought she knew nothing about.

Adam's reaction was everything she could have wished for. His whole body tautened. A vein in his temple throbbed. The muscles in his throat worked spasmodically. And something else happened. Something which, considering the level she was lying at, she couldn't help observing.

It was fascinating. She had never actually watched it happen to a man before. Mostly, the men she had dated were already in that condition before she had an opportunity to notice. The changing shape of Adam's Levi's left no doubt that he was becoming undeniably, indisputably, absolutely, completely *aroused*.

She gasped, and her eyes sought out his face to see what he intended to do about it.

Nothing! Adam thought. *He was going to do absolutely nothing about the fact this hoyden in blue jeans had him harder than a rock in ten seconds flat!*

"If you're done testing your feminine wiles, I'd like to finish showing you the house," Adam said.

Humiliated by the sarcasm in his voice, Tate quickly scooted off the bed. She had no trouble recognizing his feelings now. Irritation. Frustration. She felt the same things herself. She had never imagined how powerful desire could be. It was a lesson she wouldn't forget.

She stood before him, chin high, unwilling to admit blame or shame or regret for what she had done. "I'm ready."

Then strip down and get into that bed.

Adam clenched his teeth to keep from saying what he was thinking. He didn't know when he had felt such unbridled lust for a woman. It wasn't decent. But he damn sure wasn't going to do anything about it!

"Come on," he growled. "Follow me."

Tate followed Adam back through the house to the kitchen, where they found a short, rotund Mexican woman with snapping black eyes and round, rosy cheeks. She was chopping onions at the counter. Tate was treated to a smile that revealed two rows of brilliant white teeth.

"Who have you brought to meet me, Señor Adam?" the woman asked.

"Maria, this is Tate Whitelaw. She's going to be my new bookkeeper. Tate will be staying in the guest bedroom. Tate, I'd like you to meet my housekeeper, Maria Fuentes."

"Buenos días, Maria," Tate said.

"¡Habla usted español?" Maria asked.

"You've already heard all I know," Tate said with a self-deprecating grin.

Maria turned to Adam and said in Spanish, "She is very pretty, this one. And very young. Perhaps you would wish me to be her *dueña.*"

Adam flushed and answered in Spanish, "I'm well aware of her age, Maria. She doesn't need a chaperon around me."

The Mexican woman arched a disbelieving brow. Again in Spanish she said, "You are a man, Señor Adam. And her eyes, they smile at you. It would be hard for any man to refuse such an invitation. No?"

"No!" Adam retorted. Then added in Spanish, "I

mean, no I wouldn't take advantage of her. She has no idea what she's saying with her eyes."

Maria's disbelieving brow arched higher. "If you say so, Señor Adam."

Tate had been trying to follow the Spanish conversation, but the only words she recognized were "Maria," "chaperon," "Señor Adam" and "No." The look on Maria's face made it clear she disapproved of the fact Tate would be living in the house alone with Adam. Well, she didn't need a chaperon any more than she needed a keeper. She could take care of herself.

Fortunately, it wasn't necessary for her to interrupt the conversation. A knock at the kitchen door did it for her. The door opened before anyone could answer it, and a young cowhand stuck his head inside. He had brown eyes and auburn hair and a face so tanned it looked like rawhide.

"Adam? You're needed in the barn to take a look at that mare, Break of Day. She's having some trouble foaling."

"Sure. I'll be there in a minute, Buck."

Instead of leaving, the cowhand stood where he was, his eyes glued on the vision in a peasant blouse and skin-tight jeans standing in Adam's kitchen. He stepped inside the door, slipped his hat off his head, and said, "Name's Buck, ma'am."

Tate smiled and held out her hand. "Tate Wh—atly."

The cowboy shook her hand and then stood there foolishly grinning at her.

Adam groaned inwardly. This was a complication he should have foreseen, but hadn't. Tate was bound to charm every cowhand on the place. He quickly crossed past her and put a hand on Buck's shoulder to urge him out the door. "Let's go."

"Can I come with you?" Tate asked.

Before Adam could say no, Buck spoke up.

"Why sure, ma'am," the cowboy said. "Be glad to have you along."

There wasn't much Adam could say except, "You can come. But stay out of the way.

"What kind of trouble is the mare having?" Adam asked as they crossed the short distance to the barn, Tate following on their heels.

"She's down and her breathing's labored," Buck said.

Tate saw as soon as they entered the stall that the mare was indeed in trouble. Her features were grim as she settled onto the straw beside the mare's head. "There now, pretty lady. I know it's hard. Just relax, you pretty lady, and everything will be all right."

Adam and Buck exchanged a look of surprise and approval at the calm, matter-of-fact way Tate had insinuated herself with the mare. The mare lifted her head and whickered in response to the sound of Tate's voice. Then she lay back down and a long, low groan escaped her.

Tate held the mare's head while Adam examined her. "It's twins."

"Why that's wonderful!" Tate exclaimed.

"One of them's turned wrong, blocking the birth canal." In fact, there was one hoof from each of the twins showing.

"Surely your vet can deliver them!"

Adam's features were somber as he answered, "He's out of town at his daughter's wedding." Adam couldn't imagine a way to save either foal, entangled as they were.

Tate's excitement vanished to be replaced with foreboding. She had encountered this problem once before, and the result had come close to being disastrous. Garth had managed to save the mare and both foals, but it had been a very near thing.

"I'll have to take one foal to save the other," Adam said in a flat voice.

"You mean, destroy it?" Tate asked. She couldn't bring herself to say "dismember it" though that was what Adam was suggesting.

"There's nothing else I can do." Adam turned to the cowboy and said, "Buck, see if you can find me some rope."

Tate stroked the mare's neck, trying to keep the animal calm. She looked up and saw the dread in Adam's eyes. It was never easy to make such decisions, yet they were a constant part of ranch life.

She was hesitant to interfere, but there was the tiniest chance the second foal could be saved. "My brother Garth went through this not too long ago. He was able to save both foals by—"

Buck arrived and interrupted with, "Here's the rope, Adam. Do you need my help?"

"I'm not sure. I'd appreciate it if you'd stay."

Buck propped a foot on the edge of the stall and leaned his arms across the top rail to watch as Adam knelt beside the mare and began to fashion a noose with the rope.

Adam paused and glanced over at Tate. She was gnawing on her lower lip again while she smoothed her hand over the mare's sleek neck.

Adam found himself saying, "If you know something that can be done to save both foals, I'm willing to give it a try."

He watched Tate's whole face light up.

"Yes! Yes, I do." She quickly explained how Garth had repositioned the foals.

"I'm not sure I—"

"You can do it!" Tate encouraged. "I know you can!"

Her glowing look made him think he might be able to move mountains. As for saving two spindly foals… It was at least worth a try.

A half hour later, sweat had made damp patches under the arms and down the back of Adam's chambray shirt. He had paused in what he was doing long enough to tie a navy blue bandanna around his forehead to keep the salty wetness out of his eyes. He worked quietly, efficiently, aware of the life-and-death nature of his task.

Adam knew a moment of hope when he finished. But now that the foals had been rearranged, the mare seemed too exhausted to push. He looked across the mare to Tate, feeling his failure in every inch of his body. "I'm sorry."

Tate didn't hear his apology. She took the mare's head onto her lap and began chanting and cooing to the exhausted animal—witchcraft for sure, Adam thought—until the mare amazingly, miraculously birthed the first of the foals.

Adam knew his grin had to be as silly as the one on Tate's face, but he didn't care. Buck took care of cleaning up the first foal while Tate continued her incantations until the mare had delivered the second. Buck again took over drying off the foal while Tate remained at the mare's head, and Adam made sure the afterbirths were taken care of.

When Adam was finished, he crossed to a sink at one end of the barn and scrubbed himself clean. He dried his hands with a towel before rolling his sleeves down from above the elbow to the middle of his forearms.

Adam watched in admiration as Tate coaxed the mare onto her feet and introduced her to her offspring. The mare took a tentative lick of one, and then the other. In a matter of minutes both foals were nudging under her belly to find mother's milk.

Tate's eyes met Adam's across the stall. He opened his arms and she walked right into them. Her arms circled his waist, and she held him tightly as she gave vent to the tears she hadn't shed during the awful ordeal.

"Everything's fine, sweetheart. Thanks to you, everything's just fine," Adam said, stroking her short, silky hair. "Don't cry, sweetheart. You did just fine."

Adam wasn't sure how long they stood there. When he looked up to tell Buck he could go, he discovered the cowboy was already gone. Tate's sobs had subsided and he became aware for the first time of the lithe figure that was pressed so intimately against him.

Tate Whitelaw might be young, but she had the body of a woman. He could feel the soft roundness of her breasts against his chest, and her feminine hips were fitted tight against his masculinity. His growing masculinity.

He tried shifting himself away, but her nose buried itself more deeply at his shoulder and she snuggled closer.

"Tate." He didn't recognize the voice as his own. He cleared his throat and tried again. "Tate."

"Hmm?"

If she didn't recognize the potential danger of the situation was he honor bound to point it out to her? She felt so good in his arms!

Before he could stop himself, his hands had tangled in her hair. He tugged and her head fell back. Her eyes were limpid pools of gold and green. Her face was flushed from crying. She had been gnawing on that lip again and it was swollen. He could see it needed soothing.

He lowered his head and caught her lower lip between his teeth, letting his tongue ride the length of it, testing the fullness of it.

Tate moaned and he was lost.

His tongue slipped into her mouth, tasting her, seeking solace for a desolation of spirit he had never admitted even to himself. Her whole body melted against him, and he was aware of an excruciatingly pleasurable heat in his groin where their bodies were fitted together. He spread his legs slightly and pulled her hard against him, then rubbed them together, creating a friction that turned molten coals to fire.

Tate was only aware of sensations. The softness of his lips. The slickness of his tongue. The heat and hardness of his body pressed tightly against hers. The surge of pleasure as his maleness sought out her femaleness. The urgency of his mouth as it found the smooth column of her neck and teased its way up to her ear, where his breath, hot and moist, made her shiver.

"Please, Adam," she gasped. "Please, don't stop."

Adam's head jerked up, and he stared at the woman in his arms. Good Lord in Heaven! What was he doing?

Adam had to reach behind him to free Tate's arms. He held her at arm's length, his hands gripping hers so tightly he saw her wince. He loosened his hold slightly, but didn't let go. If he did, he was liable to pull her back into his arms and finish what he had started.

Her eyes were lambent, her face rosy with the heat

of passion. Her body was languid, boneless with desire, and it wouldn't take much to have her flat on her back beneath him.

Are you out of your mind? What's gotten into you? You're supposed to be protecting her from lechers, not seducing her yourself!

Tate could see Adam was distraught, but she hadn't the least notion why. "What's wrong?" she asked.

Her voice was still breathless and sounded sexy as hell! His body throbbed with need.

"I'll tell you what's wrong, *little girl!*" he retorted. "You may be hotter than a firecracker on the Fourth of July, but I'm not interested in initiating any virgins! Do you hear me? *Flat not interested!*"

"Could have fooled me!" Tate shot back.

Adam realized he was still holding her hands—was in fact rubbing his thumbs along her palms—and dropped them like hot potatoes. "You stay away from me, *little girl.* You're here for one reason, and one reason only—keeping books. You got that?"

"I got it, *big boy!*"

Adam started to reach for her but caught himself. He stalked over and let himself out of the stall. A moment later he was gone from the barn.

Tate curled her arms protectively around herself. What had happened to change things so quickly? One minute Adam had been making sweet, sweet love to her. The next he had become a raving lunatic. Oh, how it had stung when he called her *little girl!* She might be small in stature, but she was all grown up in every way that mattered.

Except for being a virgin.

Tate had to admit she was a babe in the woods when

it came to sexual experience. But she recognized that what had just happened between her and Adam was something special. He had wanted her as much as she had wanted him. She couldn't be mistaken about that. But their attraction had been more than sexual. It was as though when she walked into his arms she had found a missing part of herself. And though Adam might discount what had happened because she was so young, she wasn't going to let him get away with denying what had happened between them—to her or to himself.

She wasn't some *little girl* he could dismiss with a wave of his hand. Powerful forces were at work between them. Tate had to find a way to make Adam see her as a woman worthy of his love. But how best to accomplish that goal?

Because the physical attraction between them was so powerful, Tate decided she would start with that. She would put temptation in Adam's path and just see what happened.

Chapter 4

Adam watched Tate smiling up at the cowboys who surrounded her at the corral while she regaled them with another of her outrageous stories about life at Hawk's Way, as she had often done over the past three weeks. As usual, she was dressed in jeans, boots and a T-shirt with some equally outrageous slogan written on it.

Only this T-shirt had the neckline cut out so it slipped down to reveal one shoulder—and the obvious fact that she wasn't wearing a bra. Anyone with eyes in his head could see she was naked under the T-shirt. The three cowboys were sure as hell looking. The wind was blowing and the cotton clung to her, outlining her generous breasts.

Adam told himself he wasn't going to make a fool out of himself by going over there and dragging her away from three sets of ogling male eyes. However, once his ſootsteps headed in that direction, he didn't seem to be able to stop them.

He arrived in time to hear her say, "My brothers taught me how to get even when some rabbit-shy horse bucks me off."

"How's that, Tate?" one of the cowboys asked.

"Why, I just make that horse walk back to the barn all by himself!" Tate said with a grin.

The cowboys guffawed, and Tate joined in. Adam caught his lip curling with laughter and straightened it back out.

"Don't you have some work to do?" he demanded of the three cowboys.

"Sure, Boss."

"Yeah, Boss."

"Just leaving, Boss."

They tipped their hats to Tate, but continued staring at her as they backed away.

Adam swore acidly, and they quickly turned tail and scattered in three different directions.

He directed a cool stare at Tate and said, "I thought I told you to stay away from my cowhands."

"I believe your exact words were, 'Finish your work before you go traipsing around the ranch,'" Tate replied in a drawl guaranteed to irritate her already irritated boss.

"Is your work done?"

"Had you been home for lunch, I'd have offered to show you the bookkeeping system I've set up. Everything's been logged in and all the current invoices have been paid. I have some suggestions for ways—"

He interrupted with, "What the hell are you doing out here half-dressed, carousing with the hired help?"

"Carousing? I was just *talking* to them!" Tate flashed back.

"I want you to leave those boys alone."

"Boys? They looked like grown men to me. Certainly old enough to make up their minds whether or not they want to spend time with me."

Adam grabbed the hat off his head and slapped it against his thigh. "Dammit, Tate. You're a babe in the woods! You're playing with fire, and you're going to get burned! You can't run around here half naked and not expect—"

"Half naked?" she scoffed. "You've got to be kidding!"

"That T-shirt doesn't leave much to the imagination! I can see your nipples plain as day."

Tate looked down and realized for the first time that twin peaks were clearly visible beneath the T-shirt. She decided to brazen it out. "So what if you can? I assume you're familiar with the female anatomy. Besides, you're not my father or my brother. You have absolutely no right to tell me what to wear!"

Since the erotic feelings Adam was experiencing at the moment weren't the least fatherly or brotherly, he didn't argue with her. However, he had appointed himself her guardian in their stead. As such, he felt it his duty to point out to her the dangers of such provocative attire.

He explained in a reasonable voice, "When a man sees a woman looking like that, he just naturally gets ideas."

Tate looked sharply at Adam. "What kind of ideas?"

"The *wrong* kind," Adam said emphatically.

Tate smiled impishly and batted her lashes at him. "I thought you were 'flat not interested' in li'l ole me."

"Cut it out, Tate."

"Cut what out?"

"Stop batting those lashes at me, for one thing."

Tate pouted her lips like a child whose candy had been taken away. "You mean it isn't working?"

It was working all right. Too damn well. She was just precocious enough to be charming. He was entranced despite his wish not to be. He felt his body begin to harden as she slid her gaze from his eyes, to his mouth, to his chest, and straight on down his body to his crotch. Which was putting on a pretty damn good show for her.

"You're asking for it," he said through clenched teeth.

She batted her eyelashes and said, "Am I going to get it?"

"That's it!"

The next thing Tate knew she had been hefted over Adam's shoulder like a sack of wheat, and he was striding toward the house.

"Let me down!" she cried. "Adam, this is uncomfortable."

"Serves you right! You haven't been the least worried about my comfort for the past three weeks."

"Where are you taking me? What are you planning to do with me?"

"Something I'm going to enjoy very much!"

Was Adam really going to make love to her? Would he be rough, or gentle? How was she supposed to act? Was there some sort of proper etiquette for the ravishing of virgins? Not that she had ever worried too much about what was proper. But she felt nervous, anxious about the encounter to come. Finally, Adam would have to acknowledge that greater forces were at work between them than either of them could—or should—resist.

The air inside the adobe house hit her like a cooling zephyr. The dimness left her blind for an instant. Just as she was regaining her sight, they emerged once more into sunlight and she was blinded again. Several more strides and she felt herself being lowered from Adam's shoulder.

Tate barely had time to register the fact that they were in the courtyard when Adam shifted her crosswise in his arms. Grinning down into her face, he said "Maybe this will cool you off!" and unceremoniously dumped her into the pool of water that surrounded the fountain.

Tate came up spluttering. "Why you!" She blinked her eyes furiously, trying to clear the water from them.

"Why, Miss Tate, are you batting your eyelashes at me again? Guess I'll have to try another dunking."

He took one step toward her, and Tate retreated to the other side of the fountain. "I'll get you for this, you rogue! You roué!"

Adam laughed. It had been so long since he had done so, that the sound brought Maria to the kitchen window to see what Señor Adam found so funny. She shook her head and clucked when she saw the new bookkeeper standing dripping in the fountain. She grabbed a bath towel from the stack of laundry she was folding on the kitchen table and hurried outside with it.

She handed it to Adam and said in Spanish, "This is no way to treat a young woman."

Adam's eyes crinkled at the corners with laughter. "It is when she's bent on seducing an older man."

Maria hissed in a breath and turned to eye the bedraggled creature in the pool. So that was the way the wind was blowing. Well, she was not one to stand in the way of any woman who could make Señor Adam laugh once more.

"Be sure you get the *señorita* dried off quickly. Otherwise she might catch a cold."

Maria left Adam standing with the towel in his hand and a smug grin on his face.

Once the housekeeper was gone, Adam turned back to Tate. And quickly lost his smirk. Because if the T-shirt had been revealing before, it was perfectly indecent now. He could easily see Tate's flesh through the soaked cotton. The cold water had caused her nipples to peak into tight buds.

His mouth felt dry. His voice was ragged as he said, "Here. Wrap yourself in this."

Only he didn't extend the towel to her. He held it so she would have to step out of the pool and into his arms. When he encircled her with the terry cloth she shivered and snuggled closer.

"I'm freezing!" she said.

He, on the other hand, was burning up. How did she do it to him? This time, however, he had only himself to blame. He felt her cold nose burrow into his shoulder as his chin nuzzled her damp hair. The water had released the lilac scent of her shampoo. He took a deep breath and realized he didn't want to let her go.

Adam vigorously rubbed the towel up and down Tate's back, hoping to dispel the intimacy of the moment.

"Mmm. That feels good," she murmured.

His body betrayed him again, responding with amazing rapidity to the throaty sound of her voice. He edged himself away from her, unwilling to admit his need to her. In fact, he felt the distinct necessity to deny it.

"I'm not going to make love to you, Tate."

She froze in his arms. Her head lifted from his shoulder, and he found himself looking into eyes that warmed him like brandy.

"Why not, Adam? Is it because I'm not attractive to you?"

"Lord, no! Of course you're a beautiful woman, but—" Adam groaned as he realized what he had just admitted.

"I am?"

What had those brothers of hers been telling her, Adam wondered, *to make her doubt herself like this?*

"Is it because I don't dress like a lady?"

His only objection to the clothes she wore was his re-action to her in them. "Contrary to what you might have heard, clothes *don't* make the man—or the woman."

"Then it must be the fact that I'm a virgin," she said.

Adam felt himself flushing. "Tate, you just don't go around talking about things like that."

"Not even with you?"

"*Especially* not with me!"

"Why not?"

They were back to that again. He turned her so he had an arm around her shoulder, and began ushering her across the courtyard to her bedroom. "I think it's time you got out of those wet clothes."

Tate's impish smile reappeared. "Would you like to help me?"

"Not on your life!" He opened the sliding glass door and gave her a nudge inside. "I'll meet you in the of-fice in fifteen minutes and you can show me whatever bookkeeping wonders you've accomplished today." He turned and marched across the courtyard, fighting the urge to look back.

Once she was alone in her room, Tate let the towel

drop. She stared at herself in the standing oval mirror in the corner and groaned. She looked like something the cat had dragged in! No wonder Adam hadn't been interested!

Tate sat down on a wooden chair to pull off her wet boots, then yanked her T-shirt off and struggled with the wet zipper of her jeans. She peeled her silk panties down and quickly began replacing her clothing with an identical wardrobe. All except the wet boots, for which she substituted a pair of beaded Indian moccasins Charlie One Horse had given her for Christmas.

While Tate dressed, she reviewed the events of the past three weeks since she had arrived at the Lazy S. Teasing Adam had begun as a way of making him admit the sexual attraction—and something more—that existed between them. But she had discovered that kidding some folks was like teasing a loaded polecat. The satisfaction was short-lived.

Tate hadn't been enjoying the game much these days, mainly because she had begun to suffer from the sexually charged situations as much as Adam. The problem was, on her side at least, her heart followed where her hormones led.

She would give anything if Adam was as interested in her as Buck seemed to be. The lean-hipped cowboy had been asking her every day for a week if she would go out with him on Saturday night. Well, maybe she should. Maybe if Adam saw that somebody else found her worth pursuing, he would get the same idea.

Tate had a cheerful smile on her face by the time she joined Adam in his office. He already had the computer on and was perusing the statistics she had input there.

"So what do you think?" she asked, perching herself on the arm of the large swivel chair in which he was sitting.

"It looks good." Of course his office wasn't as neat as it had once been. There were half-filled coffee cups amidst the clutter on the desk, and a collection of magazines and a dirty T-shirt decorated the floor. A bridle and several other pieces of tack Tate was fixing were strewn around the room.

But he couldn't argue with what she had accomplished. Tate had set up a program to handle data on each head of stock, providing a record that would be invaluable in making buying and selling decisions. "You didn't tell me you knew so much about computers."

Tate grinned and said, "You didn't ask." She leaned across him and began earnestly discussing other ideas she had regarding possible uses of the computer in his business.

He started automatically cleaning the debris from his desk.

"Don't worry about those," Tate said, taking a handful of pebbles from him. "Aren't they pretty? I found them down by the creek." She scattered them back onto the desk. "I play with them while I'm thinking, sort of like worry beads, you know?"

"Uh-huh."

Adam forced himself to concentrate on what she was saying, rather than the way her breast was pressed up against his arm. By the time she was done talking about the projects she had in mind, she had shifted position four times. He knew because she had managed to brush some part of his anatomy with some part of hers each time she moved.

Tate was totally oblivious to Adam's difficulty, because she was having her own problems concentrating on the matters at hand. She was busy planning how she could make Adam sit up and take notice of her by accepting Buck's invitation to go out tomorrow evening. She just had to make sure that Adam saw her leaving on the date with the auburn-haired cowboy.

Her thoughts must have conjured Buck, because he suddenly appeared at the door to Adam's office.

"Need you to take a look at that irrigation system to see whether you want it repaired or replaced," Buck said.

"I'll be right there," Adam replied.

Buck had already turned to leave when Tate realized she had the perfect opportunity to let Adam know she was going out with another man. "Oh, Buck."

Buck turned and the hat came off his head in the same motion. "Yes, ma'am?"

"I've decided to take you up on your offer to go dancing tomorrow night."

Buck's face split with an engaging grin. "Yes, ma'am! I'll pick you up at seven o'clock if that's all right, and we can have some dinner first."

The thunderous look on Adam's face was everything Tate could have wished for. "I'll see you at seven," she promised.

Buck slipped his hat back on his head and said, "You coming, Boss?"

"In a minute. I'll catch up to you."

Adam's fists landed on his hips as he turned to confront Tate. "What was that all about?"

"Buck asked me to go dancing at Knippa on Saturday night, and I thought it might be fun."

Adam couldn't very well forbid her going. As Tate

had so pointedly noted, he wasn't related to her in the least. But he couldn't help having misgivings, either. There was no telling what Buck Magnesson's reaction would be if Tate subjected him to the same teasing sensuality that Adam had endured for the past three weeks. If Tate said "Please" Buck was damned likely to say "Thank you" and take what she offered.

Adam suddenly heard himself forbidding his sister Melanie from going out on a date with a boy he had thought a little wild. Heard himself telling Melanie that he knew better than she what was best for her. And remembered the awful consequences of his high-handedness. Adam didn't have to like the fact that Tate had decided to go out with Buck Magnesson. But if he didn't want to repeat the mistakes he had made with his younger sister, he had to put up with it.

"Have a good time with Buck tomorrow night," he said. Then he turned and walked out the door.

Tate frowned at Adam's back. That wasn't exactly the reaction she had been hoping for. Where was the jealousy? Where was the demand that she spend her time with him instead? Suddenly Tate wished she had thought things through a little more carefully. Agreeing to date Buck simply to make Adam realize what he was missing wasn't turning out at all as she had hoped.

She felt a little guilty that she had even considered using Buck to make Adam jealous. But since her plan had failed—quite miserably—she could at least enjoy the evening with Buck with a clear conscience.

Tate had gotten the broken water hose fixed on her '51 Chevy, and she used the pickup to drive the ninety miles east to San Antonio that afternoon to go shopping. She could have worn jeans to go dancing, but had decided that she owed it to Buck to show up for their date looking her best.

She found a pretty halter sundress that tied around the neck and had an almost nonexistent back. The bodice fit her like a glove and showed just a hint of décolletage. The bright yellow and white floral print contrasted with her dark hair and picked up the gold in her eyes. The midcalf-length skirt was gathered at the waist and flared at the hem. She whirled once in front of the mirror and saw that the dress was going to reveal a great deal of her legs if Buck was the kind of dancer who liked to twirl his partner a lot.

Buck's smile when she opened the door on Saturday night was well worth the effort spent shopping. She couldn't help feeling a stab of disappointment that Adam wasn't around to see her off. Apparently he had made plans of his own for the evening.

Tate found Buck surprisingly entertaining company. The cowboy had older brothers of his own, and Tate was quick to agree, "Nothing is harder to put up with than a good example!" He and Tate shared older brother horror stories that kept them both laughing through dinner.

The country and western band was in full swing when they crossed the threshold of the Grange Hall in Knippa. The room was fogged with cigarette smoke that battled with the overwhelming odor of sweat and cologne. The sawdusted dance floor was crowded, elbow to elbow, with men in cowboy hats partnered by ladies wearing flounced Western skirts and boots.

Just as they made their way to the dance floor, a two-step ended and the band began playing a waltz.

"Shall we?" Buck asked, making a dance frame with his arms.

"Absolutely!" Tate said, stepping into his embrace.

Tate got another welcome surprise when she and Buck began to waltz around the room. The lean cowboy was graceful on his feet. He led her into several intricate variations of the dance that left her breathless and feeling like a prima ballerina by the time the song ended.

"That was wonderful!" she exclaimed.

"Would you like something to drink?" Buck asked.

"Just a soda, please."

Buck found a seat for Tate at one of the small tables that surrounded the dance floor and forced his way through the crowd toward the bar.

Tate was tapping her foot to another two-step tune and enjoying watching the couples maneuver around the dance floor when she thought she saw someone she recognized. She followed the couple until they turned at the corner of the room.

Tate gasped aloud. It was Adam! He was dancing the two-step with a buxom redheaded woman.

As he passed by her table, Adam smiled and called out, "Hi, there! Having fun?"

Before she could answer, they had danced on past her, and she was left with the trill of the woman's laughter in her ears.

Tate felt sick. *Who was she?* The Redheaded Woman in Adam's arms was absolutely beautiful. No wonder Adam hadn't been interested in pursuing her when he was acquainted with such a gorgeous female.

"What's caught your eye?" Buck asked as he set a soda in front of Tate.

"Adam's here." She pointed him out. "See there. With that redhead."

To Tate's amazement, Buck scowled and swore under his breath.

"What's wrong?" she asked.

"Nothing I do anything about."

"That's the sort of statement that's guaranteed to get a nosy female's attention," Tate said. "Out with it."

Buck grinned sheepishly and admitted, "All right. Here goes." He took a deep breath and said, "That woman dancing with Adam is my ex-wife."

"You're kidding!"

"'Fraid not."

Tate watched Buck watching the Redheaded Woman. His feelings were painfully transparent. "You're still in love with her."

Buck grimaced. "Much good it'll do me."

"I assume Adam knows how you feel."

"He asked my permission before he took Velma out the first time."

"And you gave it to him?" Tate asked incredulously.

"She isn't my wife anymore. She can see whoever she pleases."

Tate snorted in disgust. "While you suffer in noble silence. Men!"

Tate had been so involved with talking to Buck that she hadn't realized the song was ending. She was less than pleased when Adam and Velma arrived at their table.

"Mind if we join you?" Adam asked.

Tate bit her lip to keep from saying something censorable. She slipped her arm through Buck's, put a gigantic smile on her face, and said, "Why sure! We'd love to have the company, wouldn't we, Buck?"

It was hard to say who was the more surprised by her performance, Buck or Adam. What she hadn't expected was the militant light that rose in Velma's green eyes when Tate claimed Buck's arm. Well, well, well. Maybe there was more here than met the eye.

Adam made introductions, then seated Velma and caught one of the few waitresses long enough to ask for two drinks.

"I didn't expect to see you here," Tate said to Adam.

"I enjoy dancing, and Velma's a great partner."

Tate could imagine what else Velma was great at. She had observed for herself that the redhead had a wonderful sense of rhythm.

Tate was aware of Buck sitting stiffly beside her, quieter than he had been at any time during the evening. How could Adam not be sensitive to the vibrations that arced across the table between the cowboy and his ex-wife?

In fact, Adam was eminently aware of how much Buck Magnesson still loved his ex-wife. It was why he had brought Velma here this evening. Adam knew that with Velma in the room, Buck wasn't liable to spend much time thinking about Tate.

There was more than one way to skin a cat, Adam thought with satisfaction. He had known Tate would rebel against an ultimatum, so he hadn't protested her date with Buck. He had simply sought out a more subtle way to get what he wanted.

Bringing Velma to the dance seemed like the answer to his problem. He was pretty sure Velma was as much in love with Buck as the cowboy was with his ex-wife. He didn't mind playing Cupid, especially if it meant separating Tate from the virile young cowboy.

"How about trading partners?" Adam said, rising from his chair and reaching for Tate's hand.

Before Tate could protest, Buck said, "That sounds fine to me," took Velma by the hand and headed for the dance floor.

Tate wasn't sure what to make of Adam's ploy. She waited until they were half a dance floor away from the other couple before she said, "That was a pretty sneaky thing to do."

"I wanted to dance with you."

"Are you sure you aren't matchmaking?"

Adam smiled. "You could feel it, too?"

"I think he might still love her."

"I'm sure he does."

"Then why did you bring Velma here tonight?"

"I would think that's obvious."

"Not to me."

"I enjoy her company."

"Oh."

He grinned. "And I knew Buck would be here with you."

He sent her into a series of spins that prevented her from making any kind of retort. By the time she was in his arms again the song was over and he was ushering her back toward their table, where Buck and Velma were sitting across from each other arguing vociferously.

"Buck?" Tate didn't want to interrupt, but she wasn't sure whether she should leave him alone with Velma, either.

"Let's get out of here," Buck said, jumping up and turning his back on Velma. "Good night, Adam. I'll see you tomorrow."

As Buck hurried Tate away, she heard Velma say, "I'd like to go home now, Adam. If that's all right with you?"

Tate wasn't sure where Buck was taking her when

he burned rubber on the asphalt parking lot. It was a safe guess from the dark look on his face that he had no romantic intentions toward her.

"Want to talk about it?" she asked at last.

Buck glanced quickly at her, then turned his eyes back to the road. "I don't want to bother you with my problems."

"I'm a good listener."

He sighed and said, "Velma and I were high school sweethearts. We married as soon as we graduated. Pretty soon Velma began to think she had missed something. She had an affair."

Tate bit her lip to keep from saying something judgmental. She was glad she had when Buck continued.

"I found out about it and confronted her. She asked for a divorce, and I gave it to her."

"Why?"

"Pride. Foolish damn pride!"

"And you regret it now?"

"My life's been running kind of muddy without her."

"So why don't you do something about it?" Tate asked.

"It's no use. She says that I deserve better. She doesn't believe I can ever forgive or forget what she did."

"Can you?"

The cowboy's eyes were bleak in the light from the dash. "I think so."

"But you're not sure?"

A muscle worked in his jaw. "If I were, I'd have her back home and under me faster than chain lightning with a link snapped!"

Tate had thought they were driving without direction, yet she realized suddenly that they had arrived back at the front door of Adam's house. She saw Adam's truck parked there. So, he was home. And there was a light on in the living room.

She let herself out of the truck, but Buck met her on the front porch. He put an arm around her waist and walked her away from the light.

"May I kiss you good-night, Tate?"

Tate drew a breath and held it. This was so exactly like the scene she had played out the night she had left home that it was eerie. Only there were no brothers here to protect her from the big, bad wolf.

"Of course you can kiss me good-night," she said at last.

Buck took his time, and Tate was aware of the sweetness of his kiss. And the reluctance in it. When he lifted his head their eyes met, and they smiled at each other.

"No go, huh?" he said.

Tate shook her head. "I like you an awful lot, Buck. I hope we can be friends."

"I'd like that," the cowboy said.

He leaned down and kissed her again. Both of them knew how much—and how little—it meant.

However, it was not so clear to the man watching them through a slit in the living room curtains.

Chapter 5

It had taken every ounce of willpower Adam possessed to keep from stalking out onto the front porch and putting his fist in Buck Magnesson's nose. It wasn't just the thought of his sister Melanie that kept him from doing it. There were things he couldn't offer Tate that Buck could.

But he wasn't a saint or a eunuch. If Tate persisted in tempting him, he wasn't noble enough to refuse her. He was determined to keep his hunger leashed at least until he was certain Tate knew what she *wouldn't* be getting if she got involved with him. She was too young to give up her dreams. And there was no way he could fulfill them.

Before Adam had time to examine his feelings further, the front door opened. Tate stepped inside to find him sitting in one of the large Mediterranean chairs before the blackened fireplace, nursing a half-empty glass of whiskey.

"Hello," she said. "I didn't expect to see you again tonight."

"I was waiting up for you."

Tate immediately bristled. "Look, I don't need a caretaker." She wanted a lover. But not just that. A man who loved her, as she was beginning to fear she loved him.

"Old habits die hard."

"What's that supposed to mean?"

"I used to wait up for my sister Melanie."

"You have a sister? Why haven't I met her?"

"She died ten years ago."

"I'm so sorry."

Adam had drunk just enough whiskey to want to tell her the rest of it. "Melanie ran away from home when she was seventeen. She was picked up by a stranger while hitchhiking. He raped her, and then he stabbed her to death."

"That must have been awful for you!" Tate wanted to put her arms around Adam to comfort him, but his body language posted obvious No Trespassing signs.

She used sitting on the couch as an excuse to cross closer to him, slipped off her boots and pulled her feet up under her. She folded her arms under her breasts to give herself the comfort he wouldn't accept.

Then another, more troubling thought occurred to her. "Is that why you picked me up on the road? Because of your sister?"

Adam nodded.

Tate felt as though she'd been physically struck. She hesitated and asked, "Is that why you offered me a job?"

"It seemed like a good idea at the time."

Tate swallowed over the lump that had grown in her throat. "So I'm just a charity case to you?"

Adam heard the pain in Tate's voice and realized he had handled this all wrong. If he didn't do some fast talking, he knew she would be gone by morning. "You can hardly blame me for offering help under the circumstances, can you? I couldn't take the chance that I might be responsible for another young woman's death!"

Tate wasn't so wrapped up in her own feelings that she failed to recognize the significance of what Adam had just said. "How can you blame yourself for your sister's death? What happened couldn't possibly be your fault!"

"Oh, no?" Adam's nostrils were pinched, his blue eyes like shards of ice. "Didn't you tell me that you left home because your brothers made your life miserable?"

"They only did what they did because they love me!" Tate protested.

"So that makes it all right for them to interfere in your life? To aggravate you enough to send you running in that old rattletrap truck?"

It was clear Adam was searching for answers that would release him from the guilt he suffered over what had happened to his sister. Tate found herself equally confounded by the issues he had raised. Was love a good enough excuse for the high-handed way Garth and Faron had acted? What if she had met the same fate as Adam's sister? Would they have blamed themselves for her death?

She knew they would have, just as Adam had blamed himself for Melanie's death all these years. She didn't know what to say to ease his pain. She only knew she had to do something.

Tate stood and crossed to Adam. She knelt on the cool tile floor at his feet and laid a hand on his thigh. She felt him tense beneath her touch. "Adam, I—"

He rose abruptly and stalked away from her. "I'm not in the mood for any teasing tonight."

"I was trying to offer comfort!" Tate retorted.

"Just stay away from me!"

Tate struck back like the scorned woman she felt herself to be. "There are plenty of others who'll welcome my attentions!"

"Like Buck?"

"Like Buck!" That was a lie, but told in a good cause. Saving her pride seemed of utmost importance right now.

"He'll never marry you. He's still in love with Velma."

Since Tate knew he was right, she retorted, "I don't have to marry a man to go to bed with him!"

"Is that so, *little girl?*"

Tate was gasping, she was so furious at the taunting words. But it was clear she could cut her own throat with a sharp tongue. She had certainly dug a hole for herself it was going to be hard to get out of. She took two deep breaths, trying to regain her temper.

Adam didn't give her a chance to speak before he said, "If you're smart, you'll go back home where you belong. Now, before you get hurt."

"Are you firing me?"

Tate held her breath until he said, "No."

"Then I'm staying. If you'll excuse me, I'm tired. I want to go to bed."

Tate had started for the door when Adam quipped, "What, no invitation to join you?"

Tate slowly turned back to face him. She took her

time getting from where she was to where he was. She hooked a finger into the opening at the neck of his shirt and looked up into eyes that were both wary and amused.

"I learned at my brothers' knees never to approach a bull from the front, a horse from the rear...or a damn fool from any direction. Good night, Adam."

"We'll talk about this again tomorrow," he said to her retreating back.

"Like hell we will!" she replied.

Tate spent a restless night, tossing and turning as her mind grappled with all of Adam's revelations. What she found most disturbing was the possibility that Adam had merely been tolerating her because he felt responsible for her welfare.

Surely she couldn't have been mistaken about his physical reaction to her! More likely, he was attracted to her, but his feelings of responsibility toward her were keeping him from pursuing a relationship. If so, she would soon cure him of that!

Tate felt somewhat cheered by her decision, and she made up her mind to confront Adam at breakfast. Only, when she arrived in the kitchen the next morning, she discovered that he had already eaten and left the house.

"Did he say where he was going, Maria?"

"No, *señorita*."

Tate worked hard all day in the office so she wouldn't have time to worry about where Adam had gone. He was bound to turn up sooner or later. He wasn't going anywhere. And neither was she.

However, by seven o'clock that evening there was still no sign of Adam. He hadn't even called Maria to say he wouldn't be home for dinner. Maria was washing up the dinner dishes, and to keep herself busy, Tate was drying them and putting them away. Maria had tried to start a conversation, but Tate was too distracted to keep track of what she was saying. Finally Maria gave up trying and left Tate to her thoughts.

Tate was worried. Where could Adam have gone? She had already checked once at the bunkhouse, but no one had seen him all day.

When she heard a knock at the kitchen door, Tate leaped to answer it. It wasn't until she opened the door that she realized Adam wouldn't have knocked.

"Buck! You look terrible. What's wrong?"

Buck pulled his hat off his head and wiped the sweat from his brow with his sleeve. "Um, I, um."

She put a hand on his arm and urged him inside the room. "Come in. Sit down."

He resisted her efforts to move him from his spot just inside the kitchen door. "No, I—"

"You what?" Tate asked in exasperation.

"I need your help."

"Of course, anything."

"Maybe you better not say yes until you hear what I have to say." He eyed Maria, but was too polite to ask her to leave.

Aware of the tension in the cowboy, Maria said, "I give you some time alone, so you can talk," and left the room. But she made up her mind she wouldn't be gone for long. The nice *señorita,* she was good for Señor Adam. It would not do to let cowboys like Buck Magnesson take what should not be theirs.

Tate turned a kitchen chair and sat in it like a saddle. "I'm all ears."

Buck fidgeted with the brim of his hat another moment before he said, "I've thought a lot about our conversation last night. You know, about whether or not I could forgive and forget what Velma did? And, well… I believe I can."

A smile spread on Tate's face. "I'm so glad, Buck."

"Yeah, well, that's why I need your help. I've decided to go see Velma and tell her how I feel, and I thought maybe if you were along to sort of referee—"

Tate was up and across the room in an instant. She gave the startled cowboy a big hug. "It'll be my pleasure. When would you like to go see her?"

Buck grinned. "Is right now too soon?"

Tate thought about leaving a note for Adam, then rejected the idea. It would do him good to know how it felt to worry about someone who didn't leave a message where he was going!

Maria heard the kitchen door slam closed and came back in to see what Señor Buck had wanted. She frowned and clucked her tongue in dismay when she realized that Señorita Tate had left the house with the handsome cowboy. "Señor Adam will not like this. He will not like this at all."

Maria made up her mind to stay until Señor Adam got back from wherever he had gone and tell him what had happened. Then he could go find the *señorita* and bring her home where she belonged.

Meanwhile, Buck drove Tate to a tiny house with gingerbread trim in a quiet neighborhood off Main Street in Uvalde. She waited anxiously with him to see if Velma was going to answer the doorbell.

Tate saw the light in Velma's green eyes when she saw Buck, and watched it die when she realized Tate was with him.

"I want to talk to you, Velma," Buck said.

"I don't think we have anything to say to each other." She nearly had the door closed when Buck stuck his boot in it.

"I'm not leaving until I say my piece," Buck insisted in a harsh voice.

"I'll call the police if you don't go away," Velma threatened.

"I just want to talk!"

When Velma let go of the door to run for the phone, Buck and Tate took advantage of the opportunity to come inside. Buck caught Velma in the kitchen and pried the phone receiver out of her hand.

"Please, baby, just listen to me," he pleaded.

"Please give him a chance, Velma. I know you're going to want to hear what Buck has to say."

Velma froze when she heard Tate's voice. "Why did you come here?" she demanded.

"Buck thought it might make it easier for the two of you to talk if there was someone else here to sort of mediate."

Velma looked at Buck's somber face. She took a deep breath and said, "All right. I'll listen to what you have to say. For five minutes."

Buck set her down, letting her body slide along his as he did. Tate could have lit a fire from the sparks that flew between them. They belonged together, all right. She only hoped Buck would find the right words to convince Velma he meant what he said.

Five minutes later, Velma was still listening, but Tate could see she was torn between the fervent wish to believe Buck, and the awful fear that he would soon regret what he was saying.

"I don't think I'll ever forget what happened, Velma," Buck said. "But I think I can live with it."

That wasn't exactly the same thing as *forgiving* it, Tate realized. Apparently Velma also noticed the distinction.

"That's not good enough, Buck," she said in a quiet voice.

"I love you, Velma," he said.

She choked on a sob. "I know, Buck. I love you, too."

"Then why can't we get back together?"

"It just wouldn't work."

By now Velma was crying in earnest, and Buck would have been heartless indeed if he could have resisted pulling her into his arms to comfort her. In fact, that was just what he did.

Tate suddenly realized another reason why she had been brought along. Her presence provided the only restraint on the sexual explosion that occurred whenever the two of them touched. Even that wasn't sufficient at first.

Buck already had his fingers twined in Velma's red curls, and Velma had her hand on the front of Buck's jeans when Tate cleared her throat loudly to remind them that she was still there. They broke apart like two teenagers caught necking, their faces flushed as much by embarrassment as by passion.

"Uh, sorry," Buck said.

Velma tried rearranging her hair, a hopeless task considering how badly Buck had messed it up.

"You look fine, honey," Buck said, taking a hand at smoothing her tresses himself. But the gesture turned into a caress, which turned into a fervent look of desire, which ended when Buck's lips lowered to Velma's in the gentlest of kisses.

There was no telling where things might have gone from there, except Tate said, "All right, enough is enough! We'll never get anywhere this way. Buck, you go sit over there in that chair. Velma and I will sit on the couch."

Sheepishly, Buck crossed the room and slouched down in the chair Tate had indicated. Tate joined Velma on the couch. She dragged her T-shirt out of her jeans and used it to dab at Velma's tears.

"Now it seems to me," Tate began, "that you both want to give this relationship another try. So I have a suggestion."

Tate outlined for them a plan whereby they would start from scratch. Buck would pick Velma up at her door, they would go out together and he would return her at the end of the evening. Absolutely no sex.

"You have to learn to trust each other again," she said. "That takes time."

Buck's face had taken on a mulish cast. "I'm not sure I can play by those rules. Especially that 'no sex' part."

It wasn't hard to see why. The sexual electricity between them would have killed a normal person.

"No sex," Tate insisted. "If you spend all your time in bed, you won't do as much talking. And you both have a lot you need to talk about."

Tate chewed anxiously on her lower lip while she waited to see whether they would accept her suggestion.

"I think Tate's right," Velma said.

The negotiations didn't end there. In fact it wasn't until the wee hours of the morning that all parties were satisfied. Tate felt as emotionally exhausted as she knew

Buck and Velma were. The hug Velma gave her as she was leaving, and the whispered "Thank you" from the other woman, made everything worthwhile.

Tate rubbed the tense muscles in her neck as Buck drove her back to the ranch. She knew Buck was still troubled, but at least now there was some hope that he and his ex-wife might one day end up together again.

When they arrived at the front door to Adam's house, Buck took Tate's hand in his and said, "I don't know how to thank you."

"Just be good to Velma. That'll be thanks enough for me."

He ruffled her hair as an older brother might, then leaned over and kissed her on the cheek. "You're a good friend, Tate. If I can ever do anything for you, just let me know."

"I'll remember that," Tate said. "You don't need to get out. I can let myself in."

Buck waited until she was inside the front door before he drove his truck around to the bunkhouse.

Tate had only taken two steps when the living room lights clicked on. Adam stood at the switch, his face a granite mask of displeasure.

"Where were you?" Tate accused. "I waited for you for hours, but you never came home!"

Adam was taken aback, since he had intended to ask the same question. "Dr. Kowalski had a medical emergency with one of my former patients. Susan asked me to come because Mrs. Daniels was frightened, and she thought the old lady would respond better if I was there."

"I knew it had to be something important," Tate said with a sigh of relief. "Were you able to help?"

"Yes, Mrs. Daniels is out of danger now."

Adam suddenly realized that Tate had completely distracted him from the confrontation he had planned. His eyes narrowed as he tried to decide whether she had done it on purpose.

"Where have you been all night?" he asked in a cool voice. "Do you realize it's four a.m.?"

"Is it really that late? I mean, that early," Tate said with a laugh. "I was out with Buck. Oh, Adam—"

He cut her off with a snarl of disgust as she confirmed his worst suspicions. "I don't suppose I have to ask what you were doing, *little girl*. If you were that anxious to lose your virginity you should have told me. You didn't have to drag Buck into the picture."

Tate was aghast. "You think Buck and I—"

"What am I supposed to think when you come rolling in at this ungodly hour of the morning with your T-shirt hanging out and your hair mussed up and your lower lip swollen like it's been bitten a dozen times."

"There's a perfectly logical—"

"I don't want to hear any excuses! Do you deny that you spent the night with Buck?"

"No, but something wonderful happened—"

"I don't want to hear the gory details!"

He was shouting by now, and Tate knew that if she had been any closer Adam might not have been able to control the visible anger that shook his body.

"Get out of my sight!" he said in hard, quiet voice. "Before I do something I'll regret."

Tate put her chin up. If this *fool* would give her a chance, she could explain everything! But her pride goaded her to remain silent. Adam was neither father nor brother. Yet he seemed determined to fill the role of protector. She felt the tears that threatened. Why couldn't he see that she only had eyes for one man—and that man was him!

"Some folks can't see any farther than the steam from their own pot of stew." With that pronouncement, she turned and stalked from the room.

Once Tate was gone, Adam swore a blue streak. When he was done, he felt worse instead of better. He had hoped he was wrong about what Tate and Buck had been doing out so late. He had been stunned when Tate hadn't denied losing her virginity to the cowboy. He felt absolute, uncontrollable rage at the thought of some other man touching her in ways he knew she had never been touched. And the thought that she had found it *wonderful* caused an unbearable tightness in his chest.

He tried to tell himself that what had happened was for the best. He was not a whole man. She deserved more. But nothing he said to himself took away the bitter taste in his mouth. She was his. She belonged to him.

And by God, now that her virginity was no longer an impediment, he would have her.

Chapter 6

Suddenly it was Adam who became the pursuer and Tate who proved elusive. She gave him the cold shoulder whenever she met him and made a point of smiling and recklessly flirting with Buck. Because of the way Buck's courtship was prospering with Velma, he had the look of a happy, well-satisfied man. Which left Adam seething with jealousy.

Tate suspected she could lift the thundercloud that followed Adam around if she simply told him the truth about what she had been doing the night she had spent with Buck. But she was determined that Adam would be the one to make the first move toward conciliation. All he had done for the past week was glare daggers at her.

However, there was more than anger reflected in his gaze, more than antagonism in his attitude toward her. Tate was beginning to feel frazzled by the unspoken sexual tension that sizzled between them. Something had changed since the night they had argued, and Tate felt the hairs lift on her arms whenever Adam was around. His look was hungry. His body radiated leashed power. His features were harsh with unsatisfied need. She had the uneasy feeling he was stalking her.

Tate escaped into the office by day, and played mediator for Buck and Velma at night. She refused to admit that she was hiding from Adam, but that was the case. His eyes followed her whenever they were in the same room together, and she knew he must be aware of her reaction to his disconcerting gaze.

Exactly one week from the day Tate had accompanied Buck on his pivotal visit to Velma, the cowboy took Tate aside and asked whether she minded staying home that evening instead of joining them as chaperon.

"There are some things I'd like to discuss with Velma alone," Buck said.

"Why sure," Tate replied with a forced smile. "I don't mind at all."

Once Buck was gone, Tate's smile flattened into a somber line. She was more than a little worried about what Adam might do if he found out she was home for the evening. She decided the best plan was to avoid him by staying in her room. It was the coward's way out, but her brothers had taught her that sometimes it was best to play your cards close to your belly.

Tate quickly found herself bored within the confines of her bedroom. She remembered that there was some work she could do in the office—if only she could get there without being detected by Adam. The light was on in his bedroom across the courtyard. Adam often retired early and did his reading—both ranch and medical journals—in bed.

She was already dressed for sleep in a long pink T-shirt, but it covered her practically to the knees. She decided it was modest enough even for Adam should he find her working late in the office. She tiptoed barefoot across the tiled courtyard, which was lit by both moon and stars, slipped into Adam's wing of the house via a door at the far end, and sneaked down the hall to the office.

It could have been an hour later, or two, when Tate suddenly felt the hairs prickle on her arms. She had long since finished working at the computer. Because the chair in front of the desk was more comfortable than the one behind it—which was as straight-backed and rigid as the man who usually sat there—she had plopped down in it to look over the printout of what she had done. She had one ankle balanced on the front of the desk and the other hooked on the opposite knee.

She glanced up and found herself ensnared by the look of desire in Adam's heavy-lidded blue eyes.

"Working late?" he asked in a silky voice.

"I thought I'd finish a few things."

Tate was frozen, unable to move, uncomfortably aware that her long T-shirt had rucked up around her thighs, and that her legs were bare all the way up to yonder. As Adam stared intently at her, she felt her nipples harden into dark buds easily visible beneath the pink cotton.

Adam's chest was bare, revealing dark curls that arrowed down into his Levi's. His jeans seemed to be hanging on his hipbones. His belly was ribbed with muscle, and a faint sheen of perspiration made his skin glow in the light from the single standing lamp.

Adam was no less disconcerted by Tate's appearance. He had come to his office looking for a ranch journal and found a sultry sex kitten instead. His view of Tate's French-cut panties was wreaking havoc with his self-control. Her crow-black hair was tousled, and her whiskey-colored eyes were dark with feminine allure.

"You ought to know better than to come here half-dressed," Adam said.

"I wasn't expecting to see you."

One black brow arched disbelievingly. "Weren't you?"

Adam abruptly swept the desk clear of debris with one hand while he reached for Tate with the other. Papers flew in the air, cups shattered, Tate's handful of pebbles pinged as they shot across the tile floor. The last paper hadn't landed, nor the pinging sound faded, when he set her down hard on the edge of the desk facing him.

Tate's frightened protest died on her lips. Adam's fierce blue eyes never left hers as he spread her legs and stepped between them. He yanked her toward him, fitting the thin silk of her panties snugly against the heat and hardness of his arousal.

"Is this what you had in mind?" he demanded.

"Adam, I—"

She gasped as rough hands smoothed the cotton over her breasts, revealing nipples that ached for his touch.

"Adam—"

"You've been teasing me for weeks, *little girl*. Even I have my limits. You're finally going to get what you've been asking for."

"Adam—"

"Shut up, Tate."

He seized both her hands in one of his and thrust his fingers into the hair at her nape to hold her captive for his kiss.

Tate didn't dare breathe as Adam lowered his head to hers. Her body was alive with anticipation. Though she had wanted this ever since she had first laid eyes on Adam, she was still a little afraid of what was to come. She wanted this man, and she was certain now that he wanted her. Tonight she would know what it meant to be a woman, to be Adam's woman. The waiting was over at last.

Adam's anger at finding what he considered a sensual trap in his office made him more forceful with Tate than he had intended. But after all, she was no longer the tender, inexperienced virgin of a week ago.

However, somewhere between the moment he laced his hand into her hair and the instant his lips reached hers, his feelings underwent a violent transformation. Powerful emotions were at work, soothing the savage beast. When they finally kissed, there was nothing in his touch beyond the fierce need for her that thrummed through his body.

Tate was unprepared for the velvety softness of Adam's lips as he slid his mouth across hers. His teeth found her lower lip, and she shivered as he nipped it and then soothed the hurt. His tongue teased her, slipping inside, then retreating until she sought it out and discovered the taste of him. Dark and distinctive and uniquely male.

Tate was lost in sensation as each kiss was answered by a streak of desire that found its way to her belly. Her breasts felt full and achy, yet she was too inexperienced to ask for the touch that would have satisfied her body's yearning.

Sometime while she was being kissed, Adam had released her hands. Tate wasn't quite sure what to do with them. She sought out his shoulders, then slid her hands down his back, feeling the corded muscle and sinew that made him so different from her.

Her head fell back as Adam's mouth caressed the hollow in her throat. The male hands at her waist slowly slid up under her T-shirt until Adam was cupping her breasts. Tate gasped as his thumbs brushed across the aching crests. Her body seemed alive to the barest touch of his callused fingertips.

"I want to feel you against me," Adam said as he slipped the pink T-shirt off over her head.

Before Tate could feel embarrassed, his arms slid around her.

He sighed with satisfaction as he hugged her to him. "You feel so good," he murmured against her throat.

Tate's breasts were excruciatingly sensitive to the wiry texture of Adam's chest hair. She was intimately aware of his strength, of her own softness.

Adam grasped her thighs and pulled her more snugly against him. She clutched his shoulders and held on as his maleness pressed against her femininity, evoking feelings that were foreign, yet which coaxed an instinctive response.

A guttural groan escaped Adam as Tate arched her body into his. His hands dug into her buttocks, trying to hold her still.

"You're killing me, sweetheart," he said. "Don't move!"

"But it feels good," Tate protested.

Adam half groaned, half laughed. "Too good," he agreed. "Be still. I want to be sure you enjoy this as much as I do."

"Oh, I will," Tate assured him.

Adam chuckled as he slid his mouth down her throat. He captured a nipple in his mouth, sucked on it, teased it with his tongue, then sucked again, until Tate was writhing with pleasure in his arms.

He took one of her hands and slid it along the hard ridge in his jeans, too wrapped up in the pleasure of the moment to notice her virginal reluctance to touch him. "Feel what you do to me," he said. "I only have to look at you, think about you, and I want you!" His chin rested at her temple, and he was aware of the faint scent of lilacs. He would always think of her from now on when he smelled that particular fragrance.

It didn't take Tate long to realize how sensitive Adam was to her barest touch, and she reveled in her newfound feminine power.

When he could stand the pleasure no longer, Adam brought each of Tate's hands to his mouth, kissed her wrists and her palms, then placed her hands flat on his chest. "Lift your hips, sweetheart," Adam murmured as he tucked his thumbs into her bikini panties.

She did as he asked, and an instant later Tate was naked. She hid her face in his shoulder, suddenly shy with him.

Adam's arms slipped around her. "There's no need to be embarrassed, sweetheart," he teased.

"That's easy to say when you've got clothes on," she retorted.

Adam laughed. "That can be easily remedied."

He reached between them and unsnapped his jeans.

The harsh rasp of the zipper filled a silence broken only by the sound of her labored breathing, and his.

Tate grabbed Adam's wrist to keep him from pulling his zipper down any more. "Not yet," she said breathlessly.

She couldn't help the nerves that assailed her. Adam seemed to think she knew what to do, and perhaps she had led him to believe it was so, but she was all too aware of her ignorance—and innocence.

He dragged the zipper back up but left the snap undone. "There's no hurry, sweetheart. We have all night."

Tate shivered—as much from a virgin's qualms as from anticipation—at the thought.

Adam settled her hands at his waist and lifted his own to gently cup her face. He angled her chin so that she was looking up at him. "You're so damn beautiful!" he said.

"Your eyes." He kissed them closed.

"Your nose." He cherished the tip of it.

"Your cheeks." He gave each one an accolade.

"Your chin." He nipped it with his teeth.

"Your mouth."

Tate's eyes had slipped closed as Adam began his reverent seduction. She waited with bated breath for the kiss that didn't come. Suddenly she felt herself being lifted into his arms. Her eyes flashed open in alarm.

"Adam! What are you doing? Where are we going?"

He was already halfway down the hall to his room when he said, "I want the pleasure of making love to you for the first time in my own bed."

Tate had peeked into Adam's bedroom, but she had never been invited inside. It was decorated in warm earth tones, sandy browns and cinnamon. She had remcmbered being awed by the sheer size of his bed. The antique headboard was an intricately carved master-piece, and the spindles at head and foot nearly reached to the ten-foot ceiling.

The quilt that covered the bed was an intricate box design Tate had never seen before, but the craftsman-ship was exquisite. Tate grabbed Adam around the neck to keep from falling when he reached down to yank the quilt aside, revealing pristine white sheets.

"Now we can relax and enjoy ourselves," he said.

Adam laid her on the bed and in the same motion used his body to mantle hers. He nudged her legs apart with his knees and settled himself against her so that she was left in no doubt as to the reason he had brought her here.

"Where did you get this bed?" Tate asked, postpon-ing the moment of ultimate truth.

"It's a family heirloom. Several generations of my ancestors have been conceived and born here."

But not my own, Adam thought. *Never my own.*

Tate felt the sudden tension in his body. "Adam?"

Adam's features hardened as he recalled what had happened over the past week to cause him to be here now with Tate. She had made her choice. And he had made his. He wanted her, and she was willing. That was all that mattered now.

Adam's kiss was fierce, and Tate was caught up in the roughness of his lovemaking. There was nothing brutal about his caresses, but they were not gentle, ei-ther. His kisses were fervent, his passion unbridled, as he drove her ruthlessly toward a goal she could only imagine.

Tate was hardly aware when Adam freed himself of

his clothes. She was so lost in new sensations that the feel of his hard naked body against hers was but one of many delights. The feel of his hands...*there*. The feel of his lips and tongue...*there*.

Tate was in ecstasy bordering on pain. She reached with trembling hands for whatever part of Adam she could find with her hands and her mouth.

"Adam, please!" She didn't know what she wanted, only that she desperately needed...*something*. Her body arched toward his, wild with need.

Just as Adam lifted her hips for his thrust, she cried, "Wait!" But it was already too late.

Adam's face paled as he realized what he had done.

Tate's fingernails bit into his shoulder, and she clamped her teeth on her lower lip to keep from crying out. Tears of pain pooled in the corners of her eyes.

Adam felt her muscles clench involuntarily around him and struggled not to move, fearing he would hurt her more. "You didn't sleep with Buck," he said in a flat voice.

"No," she whispered.

"You were still a virgin."

"Yes," she whispered.

"Why did you make me think— Dammit to hell, Tate! I would have done things differently if I'd known. I wouldn't have—"

He started to pull out of her, but she clutched at his shoulders. "Please, Adam. It's done now. Make love to me."

Tate lifted her hips, causing Adam to grunt with pleasure.

Now that he knew how inexperienced she was, Adam tried to be gentle. But Tate took matters out of his hands, touching him in places that sent his pulse through the roof, taunting him with her mouth and hands, until his thrust was almost savage. He brought them both to a climax so powerful that it left them gasping.

Adam slid to Tate's side and folded her in his embrace. He reached down to pull the covers over them and saw the blood on the sheet that testified to her innocence.

It made him angry all over again.

"I hope you're pleased with yourself!"

"Yes, I am."

"Don't expect an offer of marriage, because you're not going to get it," he said bluntly.

Tate fumbled for a sheet to cover herself. She sat up and stared at Adam with wary eyes. "I don't think I expected any such thing."

"No? What about all those dreams of yours—meeting the right man, having a nice home and a gaggle of children playing at your feet?"

"Geese come in a gaggle," she corrected. "And for your information, I don't think my dream is the least bit unreasonable."

"It is if you have me pictured in the role of Prince Charming."

Tate flushed. She toyed with the sheet, arranging it to cover her naked flank.

Adam watched with regret as her tempting flesh disappeared from view. "Well, Tate?"

She looked into eyes still darkened with passion and said with all the tenderness she felt for him, "I love you, Adam."

"That was lust, not love."

Tate winced at the vehemence with which he denied the rightness of what had just happened between them.

"Besides," he added, "I like my women a little more experienced."

Adam did nothing to temper the pain he saw in Tate's face at his brutal rejection of her. He couldn't give her what she wanted, and he refused to risk the pain and humiliation of having her reject what little he could offer.

"If what you want is sex, I'm available," he said. "But I'm not in love with you, Tate. And I won't pretend I am."

Tate fought the tears that threatened. She would be *damned* if she would let him see how devastated she was by his refusal to acknowledge the beautiful experience they had shared.

"It wasn't just sex, Adam," she said. "You're only fooling yourself if you think it was."

His lips curled sardonically. "When you've had a little more experience you'll realize that any man can do the same thing for you."

"Even Buck?" she taunted.

A muscle jumped in Adam's jaw. She knew all the right buttons to push where he was concerned. "You get the hankering for a little sex, you come see *me*," he drawled. "*I'll* make sure you're satisfied, *little girl*."

Tate pulled the sheet free of the mattress and wrapped it around herself as best she could. "Good night, Adam. I think I'll sleep better in my own bed."

He watched her go without saying another word. The instant she was gone he pounded a fist into the mattress.

"Damn you, Tate Whitelaw!"

She had made him wish for something he could never have. She had offered him the moon and the stars. All he had to do was bare his soul to her. And take the heart-wrenching chance that she would reject what little he could offer in return.

Chapter 7

The tears Tate had refused to let Adam see her shed fell with a vengeance once she was alone. But she hadn't been raised to give up or give in. Before long Tate had brushed the tears aside and begun to plan how best to make Adam eat his words.

If Adam hadn't cared for her at least a little, Tate reasoned, he wouldn't have been so upset by her taunt that she would seek out Buck. She was certain that Adam's jealousy could be a powerful weapon in her battle to convince him that they belonged together. Especially since Adam had admitted that he was willing to take extreme measures—even making love to her!—to keep her away from Buck. Tate intended to seek Buck out and let the green-eyed monster eat Adam alive.

It was with some distress and consternation that Tate realized over the next several days that Adam had somehow turned the tables on her. He was the one who found excuses to send her off alone with Buck. And he did it with a smile on his face.

Where was the green-eyed monster? Was it possible Adam really *didn't* care? He was obviously pushing her in Buck's direction. Was this some sort of test? Did he expect her to fall into Buck's arms? Did he *want* her to?

If Tate was unsure of Adam's intentions, he was no less confused himself. He had woken up the morning after making love to Tate and realized that somewhere between the moment she had first flashed that gamine smile at him and the moment he had claimed her with his body, he had fallen in love with her. It was an appalling realization, coming, as it had, after he had insulted and rejected her.

Loving Tate meant being willing to do what was best for her—even if it meant giving her up. He had made the selflessly noble—if absurd—decision that if, after the way he had treated her, she would rather be with Buck, he would not stand in her way. So he had made excuses for them to be alone together. And suffered the agonies of the damned, wondering whether Buck was taking advantage of the time to make love to her.

One or the other of them might have relented and honestly admitted their feelings, but they weren't given the chance before circumstances caused the tension-fraught situation to explode.

Adam had gritted his teeth and nobly sent Tate off with Buck to the Saturday night dance at the Grange Hall in Knippa, not realizing that they were stopping to pick up Velma on the way.

Tate didn't lack for partners at the dance, but she was on her way to a wretchedly lonely evening nonetheless—because the one person she wanted to be with wasn't there. She refused a cowboy the next dance so she could catch her breath. Unfortunately, that gave her time to think.

She found herself admitting that she might as well give up on her plan to make Adam jealous, mainly because it wasn't working. If he truly didn't want her, she would have to leave the Lazy S. Because she couldn't stand to be around him knowing that the love she felt would never be returned.

An altercation on the dance floor dragged Tate from her morose reflections. She was on her feet an instant later when she realized that one of the two men slugging away at each other was Buck Magnesson.

She reached Velma's side and shouted over the ruckus, "What happened? Why are they fighting?"

"All the poor man did was wink at me!" Velma shouted back. "It didn't mean a thing! There was no reason for Buck to take a swing at him."

When Tate looked back to the fight it was all over. The cowboy who had winked at Velma was out cold, and Buck was blowing cool air on his bruised knuckles. He was sporting a black eye and a cut on his chin, but his smile was broad and satisfied.

"Guess he won't be making any more advances to you, honey," Buck said.

"You idiot! You animal! I don't know when I've ever been so humiliated in my entire life!" Velma raged.

"But, honey—"

"How could you?"

"But, honey—"

Tate and Buck were left standing as Velma turned in a huff and headed for the door. Buck threw some money on the table to pay for their drinks and raced outside after her.

Velma was draped across the hood of the pickup, her face hidden in her crossed arms as she sobbed her heart out.

When Buck tried to touch her, she whirled on him. "Stay away from me!"

"What did I do?" he demanded, getting angry now.

"You don't even know, do you?" she sobbed.

"No, I don't, so I'd appreciate it if you'd just spit it out."

"You didn't trust me!" she cried.

"What?"

"You didn't trust me to let that cowboy know I'm not interested. You took it upon yourself to make sure he'd keep his distance.

"You're never going to forget the fact that I strayed once, Buck. You're always going to be watching—waiting to see if I slip up again. And every time you do something to remind me that you don't trust me—like you did tonight—it'll hurt the way it hurts right now.

"I won't be able to stand it, Buck. It'll kill me to love you and know you're watching me every minute from the corner of your eye. Take me home. I never want to see you again!"

Velma sat on the outside edge of the front seat, with Tate in the middle during the long, silent fifteen-minute drive west to Uvalde from Knippa. When they arrived in Velma's driveway, she jumped out and went running into the house before Buck could follow her.

Buck crossed his arms on the steering wheel and dropped his forehead onto them. "God. I feel awful."

Tate didn't know what to say. So she just waited for him to talk.

"I couldn't help myself," he said. "When I saw that fellow looking at her… I don't know, I just went crazy."

"Because you were afraid he would make a move on Velma?"

"Yeah."

"Is Velma right, Buck? Didn't you trust her to say no on her own?"

Buck sighed. It was a defeated sound. "No."

There wasn't anything else to say. Buck had thought he could forgive and forget. But when it came right down to it, he would never trust Velma again. The risk was too great that his trust would prove unfounded.

"I don't want to be alone right now," Buck said. "Would you mind driving up toward the Frio with me? Maybe we can find a comfortable place to sit along the riverbank and lie back and count the stars. Just for a while," he promised. "I won't keep you out too late."

Tate knew Adam might be waiting up for her, but Buck had promised he wouldn't keep her out late. Besides, Adam's behavior over the past few days— throwing her into Buck's company—suggested that he no longer cared one way or the other.

"All right, Buck. Let's go. I could use some time away to think myself."

They found a spot beneath some immense cypress trees, and lay back on the grassy bank and listened to the wind whistling through the boughs. They tried to find the constellations and the North Star in the cloud-less blue-black sky. The burble of the water over the rocky streambed was soothing to two wounded souls.

They talked about nothing, and everything. About

childhood hopes and dreams. And adult realities. About wishes that never came true. They talked until their eyes drifted closed.

And they fell asleep.

Tate woke first. A mosquito was buzzing in her ear. She slapped at it, and when it came back again she sat up abruptly. And realized where she was. And who was lying beside her. And what time it was.

She shook Buck hard and said, "Wake up! It's dawn already. We must have fallen asleep. We've got to get home!"

Buck was used to rising early, but a night on the cold hard ground—not to mention the events of the previous evening—had left him grumpy. "I'm going, I'm going," he muttered as Tate shoved him toward the truck.

Tate sat on the edge of her seat the whole way home. She only hoped she could sneak into the house before Adam saw her. She could imagine what he would think if he saw her with grass stains on her denim skirt and a blouse that looked as if she had slept in it—which she had. Adam would never believe it had been a totally innocent evening.

When Buck dropped her off, she ran up the steps to the front door—a better choice than the kitchen if she hoped to avoid Adam—and stopped dead when he opened it for her. Adam stood back so she could come inside.

"We fell asleep!" she blurted. "Oh, Lord, that came out all wrong! Look, Adam, I can explain everything. Buck and I did fall asleep, but we weren't sleeping to-gether!"

"I wouldn't have let you sleep, either," he drawled.

"Not when there are so many more interesting things to do with the time."

"I mean, we didn't have sex," she said, irritated by his sarcasm.

"Oh, really?" It was obvious he didn't believe her.

"I'm telling you the truth!"

"What makes you think I care who you spent the night with, or what you did?" he said in a voice that could have cut steel.

"I'm telling you that absolutely nothing sexual happened between me and Buck Magnesson last night," she insisted.

Adam wanted to believe her. But he couldn't imagine how Buck could have kept her out all night and not have touched her. He didn't have that kind of willpower himself. His mouth was opened and the words were out before he knew he was going to say them.

"I made you an offer once, *little girl,* and I meant it. If you're looking for more experience in bed, I'll be more than happy to provide it."

Tate's eyes widened as she realized what Adam's harsh-sounding words really meant. He was *jealous!* He *did* care! If only there was some way of provoking him into admitting how he really felt! Of course, there was something that might work. It was an outrageous idea, but then, as her brother Faron had always preached, "A faint heart never filled a flush."

Tate sat down on the brass-studded leather sofa and pulled off one of her boots. When Adam said nothing, she pulled off the other one. Then she stood up and began releasing the zipper down the side of her skirt.

"What are you doing?" he asked at last.

"I'm taking you up on your offer."

"What? Are you serious?"

"Absolutely! Weren't you?" She looked up at him coyly, batted her lashes, and had the satisfaction of seeing him flush.

"You don't know what you're doing," he said.

"I know exactly what I'm doing," she replied.

Her skirt landed in a pile at her feet, and Tate was left standing in a frilly slip and a peasant blouse that was well on its way to falling off her shoulder.

Adam swallowed hard. He knew he ought to stop her, but was powerless to do so. "Maria will be—"

"You know Maria isn't here. Sunday is her day off."

Tate reached for the hem of her blouse and pulled it up over her head.

Adam gasped. He had never seen her in a bra before—if that's what you called the tiny piece of confection that hugged her breasts and offered them up in lacy cups for a hungry man's palate.

Tate watched Adam's pulse jump when she stepped out of the circle of her skirt and walked toward him. His hand was warm when she took it in her own. "Your bedroom or mine?" she asked.

"Mine," he croaked.

Adam allowed himself to be led to his bedroom as though he had no will of his own. Indeed, he felt as though he were living some sort of fantasy. Since it was one very much to his liking, he wasn't putting up much of a struggle—none, actually—to be free.

"Here we are," Tate said as she closed the door behind her, shutting them into Adam's bedroom alone.

"I've never been made love to in the morning," Tate said. "Is there any special way it should be done?"

What healthy, red-blooded male could resist that kind of invitation?

Adam swept Tate off her feet. From then on she was caught up in a whirlwind of passion that left her breathless and panting. But now he led and she followed.

Lips reached out for lips. Flesh reached out for flesh. She was aware of textures, hard and soft, silky and crisp, rigid and supple, as Adam introduced her to the delights of sex in the warm sunlight.

This time there was no pain, only joy as he joined their bodies and made them one. When it was over, they lay together in the tangled sheets, her head on his shoulder, his hand on her hip, in a way that spoke volumes about the true state of their hearts.

Tate was aware of the fact Adam hadn't said a word since she had closed the bedroom door behind them. She didn't want to break the magic spell, so she remained silent. But it was plain from the way Adam began moving restlessly, tugging on the sheet, rearranging it to cover and uncover various parts of her body, that there was something he wanted to get off his chest.

"I don't want you to go out with Buck anymore," he said in a quiet voice.

"All right."

"Just like that? All right?"

"I don't want Buck," she said. "I want you."

Adam groaned and pulled her into his arms, holding her so tightly that she protested, "I'm not going anywhere!"

"I can hardly believe that you're here. That you want to be here," Adam said with a boyish grin. "I've been going crazy for the past week."

"Me, too," Tate admitted. "But everything is going

to be perfect now, isn't it, Adam? You do love me, don't you?"

She didn't wait for an answer, just kept on talking.

"We can be married and start a family. Oh, how I'd love to have a little boy with your blue eyes and—"

Adam abruptly sat up on the edge of the bed.

Tate put a hand on his back and he shrugged it off. "Adam? What's wrong?"

He looked over his shoulder with eyes as desolate as an endless desert. "I thought I'd made it clear that I wasn't offering marriage."

"But you love me. Don't you?"

Instead of replying to her question, he said, "I was married once before, for eight years. It ended in a bitter divorce. I have no desire to repeat the experience."

Tate couldn't have been more shocked if Adam had said he was a convicted mass murderer. "Why didn't you ever say anything to me about this before?"

"It wasn't any of your business."

"Well, now it is!" she retorted, stung by his bluntness. "You don't have to make the same mistakes this time around, Adam. Just because one marriage failed doesn't mean another will."

He clenched his teeth, trying to dredge up the courage to tell her the truth. But he wasn't willing to risk the possibility that she would choose having children over having him. And he refused to offer marriage while his awful secret lay like a wedge between them.

"I want you in my bed, I won't deny it," Adam said. "But you'll have to settle for what I'm offering."

"What's that?" Tate asked. "An affair?"

Adam shrugged. "If you want to call it that."

"And when you're tired of me, then what?"

I'll never get tired of you. "We'll cross that river when we get to it."

Tate was shaken by the revelation that Adam had been married. She wished she knew more about what had gone wrong to make him sound so bitter. Her pride urged her to leave while she still could. But her heart couldn't face a future that didn't include Adam. With the naïveté of youth, she still believed that love would conquer all, that somehow, everything would work out and that they would live happily ever after.

"All right," she said at last. "An affair it is."

She snuggled up to Adam's back. He took her arms and pulled them around his chest.

"It's a good thing my brothers can't see me now," she teased.

"I'd be a dead man for sure," he said with a groan.

"Just thank your lucky stars that I've been using a false last name. They'll never find me here."

"Let's hope not," Adam muttered.

The conversation ended there, because Adam turned and pulled Tate around onto his lap. He still didn't quite believe that she hadn't stalked out in high dudgeon, that she had chosen to stay. He straightened her legs around his lap and slipped inside her.

Tate learned yet another way to make love in the morning.

It was a mere three weeks later that their idyll came to a shocking and totally unforeseen end.

Chapter 8

Tate was pregnant. At least she thought she was. She was sitting in Dr. Kowalski's office, waiting for her name to be called so she could find out if the results of her home pregnancy test were as accurate as the company claimed. She was only eight days late, but never once had such a phenomenon occurred in the past. Who would have thought you could get pregnant the first time out!

It had to have happened then, because after that first time she had gone to see Dr. Kowalski and been fitted for a diaphragm. She had managed to use it every time she had made love with Adam over the past three weeks—except the time she had seduced him after spending the night at the river with Buck. So maybe it had happened the second time out. That was beginner's luck for you!

"Mrs. Whitelaw? You're next."

Tate sat up, then realized the nurse had said *Mrs.* Whitelaw. Besides, she had given her name as Tate Whatly. So who was this mysterious *Mrs.* Whitelaw?

The tall woman who stood up was very pregnant. The condition obviously agreed with her, because her skin glowed with health. She had curly blond hair that fell to her shoulders and a face that revealed her age and character in smile lines at the edges of her cornflower-blue eyes and the parentheses bracketing her mouth.

Tate found it hard to believe that it was pure coincidence that this woman had the same unusual last name as she did. Jesse had been gone for so long without any word that Tate immediately began weaving fantasies around the pregnant woman. Maybe this was Jesse's wife. Maybe Jesse would walk in that door in a few minutes and Tate would see him at long last.

Maybe pigs would fly.

Tate watched the woman disappear into an examining room. She was left with little time to speculate because she was called next.

"Ms. Whatly?"

"Uh, yes." She had almost forgotten the phony name she had given the nurse.

"You can come on back now. We'll need a urine specimen, and then I'd like you to strip down and put on this gown. It ties in front. The doctor will be with you in a few minutes."

Tate had had only one pelvic examination in her life—when she had been fitted for the diaphragm—and all the medical hardware attached to the examining table looked as cold and intimidating as she remembered. The wait seemed more like an hour, but actually was only about fifteen minutes. Tate had worked herself into a pretty good case of nerves by the time Dr. Kowalski came into the room.

"Hello, Tate. I understand the rabbit died."

The doctor's teasing smile and her twinkling eyes immediately put Tate at ease. "I'm afraid so," she answered.

The doctor's hands were as warm as her manner. Tate found herself leaving the doctor's office a short time later with a prescription for prenatal vitamins and another appointment in six weeks.

Tate was in the parking lot, still dazed by the confirmation of the fact she was going to have Adam's baby, when she realized that the woman who had been identified as Mrs. Whitelaw was trying to hoist her ungainly body into a pickup.

Tate hurried over to her. "Need a hand?"

"I think I can manage," the woman answered with a friendly smile. "Thanks, anyway."

Tate closed the door behind the pregnant woman, then cupped her hands over the open window frame. "The nurse called you Mrs. Whitelaw. Would you by any chance know a Jesse Whitelaw?"

The woman smiled again. "He's my husband."

Tate's jaw dropped. "No fooling! Really? Jesse's your husband! You've got to be kidding! Why, that means he's going to be a father!"

The woman chuckled at Tate's exuberance. "He sure is. My name's Honey," the woman said. "What's yours?"

"I'm Tate. Wow! This is fantastic! I can't believe this! Wait until I tell Faron and Garth!"

Tate sobered suddenly. She couldn't contact Faron and Garth to tell them she had found Jesse without taking the chance of having them discover her whereabouts. But Jesse wouldn't know she had run away from home. She could see him, and share this joy with him.

With the mention of Tate's name, and then Faron's and Garth's, Honey's gaze had become speculative, and finally troubled. When Honey had first found out she was pregnant, she had urged Jesse to get back in touch with his family. It had taken a little while to convince him, but eventually she had.

When Jesse had called Hawk's Way, he had found his brothers frantic with worry. His little sister Tate had disappeared from the face of the earth, and Faron and Garth feared she had suffered some dire fate.

If Honey wasn't mistaken, she was looking at her husband's little sister—the one who had been missing for a good two and a half months. The prescription for prenatal vitamins that Tate had been waving in her hand suggested that Jesse's little sister had been involved in a few adventures since she had left home.

"I have a confession to make," Tate said, interrupting Honey's thoughts. "Jesse—your husband—is my brother! That makes us sisters, I guess. Gee, I never had a sister. This is great!"

Honey smiled again at Tate's ebullience. "Maybe you'd like to come home with me and see Jesse," she offered.

Tate's brow furrowed as she tried to imagine what Jesse's reaction would be to the fact that she was here on her own. On second thought, it might be safer to meet him on her own ground. "Why don't you and Jesse come over for dinner at my place instead?" Tate said.

"Your place?"

Tate grinned and said, "Well, it's not exactly *mine*.

I'm living at the Lazy S and working as a bookkeeper for Adam Philips."

"Horsefeathers," Honey murmured.

"Is something wrong?"

"No. Nothing." Except that Adam Philips was the man she had jilted to marry Jesse Whitelaw.

"Well, do you think you could come?"

If Tate didn't realize the can of worms she was opening, Honey wasn't about to be the one to tell her. Honey was afraid that if she didn't take advantage of Tate's offer, the girl might run into Jesse sometime when Honey wasn't around. From facts Honey knew—that Tate obviously didn't—it was clear the fur was going to fly. Honey wanted to be there to make sure everyone came out with a whole skin.

"Of course we'll come," she said. "What time?"

"About seven. See you then, Honey. Oh, and it was nice meeting you."

"Nice meeting you, too," Honey murmured as Tate turned and hurried away. Honey watched the younger woman yank open the door to the '51 Chevy pickup her brothers claimed she had confiscated when she had run away from home.

"Horsefeathers," she said again. The word didn't do nearly enough to express the foreboding she felt about the evening ahead of her.

Meanwhile, Tate was floating on air. This was going to work out perfectly. She would introduce Adam to her brother and his wife, and later, when they were alone, she would tell Adam that he was going to be a father.

Boy was he going to be surprised!

Tate refused to imagine Adam's reaction as anything other than ecstatic. After all, just as two people didn't have to be married to have sex, they didn't have to be married to have children, either. After all, lots of movie stars were doing it. Why couldn't they?

Long before seven o'clock Tate heard someone pounding on the front door. She knew it couldn't be the company she had invited, and from the sound of things it was an emergency. She ran to open the door and gasped when she realized who was standing there.

"Jesse!"

"So it *is* you!"

Tate launched herself into her brother's arms. He lifted her up and swung her in a circle, just as he had the last time they had seen each other, when she was a child of eight.

Jesse looked so much the same, and yet he was different. His dark eyes were still as fierce as ever, his black hair still as shaggy. But his face was lined, and his body that of a mature man, not the twenty-year-old boy who had gone away when she was just a little girl.

"You look wonderful, Tate," Jesse said.

"So do you," she said with an irrepressible grin. She angled her head around his broad chest, trying to locate Honey. "Where's your wife?"

"I came ahead of her." Actually, he had snuck out behind Honey's back and come running to save his little sister from that sonofabitch Adam Philips. Jesse had never liked the man, and now his feelings had been vindicated. Just look how Philips had taken advantage of his baby sister!

"Faron and Garth have been worried to death about you," Jesse chastised.

"You've been in touch with them? When? How?"

"Honey talked me into calling them when she found

out for sure she was pregnant. Is it true what Honey told me? Are you living here with Adam Philips?" Jesse demanded.

"I work here," Tate said, the pride she felt in her job apparent in her voice. "I'm Adam's bookkeeper."

"What else do you do for Adam?"

Tate hissed in a breath of air. "I don't think I like your tone of voice."

"Get your things," Jesse ordered. "You're getting out of here."

Tate's hands fisted and found her hips. "I left home to get away from that kind of high-handedness. I don't intend to let you get away with it, either," she said tartly. "I happen to enjoy my job, and I have no intention of giving it up."

"You don't have any idea what can happen to a young woman living alone with a man!"

"Oh, don't I?"

"Do you mean to say that you and Philips—"

"My relationship with Adam is no concern of yours."

Jesse's dark eyes narrowed speculatively. His little sister glowed from the inside out. He was mentally adding one and one—and getting three. "Honey said she met you in the parking lot of Doc Kowalski's office, but she didn't say what you were doing there. What were you doing there, Tate? Are you sick?"

Jesse was just fishing, Tate thought. He couldn't know anything for sure. But even a blind pig will find an acorn once in a while. She had to do something to distract him.

"Honey's a really beautiful woman, Jesse. How did you meet her?"

"Don't change the subject, Tate."

Jesse had just grabbed Tate by the arm when Adam stepped into the living room from the kitchen. "I thought I heard voices in here." Adam spied Jesse's hold on Tate, and his body tensed. He welcomed the long overdue confrontation with Tate's brother. "Hello, Jesse. Would you mind telling me what's going on?"

"I'm taking my sister home," Jesse said.

Adam searched Tate's face, looking deep into her hazel eyes. "Is that what you want?"

"I want to stay here."

"You heard her, Jesse," Adam said in a steely voice. "Let her go."

"You bastard! It'll be a cold day in hell before I leave my sister in your clutches."

Adam took a step forward, eyes flashing, teeth bared, fists clenched.

"Stop it! Both of you!" Tate yanked herself free from Jesse's grasp, but remained between the two men, a human barrier to the violence that threatened to erupt at any moment.

"Get out of the way, Tate," Jesse said.

"Do as he says," Adam ordered.

Tate put a firm, flat palm on each man's chest to keep them apart. "I said stop it, and I meant it!"

"I'm taking you home, Tate," Jesse said. But his words and the challenge were meant for Adam.

"If Tate wants to stay, she stays!" Adam retorted, accepting the summons to battle.

Tate might as well not have been there for as much attention either man paid to her. She was merely the prize to be won. They were intent only on the conflict to come.

There was a loud knocking at the door, but before

any of them could move, it opened and Honey stepped inside. "Thank goodness I got here in time!"

Honey stepped between the two men who fell back in deference to her pregnant state. "What are you two doing to this poor girl?" She slipped a comforting arm around Tate's shoulder. "Are you all right, Tate?"

"I'm fine," Tate said. "But these two idiots are about to start pounding on each other!"

"He's got it coming!" Jesse growled. "What kind of low-down hyena seduces an innocent child!"

"Jesse!" Tate cried, mortified as much by his use of the term *child* as by his accusation. Jesse might still remember her as a child, but she was a woman now.

Adam's face had bleached white. "You're way off base, Whitelaw," he snarled.

"Can you say you aren't sleeping with her?" Jesse demanded.

"That's none of your damn business!" Adam snapped back.

Honey stepped back a pace, taking Tate with her, beyond the range of the animosity radiating from the two powerful men.

Tate turned to plead peace with her brother. "I love Adam," she said.

"But I'll bet he hasn't said he loves you," Jesse retorted in a mocking voice.

Tate lowered her eyes and bit her lip.

"I thought not!" he said triumphantly.

Tate's chin lifted and her eyes flashed defiance. "I won't leave him!"

"He's just using you to get back at me," Jesse said. "The reason I know he can't love you, is because *I* stole the woman *he* wanted right out from under his nose."

"What?" Confused, Tate looked from her brother to her lover. Adam's eyes were dark with pain and regret.

Tate whirled her head to look at Honey. The pregnant woman's arms were folded protectively around her unborn child. Her cheeks flamed. She slowly lifted her lids and allowed Tate to see the guilt in her lovely cornflower-blue eyes.

It couldn't be true! Adam wouldn't have done something so heinous as to seduce her to get back at her brother for stealing the woman he loved. But none of the three parties involved was denying it.

Her eyes sought out Adam's face again, looking for some shred of hope that her brother was lying. "Adam?"

Adam's stony features spoke volumes even though he remained mute.

"Oh, God," Tate breathed. "This can't be happening to me!"

Jesse lashed out with his fist at the man who had caused his sister so much pain. Adam instinctively stepped back and Jesse's fist swung through empty air. Before Jesse could swing the other fist, Honey had thrown herself in front of her husband.

"Please don't fight! Please, Jesse!"

It was a tribute to how much Jesse loved his wife that he held himself in check. He circled his wife's shoulder with one hand and held out the other to Tate.

"Are you coming?" he asked.

"I… I'm staying." At least until she had a chance to talk with Adam in private and hear his side of this unbelievable story. Then she would decide whether to tell him that she was going to have his child.

Honey saw that her husband was ready to argue fur-

ther and intervened. "She's a grown woman, Jesse. She
has to make her own choices."

"Dammit, this is the wrong one!" Jesse snarled.

"But it is my choice," Tate said in a quiet voice.

Honey slipped her arm around her husband's waist.
"Let's go home, Jesse."

"I'm leaving," Jesse said. "But I'll be back with Faron
and Garth." He yanked open the door, urged his wife
out of the house and quickly followed, slamming the
door after him.

Tate felt her stomach fall to her feet. She had been
surprised to see Adam stand up to her brother—
overjoyed, in fact. But if all three of the Whitelaw brothers showed up, there was no way Adam would be able
to endure against them. Her brothers would haul her
back home before she had time to say yeah, boo, or
"I'm pregnant."

"You might as well say goodbye to me now," she said
glumly. "When Faron and Garth find out where I am
they'll be coming for me."

"No one—your brothers included—is going to take
you from the Lazy S if you don't want to go," Adam
said in a hard voice.

"Does that mean you want me to stay?"

Adam nodded curtly.

She didn't want to ask, but she had to. "Is it true,
what my brother said? Did you love Honey?"

That same curt nod in response.

Tate felt the constriction in her chest tighten. "Would
you have married her if Jesse hadn't come along?"

Adam shoved a hand through his hair in agitation.
"I don't know. I wanted to marry her. I'm not so sure

she was as anxious to marry me. I asked her. She never said yes."

That was small comfort to Tate, who was appalled to hear how close Adam had come to marrying her brother's wife.

"Is that why you can't love me?" Tate asked. "Because you're still in love with her?"

The tortured look of pain on Adam's face left Tate feeling certain she had hit upon the truth. But she didn't despair. In fact, she felt a great deal of hope. Adam must realize that he could never have Honey Whitelaw now. Time was the best doctor for a wound of the heart. And time was on her side.

She very carefully did not bring up the subject of Jesse's accusation that Adam had made love to her to get revenge on her brother. In her heart she knew Adam would never use her like that. He might not be able to say he loved her—yet—but she was certain that one day he would.

"I need a hug," Tate said.

Adam opened his arms and Tate stepped into them. She snuggled against him, letting the love she felt flow over them both. But his body remained stiff and unyielding.

"Adam, I'm…" The word *pregnant* wouldn't come out.

"What is it, Tate?"

His voice sounded harsh in her ear, his tone still as curt as the abrupt nods with which he had acknowledged his love for another woman. Maybe Tate would just wait a little while before she told him she was carrying his child.

"I'm glad you want me to stay," she said.

He hugged her harder, until his hold was almost painful. Tate felt tears pool in the corners of her eyes. She blamed the phenomenon now on the heightened emotions caused by her pregnancy.

But the devil on her shoulder forced her to admit that unsettling seeds of doubt had been planted concerning whether everything would turn out happily ever after.

Chapter 9

Tate spent the night in Adam's arms. He couldn't have been more comforting. But for the first time since they had begun sleeping together, they didn't make love.

When they met across the kitchen table the next morning, an awkwardness existed between them that had not been there in the past.

"You must eat more, *señorita*," Maria urged. "You will not make it through the day on so little."

"I'm not hungry," Tate said. Actually, she had already snuck in earlier and had a light breakfast to stave off the first symptoms of morning sickness. Under Maria's stern eye, she dutifully applied herself to the bowl of oatmeal in front of her.

Tate's concentration was so complete that she paid no attention to the subsequent conversation Maria conducted with Adam in Spanish.

"The *señorita* has been crying," Maria said.

Adam glanced at Tate's red-rimmed eyes. "Her brother came to visit yesterday, the one she hasn't seen since she was a child."

"This brother made her cry?"

"He wanted her to go away with him."

"Ah. But you did not let her go."

"She chose to stay," Adam corrected.

"Then why was she crying?" Maria asked.

A muscle worked in Adam's jaw. At last he answered, "Because she's afraid I don't love her."

"Stupid man! Why don't you tell her so and put the smile back on her face?"

Adam sighed disgustedly. "I don't think she'll believe me now."

Maria shook her head and clucked her tongue. "I am going to the store to buy groceries. I will not be coming back for two—no, three hours. Tell her you love her."

Adam's lips curled sardonically. "All right, Maria. I'll give it a try."

Tate had been making shapes with her oatmeal and had only eaten about three bites when Maria whisked the bowl out from in front of her.

"I need to clear the table so I can go shopping," Maria said. She refilled Tate's coffee cup. "You sit here and enjoy another cup of coffee."

She refilled Adam's cup as well and, giving him a suggestive look, said, "You keep the *señorita* company."

Maria took off her apron, picked up her purse and left by the kitchen door a few moments later.

When she was gone, the silence seemed oppressive. Finally Adam said, "What are your plans for today?"

"I guess I'll input some more information on the computer. What about you?"

"I'm moving cattle from one pasture to another."

"Your job sounds like more fun than mine. Can I come along?"

"I don't think that would be a good idea."

"Oh."

Adam saw the look on Tate's face and realized she thought he was rejecting her—again. He swore under his breath. "Look, Tate. I think we'd better have a talk."

Tate rose abruptly. This was where Adam told her that he had thought things over and he wanted her to leave the Lazy S after all. She wasn't going to hang around to let him do it. "I'd better get going. I—"

Adam caught her before she had gone two steps. He took her shoulders in his hands, turning her to face him. She kept her eyes lowered, refusing to look at him.

"Tate," he said in a voice that was tender with the love he felt for her. "Look at me."

Her eyes were more green than gold. He couldn't bear to see the sadness in them. He grasped her nape and pulled her toward him as his mouth lowered to claim hers.

It was a hungry kiss. A kiss of longing for things that ought to be. A kiss fierce with passion. And tender with love.

Adam wanted to be closer. He pulled her T-shirt up and over her head, then yanked the snaps open down the front of his shirt and pulled the tails out of his jeans. He sighed in satisfaction as he closed his arms around her and snuggled her naked breasts tight against his chest.

"Lord, sweetheart. You feel so good!" He cupped her fanny with his hands and lifted her, rubbing himself against her, letting the layers of denim add to the friction between them.

His mouth found a spot beneath her ear that he knew was sensitive, and he sucked just hard enough to make her moan with pleasure.

Adam froze when he heard the kitchen door being flung open. He whirled to meet whatever threat was there, pulling Tate close and pressing her face against his chest protectively.

Tate felt Adam's body tense, felt his shoulders square and his stance widen. She knew who it was, who it had to be. She turned her head. There in the doorway stood her three brothers, Faron, Jesse and Garth. And Garth was carrying a shotgun.

Tate felt her face flush to the roots of her hair. She was naked from the waist up, and there could be no doubt as to what she had been doing with Adam. Or, from the looks on their faces, how her brothers felt about it. She closed her eyes and clutched Adam, knowing her brothers planned to tear them apart.

"Make yourself decent!" Garth ordered.

Tate reached across to the chair where Adam had slung her T-shirt, and with her back to her brothers, pulled it over her head. When she turned to face them, Adam put an arm around her waist and pulled her snug against his hip.

The three men crowded into the kitchen. It soon became apparent they hadn't come alone. An elderly gentleman wearing a clerical collar and carrying what Tate supposed to be a Bible followed them inside.

"You have a choice," Garth said to Adam. "You can make an honest woman of my sister, or I can kill you."

Adam cocked a brow. "That's murder."

Garth smiled grimly. "It'll be an accidental shoot-ing, of course."

"Of course," Adam said, his lips twisting cynically. "What if Tate and I aren't ready to get married?"

"Man gets a woman pregnant, it's time to marry her," Jesse snarled. "I made a point of seeing Doc Kowal-ski on the way home last night and told her Tate was my sister. She congratulated me on the fact I'll soon be an *uncle!*"

Adam froze. He turned to stare at Tate, but she re-fused to meet his gaze. His hand tightened on her waist. "Are you pregnant, Tate?"

She nodded.

Adam's lips flattened and a muscle worked in his jaw. He grabbed hold of her chin and forced it up. "Whose child is it? Buck's?"

"Yours!" Tate cried, jerking her head from his grasp.

"Not mine," he said flatly. "I'm sterile."

Tate sank into a kitchen chair at one end of the table, her eyes never wavering from Adam's granitelike ex-pression.

Meanwhile, Tate's brothers were in a quandary.

"We can't force him to marry Tate if the child's not his," Faron argued.

"But it must be his!" Jesse said. "Look how we found them today!"

Garth handed the shotgun to Faron, then crossed and sat down beside Tate on the opposite side of the table from Adam. He took Tate's hand from her lap and held it in his for a moment, gently rubbing her knuckles. "I want you to be honest with me, Tate. Have you been with another man besides Adam?"

"No! I'm carrying Adam's child, whether he believes it or not!"

"Adam says he's sterile," Garth persisted.

"I don't care what he says," Tate said through clenched teeth. "I'm telling the truth."

Garth and Faron exchanged a significant glance. Garth stood and confronted Adam. "Can you deny you've made love to my sister?"

"No, I don't deny that."

"Then my original offer still holds," Garth said.

"Given that choice, I suppose I have no choice," Adam conceded with a stony glare.

"What about me?" Tate asked. "Don't I get a choice?"

"You'll do as you're told," Garth commanded. "Or else."

"Or else what?"

"You come home to Hawk's Way."

Tate shuddered. There seemed no escape from the ultimatum Garth had given her. At least if she went through with the wedding, she would still have her freedom. Once her brothers had her safely married they would go back where they had come from—and she could figure out what to do from there.

"All right. Let's get this over with," she said.

"Reverend Wheeler, if you please?" Garth directed the minister to the head of the table, arranged Tate and Adam on one side, and stood on the other side with Faron and Jesse.

He told Adam, "I had to cut a few corners, but I've taken care of getting the license." He gestured to the minister. "Whenever you're ready, Reverend."

If Reverend Wheeler hadn't baptized Tate and presided at her confirmation, he might have had some qualms about what he was about to do. Never had bride and bridegroom looked less happy to be wed. But he firmly believed in the sanctity of home and family. And Garth had promised a large donation to build the new Sunday school wing.

The reverend opened the Bible he had brought along and began to read, "Dearly Beloved…"

Tate listened, but she didn't hear what was being said, spoke when called upon, but was unaware of the answers she gave. She had fallen into a deep well of despair.

Tate had never really thought about having a big wedding, but a white T-shirt was a poor substitute for a wedding gown. She wouldn't have minded giving up the festive trappings, if only she were sure the man standing beside her wanted to be her husband.

Adam did not.

How had things gone so wrong? Tate had never meant to trap Adam. It was clear he thought she had slept with Buck, and that the baby wasn't his. She knew from her experience with Buck and Velma that a marriage that lacked trust—on both sides—was in deep trouble. If Adam believed she had lied about the child's father, wouldn't he expect her to lie about other things? Would he, like Buck, overreact from now on if she so much as looked at another man? Of course Buck was jealous because he loved Velma. Tate wasn't so sure about Adam's feelings. He had never once said he loved her.

Tate would have given anything if she had just told Adam about the baby last night. Then, they would have had a chance to discuss things alone. Such as why a man who was obviously able to sire children thought he was sterile.

"Tate?"

"What?"

"Hold out your hand so Adam can put the ring on your finger," Garth said.

What ring? Tate thought.

"With this ring I thee wed," Adam said. He slipped the turquoise ring he usually wore on his little finger on the third finger of Tate's left hand.

Tate was lost. What had happened to the rest of the ceremony? Had she said "I do"?

Reverend Wheeler said, "I now pronounce you man and wife. You may kiss the bride."

When neither of the newlyweds moved, Faron said in a quiet—some might have said gentle—voice, "It's time to kiss your bride now, Adam."

Adam wanted to refuse. It was all a sham, anyway. But when Tate turned her face up to him she looked so bewildered he felt the urge to take her in his arms and protect her.

Garth cleared his throat at the delay.

Adam's jaw tightened. Tate already had three very efficient guardians. She didn't need him. But he found himself unable to resist the temptation of her lips, still swollen from his earlier kisses. Her eyes slid closed as he lowered his head. He touched his lips lightly to hers, taking the barest taste of her with the tip of his tongue.

If this had been a real wedding he would have wanted to cherish this moment. From the shuffling sounds across the table, Adam was reminded that it was real enough. So he took what he wanted from Tate, ravaging her mouth, letting her feel his fury and frustration at what her brothers had robbed them of when they had insisted on this forced marriage.

As soon as he lifted his head Adam saw that Garth had crossed around the table. Instead of the punch in the nose Adam expected, Tate's oldest brother held out his hand to be shaken. To Adam's further surprise, Garth had a grin on his face.

"Welcome to the family," Garth said. He gave Tate a fierce hug. "Be happy!" he whispered in her ear.

Faron was next to shake Adam's hand. "How about a drink to celebrate?" he asked. "I've got champagne on ice outside in the pickup."

"I guess that would be all right," Adam said, still stunned by the abrupt change in attitude of Tate's brothers.

Faron headed outside as Jesse approached Adam. The two men eyed each other warily.

At last Jesse held out his hand. "Truce?"

When Adam hesitated, Jesse said, "Honey will kill me if we don't make peace." When Adam still hesitated, Jesse added, "For Tate's sake?"

Adam shook hands with Tate's middle brother. They would never be good friends. But they were neighbors, and now brothers-in-law. For their wives' sakes, they would tolerate one another.

The wedding celebration was a lively affair. Now that Adam had done the right thing by Tate, her brothers were more than willing to treat him like one of the family.

As the morning wore on and Adam had a few glasses of champagne—and more than a few glasses of whiskey—he began to think maybe things hadn't turned out so badly after all.

Now that he and Tate were married, there was no reason why they couldn't make the best of the situation. He couldn't feel sorry about the baby, even if it meant Tate had lied to him about sleeping with Buck. He had always wanted children, and this one would be especially beloved because it would belong to him and Tate.

After he made love to his wife, Adam would tell her that he loved her. They could forget what had happened in the past. Their lives could begin from there.

Tate's brothers might have stayed longer, except Honey called to make sure everything had turned out all right. When Jesse hung up the phone, he said to his brothers, "I know you don't want to be reminded, but I have work that has to get done today."

Faron guffawed and said, "Tell the truth. What you're really concerned about is getting home to your wife."

The three brothers kidded each other good-naturedly all the way out the door. Once they and the preacher were gone, Tate closed the door and leaned her forehead against the cool wood frame.

"I'm sorry, Adam."

He crossed to her and slipped his arms around her waist from behind. "It's all right, Tate. It wasn't your fault."

"They're *my* brothers."

"They only did what they thought was best for you." Despite the fact he was a victim of their manipulation, Adam could sympathize with her brothers. If Melanie had lived…if he had found her in the same circumstances…he might have done the same thing. And hoped for the best. As Adam was hoping for the best now with Tate.

He kissed her nape and felt her shiver in his arms. "Come to bed, Tate. It's our wedding day."

She kept her face pressed to the door. She was too intent on giving Adam back his freedom to hear the message of love in his words and his caress. "I can't stand it—knowing you were trapped into marrying me." She felt his body stiffen, and said, "I promise I'll give you a divorce. As soon as the baby is born I—"

Adam grabbed her by the arm and jerked her around to face him. "Is that the reason you agreed to marry me? So you can have a name for your bastard?"

"Please, Adam—"

"Don't beg, Tate, it doesn't become you."

Tate had slapped him before she was aware she had raised her hand. She gasped when she saw the stark imprint her fingers had left on his cheek.

Adam grabbed her wrist. Tate could feel him trembling with rage. She waited to see what form his retaliation would take.

"All right," Adam said in the harshest voice she had ever heard him use. "I'll give you what you want. Your baby will have my name and you can have your divorce. But there's something I want in return, Tate."

"What?" she breathed.

"You. I want you in my bed every night." His grasp on her wrist tightened. "Warm. And willing. Do I make myself understood?"

Oh, she understood, all right. She had offered him the divorce hoping he would refuse. His ultimatum made it clear what he had wanted from her all along. Well, she would just show him what he was so willing to give up!

"Believe me, you're going to get what you're asking for, Adam," she said in a silky voice. *And a whole lot more!*

He started for the bedroom, his hand firmly clamped around her wrist. Tate hurried to catch up, afraid that if she fell, he would simply drag her behind him.

When they arrived in the bedroom he closed the door behind her. Only then did he release her. "Get undressed," he ordered. He crossed his arms and stood there, legs widespread, staring at her.

Tate held herself proudly erect. Sooner or later Adam was going to realize the truth. The child she carried was his. Meanwhile, he was going to get every bit of what he had demanded—and perhaps even more than he had bargained for.

Tate had never stripped to tease a man. She did so now.

The T-shirt came off first. Slowly. She let it hang by one finger for a moment before it dropped to the floor. She looked down at her breasts and saw the aureoles were pink and full. She reached down to brush her fingertips across her nipples, then returned to tease the pink buds until they stood erect.

Adam hissed in a breath of air.

Tate didn't dare look at him, afraid she would lose her nerve. Instead she smoothed her hands over her belly and down across the delta of her thighs, spreading her legs so that her hand could cup the heat there. She glided her hands back up the length of her body, feeling the textures of her skin, aware of the prickles as her flesh responded to the knowledge that Adam was watching every move she made.

She shoved her hands into her hair at the temples and then gathered her hair and lifted it off her nape, knowing that as she raised her arms her breasts would follow. She arched her back in a sensuous curve that thrust breasts and belly toward Adam.

She actually heard him swallow. Then she made the mistake of looking at him—at his bare chest. His nipples were as turgid as hers. As she relaxed her body into a more natural pose, she met blue eyes so dark with passion they were more the hue of a stormy sky.

His nostrils were flared to drink in the scent of her. His body was wired taut as a bowstring, fists clenched at his sides. His manhood was a hard ridge that threatened the seams at the crotch of his jeans. As his tongue reached out to lick at the perspiration on his upper lip, she felt her groin tighten with answering pleasure.

Tate felt exultant. Powerful. And oh, so much a woman. Encouraged by her success, she reached down for the snap of her jeans. Adam's whole body jerked when it popped free. The rasp of her zipper as she slid it down was matched by the harsh sound of Adam's breathing.

She slowly turned down each side of her jeans in front, creating a V through which the white of her panties showed. Then she spread her legs, stuck her thumbs into her panties and let her fingers slide down inside the jeans, pulling her underwear down and slowly exposing a V of flesh on her belly.

Adam swore under his breath. But he didn't move an inch.

Tate took a deep breath and shoved both panties and jeans down low on her hips, revealing her hipbones and belly and a hint of dark curls at the crest of her thighs. She put her hands behind her and rubbed her buttocks, easing the jeans down a little more with each circular motion.

She stuck her thumbs back in the front of the jeans, and met Adam's gaze before skimming her fingers across her pubic arch. A pulse in his temple jumped. His jaw clenched. But otherwise he didn't stir from where he was standing.

Tate smiled, a feminine smile of enjoyment and satisfaction. She gave one last little shove and both panties and jeans began the slide down to her ankles, where she stepped out of jeans, panties and moccasins all at once.

At last Tate stood naked before Adam. Her body felt languid, graceful as it never had. She realized it was because Adam adored her with his eyes. Because he desired her with his body. She made no move to hide herself from him.

It wasn't until she took a step toward him that Adam finally moved.

He glided toward her like a stalking tiger. Tate felt the sexual energy radiating from him long before their bodies met. His kiss was fierce, consuming. His hands seemed to be everywhere, touching, demanding a response. She arched against him, feeling the swollen heat and hardness beneath the denim.

Adam didn't bother taking her to bed. He backed her up against the wall, unsnapped his jeans to free himself, then lifted her legs around him and thrust himself inside.

Tate clung to Adam's neck with her arms and to his hips with her legs. His mouth sought hers, and his tongue thrust in rhythm with his body. His hand slipped between them and sought out the tiny nubbin that was the source of her pleasure. His thumb caressed her until he felt the waves of pleasure tightening her inner muscles around him. He threw his head back in ecstasy as his own powerful orgasm spilled inside her.

Then his head fell forward against her shoulder as he struggled to regain his breath. He finally released her legs so that she could stand, but found he had to hold her to keep her from falling, her knees were so wobbly. He lifted her into his arms and carried her to bed, throwing the sheets back and setting her down gently before joining her there.

He pulled the covers up over them both and found he could barely keep his eyes open. But there was something he wanted to say before he fell asleep.

"Tate? Are you awake?"

"Mmm. I guess so," she murmured against his throat.

"You can admit the truth about sleeping with Buck. It isn't going to make a difference in how I feel about you." *Or the baby,* he thought.

Tate pushed herself upright. The sheet that had covered her fell to her waist. "I'm telling the truth, Adam, when I say I never slept with Buck. Why won't you believe me?"

Adam levered himself up on his elbow and met her gaze with a flinty one of his own. "Because I have the medical tests to prove you wrong."

"Then your tests are mistaken!" Tate retorted. She leaned back against the headboard and yanked the covers up to her neck.

Tate had never looked more beautiful. Adam had to lie back and put his hands behind his head to keep from reaching for her again. The three hours Maria had promised to stay gone were nearly up, and he had no doubt the housekeeper would come looking for him to find out whether he had told Tate that he loved her.

He was glad now that he hadn't. At least he had been spared the humbling experience of confessing his love to a woman who had married him only to have a name for her child. Adam lay there trying to figure out why Tate persisted in lying about the baby.

"Does Buck know about the baby?" he asked.

"He guessed," Tate admitted. Buck had known from the glow on her face that something was different and had confronted her about it. She had told him the truth.

"I suppose he refused to marry you because he's still in love with Velma," Adam said.

Tate lurched out of bed and stomped over to where her clothes lay in a pile on the floor. She kept her back to Adam as she began dressing.

"Where are you going?" he asked.

"Anywhere I can be away from you," she retorted.

"Just so long as you stay away from Buck, I don't care—"

Tate whirled and said, "Buck is my friend. I'll see him when and where and as often as I please."

Adam shoved the covers out of the way and yanked on his jeans. "You took vows to me that I don't intend to see you break," he said.

"You're a fool, Adam. You can't see what's right in front of your face."

"I know a whore when I see one."

Adam was sorry the instant the words were out of his mouth. He would have given anything to take them back. He was jealous, and hurt by her apparent devotion to Buck. He had said the first thing that came into his head that he knew would hurt her.

And he was sorry for it. "Tate, I—"

"Don't say anything, Adam. Just get away from me. Maybe someday I'll be able to forgive you for that."

Adam grabbed his shirt, underwear, socks and boots and left the room, closing the door quietly behind him.

Tate sank onto the bed, fighting sobs that made her chest ache. This was worse than anything she had ever imagined. She had ample evidence in Buck's case of how suspicion and mistrust could make a man act irrationally. She had just never expected to see Adam behave like a jealous jackass.

What was she going to do now?

Adam had ample time all through the day and overnight to regret his outburst. He had snapped at Tate
like a wounded bear when she...leaving out...
...Maria was...living room to put away...he realized...
...he put down his head and headed out to the...

Chapter 10

Adam had ample time all through the day and overnight to regret his outburst. Tate had spent the rest of the
day in the office, then retreated to her own bedroom for
the night. He had decided it would be best to meet her
over the breakfast table and try to mend fences when
Maria was there to act as a buffer.

But morning sickness had once again brought Tate
to the kitchen early. Instead of waiting to have coffee
with Adam, she left the house to go for a walk, hoping
it might settle her stomach. Buck waved to her from
the loft of the barn, where he was forking down hay.
After looking back once at the house, Tate headed toward the barn to talk to him. She had better give him
fair warning that Adam was on the warpath and looking for scalps.

Adam's mood wasn't improved when he realized,

after sitting at the table for half an hour alone, that Tate wasn't coming to breakfast. He had snapped at Maria like a wounded bear when she started asking questions, and now she wasn't talking to him, either. He shoved his hat down on his head and headed out to the barn to work off some steam by cleaning out stalls.

Adam's eyes had barely adjusted to the shadows in the barn when he spied Tate standing next to the ladder that led to the loft. His heart gave a giant leap—then began to pump with adrenaline when he realized that Buck was standing right beside her. And that the lanky cowboy had his arm around Tate's shoulder.

Adam marched over to Buck and ordered, "Get your hands off my wife."

Buck grinned. "Jealous, huh? You've got no reason—"

Adam thought he had damned good reason to be jealous. After all, his wife was carrying Buck's child. His fist swung hard and fast, straight for Buck's nose.

Buck fell like a stone, his nose squirting blood. Tate quickly knelt beside him, grabbing the bandanna out of her back pocket to staunch the bleeding.

"You idiot!" she snapped at Adam. "Go stick your head in a bucket of water and cool off!"

Adam wanted to yank Tate away from the other man's side, but it was plain he would have a fight on his hands if he tried. His pride wouldn't allow him to ask her nicely to come with him. Not that he could have forced the words past the lump in his throat. "Do as you please," he snarled. "You always have."

With that, he turned and marched right back out of the barn. They heard gravel fly in the drive as he gunned his pickup and drove away.

"Who put a burr under his saddle?" Buck asked, dabbing gently at his nose with the bloody bandanna.

"How did you like the way he treated you?" Tate asked.

"Damn near hated it," Buck replied.

"Think about it the next time you see Velma with another man and decide to take a punch at him. Because that's what an unreasonable, mistrustful, paranoid sonofabitch looks like in action."

Buck's lips quirked at the corners. "Are you saying that's the way I act around Velma?"

"Bingo."

Buck tested the bridge of his nose to see if it were broken. "Maybe this bloody nose wasn't such a bad thing after all."

"Oh?"

"Adam might have knocked some sense into me. I know damn well he has no reason to be jealous, even though he thinks he does. He should have trusted you." Buck struggled to his feet. "Maybe I'll just go see Velma again."

"Is there any chance she'll speak to you?"

"If she's been as miserable as I have the past few weeks, she will," Buck said, a determined light in his brown eyes.

"I wish you luck," Tate said.

"I don't think I'm going to need luck," Buck said. "I've got something even better."

"What's that?"

"I think I just might have had some trust pounded into me."

Tate gave Buck a hug, which he was quick to escape with the excuse of dusting the hay off his britches.

"I may have become a trusting soul," he said, "but Adam's still crazy as a loon. No telling when he'll turn right around and come looking for you. I'd feel a mite safer if you go on back to the house."

Tate did as he asked. She hoped Buck's experience with Adam had shown Buck once and for all the folly of being needlessly jealous. Because if Buck could learn to trust Velma, there was some hope that Adam would one day come to trust her.

Meanwhile, Adam had driven north toward Fredericksburg and was almost into the hill country before he calmed down enough to look around and see where he was. He made a U-turn in the middle of the highway and headed back the way he had come.

Jealousy. Adam had never before had to cope with the feeling, and he had been doing a pretty rotten job of it so far. He could spend the little time he and Tate had together before she sought out a divorce condemning her for what was past. Or he could simply enjoy the company of the irrepressible, lively hoyden he had come to know and love. Between those two choices, the latter made a whole lot more sense.

When Adam arrived back at the ranch house he sought Tate out first in the barn. He found Buck working there.

The lanky cowboy leaned on the pitchfork and said, "You finally come to your senses?"

Adam grinned ruefully. "Yeah. About that punch—"

"Forget it." Buck had been working out how he could use his swollen nose to get Velma's sympathy, and then explain to her the lesson it had taught him. "Believe me, I can understand how you must have felt when you saw me with Tate."

"Because of Velma?" Adam remembered how devastated Buck had been when he had found out his wife
was cheating on him.

"Yeah."

"Uh, have you seen Tate?" Adam asked.

"She went back to the house. Look, Adam, you don't—"

"You don't have to explain, Buck. It doesn't matter."
Adam turned and headed back to the house. He found
Tate working in his office at the computer.

"Busy?"

Tate jumped at the sound of Adam's voice. She
looked over her shoulder and found him leaning negli-
gently against the door frame, one hip cocked, his hat
in his hands. The anxious way his fingers were working the brim betrayed his nerves.

"Not too busy to talk," she said. She turned the
swivel chair in his direction, leaned back, put her ankles on the desk and crossed her arms behind her head.
It was a pose intended to be equally carefree. In Tate's
case, her bare toes—which wiggled constantly—gave
her away.

In his younger days, Adam had ridden bucking
broncs in the rodeo. His stomach felt now as it did when
he was on the bronc and the chute was about to open.
Like the championship rider he was, he gave himself
eight good seconds to make his point and get out.

"I'm sorry. I was out of line—with what I said last
night and today with Buck. I'm not asking you to forgive
me. I'd just like a chance to start over fresh from here."

Tate sat there stunned. *Adam apologizing?* She had
never thought she would see the day. But like Velma,
once burned, twice chary. "Does this mean you're re-
scinding the bargain we made?"

Adam swallowed hard. "No."

So, he still wanted her, even though he was convinced the baby was Buck's. And he was willing to keep his mouth shut about her supposed indiscretion—and give his name to Buck's child—in return for favors in bed.

A woman had to be out of her mind to accept a bargain like that.

"All right," Tate said. "I accept your apology. And I agree to abide by the bargain we made yesterday."

Adam noticed she hadn't forgiven him. But then he hadn't asked for forgiveness. More to the point, she had agreed that their marriage continue to be consummated.

Tate thought she must be an eternal optimist, because she took Adam's appearance at her door as a good sign. She hadn't given up hope that she could somehow convince him of the truth about the baby, and that they would live happily ever after. It might never happen, but at least now they would be living in amity while they tried to work things out.

"It's beautiful out today," Adam said. "How would you like to take a break and come help me? I still have to move those cattle from one pasture to another." Work that hadn't been done yesterday because they had gotten married instead.

A broad smile appeared on Tate's face. "I'd like that. Just let me save this material on the computer."

She dropped her feet and swiveled back around to face the computer. She was interrupted when Adam loudly cleared his throat.

"Uh. I didn't think to ask. Did Dr. Kowalski say everything's okay with the baby? There's no medical reason why you can't do strenuous exercise, is there?"

Tate turned and gave him a beatific smile. "I'm fine. The baby will enjoy the ride." ¬

Nevertheless, Adam kept a close eye on Tate. When he saw her eyelids begin to droop late in the afternoon he suggested they take a siesta. He led her to a giant live oak that stood near the banks of a creek on his property. There he spread a blanket he had tied behind the saddle and provided a picnic he had packed in his saddlebags.

Tate pulled off her boots and wiggled her toes. Then she lay back on the blanket with her hands behind her head and stared up at the freckles of sun visible through the gnarled, moss-laden limbs of the live oak. "This is wonderful! A picnic! I had no idea you had this in mind when you asked me to come with you today."

Actually, Maria was responsible for the impromptu picnic. Adam had thought of the blanket himself. The delight on Tate's face was its own reward. Adam sat down cross-legged across from her and passed out ham and cheese sandwiches, deviled eggs and pickles. There was a thermos of iced tea to drink.

"I don't usually care for pickles," Tate said, crunching into the sweet gherkin in her hand. "But you know, this tastes pretty good."

Adam smiled to himself. In his experience, pregnant women had odd cravings. He had once had a patient who'd eaten liver with peanut butter.

Soon after she had finished her lunch, Tate yawned. "I can't believe how tired I feel lately."

"Your body is going through a lot of changes."

"Is that a medical opinion, Doctor?" Tate asked, eyeing him through half-closed lids. But she didn't hear his answer. The moment she laid her head on her hand and closed her eyes, she fell sound asleep.

Adam cleared away the picnic and lay down beside her to watch her sleep. He had never realized how very long her lashes were, or how very dark. She had a tiny mole beside her ear that he hadn't detected before. And dark circles under her eyes, which he also hadn't noticed.

As a doctor he knew the strain pregnancy put on a woman's body and her emotions. He made a vow to himself to take care of Tate, to make sure that the dark circles disappeared and that the smile stayed on her face.

He knew how she would resent it if she thought he had taken on the role of caretaker. After all, she had fled her brothers because they had been overprotective. He knew he would have to be subtle if he were going to get her to rest. Like the picnic today. He was sure she had no idea she was being manipulated for her own good.

When Tate awoke, she stretched languorously, unaware that she had an appreciative audience. When she blinked open her eyes she realized it was nearly dusk. She sat up abruptly and made herself dizzy.

Adam was beside her instantly, his arm around her shoulder to support her. "Are you all right?"

"Just a little woozy. I guess I sat up too quickly. Why did you let me sleep so long?"

"You were tired."

Tate leaned her head on his shoulder. "I guess I was. Hadn't we better head back now?"

He nuzzled her neck, searching out the mole near her ear. "I don't have anything planned for this evening. Do you?"

Tate chuckled. "No, I can't say that I have."

Adam slowly laid her back down and found her

mouth with his. He brushed his cheek against her long
lashes and slid his hands into her hair, smoothing it back
where the breeze had ruffled it into her face.

As the sun slipped from the sky, Adam made sweet
love to his wife. They rode home by moonlight, and
after they had taken care of the horses, Adam made
sure Tate went right to bed. In his room. With his arms
around her.

"I'll have Maria move your things to my room," he
murmured in her ear. "It'll be more convenient since
you'll be sleeping in here."

Tate opened her mouth to object and shut it again.
After all, she wanted this marriage to work. It made
sense that the more time she spent with Adam, the better chance she had of making that happen. She intended
to become absolutely irreplaceable in his life.

But as the days turned into weeks, and the weeks into
months, the invisible wall of mistrust between them did
not come down. Though she made love with Adam each
evening, the words "I love you" stuck in Tate's throat
whenever she tried to say them. It was too painful to
expose her need to him. Especially since she didn't want
to put him in the position of feeling he had to say the
words back. Which she was afraid he wouldn't.

Adam was equally aware of how much he had gained
when he had moved Tate into his bedroom, and how
little things had really changed between them. He found
himself enchanted by her constant delight in the baby.
He tried to be happy with each stage of her pregnancy.
Mostly he was successful.

But he watched her and wondered if she ever thought
of Buck. The cowboy hadn't been spending much of
his free time around the ranch lately. But Adam was

watching. Which meant that he still didn't trust her not to seek Buck out if she got the chance.

Meanwhile, he had waited for Tate to tell him again that she loved him. She hadn't said the words lately. Not once, in fact, since they had gotten married. And he found he wanted—needed—to hear those words.

Tate was in bed with Adam when she felt the baby move for the first time. She grabbed his hand and placed it on her belly. "Can you feel that? Kind of a fluttery feeling."

"No." He tried to remove his hand.

"Wait. Maybe it'll happen again."

"Feel here," Adam said, putting her hand on his arousal. "I think I've got a little fluttery feeling of my own."

Tate couldn't help giggling as Adam's body pulsed beneath her hand. "You've got a one track mind, Dr. Philips."

"Oh, but what a lovely track it is," he murmured, kissing his way down her body. His head lay against her belly when he felt a slight movement against his cheek. He came up off her like a scalded cat.

"I felt it! I felt the baby move!"

Tate smiled triumphantly. "I told you so!"

Adam found himself suddenly uncomfortable. As a doctor he had described the stages of pregnancy to his patients hundreds of times. Yet he found himself overwhelmed by the reality of it. That feather-light touch against his cheek had been an actual human being. Growing inside Tate. A baby that would have his name. A baby that Tate planned to take away with her when she divorced him.

Adam was reminded why he shouldn't let himself

care too much about either Tate or the baby. It was going to be bad enough when Tate left him. He wouldn't be able to bear it if he got attached to the child, as well.

Adam didn't say anything about what he was thinking, but from that night onward Tate noticed a distinct difference in his behavior whenever she mentioned the baby. Adam seemed indifferent. Nothing she said got him excited or brought a smile to his face. It was as if the baby had become a burden too heavy for him to bear.

Tate had conveniently forgotten that she had promised Adam a divorce as soon as the baby was born. So she was certain the only possible explanation why Adam wasn't allowing himself to get involved with anything having to do with the baby was because he believed it wasn't his child. She decided to try, once more, to convince him that he was the baby's father.

She chose her moment well. She and Adam had just made love and were lying with their bodies still tangled together. Their breathing had eased and Adam's nose was nuzzled against her throat. The baby was active now, and she pressed her belly against his, knowing Adam couldn't help but feel the movement.

"Adam?"

"Hmm."

"The baby's kicking a lot tonight."

"Hmm."

She threaded her fingers through Adam's hair. "You know, I think he's going to be a lot like his father."

She felt Adam stiffen.

"Like you, Adam. He's going to be a lot like you."

Adam's voice was weary as he said, "You don't have to do this Tate. It's not necessary to try and make me believe the baby's mine. I—" *I'll love it anyway.* Adam bit his lip on that admission. No sense revealing the pain she would be causing him when she took the child away.

"But the baby *is* yours, Adam."

"Tate, we've been through this before. I took tests—"

"What about your wife? Did she take tests, too? Maybe it was her fault and not yours."

"Anne was tested. There was nothing wrong with her."

"Maybe they got your test results mixed up with someone else's," Tate persisted. "I mean, you're a doctor. You know those things happen. Did you see the results yourself?"

"Anne called me from the doctor's office," Adam said.

"You mean you weren't there?"

"I had a medical emergency. I—"

"Then she could have lied!" Tate said.

"Why? She wanted children as much as I did. What earthly reason would she have had to lie?"

"I don't know," Tate said. "All I do know is that a child is growing in my body, and the only man who's put his seed inside me is you!"

For an instant Adam felt a wild surge of hope. Maybe there had been some mistake. Maybe Anne had not lied, but been mistaken. He couldn't believe she would have lied about a thing like that. He had seen her tests himself. The problem did not lie with Anne. So something must have been wrong with him for them to remain childless for eight years.

He felt the hope die as painfully as it had been born. "You're making wishes that can't come true, Tate," he said. "This child isn't mine. I'm sterile."

Tate could have screamed, she was so frustrated. "Is that why you refuse to get involved with anything having to do with the baby?" she demanded. "Because you think it isn't yours?"

"Have you forgotten that you promised me a divorce as soon as it's born?" Adam reminded her.

"What if I said I didn't want a divorce? Would you feel differently about the baby then?" Tate persisted.

"What do you want me to say, Tate? That I'll be a father to your child? I will. What more do you want from me?" The words seemed torn from someplace deep inside him.

Tate felt frozen inside. It was clear Adam wouldn't ever be able to accept the baby she carried as his own. And she wouldn't subject her child to a lifetime of rejection by its father, the one person who should love and protect it above all others. That knowledge, on top of her doubts about whether Adam loved her, made it plain that she would be better off away from here.

She didn't say another word, just allowed Adam to pull her into his embrace and hold her one last time. Once he was asleep, she carefully disentangled herself. She turned and looked at him once before she left the room—and his life—forever.

Chapter 11

Garth and Faron were shocked—to put it mildly—when Tate showed up on the doorstep at Hawk's Way.

"What happened?" Garth demanded. "What did that bastard do to you?"

"You look awful, Tate," Faron said, putting an arm around her shoulder and leading her inside.

"If that man hurt you I'll—"

"Don't, Garth!" Tate pleaded. "Just leave it alone. Adam and I are both better off this way."

"Do you want to talk about it?" Faron asked.

"I just want to go to bed and sleep for a week," Tate said.

Faron and Garth exchanged a sober look. There were deep shadows under Tate's eyes. Her face looked gaunt and unhappy.

"He'll pay for the way he's treated you," Garth said.

"No! Listen to me!" Tate said, her voice sharp with fatigue and anxiety. "You have to trust me to know what's best." There it was again. That word *trust.* "This marriage was a horrible mistake. I'm going to file for a divorce."

"Don't be hasty," Faron urged.

"You're dead on your feet. You have no idea what you're saying," Garth countered.

"Stop it! Both of you! *I'm a grown woman.*" She laughed hysterically. "Don't you see? I'm going to be a mother myself! Surely it's time for you to admit that I can manage my own life. You have to love me enough to let go."

Tate didn't wait to hear whether they were willing to concede to her wishes. She was too distressed to deal with them anymore. She ran up the stairs to her bedroom, her rigid bearing defying either one of her brothers to come after her.

"She's changed," Faron said.

"And not for the better," Garth noted.

Faron frowned. "I'm not so sure about that. She's grown up, Garth. She's not a little girl anymore. Six months ago she wouldn't have stood up to you like that. I think she had to be in a lot of pain to leave here in the first place, and a helluva lot more pain to come back. I think maybe we're at least partly responsible."

"I blame the bastard who got her pregnant," Garth said.

"None of this would have happened if she hadn't run away from home. And she wouldn't have run away from home if we hadn't kept such a tight rein on her."

"It was for her own good."

"It doesn't seem that way now, does it?" Faron asked.

"I think maybe our little sister grew up in spite of us. And I, for one, am not going to interfere anymore in her life."

Adam had been scowling ever since he had woken up to find Tate gone from his bed—and his life. The first thing he had done was to go hunting Buck. His fury had been boundless when the lanky cowboy was no-where to be found. Finally, one of the other hands told him Buck had been spending nights with his ex-wife.

That news had confounded Adam. He had doggedly made the trip to Velma's house and knocked on the door in the early hours of the morning. Buck had answered the door wearing low-slung jeans and scratching a head of auburn hair that stood out in all directions.

"Adam! What are you doing here this hour of the morning?"

"Where's Tate?"

"How the hell should I know?" Buck retorted.

By now Velma had joined him, wearing a flashy silk robe, and with her red tresses equally tangled. "What's going on, Adam?"

It was obvious to Adam that Tate wasn't here. But he didn't know where else to look. "Do you mind if I come in?"

"Come on in and I'll make us some coffee," Velma said. "You can tell us what's got you running around at this hour like a chicken with its head cut off."

While Velma was in the kitchen making coffee, Adam put his elbows on the table and wearily rubbed his forehead. Buck waited patiently for Adam to speak his piece.

"Tate's gone. Run away," Adam said at last.

Buck whistled his surprise. "Thought that little filly loved you too much ever to leave you."

Adam's head came up out of his hands. "What?"

"Sure. You and that baby of yours was all she ever talked about."

"*My* baby?"

"Sure as hell wasn't mine!" Buck said.

Adam's eyes narrowed. "She spent nearly the whole night with you. Twice."

Buck laughed in Adam's face. "We were here at Velma's house the first night. And we fell asleep on the banks of the Frio after Velma and I had an argument on the second. There's only been one woman for me. And that's my wife."

"You mean your ex-wife."

Buck grinned and held up his left hand, which bore a gold wedding band. "I mean my wife. Velma and I got married again last Sunday."

"Congratulations. I guess." Adam was confused. "But if you're not the father of Tate's baby, then who is?"

Buck pursed his lips and shook his head. "I would think that has to be pretty obvious even to a blind man."

"But I—" Adam swallowed and admitted, "I can't father children."

"Whoever told you that," Buck said, "is a whopping liar."

"But—" Adam shut his mouth over the protest he had been about to make. Was it really possible? Could Anne have lied to him? It was the only answer that would explain everything.

Adam jumped up from his chair just as Velma brought in the coffeepot.

"You're not staying?" she asked.

"I've got to get in touch with someone in San Antonio." He was going to see the doctor who had done those fertility tests and find out the truth for himself.

"When you're ready to go after Tate, I have a suggestion where you might look," Buck said.

"Where?"

"I figure she went home to her brothers. You'll probably find her at Hawk's Way."

"Damn."

Buck laughed. "I'd like to be a fly on the wall when you try to take her out of there."

Adam wasn't able to think that far ahead. Right now he had a doctor to visit in San Antonio.

Early the next afternoon Adam came out of a glass-walled office building feeling like a man who had been poleaxed.

"Your sperm count was low," the doctor had said. "But certainly still within the range that would allow you to father children."

"But why didn't Anne and I ever conceive children?" he had demanded.

The doctor had shrugged. "It was just one of those things that happens with some couples."

Anne had lied to him. Whatever her reasons—maybe she just hadn't wanted to keep on trying—she had lied to him.

I'm going to be a father! Tate is pregnant with my child!

The realization was only just hitting him. Adam was floating on air. He had always intended to love the child because it was Tate's, but the knowledge that the baby Tate was carrying was a part of him filled his cup to overflowing.

There was only one problem. Tate was at Hawk's

Way. And he was going to have to fight her brothers to get her back.

An hour later, he was in his pickup traveling north.

Adam shouldn't have been surprised when he discovered the vastness of Hawk's Way, but he was. The cliffs and canyons in northwest Texas were a startling contrast to the rolling prairies found on the Lazy S.

The ranch house was an imposing two-story white frame structure that looked a lot like an antebellum mansion with its four, twenty-foot-high fluted columns across the front and its railed firstand secondstory porches. The road leading to the house was lined with magnolias, but the house itself was shaded by the branches of a moss-laden live oak.

Adam was glad to see that the barn and outbuildings were a good distance from the house. He was hoping to catch Tate alone and talk with her before he had to confront her brothers. He went around to the kitchen door, knocked softly and let himself inside.

Tate was standing at the sink peeling potatoes. She was wearing an apron, and sweat from the heat of the kitchen made her hair curl damply at her nape.

"Hello, Tate."

Tate dropped both potato and peeler in the sink and turned to face Adam. Once she had wiped her hands dry, she kept them hidden in the folds of the apron so Adam wouldn't see how much they were trembling.

"Hello, Adam," she said at last. "I was just peeling potatoes for tonight's pot roast."

"You look tired," he said.

"I haven't been sleeping much the last couple of days." She swallowed over the ache in her throat and asked, "What are you doing here, Adam?"

"I've come to get you. Go upstairs and pack your things. I'm taking you home with me."

"I am home."

"Like hell you are! This is where you grew up, Tate. It isn't your home. Your home is with me and our child."

Tate felt her heart racing with excitement and with hope. Adam's words now were a far cry from what she had heard a mere forty-eight hours ago. It appeared he intended to be a father to the baby after all.

Before Adam could say more, the kitchen door opened and Tate remembered she had told her brothers to come to the house early for lunch because she wanted to take a long afternoon nap. She quailed at the confrontation she knew was coming.

"What the hell are you doing here?" Garth demanded.

"I've come for my wife."

"Tate's not going anywhere," Garth said.

Adam wasn't about to be said nay. He grabbed Tate by the wrist. "Forget your things," he said. "We can get them later." He dragged her two steps, but could go no farther.

Faron and Garth were blocking the way out.

"Get out of my way," Adam said.

"Look, Adam," Faron began in a reasonable voice. "If you'll just—"

But Adam was in no mood to be reasonable. He twisted around to shove Tate out of the way, then reversed the arc with his fist. Faron was felled by the powerful blow, which caught him completely unprepared to defend himself.

Adam stood spread-legged, facing Tate's eldest brother. "I'm telling you to get out of my way."

"You're welcome to leave," Garth said. "But Tate stays here."

"I'm taking her with me."

"That remains to be seen."

Tate knew her brother's strength. He had at least three inches of height and thirty more pounds of muscle than Adam. "Garth, please don't—"

"Shut up, Tate," Adam ordered. "I can handle this on my own." He was fighting for his life—the right to cherish his wife and raise his child—and he had no intention of losing.

The fight that followed was vicious, but mercifully short. When it was finished, Adam was still standing, but it was a near thing. He grabbed Tate's wrist and helped her step over Garth's body on the way out, letting the screen door slam behind her.

Once Tate and Adam were gone, the two brothers, still sprawled on the floor where Adam had left them, had trouble meeting each other's eyes. Two against one and they were the ones dusting themselves off.

Garth cradled his ribs as he sat up and leaned back against the kitchen cupboards. He pulled his shirttail out and pressed the cloth against a cut over his cheekbone.

Faron stretched his legs out in front of him as he leaned back against the refrigerator. He rubbed his sore chin, then opened his mouth and moved his jaw around to make sure no bones were broken.

"Guess our little sister is married to a man who loves her after all," Faron said.

"One with a damned fine right hook," Garth agreed, dabbing gently with his shirttail at the bruised skin around his eye.

The two brothers looked at each other and grinned. Garth yelped when his split lip protested.

"Guess that's one suitor you couldn't scare off," Faron said.

"I always said Tate would know the right man when he came along."

"Seems you were the one needed convincing," Faron said, eyeing Garth's battered face.

Garth guffawed, then moaned when his head protested. "By the way, who do you think's going to be godfather to that baby of hers?"

"Me," Faron said, hauling himself off the floor. "You get to be godfather to Jesse's firstborn."

"Jesse's next oldest. It ought to be him."

"Jesse and Adam don't get along. I'm a better choice," Faron said.

The two brothers headed out to the barn, arguing all the way. Neither of them mentioned the fact that they had been relegated to a new role in Tate's life. Their little sister had found a new protector.

Meanwhile, Tate was aware of every move Adam made, every word he spoke. She had him stop at the first gas station they came to with the excuse she had to use the bathroom. She used the opportunity to clean the blood off his face and bought some bandages in the convenience store to put across the cuts on his cheek and chin.

Once they were back in the car, she said, "You were wonderful, you know. I don't think anybody's ever beaten my brother Garth in a fight."

"I had more at stake than he did," Adam mumbled through his split lips.

Tate's spirits soared at this further evidence that

Adam's attitude toward both her and the baby had some-how changed.

It was a long ride back home to the Lazy S, broken frequently by stops to allow Tate to use rest room fa-cilities.

"It's the baby," she explained.

"I know about these things," Adam replied with an understanding smile. "I'm a doctor, remember?"

It was dark by the time they arrived back at the Lazy S. Maria greeted them both at the door with a big hug.

"It is so good to see you back where you belong, *señora!*"

In Spanish she said to Adam, "I see you have put the smile back on her face. You will tell her now you love her, yes?"

"When the time is right," Adam said.

Maria frowned. "The time, she is *right now.*"

Adam refused to be pressed. He excused himself and ushered Tate to his bedroom. He lifted her into his arms and carried her across the threshold.

"Our marriage begins now," he said, looking into her eyes. "The past is past."

Tate could hardly believe this was happening. "I love you, Adam."

She waited for the words she knew he would say back to her. But they didn't come.

There was nothing very difficult about saying those three little words, but Adam felt too vulnerable at the moment to admit the depth of his feelings for Tate. He hadn't really given her a choice about coming back with him. It seemed more appropriate to *show* her that he loved her, rather than to tell her so in words.

He made love to her as though she were the most precious being in the world. He kissed her gently, indifferent to his split lip, tasting her as though he had never done so before, teasing her with his teeth and tongue. Her soft whimper of pleasure rolled through him, tightening his body with need.

His hand slid down to her rounded belly. "My child," he whispered in her ear. "Our child."

"Yes. Yes, our child," Tate agreed, glad that he was ready to accept the baby as his own.

"I mean, I know it's mine," Adam said.

Tate was jerked abruptly from her euphoria. "What?" She turned to face him, her eyes still wide and dilated with pleasure. "What did you say?"

Adam's thumb caressed her belly as his eyes met hers. "I went back to that doctor in San Antonio. The one who did the fertility tests on Anne and me. I'm not sterile, Tate. Anne lied to me."

Tate's eyes widened in horror as she realized what this meant. No wonder Adam hadn't said he loved her. He hadn't come to Hawk's Way for her at all. He hadn't fought Garth for the purpose of getting her back. He had fought to get back his child!

Chapter 12

Tate pleaded fatigue from her pregnancy as an excuse not to make love to Adam, and the damned man fell all over himself being understanding. Naturally he wanted to make sure she took good care of herself so *his child* would be born healthy!

But the next morning, when Adam stood blocking her way into the office—because she shouldn't have to work in her delicate condition—Tate let him have it with both barrels.

"I'm just as capable of working with *your* child growing inside me as I was when it was just *my* child!" she snapped.

"But—"

"No buts! I'll eat right, get enough rest and come through this pregnancy with flying colors. Even if it is partly *your* child growing inside me and not just *mine*."

Adam wasn't sure what he had done wrong, but Tate obviously had a bee in her bonnet about something. "What's all this *your* child and *my* child business? What happened to *our* child?"

"That was before you found out you can father as many children as you want. Well, you can go father some other fool woman's kids. This baby's *mine!*"

With that, she shoved him out of the office and slammed the door in his face.

Adam could hear her crying on the other side of the door. He tried the handle and found it was locked. He pounded on the door. "Tate, let me in!"

"I don't want to talk to you. Go away!"

He pounded on the door again. "If you don't open this door, I'm going to break it down," he threatened.

He had just turned his shoulder toward the door when it opened, and he nearly fell inside. "That's better," he said, walking in and shutting the door behind him. "I think maybe we better talk about this...difference of opinion. What's important—"

"I'm not a baby that needs coddling. I'm fully capable of taking care of myself. You have to trust me to— oh, what's the use?" she said, throwing up her hands in disgust. "Trust was never a part of our relationship in the past. I don't suppose that just because you've found out I didn't lie to you about the baby, it's going to change anything between us."

"What does trust have to do with this?"

"Everything!" Tate was quivering she was so upset. "Buck and Velma—"

"Whoa there! What do Buck and Velma have to do with this?" Adam was getting more confused by the minute.

"It doesn't matter," Tate said.

Adam grabbed her by the shoulders. "It obviously *does* matter. Now I want an explanation and I want it now!"

"You sure about that? Food for thought gives some folks indigestion!"

Adam shoved Tate down in the swivel chair and settled his hip on the desk in front of her. "Settle down now. This kind of agitation isn't good for the baby. I—"

Tate leaped out of the chair and poked a finger at Adam's chest. *"The baby! The baby!"* she mimicked back at him. "That's all you really care about, isn't it? I'm nothing more than a vessel for your seed. I could be a test tube for all the difference it would make to you! Well, I've got news for you, *buster!* I want more than a father for my child, I want a husband to love me and hold me and—" Tate choked back a sob.

"Tate, I do love—"

"Don't say it! If you really loved me, you've had plenty of opportunities to say so. If you say it now I'll know you're just doing it to calm me down for the sake of the baby."

"I'm telling the truth!"

"So was I! When I told you months ago that this baby was yours and mine—*ours!* But you didn't trust me then. And I don't believe you now! Just like Buck and Velma—"

"Are we back to them again?"

"Yes-s-s!" she hissed. "Because Buck and Velma are a perfect example of what happens when there's no trust in a relationship. You hurt each other, and you're miserable and unhappy together.

"If you love somebody you have to be willing to

trust them enough to be honest with them. To lay yourself open to the pain of rejection by admitting how you really feel about them. And you have to trust in their love enough to know that they would never do anything purposely to hurt you. Like lying to you. Or sleeping with another man.

"Without trust, love will just wither and die." Tate swallowed another sob and said, "Like it did with Buck and Velma."

"Are you finished?" Adam asked.

Tate sniffled and wiped her nose with the hem of her T-shirt. "I'm finished."

"First of all, I think you should know that Buck and Velma got remarried on Sunday."

Tate's eyes went wide. "They did?"

"Second of all, whether you believe me or not, I do love you. I've loved you for a long time. I never said anything because…"

"Because you didn't trust me," Tate finished in a small voice.

He couldn't deny it, because it was true. "I guess it's my turn to point to Buck and Velma," Adam said ruefully.

"Why?"

"Aren't they proof that people can change? That mistakes aren't irrevocable?"

Tate's brow furrowed. "I suppose."

"Then will you give me a chance to prove how I feel? To prove that I do love you enough to trust you with my heart?"

Tate felt her throat swelling closed with emotion. "I suppose."

"Come here." Adam opened his arms and Tate

walked into them. He tipped her chin up and looked deep into her eyes. "We start from here. Our baby, our marriage—"

"Our trust in each other," Tate finished.

They shared a tender kiss to seal the bargain. But it turned into something much more. Or would have, if Maria hadn't interrupted them.

"Señor Adam, there is a man here with the new rodeo bull he says you must sign for."

"I'm coming, Maria."

Adam gave Tate another quick, hard kiss. "Until tonight."

"Until tonight." Tate managed a smile as he turned and left her. He had given her an awful lot to think about. But it was better to confront these issues now, before the baby came, than later. Garth had always said, "If you have a hill to climb, waiting won't make it smaller."

As Adam began to realize over the next several weeks, it was one thing to believe yourself trustworthy; it was quite another thing to earn someone's trust.

He made love to Tate each night, revering her with words and gestures. But he never told her that he loved her. It was plain from the cautious way she watched him when she thought he wasn't looking, that she wasn't yet ready to hear the words—and believe them.

Maria got thoroughly disgusted watching Señor Adam and Señora Tate tiptoe around each other. She nagged at him in Spanish to tell Señora Tate he loved her and be done with it. "If you say it often enough, she will believe it," Maria advised.

"Do you think so?" Adam asked. "Even if she thinks I'm lying through my teeth?"

"But you would not be lying!" Maria protested. "She will see what is in your eyes. And she will believe."

Adam truly wished it were that simple. He was beginning to despair of ever convincing Tate that he loved her enough to want her both as his wife and the mother of his child.

The situation might have gone on unresolved, with both Adam and Tate less than happy, if Maria hadn't decided to take matters into her own hands.

As far as Maria was concerned, it was as plain as white socks on a sorrel horse that Señor Adam loved the little *señora,* and that she loved him. The problem was getting the two of them to recognize what was right in front of their noses.

So right after lunch one day she sent Señor Adam off to the store to buy some spices she needed for dinner. She waited a half hour, then raced into the office where the *señora* was working.

"Señora Tate, come quick! There's been an accident! Señor Adam—"

By the time Adam's name was out of Maria's mouth, Tate had already left her chair. She grabbed hold of Maria's sleeve and demanded, "How badly is he hurt? What happened? Where is he?"

"It was the new Brahma bull, the one he has penned in the far pasture," Maria said. "He was not watching closely enough and—"

"The bull stomped him? My God! How did you find this out? I never even heard the phone ring! Has somebody called an ambulance? We have to get Adam to a doctor!"

"Señor Buck has already called the doctor. He is with Señor Adam now." Maria smiled inwardly. She hadn't even had to invent an injury for Señor Adam. The *señora* had done that herself. She said, "Señor Buck—"

"Thank God, Buck's with him!" Tate headed for the kitchen to get the keys to her pickup from the peg where she usually left them. But they weren't there.

"Where are my keys? Maria, have you seen my keys?"

Maria closed her hands around the set of keys in her pocket. "No, *señora*. But your horse, she is saddled already for the ride you wished to take this afternoon."

"That'll probably be faster anyway. I can go crosscountry. Thanks, Maria. You're a lifesaver!"

Tate had barely been gone ten minutes when Maria heard Señor Adam's pickup pull up in back of the house. She sniffed the onion she had ready and waiting and went running out to the truck, tears streaming, waving her hands frantically to attract his attention.

"Señor Adam! The *señora!* Hurry!" Maria hid her face in her apron and pretended to cry.

"What's wrong, Maria? What happened to Tate? Is she all right?" He didn't wait for an answer, but bounded up the back steps toward the house.

"She is not there!" Maria cried.

Adam's face bleached white. "She's gone? She left me?"

Maria saw she had made a serious mistake and said, "Oh, no! But she went riding toward the pasture where you are keeping that big-humped bull. Her horse must have been frightened. Señor Buck found her there on the ground."

"She's hurt? Has she been taken to the doctor?"

"She is still there. Señor Buck is with her—"

Adam didn't wait to hear more. He jumped back into

his pickup and gunned the motor, heading down the gravel road, hell-bent-for-leather toward the opposite end of the Lazy S.

Maria dabbed with her apron at the corners of her eyes where the onion had done its work. Well, she would soon see the results of her meddling. If she was right, there would be more smiles and laughter around this house in the future. When *el bebé* arrived, Tía Maria would tell the story of the day Papa rescued Mama from the big bad bull and brought her home to live here happily ever after.

Tate managed to get through the gate that led to the new bull's pasture without dismounting, but she still begrudged the time it took the mare to respond to her commands as she opened the metal gate and closed it behind her.

Once she was inside the pasture she kept a sharp lookout for the huge Brahma. She wasn't sure what Buck had done to secure it after it had stomped Adam. The chance that it might still be roaming free in the pasture made her shudder in fear.

Tate hadn't gone far when she heard the sound of a truck spinning gravel somewhere beyond the pasture gate. There was no siren, but she thought it might be the ambulance. Maybe they would know exactly where to find Adam. Tate turned the mare back toward the gate and headed there at a gallop.

She was almost to the gate when she realized the huge Brahma bull, with its thick horns and humped back, was standing there, apparently drawn by the sound of the truck, which usually brought hay and feed. When the bull heard the horse behind him, he whirled to confront the interloper on his territory. Tate found herself trapped, with no way out. She yanked the mare to a halt, holding her perfectly still, knowing that any movement would make the Brahma charge.

Adam swore loudly and fluently when he realized Tate's predicament. He slammed on the brakes, grabbed a rope from the bed of the truck, and hit the ground running.

"Don't move!" he yelled. "I'm coming."

"Wait!" Tate yelled back. "Don't come in here! It's too dangerous!"

Adam didn't bother with opening the gate, just went over the top and down inside. The rattle of the fence had the bull turning back, certain dinner was about to be served. He stopped, confused when he saw the man on foot inside the fence. He nodded his lowered head from Tate to Adam and back again, uncertain which way he wanted to go.

Adam shook out the lasso and started looking for something he could use as a snubbing post. Not too far away stood a medium-size live oak.

Adam didn't hesitate. He walked slowly toward the Brahma, which began to snort and paw at the ground in agitation. The bull's attention was definitely on Adam now, not Tate.

"Please don't come any closer, Adam," Tate said quietly.

"Don't worry. I've got this all worked out." If he missed his throw, he was going to run like hell and hope he got to the fence before the Brahma got to him.

But Adam's loop sang through the air and landed neatly around the Brahma's horns. He let out the rope as he ran for the live oak. He circled the tree several times, enough to make sure the rope was going to hold when the bull hit the end of it.

By then, Tate had realized what he was doing. She raced her mare to the live oak, took her foot out of the stirrup so Adam could quickly mount behind her, then kicked the mare into a gallop that took them out of harm's way.

The Brahma charged after them, but was brought up short by the rope that held it hog-tied to the tree.

Tate rode the mare back to the gate, where Adam slipped over the horse's rump, and quickly opened the gate for her. Once she was through, he fastened the gate, and reached up to pull her off the mare.

They clutched each other tightly, well aware of the calamity they had barely escaped. As soon as their initial relief was past, they began talking at the same time, amazed by the fact that they had found each other alive and well and unhurt.

"Maria told me the bull had stomped you!"

"She told me you had been thrown from your horse!"

"I wasn't thrown!"

"I wasn't stomped!"

The realization dawned for both at the same time that they had been manipulated into coming here under false pretenses.

"I'll kill her!" Adam said.

"I think you should give her a raise," Tate said with a laugh.

"Why? She nearly got us both killed!"

"Because she made me realize I've been a fool not to believe what I know in my heart is true."

"I do love you, Tate," Adam said. He pulled her into his arms and kissed her hard. "I do love you."

"I know. And I love you. When I thought you might be dying—or dead—I realized just how much."

"When I thought something might have happened to you, I felt the same," Adam said. "I should have been saying 'I love you' every day. I love you, Tate. I love you. I love you."

Adam punctuated each statement with a kiss that was more fervent than the one before.

Tate was having trouble catching her breath. She managed to say, "Adam, we have to do something about that bull."

"Let him find his own heifer," Adam murmured against her throat.

Tate laughed. "We can't just leave him tied up like that."

"I'll send Buck and the boys back to take care of him and to pick up your mare. We have more important things to do this afternoon."

"Like what?"

"Like plotting how we're going to get even with Maria."

As they drove back toward the ranch house, Adam and Tate plotted imaginative punishments they could wreak on the housekeeper for lying to them. It wasn't an easy job, considering how they had to balance her dubious methods against her very satisfying results.

"I think the best thing we could do is have about five children," Adam said.

Tate gulped. "Five?"

"Sure. That'll fix Maria, all right. She'll have the little devils sitting on her lap and tugging at her skirts for a good long while!"

"Serves her right!" Tate agreed with a grin.

Adam stopped the pickup in front of the ranch house, grabbed Tate's hand and went running inside to find the housekeeper.

"Maria!" he shouted. "Where are you?" He headed for the kitchen, dragging Tate along behind him.

"Here's a note on the refrigerator," Tate said.

"What's it say?"

Tate held the note out to Adam.

Dear Señor Adam,

Tell her you love her. I'll be gone for two—no, three—hours.

Love, Maria

Adam laughed and pulled Tate into his embrace— where the first of Maria's little devils promptly kicked his father in the stomach.

* * * * *

"I appreciate you coming," he said.

"You said it was important."

Paul nodded as he gestured for her to take a seat. Sitting down, Simone stole another quick glance toward the bar. The two strangers were both staring blatantly, not bothering to hide their interest in the two of them.

Simone rested an elbow on the tabletop, turning flirtatiously toward her friend. "Do you know Tom and Jerry over there at the bar?" she asked softly. She reached a hand out, trailing her fingers against his arm.

Her touch was just distracting enough that Paul didn't turn abruptly to stare back, drawing even more attention in their direction. His focus shifted slowly from her toward the duo at the bar. He eyed them briefly before turning his attention back to Simone. He shook his head. "Should I?"

"It might be nothing, but they seem very interested in you."

Paul's gaze danced back in their direction and he took a swift inhale of air. One of the men was on a cell phone and both were still eyeing him intently.

"We need to leave," he said, suddenly anxious. He began to gather his papers.

"What's going on, Paul?"

"I don't think we're safe, Simone."

"What do you mean we're not safe?" she snapped, her teeth clenched tightly. "Why are we not safe?"

"I'll explain, but I think we really need to leave."

Simone took a deep breath and held it, watching as he repacked his belongings into his briefcase.

"We're not going anywhere until you explain," she started, and then a commotion at the door pulled at her attention.

Don't miss
Reunited by the Badge *by Deborah Fletcher Mello*
available October 2019 wherever
Harlequin® Romantic Suspense
books and ebooks are sold.

www.Harlequin.com

Need an adrenaline rush from nail-biting tales
(and irresistible males)?

Check out **Harlequin Intrigue**®,
Harlequin® **Romantic Suspense** and
Love Inspired® **Suspense** books!

New books available every month!

CONNECT WITH US AT:

Facebook.com/groups/HarlequinConnection

 Facebook.com/HarlequinBooks

Twitter.com/HarlequinBooks

Instagram.com/HarlequinBooks

Pinterest.com/HarlequinBooks

ReaderService.com

**ROMANCE WHEN
YOU NEED IT**

SGENRE2018R

SPECIAL EXCERPT FROM

◆ HARLEQUIN®
™

I N T R I G U E

*Waking in the middle of a war zone, Jane Doe
has no memory of who she is or who she can trust.
When she meets former elite Force Recon member
Gus Walsh, she finds that trusting him is her only
chance at finding answers.*

Read on for a sneak preview of
Driving Force,
the fourth installment of the thrilling
Declan's Defenders series by New York Times
and USA TODAY *bestselling author Elle James.*

CHAPTER ONE

She struggled to surface from the black hole trying to suck
her back down. Her head hurt and she could barely open her
eyes. Every part of her body ached so badly she began to
think death would be a relief. But her heart, buried behind
bruised and broken ribs, beat strong, pushing blood through
her veins. And with the blood, the desire to live.

Willing her eyes to open, she blinked and gazed through
narrow slits at the dirty mud-and-stick wall in front of her.
Why couldn't she open her eyes more? She raised her hand
to her face and felt the puffy, blood-crusted skin around
her eyes and mouth. When she tried to move her lips, they
cracked and warm liquid oozed out on her chin.

Her fingernails were split, some ripped down to the quick,
and the backs of her knuckles looked like pounded hamburger

meat. Bruises, scratches and cuts covered her arms.

She felt along her torso, wincing when she touched a bruised rib. As she shifted her search lower, her hands shook and she held her breath, feeling for bruises, wondering if she'd been assaulted in other ways. When she felt no tenderness between her legs, she let go of the breath she'd held in a rush of relief.

She pushed into a sitting position and winced at the pain knifing through her head. Running her hand over her scalp, she felt a couple of goose egg–sized lumps. One behind her left ear, the other at the base of her skull.

A glance around the small cell-like room gave her little information about where she was. The floor was hard-packed dirt and smelled of urine and feces. She wore a torn shirt and the dark pants women wore beneath their burkas.

Voices outside the rough wooden door made her tense and her body cringe.

She wasn't sure why she was there, but those voices inspired an automatic response of drawing deep within, preparing for additional beatings and torture.

What she had done to deserve it, she couldn't remember. Everything about her life was a gaping, useless void.

The door jerked open. A man wearing the camouflage uniform of a Syrian fighter and a black hood covering his head and face stood in the doorway with a Russian AK-47 slung over his shoulder and a steel pipe in his hand.

Don't miss
Driving Force *by Elle James,*
available October 2019 wherever
Harlequin® books and ebooks are sold.

www.Harlequin.com